ANCESTORS OF AVALON

Marion Zimmer Bradley is the creator of the popular *Darkover* universe as well as the critically acclaimed author of the bestselling *The Mists of Avalon*, its sequel, *The Forest House*, and *Priestess of Avalon* with her long-time collaborator Diana L. Paxson. She died in Berkeley, California on September 25, 1999.

Diana L. Paxson was born in Detroit, Michigan in 1943, but moved to Los Angeles at the age of three and has been a Californian ever since. After attending Mills College in 1960, she received a Masters degree in Comparative (Medieval) Literature from U.C. Berkeley. She married and became the mother of two children. In 1971 she began writing seriously. Her first short story was published in 1978 and her first novel in 1981. Following the death of Marion Zimmer Bradley, she took up the draft of this long-planned novel to complete the story-cycle.

For automatic updates on your favourite authors visit Voyager-books.co.uk and register for AuthorTracker.

Other books in this series

Voyager

MARION ZIMMER BRADLEY
and DIANA L. PAXSON

Ancestors of Avalon

HarperCollins*Publishers*

Voyager
An Imprint of HarperCollins*Publishers*
77–85 Fulham Palace Road,
Hammersmith, London W6 8JB

www.voyager-books.com

This paperback edition 2005
1

First published in Great Britain by *Voyager* 2004

Map drawn by Jeffrey L. Ward

ISBN 0 00 713845 8

Set in Sabon by Palimpsest Book Production Limited,
Polmont, Stirlingshire

Printed and bound in Great Britain by
Clays Limited, St Ives plc

To David Bradley

Without whom this book
could not have been written

PEOPLE IN THE STORY

PEOPLE WHO DO NOT ESCAPE ATLANTIS

Aldel – of Ahtarrath; an acolyte, betrothed to Elis, killed in rescue of Omphalos Stone

Deoris [temple name, 'Adsartha'] – a former priestess of Caratra, mother of Tiriki, wife of Reio-ta

(*Domaris* – a Vested Guardian, priestess of Light, mother of Micail)

Gremos – a priestess, housemother to the acolytes

Kalhan – of Atalan; an acolyte, betrothed to Damisa

Kanar – chief astrologer of the Temple on Ahtarrath, Lanath's first teacher

Lunrick – a merchant of Ahtarra

Mesira – chief of the healers, a priestess of the cult of Caratra

(*Micon* – Prince of Ahtarrath, father of Micail)

(*Mikantor* – Prince of Ahtarrath, father of Micon and Reio-ta)

Pegar – a landowner of Ahtarrath

(*Rajasta* – mage, priest of Light, and Vested Guardian in the Ancient Land)

CAPITALS = major characters

( ) = dead before story begins

Reio-ta – regent of Ahtarrath and governor of the Temple of Light on Ahtarrath, priest, uncle of Micail and stepfather of Tiriki

(*Riveda* – biological father of Tiriki, healer, mage, and chief of the Grey Robe Order in the Ancient Land; executed for sorcery)

PEOPLE AT THE TOR

Adeyna – wife of the merchant Forolin

Alyssa [Temple name, 'Neniath'] – of Caris; a Grey Robe priestess (the Grey Mage), seeress, and adept

Arcor – of Ahtarrath, a sailor on the *Crimson Serpent*

Aven – an Alkonan sailor on the *Crimson Serpent*

Cadis – an Ahtarran sailor on the *Crimson Serpent*

CHEDAN ARADOS – originally of Alkonath; son of Naduil, an acolyte in the Ancient Land before its fall, former Vested Guardian, and now a mage

DAMISA – of Alkonath; eldest of the acolytes, a cousin of Prince Tjalan, betrothed to Kalhan

Dannetrasa of Caris – a priest of Light who assisted Ardral in the library; arrives at the Tor on the second ship

Domara – daughter of Tiriki and Micail, born at the Tor

Eilantha – Tiriki's Temple name

Elis – of Ahtarrath; one of the acolytes, especially good with plants

Forolin – a merchant of Ahtarrath and late arrival to the Tor

Heron – headman of the marsh folk

Iriel – of Arhaburath; youngest of the acolytes (age twelve at the time of the Sinking), betrothed to Aldel

Jarata – a merchant of Ahtarrath

Kalaran – an acolyte, betrothed to Selast

Kestil – daughter of Forolin and Adeyna, five years old when she arrives at the Tor

Larin – a sailor on the *Crimson Serpent*, later inducted into the priesthood

Liala [Temple name, 'Atlialmaris'] – of Ahtarrath; a Blue Robe priestess and healer

Linnet – daughter of Nettle, of the marsh folk

Malaera – a lesser Blue Robe priestess

Metia – senior saji woman, nursemaid to Domara

Mudlark – son of Nettle, of the marsh folk

Nettle – wife of Heron, headman of the marsh folk

Otter – son of the headman, Heron

Reidel – of Ahtarrath; son of Sarhedran, captain of the *Crimson Serpent;* later, a priest of the Sixth Order

Redfern – a woman of the marsh folk

Rendano – of Akil, a lesser priest in the Temple of Light and a sensitive

Selast – of Cosarrath, one of the acolytes

Taret – wisewoman of the marsh folk at the Tor

Teiron – an Alkonian sailor assigned to the *Crimson Serpent*

Teviri – one of the saji women, attendant to Alyssa

TIRIKI [Temple name, 'Eilantha'] – of Ahtarrath, a Guardian in the Temple of Light, wife of Micail; she will become the Morgan of Avalon

Virja – one of the saji women, attendant to Alyssa

PEOPLE AT BELSAIRATH AND AZAN

Aderanthis – of Tapallan; midlevel priestess from the Temple at Ahtarrath

Anet – daughter of the high priestess Ayo and King Khattar of the Ai-Zir

Antar – bodyguard to Prince Tjalan

ARDRAL [Temple name, 'Ardravanant,' meaning *Knower*

of the Brightest] – of Atalan; an Adept, Seventh Vested Guardian of the Temple of Light at Ahtarrath, custodian of the library

Ayo – Sacred Sister for the Ai-Zan, high priestess at Carn Ava

Baradel – Tjalan's older son, seven years old at the time of the Sinking

Bennurajos – of Cosarrath, a singer from the Temple of Light on Ahtarrath, expert on plants and animals

Chaithala – Princess of Alkonath, wife of Tjalan

Cleta – of Tarisseda Ruta; an acolyte, herbalist, betrothed to Vialmar, fifteen years old at the time of the Sinking

Cyrena – Princess of Tarisseda, betrothed to Baradel, nine years old at the time of the Sinking

Dan – one of the three swordsmen known as Prince Tjalan's Companions

Dantu – captain of the *Royal Emerald*, Tjalan's flagship

Delengirol – of Tarisseda; a singer from the Temple in Ahtarra

Domazo – keeper of the inn in Belsairath, heir to the local chieftain

Droshrad – shaman of the Red Bulls

ELARA [Temple name, 'Larrnebiru'] – of Ahtarrath; second eldest of the acolytes, also an initiate of Caratra, betrothed to Lanath

Galara – half-sister to Tiriki, daughter of Deoris and Reio-ta, a junior scribe

Greha – Ai-Zir warrior, bodyguard to Heshoth

Haladris – of Atalan; First Vested Guardian in the Temple of Light on Alkonath, formerly an archpriest in the Ancient Land

Heshoth – a native trader

Jiritaren – of Tapallan; priest of Light, astronomer

Karagon – of Mormallor; a chela to Valadur

Khattar – chief of the Red Bulls, high king of the Ai-Zir

Khayan-e-Durr – sister of Khattar, queen of the Red Bull tribe

Khensu – Khattar's nephew and heir

Kyrrdis – of Ahtarrath; singer and priestess of Light

Lanath – of Tarisseda Ruta; an acolyte, former apprentice to Kanar, betrothed to Elara

Li'ija – of Alkonath; a chela, Ocathrel's eldest daughter, nineteen years old at the time of the Sinking

Lirini – of Alkonath; a chela in the Scribes' School, middle daughter of Ocathrel, seventeen years old at the time of the Sinking

Lodreimi – of Alkonath; a Blue Robe priestess in Timul's Temple

Mahadalku – of Tarisseda Ruta; First Vested Guardian of the Tarissedan Temple of Light

Marona – of Ahtarrath; a Blue Robe priestess and healer

Metanor – of Ahtarrath; Fifth Vested Guardian in the Temple of Light

MICAIL – Prince of Ahtarrath; First Vested Guardian in the Temple of Light

Naranshada [Temple name, 'Ansha'] – of Ahtarrath; Fourth Vested Guardian in the Temple of Light, an engineer

Ocathrel – of Alkonath; Fifth Vested Guardian in the Temple of Light

Osinarmen – Micail's Temple name

Ot – one of the three swordsmen known as Prince Tjalan's Companions

Reualen – of Alkonath; Priest of Light, husband of Sahurusartha

Sadhisebo and *Saiyano* – saji priestesses in Timul's Temple, skilled in herblore

Sahurusartha – of Alkonath; priestess of Light, singer, wife of Reualen

Stathalkha – of Tarisseda Ruta; Third Guardian of the Tarissedan Temple, a powerful sensitive

Timul – of Alkonath; second to the high priestess of the Temple of Ni-Terat in Alkonath, head of the Blue Robes in Belsairath

TJALAN – Prince of Alkonath; leader of the colony in Belsairath, cousin of Micail

Valadur – of Mormallor; a Grey Adept

Valorin – of Tapallan; priest of Light in the Temple at Alkonath, a naturalist

Vialmar – of Arhurabath; an acolyte, betrothed to Cleta

HEAVENLY POWERS

Banur – the four-faced god, destroyer-preserver; ruler of winter

The Blood Star – Mars

Caratra – daughter or nurturing aspect of Ni-Terat, the Great Mother; Venus is her star

Dyaus – the Sleeper, also known as the 'Man with Crossed Hands,' the force of chaos that brings change; sometimes referred to as 'That One'

Manoah – the Great Maker, Lord of the Day, identified with the sun; ruler of Summer, and with Orion ('The Hunter of Destiny')

Nar-Inabi – 'Star Shaper,' god of the night, the stars, and the sea; ruler of harvest time

---

[A note on Atlantean astrology: Four millennia ago, the sky was different in many ways. Due to the precession of the equinoxes, for instance, the solstices fell in early January and July, and the equinoxes in early April and October. The signs of the zodiac were also different, so that the winter solstice occurred when the sun entered Aquarius, and the spring equinox when it entered Taurus. The constellation names, in the Sea Kingdoms and the ancient civilizations around them, were different as well.]

Ni-Terat – Dark Mother of All, Veiled aspect of the Great Mother, goddess of the Earth; ruler of planting time

The Peacemaker – Virgo

The Sorcerer – Saturn

The Sovereign – Jupiter

The Torch – Leo, also called the Scepter or the Great Fire

The Wheel – Ursa Major, also called the Seven Guardians or Chariot

Winged Bull – Taurus

PLACES IN THE STORY

Ahtarra – capital city of Ahtarrath
Ahtarrath – the last isle of the Sea Kingdoms to fall;
  home of the House of the Twelve (acolytes)
Ahurabath – an isle of the Sea Kingdoms
Alkona – capital of Alkonath
Alkonath – one of the mightiest of the Ten Island
  Kingdoms, famed for its seafarers
Aman River – the Avon, in Britain
Amber Coast – coast of the North Sea
Ancient Land – ancestral realm of the Atlanteans, located
  somewhere near what is now the Black Sea
Atlantis – a general name for the Sea Kingdoms
Azan – the 'Bull-pen,' territory of the five tribes of the
  Ai-Zir, from Weymouth northeast to the Salisbury
  Plain in Wessex, Britain
Azan-Ylir – capital of Azan, modern Amesbury
Beleri'in [Belerion] – modern Penzance, in Cornwall
Belsairath – an Alkonan trading outpost where
  Dorchester is now
Belsairath fortress – Maiden Castle, Dorset
Carn Ava – Avebury
Casseritides – 'Isles of Tin,' a name for Britain
City of the Circling Snake – capital of the Ancient Land
Cosarrath – an isle of the Ten Kingdoms
Hellas – Greece

Hill of the Ghosts – Hambledon Hill, Dorset

Isle of the Mighty, Isle of Tin, Hesperides – British Isles

Khem – Egypt

Mormallor – one of the Ten Kingdoms, called the 'holy isle'

Olbairos – an Ahtarran trading station on the continent

Oranderis – an isle of the Sea Kingdoms

The Sea Kingdoms – the islands of Atlantis

Tapallan – an isle of the Ten Kingdoms

Tarisseda – an isle of the Ten Kingdoms

The Ten Kingdoms – the alliance of Sea Kingdoms that replaced the Bright Empire

The Tor – Glastonbury Tor, Somerset

Zaiadan – a land on the coast of the North Sea

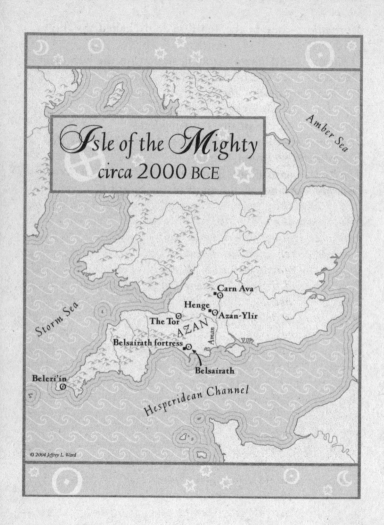

Isle of the Mighty
circa 2000 BCE

Amber Sea

Carn Ava

Henge
Azan-Ylir

The Tor

Storm Sea

AZAN

Aman

Belsairath fortress
Belsairath

Beleri'in

Hesperidean Channel

© 2004 Jeffrey L. Ward

Morgaine speaks . . .

The people of Avalon bring to their Lady their troubles, both great and small. This morning the Druids came to me to say that there has been a rockfall in the passage that leads from their Temple to the chamber that holds the Omphalos Stone, and they do not know how it is to be repaired. Their numbers here are small now, and most of those who remain are old. So many of those who might have renewed their Order were killed in the Saxon wars or have gone instead to the monks who tend the Christian chapel that is on that other Avalon.

And so they come to me as they all come to me, those who remain, to tell them what they must do. It has always seemed odd to me that the way to a mystery that is buried so deeply in the earth begins in the Temple of the Sun, but they say that those who first brought the ancient wisdom to these isles, long before the Druids, honored the Light above all things.

The Sight no longer comes to me as it did when I was young and we fought to bring the Goddess back into the world. I know now that She was already here, and always will be, but the Omphalos is the egg stone, the navel of the world, the last magic of a land sunk beneath the seas so long that even to us it is a legend.

When I was a girl, there were tapestries in the Druids'

1

Temple that told the story of how it came here. They have fallen to threads and dust, but I myself once followed that passage to the heart of the hill and touched the sacred stone. The visions that came to me then are more vivid now than many of my own memories. I can see once more the Star Mountain crowned with fire and Tiriki's ship poised trembling on the wave as the Doomed Land is engulfed by the sea.

But I do not believe that I was on that ship. I have had dreams in which I stood, hand in hand with a man I loved, and watched as my world tore itself to pieces, just as Britannia did when Arthur died. Perhaps that was why I was sent back in this time, for Avalon is surely as lost as Atlantis, though it is mist, not smoke that veils it from the mortal world.

Once, there was a passage that led to the Omphalos Stone from the cave where the White Spring flows out from the Tor, but tremors in the earth blocked that way a long time ago. Perhaps it is not meant that we should any longer walk there. The Stone is being withdrawn from us, like so many other Mysteries.

I know all about endings. It is beginnings that elude me.

How did they come here, those brave priestesses and priests who survived the Sinking? Two millennia have passed since the Stone was brought to this shore, and five hundred more, and though we know little more than their names, we have preserved their legacy. Who were those ancestors who first brought the ancient wisdom and buried it like a seed in the heart of this holy hill?

If I can understand how they survived their testing, then perhaps I will find hope that the ancient wisdom we preserved will be carried into the future, and that something of the magic of Avalon will endure . . .

ONE

Tiriki woke with a gasp as the bed lurched. She reached out for Micail, blinking away tormenting images of fire and blood and falling walls and a faceless, brooding figure writhing in chains. But she lay safe in her own bed, her husband by her side.

'Thank the gods,' she whispered. 'It was only a dream!'

'Not entirely – look there—' Raising himself on one elbow, Micail pointed to the lamp that swung before the Mother's shrine in the corner, sending shadows flickering madly around the room. 'But I know what you dreamed. The vision came to me, too.'

In the same moment the earth moved again. Micail seized her in his arms and rolled her toward the protection of the wall as plaster showered down from above. From somewhere in the distance came a long rumble of falling masonry. They clung, scarcely breathing, as the vibration peaked and eased.

'The mountain is waking,' he said grimly when all was still. 'This makes the third tremor in two days.' He released her and got out of the bed.

'They're getting stronger—' she agreed. The palace was solidly built of stone and had withstood many tremors over the years, but even in the uncertain light Tiriki could see a new crack running across the ceiling of the room.

'I must go. Reports will be coming in. Will you be all

right here?' Micail stepped into his sandals and wrapped himself in a mantle. Tall and strong, with the lamplight striking flame from his red hair, he seemed the most stable thing in the room.

'Of course,' she answered, getting up herself and pulling a light robe around her slim body. 'You are prince as well as priest of this city. They will look to you for direction. But do not wear yourself out on work that can be done by other men. We must be ready for the ritual this afternoon.' She tried to hide her shiver of fear at the thought of facing the Omphalos Stone, but surely a ritual to reinforce the balance of the world had never been so necessary as now.

He nodded, looking down at her. 'You seem so fragile, but sometimes I think you are the strongest of us all . . .'

'I am strong because we are together,' Tiriki murmured as he left her.

Beyond the curtains that screened the balcony a red light was glowing. Today marked the midpoint of spring, she thought grimly, but that light was not the dawn. The city of Ahtarra was on fire.

In the city above, men struggled to shift rubble and put out the last of the fires. In the shrine where the Omphalos Stone lay hidden, all was still. Tiriki held her torch higher as she followed the other priests and priestesses into its deepest chamber, suppressing a shiver as the hot flame became its own shadow, greenish smoke swirling around the pitch-soaked brand.

The Omphalos Stone glimmered like occluded crystal in the center of the room. An egg-shaped thing half the height of a man, it seemed to pulse as it absorbed the light. Robed figures stood along the curving wall. The torches they had set into the brackets above them flickered bravely, yet the shrine seemed shrouded in gloom. There was a chill here, deep beneath the surface of the island of Ahtarrath, that no ordinary fire could ease. Even the smoke of the incense that smoldered on the altar sank in the heavy air.

All other light faded before the glowing Stone. Even without their hoods and veils, the faces of the priests and priestesses would have been difficult to see, but as she felt her way to her place against the wall, Tiriki needed no sight to identify the hooded figure beside her as Micail. She smiled a silent greeting, knowing he would feel it.

Were we disembodied spirits, she thought warmly, *still I would know him . . .* The sacred medallion upon his breast, a golden wheel with seven spokes, gleamed faintly, reminding Tiriki that here he was not only her husband, but the High Priest Osinarmen, Son of the Sun; just as she was not only Tiriki but Eilantha, Guardian of Light.

Straightening, Micail began to sing the Invocation for the Equinox of Spring, his voice vibrating oddly. '*Let Day be bounded by the Night . . .*'

Other, softer voices joined the chant.

> '*Dark be balanced by the Light.*
> *Earth and Sky and Sun and Sea,*
> *A circled cross shall ever be.*'

A lifetime of priestly training had taught Tiriki all the ways of setting aside the demands of the body, but it was hard to ignore the dank subterranean air, or the eerie sense of pressure that set goose bumps in her skin. Only by supreme effort could she focus again on the song as it began to stir the stillness into harmony . . .

> '*Let sorrow make a space for joy,*
> *Let grief with jubilance alloy,*
> *Step by step to make our way,*
> *Till Darkness shall unite with Day . . .*'

In the desperate struggle that had caused the destruction of the Ancient Land a generation earlier, the Omphalos

Stone had become, if only briefly, the plaything of black sorcery. For a time it had been feared that the corruption was absolute; and so the priests had circulated the story that the Stone had been lost, with so much else, beneath the vengeful sea.

In a way, the lie was truth; but the deep place in which the Stone lay was this cavern beneath the temples and the city of Ahtarra. With the arrival of the Stone, this midsize island of the Sea Kingdoms of Atlantis had become the sacred center of the world. But though the Stone was far from lost, it was hidden, as it had always been. Even the highest in the priesthood rarely found cause to enter this shrine. Those few who dared consult the Omphalos knew that their actions could upset the equilibrium of the world.

The song changed tempo, growing more urgent.

> 'Each season by the next is bound,
> Meetings, partings, form the round,
> The sacred center is our frame,
> Where all is changing, all the same . . .'

Tiriki was losing focus again. *If it* was *all the same*, she thought in sudden rebellion, *we wouldn't be here now!*

For months, news of earthquakes and rumors of worse destruction to come had been running like wildfire throughout the Sea Kingdoms. In Ahtarrath, such terrors had at first seemed distant, but the past few nights, Temple dwellers and city folk alike had been plagued by faint tremors in the earth, and persistent, dreadful dreams. And even now, as the song continued, she could sense uneasiness in the other singers.

Can this truly be the prophesied Time of Ending? Tiriki wondered silently. *After so many warnings?*

Resolutely, she rejoined her voice to the rising architecture of sound, whose manipulation was perhaps the most powerful tool of Atlantean magic.

> '*Moving, we become more still,*
> *Impassioned, we are bound by will,*
> *Turning in perpetuity*
> *While Time becomes Eternity . . .*'

The shadows thickened, contorting the swirls of incense that at last spiraled into the chill air.

The music stopped.

Light blazed forth from the Stone, filling the shrine as completely as darkness had before. Light was everywhere, so radiant that Tiriki was surprised to find that it carried no heat. Even the torches shone more brightly. The singers released a collective sigh. Now they could begin.

First to take off his hood and move toward the Stone was Reio-ta, governor of the Temple. Beside him the blue-robed Mesira, leader of the healers, lifted her veil. Tiriki and Micail stepped out to face them across the Stone. In that light, Micail's red hair shone like flame, while the wisps that escaped Tiriki's coiled braids glistened gold and silver.

Reio-ta's rich tenor took up the invocation . . .

> '*In this place of Ni-Terat, Dark Queen of Earth,*
> *Now bright with the Spirit of Manoah's Light,*
> *Confirm we now the Sacred Center,*
> *The Omphalos, Navel of the World.*'

The richness of her husky contralto belied Mesira's age. 'The center is not a place, but a state of being. The Omphalos is of another realm. Many ages the Stone lay undisturbed in the sanctuaries of the Ancient Land, but the center was not there, nor is it in Ahtarrath.'

Micail voiced the formal response, 'Mindful that all here have vowed that what is, is worth preserving, and to that end bending might and will . . .' He smiled at Tiriki, and reached again for her hand. Together they drew breath for the closing words.

7

'We arrive forever in the Realm of the True, which can never be destroyed.'

And the rest responded in chorus, 'While we keep faith, Light lives in us!'

The otherworldly illumination throbbed as Mesira spoke once more.

'So we invoke the Equilibrium of the Stone, that the people may know peace once more. For we cannot ignore the portents we have seen. We meet in a place of wisdom to seek answers. Seeress, I summon thee—' Mesira extended both arms to the grey figure who now stepped forward. 'The time is come. Be thou our eyes and our voice before the Eternal.'

The seeress drew back her veils. In the intense brilliance of the Stone's light it was not difficult to recognize Alyssa, her black hair hanging loose around her shoulders, her eyes already dilated by trance. With strange, half-bowing steps, she moved into the altar's radiance.

The singers watched nervously as the seeress rested her fingertips upon the Stone. Translucent patterns of power pooled and eddied within. Alyssa stiffened, but instead of retreating, she moved even nearer.

'It is . . . it is so,' she whispered. 'One with the Stone am I. What it knows, ye shall know. Let the sacred song bear us to the doors of Fate.'

As she spoke, the singers began to hum softly. Micail's voice soared in the cadence of Command, calling the seeress by her Temple name.

> *'Neniath, seeress, dost thou know me?*
> *I, Osinarmen, do address thee.*
> *Part us from dreams as thou dost wake*
> *By the answer thou wilt make.'*

'I hear.' The voice was quite different from Alyssa's, sharp and ringing. 'I am here. What wouldst thou know?'

'Speak if it please thee, and we shall attend.' Micail sang

the formal phrase in one sustained exhalation, but in his voice, Tiriki could hear the strain. 'We come because the Stone has called us, whispering secretly in the night.'

A moment passed. 'The answer, thou dost already know,' the seeress murmured. 'The question lies before the truth. Yet the door that was cast open will not be shut. Stone upon stone rises higher, doomed to fall. The forests fill with tinder. The power which has waited at the heart of the world shifts . . . and *it hungers*.'

Tiriki felt a momentary unsteadiness, but could not tell if it came from beneath the flooring stones, or from her own heart. She looked to Micail, but he stood frozen, his face a grimacing mask.

Reio-ta forced out words. 'Darkness has broken loose before,' he said with grim concentration, 'and always, it has been contained. What must we do this time to bind it?'

'Can you do aught but sing again while silence grows?' Alyssa shook with unexpected, bitter laughter; and this time the earth shuddered with her.

A ripple of fright shook the singers. They cried out as one, 'We are servants of Light Unfailing! The Darkness can never prevail!'

But the tremors did not cease. The torches flickered out. Scarlet lightnings shot from the Stone. For a moment Tiriki thought the cavern around them was groaning, but it was Alyssa's throat from which those horrific sounds came.

The seeress was speaking, or trying to, but the words came garbled and unintelligible. Fighting their dread, the singers inched closer to Alyssa, straining to hear; but the seeress shrank away from them, arms flailing against the Stone.

'*It climbs!*' Her shrieks echoed far beyond the circular chamber. '*The foul flower! Blood and fire! YOU ARE TOO LATE!*'

As the echoes diminished, the strength faded from the taut body of the seeress. Only Micail's swift movement prevented her from falling.

'Take her—' Reio-ta gasped. 'Mesira, go with them! We will f-finish here—'

Nodding, Micail bore the seeress from the chamber.

The alcove by the entrance to the shrine where they brought the seeress seemed strangely quiet. While the earth beneath them had finally stilled, Tiriki's spirit was still shaken. As she entered, her acolyte Damisa, who had waited here with the other attendants during the ceremony, looked up with anxious green eyes.

Micail pressed past her, touching Tiriki's hand in a swift caress that was more intimate than an embrace. Eyes met in an unspoken assurance – *I am here . . . I am here. We will survive, though the heavens fall.*

From the chamber beyond came a babble of voices.

'How are they?' murmured Micail, with a nod toward the sound.

Tiriki shrugged, but held on to his hand. 'Half of them are assuring one another that we did not understand Alyssa's words, and the others are convinced that Ahtarra is about to fall into the sea. Reio-ta will deal with them.' She looked at Alyssa, who lay upon a bench with Mesira beside her. 'How is she?'

The face of the seeress was pale, and the long hair which this morning had shone like a raven's wing was now brindled with streaks of grey.

'She sleeps,' Mesira said simply. In the soft light that came through the doorway, the healer's face showed all its years. 'As for her waking . . . it will be some time, I believe, before we know whether this day's work has harmed her. You may as well go. I think we have received all the answers we are going to get. My chela is fetching a litter, that we may take her back to the Healers Hall. If there is any change, I will send word.'

Micail had already removed his vestments and slipped the emblem of his rank beneath the neck of his sleeveless tunic. Tiriki folded her veil and outer robe and handed them to Damisa. 'Shall we too call for bearers?' she asked.

Micail shook his head. 'Are you up to walking? I need to feel the touch of honest daylight on my skin.'

The hot bright air of the outdoors was a blessing, baking the chill of the underground chambers from their bones. Tiriki felt the tightness easing from her neck and shoulders, and lengthened her steps to keep up with her husband's longer stride. Through the red and white stone columns of the Temple that marked the entrance to the underground shrine, she glimpsed a string of roofs tiled in blue. Farther down the slope, a scattering of newly built domes in cream and red were set amid the gardens of the city. Beyond them, the glittering sea stretched away to infinity.

As they emerged from the portico, the sounds and smells of the city rose around them – barking dogs and crying babies, merchants calling out their wares, the spicy smell of the seafood stew that was a local favorite, and the less salubrious odors from a nearby sewer. The fires started by last night's quake had been put out, and the damage was being dealt with. The destruction had been less than they had feared. Indeed, fear was now their greatest enemy. Even the stinks were an affirmation of ordinary life, reassuring after their confrontation with the uncanny power of the Stone.

Perhaps Micail felt the same. At any rate, he was leading her the long way around, away from the tall buildings of the Temple complex and down through the marketplace, instead of following the white-paved Processional Way that led to the palace. The gleaming flanks of the Three Towers were hidden as they turned down a side street that led toward the harbor, where shopkeepers haggled with customers as they would on any normal day. They attracted a few looks of admiration, but no one pointed or stared. Without their ritual robes, she and Micail looked like any ordinary couple doing errands in the marketplace, though they were taller and fairer than most of the people of the town. And had anyone considered troubling them, the decision in Micail's strong features and the energy in his stride would have been deterrent enough.

'Are you hungry?' she asked. They had fasted for the ritual, and it was now close to noon.

'What I really want is a drink,' he responded with a grin. 'There used to be a taverna near the harbor that served good wine – not our local rough red, but a respectable vintage from the land of the Hellenes. Don't worry – the food will not disappoint you, either.'

The taverna had an open loggia shaded by trellised vines. Around its edges grew the crimson lilies of Ahtarrath. Their delicate fragrance scented the air. Tiriki tipped back her head to allow the breeze from the harbor to stir her hair. If she turned, she could see the slopes of the Star Mountain – the dormant volcano that was the island's core, shimmering in the heat-haze. Down the slope there was a band of forest, and then a patchwork of field and vineyard. Sitting here, the events of the morning seemed no more than gloomy dreams. Micail's fathers had ruled here for a hundred generations. What power could overwhelm a tradition of such wisdom and glory?

Micail took a long swallow from his earthenware goblet and let out a breath with an appreciative sigh. Tiriki was surprised to feel a bubble of laughter rising within. At the sound, her husband lifted one eyebrow.

'For a moment you reminded me of Rajasta,' she explained.

Micail grinned. 'Our old teacher was a noble spirit, but he did appreciate good wine! He has been in my mind today as well, but not because of the wine,' he added, sobering.

She nodded, agreeing. 'I've been trying to remember all he told us of the doom that claimed the Ancient Land. When the land began to sink, they had warning enough to send the sacred scrolls here, along with the adepts to read them.

12

But if disaster should destroy all the Sea Kingdoms . . . where would a refuge for the ancient wisdom of Atlantis be found?'

Micail gestured with his goblet. 'Is it not for that very purpose that we send out emissaries to the eastern lands of Hellas and Khem, and north as far as the Amber Coast, and the Isles of Tin?'

'And what of the wisdom that cannot be preserved in scrolls and tokens?' she mused. 'What of those things that must be seen and felt before one can understand? And what of the powers that can be safely given only when a master judges the student to be ready for them? What of the wisdom that must be transmitted soul to soul?'

Micail frowned thoughtfully, but his tone was relaxed. 'Our teacher Rajasta used to say that however great the cataclysm, if only the House of the Twelve was preserved – not the priesthood, but the six couples, the youths and maidens who are the chosen acolytes – by themselves they could re-create all the greatness of our land. And then he would laugh . . .'

'He must have been joking,' said Tiriki, thinking of Damisa and Kalhan, Elis and Aldel, Kalaran and Selast, and Elara and Cleta, and the rest. The acolytes had been bred to the calling, the offspring of matings ordained by the stars. Their potential was great – but they were all so terribly *young*.

Tiriki shook her head. 'No doubt they will surpass us all when they complete their training, but without supervision, I fear they would find it hard to resist the temptation to misuse their powers. Even my father—' She stopped abruptly, her fair skin flushing.

Most of the time she was able to forget that her real father was not Reio-ta, her mother's husband, but Riveda, who had ruled over the Order of Grey Robe mages in the Ancient Land; Riveda, who had proved unable to resist the temptations of forbidden magic and had been executed for sorcery.

13

'Even Riveda did good as well as evil,' Micail said softly, taking her hand. 'His soul is in the keeping of the Lords of Fate, and through many lifetimes he will work out his penance. But his writings on the treatment of sickness have saved many. You must not let his memory haunt you, beloved. Here he is remembered as a healer.'

A dark-eyed youth arrived with a platter of flat cakes and little crisply fried fishes served with goat cheese and cut herbs. His eyes widened a little as he took in Tiriki's blue eyes and fair hair, her only legacy from Riveda, who had originally come not from the Ancient Land, but from the little-known northern kingdom of Zaiadan.

'We must try not to be afraid,' Micail said, when the servant had gone. 'There are many prophecies other than Rajasta's that speak of the Time of Ending. If it has come, we will be at great risk, but the foreshadowings have never suggested that we are wholly doomed. Indeed, Rajasta's vision has assured us that you and I will found a new Temple in a new land! I am convinced that there is a Destiny that will preserve us. We must only find its thread.'

Tiriki nodded, and took the hand he held out to her. *But all this bright and beautiful life that surrounds us must pass away before the prophecy can be fulfilled.*

But for now, the day was fair, and the aromas rising from her plate offered a pleasant distraction from whatever fate might have in store. Willing herself to think only of the moment, and of Micail, Tiriki sought for a more neutral subject.

'Did you know that Elara is a fine archer?'

Micail raised an eyebrow. 'That seems an odd amusement for a healer – she's apprenticed to Liala, is she not?'

'Yes, she is, but you know that a healer's work requires both precision and nerve. Elara has become something of a leader among the acolytes.'

'I would have expected the Alkonan girl – your acolyte Damisa – to take that role,' he replied. 'Isn't she the oldest?

And she's some relation to Tjalan, I believe. That family does like to take charge.' He grinned, and Tiriki remembered that he had spent several summers with the Prince of Alkonath.

'Perhaps she is a little *too* aware of her royal background. In any case, she was the last of them to arrive here, and I think she's finding it hard to fit in.'

'If that is the hardest thing she has to deal with she may count herself fortunate!' Micail downed the last of his wine and got to his feet.

Tiriki sighed, but indeed, it was time for them to go.

When the innkeeper realized that the couple who had been occupying the best table on his terrace for so very long were the prince and his lady, he tried to refuse payment, but Micail insisted on impressing his signet on a bit of clay.

'Present that at the palace and my servants will give you what I owe—'

'You are too kind,' Tiriki jested softly, as they were at last permitted to leave the taverna. 'The man plainly felt honored by a visit from the prince and wished to make you a gift in return. Why did you not allow it?'

'Think of it as an affirmation,' Micail smiled, a little grimly. 'That bit of clay represents my belief that someone *will* be here tomorrow. And if, as you say, he would prefer the honor, well, there is nothing to force him to redeem the debt. Memory fades. But he has my seal for a keepsake—'

Slowly, they walked back to the palace, speaking of ordinary things, but Tiriki could not help recalling how the screams of the seeress had echoed from the crypt.

When Damisa returned to the House of the Falling Leaves, the other acolytes were just finishing a lesson. Elara of Ahtarrath was the first to see her come in. Elara, dark-haired and buxom, was a native of this island, and it had fallen to her to make the newcomers from the other Sea Kingdoms welcome as they arrived.

On each island, the temples trained priests and priestesses. But from among the most talented young people in each generation, twelve were chosen to learn the greater Mysteries. Some would one day return to their own islands as senior clergy, while others explored specialties such as healing or astrology. From the Twelve came the adepts, who served all Atlantis as Vested Guardians in the Temple of Light.

The house was a low, sprawling structure of oddly aligned corridors and oversize suites, rumored to have been built a century or more ago for a foreign dignitary. The acolytes often amused themselves with suggesting other explanations for the stone mermaids in the weathered fountain in the central courtyard. Whatever its origins, until quite recently the strange old villa had served as a dormitory for unmarried priests, pilgrims, and refugees. Now it was the House of the Twelve.

Some of the acolytes welcomed Elara's help while others resisted her, but Damisa, who was a cousin of the prince of Alkonath, was usually the most self-sufficient of them all. Right now, thought Elara, she looked terrible.

'Damisa? What has happened to you? Are you ill?' She flinched as the other girl turned to her with a blind stare. 'Did something happen at the ceremony?' Elara took a firm grip on Damisa's elbow and made her sit down by the fountain. She turned to get the attention of one of the others. 'Lanath, go get her some water!' Elara said in a low voice as all the acolytes surrounded them. Elara sat down, pushing back the black curls that kept falling into her eyes. 'Be quiet, all of you!' she glared until they moved back. 'Let her breathe!'

She knew that Damisa had been called to attend Lady Tiriki early that morning, and she had envied her. Elara's role as chela to the Blue Robe priestess Liala in the Temple of Ni-Terat was a pleasant enough assignment, but hardly glamorous. The acolytes had been told that their apprenticeships were determined by the placement of their stars and the will of the gods. It made sense that Elara's betrothed, Lanath, was assigned to the Temple astrologer because he had a good head for figures, but Elara had always suspected that Damisa's royal connections had got her the place with Tiriki, who was not only a priestess but Princess of Ahtarrath, after all. But she did not envy Damisa now.

'Tell us, Damisa,' she murmured as the other girl drank. 'Was someone hurt? Has something gone wrong?'

'Wrong!' Damisa closed her eyes for a moment, then straightened and looked around the circle. 'Haven't you heard the rumors that have been going around the city?'

'Of course we have. But where were you?' asked little Iriel.

'At an equinox ritual, attending my lady,' Damisa replied.

'Those rituals are usually held in the Great Temple of Manoah,' observed Elis, who was also a native of the city. 'It wouldn't take you this long to get back from there!'

'We weren't at the Temple of Light,' Damisa said tightly. 'We went to another place, a sanctuary built into the cliffs at the eastern edge of the city. The portico looks ordinary enough, but the actual Temple is deep underground. Or at least I suppose so. I was told to wait in the alcove at the head of the passage.'

'Banur's bones!' Elara exclaimed, 'That's the Temple of – I don't know what it is – no one ever goes there!'

'I don't know what it is, either,' Damisa responded with a return of her usual arrogance, 'but some Power is down there. I could see odd flashes of light all the way up the passageway.'

'It's the Sinking . . .' said Kalaran in a dull voice. 'My own island is gone and now this one is going to go, too. My parents migrated to Alkonath, but I was chosen for the Temple. They thought it was an honor for me to come here . . .'

The acolytes looked at one another, shaken.

'We don't *know* that the ritual failed,' Elara said bracingly. 'We must wait – we will be told—'

17

'They had to carry the seeress out of that chamber,' Damisa interrupted. 'She looked half dead. They've taken her to Liala and the healers at the House of Ni-Terat.'

'I should go there,' said Elara. 'Liala may need my assistance.'

'Why bother?' glowered Lanath. 'We're all going to die.'

'Be still!' Elara rounded on him, wondering what had possessed the astrologers to betroth her to a boy who would run from his own shadow if it barked at him. 'All of you – calm down. We are the Chosen Twelve, not a pack of backcountry peasants. Do you think our elders have not foreseen this disaster and made some kind of plan? Our duty is to help them however we can.' She pushed her dark hair back again, hoping that what she had said was true.

'And if they haven't?' asked Damisa's betrothed, a rather stodgy, brown-haired lad called Kalhan.

'Then we will die,' Damisa recovered herself enough to scowl at him.

'Well, if we do,' said little Iriel, with her irrepressible smile, 'I am going to have a few strong words to say to the gods!'

When Micail and Tiriki returned to the palace they found a blue-robed priestess waiting at the gate, bearing news from Mesira. Alyssa had awakened and was expected to make a good recovery.

If only, Tiriki thought darkly, *we could do so well at healing her prophecy* . . .

Yet she kept a smile on her lips as she accompanied Micail upstairs to the suite of rooms they shared on the upper floor. The veil before the alcove that held the shrine to the goddess, and the hangings that curtained the doors to the balcony stirred in the night wind from the sea. The whitewashed walls were frescoed with a frieze of golden falcons above a bed of crimson lilies. In the flickering light of the hanging lamps, the birds soared and the flowers seemed to bend in an invisible breeze.

When he had changed into a fresh robe, Micail went off to confer with Reio-ta. Left alone, Tiriki ordered soft-footed servants to fill her bath with cool, scented water. When she had bathed, they waited to pat her dry. When they had gone, she walked out onto the balcony and gazed at the city below. To the east, the Star Mountain loomed against the crisp night sky. Groves of cypress covered the lower slopes, but the cone rose sharply above. The perpetual flame in the Temple at its summit appeared as a faint, pyramidal glow. Scattered points of light marked outlying farmsteads on the lower slopes, dimming one by one as the inhabitants sought their beds. In the city, folk stayed up later. Bobbing torches moved along the streets in the entertainment quarter.

As the air cooled, the land gave up scents of drying grass and freshly turned earth like a rich perfume. She gazed out upon the peace of the night and in her heart, the words of the evening hymn became a prayer—

> *Oh Source of Stars in splendor*
> *Against the darkness showing,*
> *Grant us restful slumber*
> *This night, Thy blessing knowing.*

How could such peace, such beauty, be destroyed?

Her bed was hung with gauze draperies and covered with linen so fine it felt like silk against the skin. No comfort that Ahtarrath could provide was denied her, but despite her prayer, Tiriki could not sleep. By the time Micail came to bed, it was midnight. She could feel him gazing down at her and tried to make her breathing slow and even. Just because she was wakeful was no reason he should be deprived of sleep as well. But the bond between them went beyond the senses of the flesh.

'What is wrong, beloved?' His voice was soft in the darkness.

She let out her breath in a long sigh. 'I am afraid.'

'But we have known ever since we were born that doom might come to Ahtarrath.'

'Yes – at some time in the distant future. But Alyssa's warning makes it *immediate!*'

'Perhaps . . . perhaps . . .' The bed creaked as he sat down and reached to caress her hair. 'Still, you know how hard it is to know the timing of a prophecy.'

Tiriki sat up, facing him. 'Do you truly believe that?'

'Beloved . . . none of us can know what our knowing may change. All we can do is to use what powers we have to face the future when it comes.' He sighed, and Tiriki thought she heard an echo of thunder, although the night was cloudless.

'Ah, yes, your powers,' she whispered bitterly, for what use were they now? 'You can invoke the wind and the lightning, but what of the earth beneath? And how will *that* be passed on, if all else falls? Reio-ta has only a daughter – and I – I am unable to bear you a child!'

Sensing her tears, he clasped her closer to him. 'You have not done so – but we are still young!'

Tiriki let her head rest against his shoulder and relaxed into the strength of his arms, drawing in the faint spicy scent of his body mixed with the oils of his own bath.

'Two babes have I laid upon the funeral pyre,' she whispered, 'and three more I lost before they could be born. The priestesses of Caratra have no more help for me, Micail.' She felt her hot tears welling up as his arms tightened around her. 'Our mothers were sisters – perhaps we are too close kin. You must take another wife, my beloved, one who can give you a child.'

She felt him shake his head in the darkness.

'The law of Ahtarrath allows it,' she whispered.

'And the law of love?' he asked. He grasped her shoulders, looking down at her. She felt, rather than saw, the intensity in his gaze. 'To beget a son worthy to bear my powers, I must give not only my seed but my soul. Truly, beloved, I do not think I would even be – capable – with a woman who was not my match in spirit as well as in body. We were destined for each other, Tiriki, and there can never be anyone for me but you.'

She reached up to trace the strong lines of his cheek and brow. 'But your line will end!'

He bent his head to kiss away her tears. 'If Ahtarrath itself must cease to be, does it matter so greatly if the magic of its princes is lost as well? It is the wisdom of Atlantis we must preserve, not its powers.'

'Osinarmen . . . do you know how much I love you?' She lay back with a sigh as his hands began to move along her body, each touch awakening a sensation to which her body had learned to respond as the spiritual exercises of the Temple had trained her soul.

'Eilantha . . . Eilantha!' he answered and closed his arms around her.

At that summons, spirit and body opened together, over-whelmed and transfigured in the ultimate union.

TWO

Damisa peered through the foliage of the garden of the House of the Twelve, wondering if she would be able to see any of the earthquake damage from here. Since the ritual in the underground Temple, the earth had been quiet, and Prince Micail had ordered his guards to help with the reconstruction. Ahtarrath's capital had grown from the remnants of a more ancient settlement. The Three Towers, sheathed in gold, had stretched toward the sky for a thousand years. Almost as venerable were the Seven Arches, in whose weathered sides students strove to trace hieroglyphs long since worn away.

The clergy of Ahtarra had done their best to prepare the old rooms of the House of the Falling Leaves for the twelve acolytes, but it was the gardens that made the location ideal, for they set the house well apart from the city and the temple. Damisa stepped back, letting the branches of the laurel hedge swing down. From here, no other building could be seen.

She turned to watch the group on the lawn a little distance away. Priestly inbreeding could produce weakness as well as talent. She often wondered if she herself had been chosen as an acolyte because of her royal grandmother's influence rather than her own merit, but half the others would have run screaming had they seen those lights flickering up the passageway of the underground Temple. It occurred to her now that the guardians might have seen some benefit in adding the robust blood of Alkonath to the priestly lineage.

But why had they decided that the detestable Kalhan, with his blunt features and equally blunt sense of humor, was a fit mate for her? Surely he would have been a better match for Cleta, who had no sense of humor at all. As a minor princess, Damisa would have expected an arranged marriage, but at least her husband should be a man of power. Tiriki had said Kalhan would probably improve with age, but Damisa could see no signs of it now.

There he was, leaping about on the lawn, leading a cluster of other acolytes in boisterous cheers, while Aldel, who she had decided was the nicest of the boys, and Lanath, who was better with his head than his hands, wrestled fiercely. Even Elara, usually the most sensible of the female acolytes, was watching them with an amused smile. Selast, on the other hand, looked as if she wanted to join the battle. She could probably win, thought Damisa, as she considered the younger girl's wiry frame. Damisa turned away. She could not tell if the fight was in fun or fury, and for the moment she did not care.

They all seem to have forgotten to worry about the end of the world, she thought moodily. *How I wish I was home! It's an honor to be Chosen and all of that – but it's always so hot here, and the food is strange. But would it be any safer there? Are we even allowed to run away? Or are we expected to just nobly stand here and let the world fall to pieces around us?*

Battling sniffles, Damisa let her wandering feet take her up the grassy slope. In moments, she emerged onto the outermost of the garden's many terraces – a long, broad retaining wall with a sweeping view of the city and the sea.

Only two days ago Damisa had discovered this spot, which she was certain could not be seen even from the roof of the House of the Twelve. With any luck, the others did not yet know about it.

As always, the sea wind dispelled her ill temper. Every salty gust felt like a secret love letter from her faraway home. Minutes passed before she noticed how many boats were out on the water today – no, not boats, she realized, but ships, and not just any ships, but a fleet of three-masted wingbirds, the pride and the might of Atlantis. High in the water, their wicked prows sheathed in hardened bronze, they could be rowed to ramming speed, or ride the wind under sail. In precise formation they made the turn around the headland.

Nestled almost directly below her vantage point was a small harbor. It was rarely used and ordinarily quiet enough for one to sink into trance while staring at its clear blue waters. But now, one by one, the tall wingbirds cast out their anchors as their brilliantly colored banners fluttered and settled to rest in the calm of the bay. The largest was already moored by the quay, furling purple sails.

Damisa rubbed her eyes again. *How can it be?* she asked herself, but there was no fault in her vision. From each proud mainmast flew the Circle of Falcons, the sovereign banner of her homeland. A surge of longing brought tears to her eyes.

'Alkonath,' she breathed; and without a second thought, lifted her robes and began to run, her long auburn hair streaming behind her as she passed the ongoing wrestling match and flew out of the garden to the stairway that led down to the harbor.

The largest of the wingbirds had dropped anchor at the main docks, but had not yet lowered its gangplank. Merchants and city folk had already convened on the pier, chattering excitedly as they waited to see what would happen next. But even with their servants, they were almost outnumbered by the white-clad men and women of the priests' caste.

Tiriki was at the very forefront, swathed in fine layers of colorless fabric, her headdress dangling flowers of gold across her hair. Her two companions were covered by mantles of Ahtarrath's royal purple. The rubies in their diadems burned like fire in the sun. It took Damisa a moment to recognize them as Reio-ta and Micail.

The ships were expected, then, the acolyte deduced, knowing well how long it took to put the ceremonial garments on. *The fleet must have been sighted from the mountain, and a runner sent down to warn them that visitors were coming.* She pressed through the crowd until she had reached her mentor's side.

Tiriki inclined her head slightly in greeting. 'Damisa, what a sense of timing!' But before Damisa could wonder if Tiriki was poking fun at her, a collective cheer announced that the visitors had begun to debark.

First to emerge were the green-cloaked soldiers armed with pikes and swords. They escorted two men in traveler's cloaks of simple wool, accompanied by a priest whose robe was cut in an unfamiliar style. Reio-ta stepped forward, raising his ceremonial staff to trace the circle of blessing. Tiriki and Micail had moved closer together. Damisa had to crane her neck to see.

'In the name of Manoah, Maker of All, whose radiance fills our hearts as He illuminates the sky,' Reio-ta said, 'I welcome you.'

'We give thanks to Nar-Inabi, the Star Shaper, who has brought you safely across the sea,' Micail added. As he lifted his arms to make a formal obeisance, Damisa caught sight of the gleaming serpent bracelets that could be worn only by a prince of the Imperial lineage.

Tiriki stepped forward, offering a basket of fruit and flowers. Her voice was like a song. 'Ni-Terat, the Great Mother, who is also called Caratra, welcomes all her children, young and old.'

The tallest of the travelers threw back the hood of his cloak, and Damisa's cheer became a delighted squeal. *Tjalan!* She could not have said if she cared more that he was Prince of Alkonath or that he was her own cousin who had always

25

been kind to her. She had barely enough discipline to stop herself from running to him and flinging her arms about his knees, as she had done when she was a child. But she controlled herself, and it was just as well that she did, for at the moment, Tjalan was entirely a lord of the empire, with the great emerald blazing from his diadem and the royal bracelets entwined around his forearms.

Lean and bronzed, he stood with the confidence of one who had never doubted his right to command. There was silver at his temples – that was new – but Damisa thought it added distinction to her cousin's dark hair. Still, Tjalan's far-seeing eyes were the same – green as the Emerald of Alkona, though there were times, she knew, when they could show all the colors of the sea.

As the strangely robed priest came forward Tiriki laid her hand upon her heart and then her forehead in the salute offered only to the very highest of initiates.

'Master Chedan Arados,' she murmured, 'may you walk in Light.'

Damisa surveyed the priest with interest. Throughout Atlantis, in the priests' caste at least, the name of Chedan Arados was well known. He had been an acolyte in the Ancient Land, schooled at the same time as Tiriki's mother, Deoris; but Chedan had carried his studies further to become a Free Mage. After the destruction of the City of the Circling Snake, he had traveled widely. But despite his several visits to Alkonath, Damisa had never seen him.

The mage was tall with warm but piercing eyes, and the full beard of a mature man. There was already a strong hint of roundness to his belly, but he could not fairly have been called stout. His robe, made of the same fine white linen as those worn by ordinary priests of Light, was of a distinctly different design, fastened with loops and buttons on one shoulder and hanging loose to the ankle. Upon his breast was a disk of crystal, a lens in which thin blue-white glimmers darted and sparkled like fish in a pool.

'I do walk in Light,' said the mage to Tiriki, 'but too often, what I see is darkness. And so it is today.'

Tiriki's smile froze. 'We see what you see,' she said, very softly, 'but we should not speak of it here.'

Micail and Tjalan, having completed the more formal greetings between princes, clasped wrists forcefully. As their bracelets clinked, the severe lines of their similarly large-nosed faces gave way to the warmest laughter.

'You had a good voyage?' Micail asked as the two turned, arms linked, making their way along the quayside.

'The *sea* was calm enough,' Tjalan quipped wryly.

'Your lady did not want to leave Alkonath?'

Tjalan suppressed a snort of laughter. 'Chaithala is convinced that the Isles of Tin are a howling wilderness inhabited by monsters. But our traders have been preparing a refuge at Belsairath for many years. She will not fare so ill. Knowing she and the children are safe frees my mind for the task here.'

'And if we are all mistaken and no disaster occurs?' asked Micail.

'Then she will have had an unusual vacation and will likely never forgive me. But I have been speaking much with Master Chedan on the voyage, and I fear your forebodings are only too sure . . .'

Damisa suppressed a shiver. She had assumed that the ritual in the deep Temple had been successful, despite Alyssa's collapse, because the earthquakes and the nightmares had ceased. Now she was uneasy. Had such tremors been felt in Alkonath, too? It was becoming difficult to assure herself that Tjalan's visit was no more than a social call.

'And who is this? Can this be little Damisa, grown woman-high?'

The voice brought Damisa's head around. The third traveler stood before her with his cloak now thrown back to reveal a sleeveless tunic and kilt so emblazoned with embroidery she blinked as the bright garments caught the sun. But she knew the gaudy clothing covered a muscular body, and the long dagger sheathed at the man's side, however ornate, was not aristocratic frippery. He was Antar, Tjalan's body-guard from the time they were boys.

'It *is* Damisa,' Antar answered himself, his dark eyes, as always, in constant motion, watching for any threat to his lord.

Damisa blushed, realizing that the others were now looking at her, too.

'Trust you, Antar, to see her first,' said Micail, smiling.

'I trust Antar to see everything first,' Tjalan commented, with a grin no less wide. 'Damisa. What a pleasure, sweet cousin, to find a flower of Alkona amid so many lilies.' His attitude was warm and welcoming, but as Damisa walked forward she knew that the days of childish hugs were forever gone. She held out her hand, and her prince bent to it respectfully – if with a twinkle in his sea-colored eyes.

'Damisa, you are become a woman indeed,' said Tjalan appreciatively. But he let go her hand, and turned once more to Tiriki. 'You have taken good care of our flower, I see.'

'We do what we may, my noble lord. And now—' Tiriki handed the basket of fruit and flowers to Damisa as she said, in a ringing voice, 'Let the officers of the city make the Prince of Alkonath most welcome.' She gestured toward the open square at the entrance to the quay where, as if by magic, crimson pavilions had sprung up to shade tables full of food and drink.

Tjalan frowned. 'I hardly think we have time—'

Tiriki delicately took his arm. 'We must delay all serious discussion until the lords arrive from the estates in the countryside. And if the people see us eat and drink together, it will hearten the city. Indulge us, my noble lord, I pray.'

As ever, beneath Tiriki's words rang the cadence of a song. A man would have to be made of stone, Damisa thought, to resist the sweetness in that plea.

* * *

Micail glanced around the great hall to ascertain that the servants had finished setting out the earthenware pitchers of lemon-water and the silver goblets, and then nodded his permission for them to retire. The last of the daylight shafted through narrow windows beneath the soaring dome of the Council Hall, illuminating the circular table and the worried faces of the traders, landowners, and leaders who sat around it. Would the strength of Atlantis ever again be arrayed in such order and dignity?

Micail arose from his couch and waited for the conversations to fade. For this meeting, he retained the regalia that marked him as a prince, although Tiriki had resumed the white robe and veil of a simple priestess and sat a little to one side. Reio-ta, robed as governor of the Temple, had taken a place on the left with the other rulers.

Once again, Micail felt acutely that he stood between two realms, the worldly and the spiritual. Over the years he had often found his identities as a Vested Guardian and as Prince of Ahtarrath in conflict, but tonight, perhaps, his royalty might give him the authority to enforce the priesthood's wisdom.

If even that will be enough. At the moment, what Micail felt most strongly was fear. But the die was cast. His friend Jiritaren gave an encouraging nod. The room had silenced. All eyes were on him, tensely expectant.

'My friends, heirs of Manoah, citizens of Atlantis, we all have felt the tremors that shake our islands. Yes, *islands*,' he repeated sharply, seeing the eyes of some of the landowners widen, 'for the same forerunners of disaster have shook Alkonath, Tarisseda, and other kingdoms as well. So we gather together to take counsel against the threat that now faces us all.' Micail paused and looked slowly about the table.

'There is still much that we can do,' he said encouragingly, 'for as you surely know, the Empire has faced circumstances no less dire, and has survived to see this day.

Master Chedan Arados—' Micail paused, permitting a flurry of whispers to run through the hall. 'Master Chedan, you were among those who escaped the Ancient Land's destruction. Will you speak to us now of the prophecies?'

'I will.' Ponderously, the mage got to his feet and eyed the gathering sternly.

'It is time for the veil to be set aside,' he said. 'Some secrets will be shared which have hitherto been spoken only under seal of initiation; but that was done to preserve the truth, that it might be revealed at the appointed hour. To keep these things hidden now would be the true sacrilege. Indeed, for the threat we face has its deepest roots in a sacrilege committed almost thirty years ago in the Ancient Land.' As Chedan drew breath, the bar of sunlight that had haloed his head moved, leaving him in sudden shadow. Micail knew it was only because the sun was sinking, but the effect was disquieting.

'And it was not ordinary men but priests,' Chedan said clearly, 'who in the misguided quest for forbidden knowledge, destabilized the magnetic field that harmonizes the conflicting forces within the earth. All our wisdom and all our power was only enough to delay the moment when the fault gave way; and when at last the City of the Circling Snake sank beneath the inland sea, there were no few who said it was only justice. The city that had permitted the desecration *should* pay the price, they said. And when, soon after, the Ancient Land itself was swallowed up by the sea, although the seers gave us warning that the repercussions would continue, that the unraveling would expand along the fault line, perhaps to crack the world open like an egg – yet we dared hope we had seen the worst of the destruction.'

The priests looked grim – they knew what was coming. On the faces of the rest, Micail read growing apprehension as Chedan continued.

'The recent tremors in Alkonath, as here, are a final

warning that the Ascent of Dyaus – the Time of Ending, as some call it – is very near.'

By now, much of the hall was in darkness. Micail signaled to a servant to light the hanging lamps, but their illumination seemed too meager for the room.

'Why were we not told?' cried a merchant. 'Did you mean to keep this secret so only the priesthood might be saved?'

'Were you not listening?' Micail overrode him. 'The only *facts* we had were made known as we received them. Should we have created useless panic by proclaiming predictions of a disaster that might not have come to pass for a century?'

'Of course not,' Chedan agreed. 'That was in fact the mistake made in the Ancient Land. Until the foreseen is seen again, its signs cannot be recognized. This is why the greatest seers are helpless against true destiny. When men are braced too long against a danger that does not come, they grow heedless, and cannot respond when the moment does arrive.'

'If it *has* arrived,' scoffed a prominent landowner. 'I am a simple man, I don't know anything about the meaning of lights in the sky. But I do know that Ahtarrath is a volcanic island. It is entirely natural for it to shake at times. Another layer of ash and lava will only serve to enrich the soil.'

Hearing murmurs of agreement from the village lords, Micail sighed.

'All that the priesthood can do is to give warning,' he said, striving to keep rising irritation from his voice. 'What you do about this is up to you. I will not force even my own servants to abandon their homes. I can only advise all here that the majority of the Guardians of the Temple have chosen to entrust ourselves and our goods to the sea, and return to land only when the cataclysm ends. As a prince of the blood I say it, and we shall endeavor to take with us as many as we can.'

Reio-ta rose, nodding affirmation. 'We must not allow the truth that the Temple safeguards to . . . die. We will send forth our Twelve Acolytes and as . . . many more as we can

31

find ships for, with our hopes that at least some of them will come safely to . . . lands where new temples may rise.'

'What lands?' someone exclaimed. 'The barren rocks where savages and animals rule? Only fools trust to the wind and the sea!'

Chedan spread his arms. 'You forget your own history,' he chided. 'Though we have stood apart from the world since the war with the Hellenes, we are not ignorant of other lands. Wherever there are goods to be bought or sold, the ships of Atlantis have gone – and since the fall of the Ancient Land, many of our priests have gone with them. In trading stations from Khem and Hellas to the Hesperides and Zaiadan, they have endured a lonely exile, learning the ways of the native peoples, studying their alien gods in search of beliefs held in common, teaching and healing, preparing the way. I believe that when our wanderers arrive, they will find a welcome.'

'Those who choose to remain need not fear idleness,' said the priestess Mesira, unexpectedly. 'Not all who are of the Temple believe that disaster is inevitable. We will continue to work with all our powers to maintain the balance here.'

'That, I am glad to hear,' came a sardonic voice from the western quarter. Micail recognized Sarhedran, a wealthy shipmaster, with his son Reidel behind him. 'Once Ahtarrath ruled the seas, but as my noble lord has reminded us, our gaze turned inward. Even if people could be persuaded to go to these foreign lands, we have not the vessels to carry them.'

'That is just why we come now, with half the fleet of great Alkonath, to offer help.' The speaker was Dantu, captain of the ship in which Tjalan had arrived. If his smile was less tactful than triumphant, there was reason for it. The traders of Alkonath and Ahtarrath had been fierce rivals in the past.

Now Tjalan spoke. 'In this time of trial, we remember that we are all children of Atlantis. My brothers remain to supervise the evacuation of Alkonath. It is my honor and my great personal pleasure to commit eighty of my finest wingbirds to the preservation of the people and the culture of *your* great land.'

Some at the table looked a little sour still, but most faces had begun to blossom in smiles. Micail could not repress a grin at his fellow prince, though even eighty ships, of course, could not save more than a tithe of the population.

'Then let this be our resolution,' Micail said, taking charge again. 'You shall go back to your districts and followers, and give them this news in whatever manner you see fit. Where needed, the treasury of Ahtarrath will be opened to secure supplies for the journey. Go now, make your preparations. Do not panic, but neither should anyone needlessly delay. We will pray to the gods that there is time.'

'And will *you* be on one of those ships, my lord? Will the royal blood of Ahtarrath abandon the land? Then we are lost indeed.' The voice was that of an old woman, one of the principal landowners. Micail strove to remember her name, but before he could, Reio-ta stirred beside him.

'The gods ordain that Micail must . . . go into exile.' The older man took deep breaths to control the stammer that still sometimes afflicted him. 'But I too am a Son of the Sun, blood-bound to Ahtarrath. Whatever fate befalls those remaining here, I will remain and share.'

Micail could only stare at his uncle, as Tiriki's shock amplified his own. Reio-ta had said nothing of this! They scarcely heard Chedan's concluding words.

'It is not for the priesthood to decide who shall live and who shall die. There is no one fit to say whether those who depart will do better than those who stay. Our fates result from our own choices, in this life and every other. I bid you only remember that, and choose mindfully, according to the wisdom that is within you. The Powers of Light and Life bless and preserve you all!'

*　　*　　*

Chedan took off his headdress and tucked it under his arm as he emerged from the Council Hall onto the portico. The wind from the harbor was a blessed breath of coolness.

'That went better than I . . . expected,' said Reio-ta, watching the others streaming down the stairs. 'Chedan, I thank you for your . . . words and efforts.'

'I have done little so far,' said Chedan, with a wave toward Tjalan, who had come out to join them, 'but even that would have been impossible without the limitless generosity of my royal cousin.'

Prince Tjalan clenched his fists to his heart and bowed before replying. 'My best reward is the knowledge that I have served the cause of Light.' Suddenly he grinned at the mage. 'You have been my teacher and my friend, and have never led me falsely.'

The door opened again and Micail, having calmed the immediate fears of the most anxious councillors, joined them. He looked worried. Until he actually set foot onboard ship, he would carry the responsibility not only for the evacuation but also for the welfare of those who decided to stay behind.

'We thank you, my lords,' Micail said, with a gesture. 'I know I would not wish to endure such a council after a sea voyage. You must be weary. The hospitality of Ahtarra can still provide a bit of food and shelter—' He managed a smile. 'If you will come with me.'

I think you need the rest more than I do, boy, thought Chedan, but he knew better than to show his pity.

The rooms allotted to the mage were spacious and pleasant, with long windows to admit a cooling breeze from the sea. He sensed that Micail would have liked to linger, but Chedan pretended exhaustion and was soon left alone.

As the sound of footsteps receded, the mage unstrapped his bag and rummaged within it for a pair of brown boots and a dull-colored robe such as any traveler might wear. Donning them, he briskly descended to the street, taking care to remain unnoticed, and set off into the murky twilight with such calm self-assurance that any who saw him pass would have thought he was a lifelong denizen of the tangled alleys and byways of the Temple precincts.

In fact, Chedan had not visited Ahtarra for many years, but the roads had changed little. Every other step he took was dogged by echoes of lost youth, lost love, lost lives . . . Chedan paused alongside the vine-draped northern wall of the new Temple. Hoping he was in the right place, he swept aside a handful of vines and found a side door. It opened easily enough. It was more difficult to close it again.

Inside it was dark, save for a faintly glowing line of stones in the floor that delineated the way through a narrow service corridor lined with unmarked doorways. Chedan was able to move along the path quickly, until he suddenly came to the low stone archway at its end.

I am getting too old for such shortcuts, the mage thought ruefully as he rubbed his head. *I might have gotten there faster by the front door.*

Beyond the archway was a cramped, vaulted chamber, lit by the glowing steps of a spiral stair. Chedan carefully ascended two flights and emerged through another arch to reach the common reading room, a broad pyramidal room almost at the top of the building. Designed to catch the maximum daylight, it was now almost entirely in shadow. Only a few reading lamps burned here and there.

Beneath one such glow, the Vested Guardian Ardral sat alone at a broad table, examining the contents of a wooden chest. Moving closer, Chedan could hardly see the tabletop for the clutter that covered it: tattered scrolls, fragments of inscribed stone tablets, and what looked like strings of colorful beads.

Ardral's attention was bent upon the prize of the collection, a curious sort of long, narrow book made of bamboo strips sewn together with silken threads.

'I didn't know you had the *Vimana Codex* here,' Chedan

commented, but Ardral ignored the attempt at polite interruption.

With a grimace, the mage appropriated a small bench nearby and dragged it noisily to a spot beside Ardral. 'I can wait,' he announced.

Ardral looked up, with an outright grin. 'Chedan,' he said softly, 'I really was not expecting you until—'

'I know.' Chedan looked away. 'I suppose I should have waited, but I've just come from the council meeting.'

'My condolences,' Ardral interjected. 'I hope I succeeded in providing everyone with whatever information they needed.'

'I thought I saw evidence of your work,' Chedan put in.

'But I simply could not face another rehearsal of the inevitable platitudes.'

'Yes, there was a lot of that. They're afraid,' said Chedan.

Ardral rolled his eyes. 'Afraid they might remember why they still aren't ready? This has been coming for a long time, nephew. And it's just as Rajasta predicted – even if he was a little wrong about the date. With the best will in the world, in the Temple as on the farmstead, most people simply cannot go on year after year, looking for a way out of an impossible situation that fails to develop at the expected time! The urge to resume the routine of life—' Ardral broke off. 'Well there, you see, even I do it. Speaking of which, I have something put aside that you used to enjoy very much. Perhaps we could go solve the world's problems in private, eh?'

'I—' Chedan blinked, then looked about the gloomy chamber . . . For a moment, seeing his uncle, he felt very young again. 'Yes,' he said, with a chuckle, and then a real smile. 'Thank you, Uncle.'

'That's the spirit,' Ardral approved, and standing up, proceeded to put the strange book into the wooden chest. 'Just because eternity is trampling our toes, doesn't mean we can't live a little before—' Locking the chest, he gave Chedan a wink. 'We do whatever dance comes next.'

During Chedan's last visit, Ardral had occupied a rather decrepit dormitory, some little distance from the temple. Now, as curator of the library, he had a spacious room within its very walls.

A fire blazed up in the hearth as they entered, or perhaps it had already been burning. Chedan glanced at the sparse but tasteful furnishings, while Ardral brought out two fili-greed silver cups, and opened a black and yellow jar of honey wine.

'*Teli'ir?*' the mage exclaimed.

Ardral nodded. 'I daresay there are no more than a dozen bottles in existence.'

'You honor me, Uncle. But I fear the occasion will not be worthy of it.' With a sigh, Chedan settled upon a cushioned couch.

In his uncle's company, drinking teli'ir, it was almost as if the Bright Empire still ruled both horizons. Time had hardly passed at all. He was no longer the learned Chedan Arados, the great Initiate of Initiates, the one who was expected to set forth answers, solutions, hope. He could be himself.

Although the two had not been particularly close before the fall of the Ancient Land, Chedan had known Ardral all his life – indeed, years before he became an acolyte, his uncle had briefly been his tutor. Many years had passed since then, yet Ardral seemed no older. There were, no doubt, new lines and creases in the mobile, expressive face, and the shock of brown hair had faded and thinned . . . If Chedan looked closely, he could find such marks of age, but these slight details did not change his inner identity which had somehow remained exactly the same.

'It *is* good to see you, Uncle,' he said.

Ardral grinned and refilled their cups. 'I am glad you got here,' he answered. 'The stars have not been reassuring for travelers.'

'No,' Chedan agreed, 'and the weather is little better,

though Tjalan tells me not to worry. But since you raised the subject, let me ask you – *your* head is always clear—'

'For another moment only,' Ardral joked, and quickly sipped more wine.

'Hah!' Chedan scoffed. 'You know what I mean. You have never been one who is easily misled by presumptions or legends. You see only what is actually before you, unlike some – but never mind that.

'Once, years ago,' Chedan persisted, 'you spoke to me of Rajasta's *other* prophecies, and your own reasons for believing them. Have those reasons changed? . . . *Have they?*' he repeated, leaning closer to his uncle. 'No one living knows Rajasta's works better than you.'

'I suppose,' said Ardral distantly, as he ate a bit of cheese.

Undeterred, Chedan continued, 'Everyone else has focused on the tragic elements of the prophecy. The destruction of Atlantis, the inevitable loss of life, the slim chance of survival. But you if anyone understands the larger scale of the prophecy – what was, and what is, and—'

'You are going to be a pest about this, aren't you?' Ardral growled, without his usual smile. 'All right. *Just this once*, I will answer the question you cannot bring yourself to ask. And then we will put the matter aside, for this night at least!'

'As you will, Uncle,' said Chedan, as meekly as a child.

With a sigh, Ardral ran his fingers through his hair, further disarranging it. 'The short answer is yes. It is as Rajasta feared. The inevitable is happening, and worse, it occurs under just the sort of conditions that give mediocre horologers fits. Bah. They're so easily distracted from the many positive influences – it's as if they *want* to think the worst. But yes, yes, we can't deny it, Adsar the Warrior Star has definitely changed its course toward the Ram's Horn. And this is precisely the alignment the ancient texts call the War of the Gods. But the ancients plainly do *not* say that such a configuration will mean anything to the *mortal* world! The usual human vanity. So predictable.'

For some moments there was silence, as Ardral once more refilled his cup, and Chedan tried to think of something to say.

'You see?' said Ardral, rather gently. 'It does no good to think on such things. We only see the hem of the garment, as they say. So let it go. Things are going to be hectic enough in the next few days. There won't be a lot of time for sitting quietly and doing nothing. And yet—' He raised his cup, mock-solemn. 'In times like these—'

Laughing in spite of his dark thoughts, Chedan joined him in the old refrain, *'There's nothing like nothing to settle the mind!'*

THREE

How does one pack a life?

Micail looked down at the confusion of items piled upon his couch and shook his head. It seemed a sad little assortment in the early morning light. *Three parts need to one part nostalgia?*

Every ship, of course, would be provisioned with practical items such as bedding and seeds and medicines. Meanwhile, the acolytes and a few trusted chelas had been given the task of packing scrolls and regalia, using lists the Temple had prepared long ago. But those items, really, were all for public use. It was left to each passenger to choose as many personal belongings as would fit into a sack to go with him or her across the sea.

He had done this once before, when he was twelve, leaving the Ancient Land where he had been born to come to this island that was his heritage. Then he had left his boyhood behind.

Well, I will no longer need to lead processions up the Star Mountain. For a moment longer, he examined the ceremonial mantle, beautifully embroidered with a web of spirals and comets . . . With the merest twinge of regret, he cast it aside and began to fold a pair of plain linen tunics. The only mantle of office he packed was one woven of white silk, so fine that it was luminous, and the blue mantle that went with it. With the ornaments of his priesthood, it would suffice for ritual work. *And without a country I will no longer be a prince.* Would that be a relief, he wondered, or would he miss the respect that his title brought him?

The symbol is nothing, he reminded himself; *the reality is everything.* A true adept should be able to carry on without any regalia. '*The most important tool of the mage is here*,' old Rajasta used to say, tapping his brow with a smile. For a moment Micail felt as if he were back in the House of the Twelve in the Ancient Land. *I miss Rajasta sorely*, thought Micail, *but I am glad he did not live to see this day.*

His gaze drifted to the miniature feather tree in its decorous pot on the windowsill, pale green foliage gleaming in the morning sun. It had been a gift from his mother, Domaris, not long after he had arrived on Ahtarrath, and since then he had watered it, pruned it, cared for it . . . As he picked it up he heard Tiriki's light step in the hall.

'My darling, are you really planning to take that little tree?'

'I . . . don't know.' Micail returned the pot to the window and turned to Tiriki with a smile. 'It seems a pity to abandon it after I have watched over it for so long.'

'It will not survive in your sack,' she observed, coming into his arms.

'That's so, but there might be room for it somewhere. If deciding whether to bring a little tree is my hardest choice . . .' The words died in his throat.

Tiriki raised her head, her eyes seeking his and following his gaze to the window. The delicate leaflets of the little tree trembled, quivering, though there was no wind.

Sensed, rather than heard, the subsonic groaning below and all around them became a vibration felt in the soles of their feet, more powerful by far than the tremor they had felt the day before.

Not again! Micail thought, pleading, *not yet, not now . . .*

From the mountain's summit, a trail of smoke rose to stain the pale sky.

The floor rolled. He grabbed Tiriki and pulled her toward the door. Braced beneath its frame, they would have some protection if the ceiling fell. Their eyes locked again, and without need of words, they synchronized their breathing, moving into the focused detachment of trance. Each breath took them deeper. Linked, they were both more aware of the unraveling stresses within the earth, and less vulnerable to them.

'Powers of Earth be still!' he cried, drawing on the full authority of his heritage. 'I, Son of Ahtarrath, Royal Hunter, Heir-to-the-Word-of-Thunder, command you! Be at peace!'

From the empty sky came thunder, echoed by a rumble that sounded far away. Tiriki and Micail could hear the tumult and outcry in the palace and the sounds of things crashing and breaking everywhere.

The shaking finally ceased, but the tension did not. Through the window, Micail could see that the Star Mountain's summit was gone – no, not gone, *displaced*. Smoke, or dust, rose all about the distinctive little pyramid as, still lighted, it slid slowly toward the city.

Micail closed his eyes tight and reached beyond himself again as a roiling onslaught of energies whipped through him. He tried to visualize the layers of rock that made up the island, but the restraining vision only flickered and shifted, until finally it became the image of the crossed arms of the faceless man, bound and chained but stirring, that had haunted their dreams. His muscles flexed and links popped as the man strained against his bonds.

'Who are you? WHAT DOES THIS MEAN?' He did not realize he had been shouting until he felt Tiriki's thoughts within his own.

'*It is – the Unrevealed!*' came her mental cry. '*Dyaus! Do not look at his eyes!*'

At this, the vision rose, snarling. The floor shook anew, more roughly than before, and would not stop. Micail had grown up with the whispered tales of the god Dyaus, invoked to bring change by Grey Mages of the Ancient Land. Instead, he had brought chaos whose reverberations had eventually destroyed that land and now seemed about to destroy Atlantis as well. But he had never been to the crypt where that image was chained.

'*I cannot hold him! Help me!*'

At once Micail felt Tiriki's unflinching rush of compassion.

'*Let Light balance Darkness—*' Her thought became a song.

'*And Reaction, Rest—*' he followed.

'*Let Love balance Hatred—*' Warmth built between their clasped hands.

'*The Male, the Female—*' Light grew between them, generating power to transform the tensions of the opposing forces.

> '*There is Light – There is Form*
> *There is Shadow and Illusion*
> *and Proportion—*'

It seemed a long time that they stood so, while the vacant howling of the chained god receded, gradually, grudgingly, sullenly.

When the shaking ceased at last, Micail drew a deep breath of relief, although his sensitized awareness felt the constant tremors beneath the equilibrium they had imposed upon the island.

'It's over.' Tiriki opened her eyes with a sigh.

'No,' he said heavily, 'only restrained, for a little while. Beloved—' Words failed him, and he clasped her more tightly. 'I could not have held back that power alone.'

'Do we have – time?'

'Ask the gods,' Micail replied. 'But at least no one will doubt our warning now.' He looked past her, his shoulders slumping as he saw on the floor beneath the window the shattered pot, spilled earth, and naked roots of his little feather tree.

People died in that quake, he told himself. *The city is burning. This is no time to weep over a tree.* But as he shoved his spare sandals into the bag, his eyes burned with tears.

The mood of the city had certainly altered, thought Damisa as she picked her way around a pile of rubble and continued toward the harbor. After the terror of the early morning, the bright sunlight seemed a mockery. The smoke from a dozen burning buildings had turned the light a strange, rich gold. Now and again, a vibration in the earth reminded her that though the dust from its toppled summit had dispersed, the Star Mountain was still wakeful.

The taverns were doing a roaring business, selling wine to those who preferred to drown their fear rather than take steps to save themselves from the sea, but otherwise the marketplace looked deserted. A few insisted that the morning's quake would be the last, but most people were at home, packing valuables to take on the ship or into the countryside. From the roof of the House of the Twelve, Damisa had seen the roads jammed with wagons. People were heading for the harbors or the inland hills, or anywhere away from the Star Mountain, whose crowning pyramid had come to a precarious stop about halfway down the slope. From the new, flattened summit, a plume of smoke continued to rise, a constant promise of more violence to come.

And to think that there had been moments when she had resisted the Temple's orderly serenity, its incessant imposition of patience and discipline. If this morning was a taste of what was coming, she suspected she would soon be remembering her life here as a paradise.

In the emergency, even the twelve acolytes had been pressed into service as common messengers. Damisa had claimed the note meant for Prince Tjalan, and she meant to deliver it. Determined, she tiptoed around a pool of noxious liquids spilling from a market, and she headed down a reeking alley to the waterfront.

The harbor yards were crowded and noisy as on any normal day, but now there was a barely restrained hysteria. She tugged her veil into place, and hastened her steps into the hubbub. She heard the drawling accents of Alkonath everywhere she turned. It must have been some kind of instinct that allowed her to distinguish Tjalan's voice, ringing above the babble of men who toiled to stow a hundred different kinds of gear.

As she drew nearer, she heard the sailor to whom the prince was speaking. 'What does it matter if the seed grain goes above or below the bales of cloth?'

'Do you eat cloth?' Tjalan asked sharply. 'Wet linen will dry, but salt-soaked barley will mold, not grow. So get back down there, man, and do it right this time!'

Damisa was relieved to see the prince's expression lighten as he recognized her.

'My dear – how goes it up there?' A wave of his hand indicated the temples and the palace on the hill.

'How is it everywhere?' Damisa tried to keep her voice even, but had to look away. 'Oh!' she brightened. 'But there *is* good news! The priests who serve at the summit of the Star Mountain actually survived! They came in an hour ago, all except their leader. He sends word that he dwelled on that peak since he was a boy, so if the mountain wishes to be rid of the pyramid, he will return to the summit without it.'

Tjalan laughed. 'I have known men like him – *"deep in the Mercy of the Gods,"* as they say. He may outlast all of us!'

'There are some,' she found herself saying, 'who believe that when the earth began to shake, we should have made . . . a special offering . . .'

Tjalan blinked, brows furrowing. 'Sweet child – do not

even think such things!' His bronzed face had gone taut and pale. 'We are not barbarians who sacrifice children! The gods would be right to destroy us if we were!'

'But they *are* destroying us,' she muttered, unable to tear her gaze from the flattened, smoking peak.

'They are certainly unmaking the islands,' Tjalan corrected gently. 'But they granted us warning first, did they not – first by the prophecies and now by the tremors? We were given time to prepare an escape—' His gesture embraced the ships, the people, the boxes, bags, and barrels of provisions. 'Even the gods cannot do everything for us!'

He is as wise as any priest. Damisa admired the strength in his profile as he turned to answer a question from the captain, a man called Dantu. *I can be proud to be kin to such a man*, she thought, and not for the first time. She had not originally been destined for the Temple – it was her grandmother who proposed her as a candidate for the Twelve. When she had dreamed of a royal marriage as a little girl, Tjalan had been her model for a worthy consort. It was a relief to find that a more mature judgment justified her original opinion. He made Kalhan look like the boy he was!

'Mind yourselves!' The prince was glaring at a group of sailors who stopped work to goggle at two buxom, saffron-draped saji girls who were pulling a cart full of parcels from the Temple of Caratra.

One of the men smacked his lips and made a kissing noise at the girls, who giggled behind their veils. 'Wouldn' mind packing *you* into my hold . . .'

'You there!' Tjalan repeated, 'back to work. They're not for such as you!'

What the sajis *were* for had been the subject of much wild-eyed speculation among the acolytes. In the old days, it was said, sajis had been trained to assist in certain kinds of magic that involved the sexual energies. Damisa shuddered, glad that she had not experience enough to guess what those might be. The acolytes were free to take lovers before they married, but she had been too fastidious to do so, and Kalhan, chosen as her betrothed by some arcane procedure of astrology, had not tempted her to experiment ahead of time.

'I almost forgot!' she exclaimed. 'I have brought a list of candidates to sail in the royal vessel, with – with you.' As Prince Tjalan turned to her again, she opened her scroll case and gave him the parchment.

'Ah yes,' he murmured, running a finger down the list of names. 'Hmm. I don't know if this is a relief or not—' He waved the paper at her. 'I can see beside it like a shadow the list of those who will not escape – either because they choose to stay, or because there is not enough room. I had hoped that the only decisions required of me would be where to stow their gear.'

Damisa heard his bitterness and had to quell a powerful impulse to reach out to him. 'Lord Micail and Lady Tiriki will be sailing with Captain Reidel, but I am on *your* list,' she said softly.

'Yes, little flower, and I am very glad of it!' Tjalan's gaze returned to her face, and his grim look lightened. 'Who would have thought my skinny little cousin would have grown so—'

Another call from Dantu cut off whatever he had been about to say, but Damisa was to cherish those parting words for a long time. He had noticed that she was grown up. He had really *seen* her. Surely, the word he had not had the chance to say was 'fair,' or 'lovely,' or even 'beautiful.'

The house where Reio-ta dwelt with Deoris was set into a hillside close to the Temple, with a view of the sea. As a small child, Tiriki had lived in the house of the priestesses with her aunt Domaris. They had brought her to Ahtarrath as an infant to save her from the danger she faced as the child of the Grey Mage whose magic had awakened the evil of Dyaus. Deoris had feared her daughter dead until she came to Ahtarrath and they met once more. By then, Tiriki thought of Domaris as her mother, and it was only after Domaris's death that Tiriki lived with Deoris.

Now, as she climbed the broad steps of the house, arm in arm with Micail, she could not restrain a sudden sigh of appreciation for the harmony of the building and the gardens around it. As a child, confused and grieving, she had taken little notice of her surroundings, and by the time the pain of loss had faded, she had learned her way about too well to really see the place for what it was.

'How glorious.' Chedan, ascending close behind them, echoed her thought. 'It is a sad fact that we often appreciate things most deeply when we are about to lose them.'

Tiriki nodded, surreptitiously wiping away a tear. *When this is gone, how often will I regret all the times I passed this way without stopping to really look?*

For a moment the three paused, gazing westward. From here, the greater part of the broken city was hidden by the glittering roofs of the Temple district. Beyond them was only the ambiguous blue of the sea.

'It looks so peaceful,' Chedan said.

'An illusion,' Micail gritted, as he led them through the portico. Tiriki shivered as they crossed the decorative bridge that had, she reminded herself, always swayed slightly beneath the lightest step, but since the morning's quake, she had become preternaturally aware of the leashed stresses in the earth. Whenever *anything* shook, she tensed and wondered if the horror was about to begin again.

Here, she observed, there were no chaotic piles of keepsakes and discards, none of the frantic bustling that rippled through the rest of the city, just a soft-voiced servant, waiting to escort the visitors to Reio-ta and Deoris. Tiriki's heart sank with a premonition that their errand here would fail. Clearly, her parents did not intend to leave.

Chedan had gone ahead of her into the wide chamber

that looked out on the gardens, and stood, saluting Deoris. It seemed to Tiriki that his voice trembled as he spoke the conventional words. What had Chedan been to her mother, she wondered, when they were young together in the Ancient Land? Did he see the mature priestess, with silver threading auburn-black braids coiled like a diadem above her brow, or the shade of a rebellious girl with stormy eyes and a tangle of dark curls – the girl Domaris had described when she spoke of Tiriki's mother, before Deoris came to Ahtarrath from the Ancient Land?

'Have you . . . finished packing?' Reio-ta was asking. 'Is the Temple prepared for evacuation, and the acolytes ready to . . . go?' The governor's speech stumbled no more than usual. From his tone, it might have been a perfectly ordinary day.

'Yes, all is going well,' Micail answered, 'or as well as can be expected. Some of the vessels have departed already. We expect to sail out on the morning tide.'

'We have saved more than enough space on Reidel's ship for both of you,' added Tiriki. 'You must come! Mother – Father—' she held out her hands. 'We will need your wisdom. We will need *you!*'

'I love you too, darling – but don't be foolish.' Deoris's voice was low and vibrant. 'I need only see the two of you to know that we have already given you all that you need.'

Reio-ta nodded, his warm eyes smiling. 'Have you forgotten, I . . . gave my word, in council? So long as any of my beloved people hold the land, I . . . I, too, shall stay.'

Tiriki and Micail exchanged a quick but meaningful glance. *Time to try the other plan.*

'Then, dear Uncle,' Micail said reasonably, 'we must drink deep of your advice while we can.'

'G-gladly,' said Reio-ta, with a modest inclination of his head. 'Perhaps you, Master Chedan, will . . . drink, of something sweeter? I can offer several good vintages. We have had some . . . banner years, in your absence.'

'You know me too well,' the mage said softly.

Micail laughed. 'If Reio-ta hadn't offered,' he went on, disingenuously, 'no doubt Chedan would have asked.' Catching Tiriki's eye, Micail jerked his head slightly in the direction of the garden, as if to say, *The two of you could talk alone out there.*

'Come, Mother,' Tiriki said brightly, 'let the men have their little ceremonies. Perhaps we might walk in your garden? I think that is what I will miss most.'

Deoris lifted an eyebrow, first at Tiriki and then at Micail, but she allowed her daughter to take her arm without comment. As they passed through the open doors, they could hear Chedan proposing the first toast.

The courtyard garden Reio-ta had built for his lady was unique in Ahtarrath, and since the fall of the Ancient Land, perhaps in the world. It had been designed as a place of meditation, a re-creation of the primal paradise. Even now the breeze was sweet with the continual trilling of songbirds, and the scent of herbs both sweet and pungent perfumed the air. In the shade of the willows, mints grew green and water-loving plants opened lush blossoms, while salvias and artemisia and other aromatic herbs had been planted in raised beds to harvest the sun. The spaces between the flagstones were filled with the tiny leaves and pale blue flowers of creeping thyme.

The path itself turned in a spiral so graceful that it seemed the work of nature rather than art, leading inward to the grotto where the image of the Goddess was enshrined, half-veiled by hanging sprays of jasmine, whose waxy white flowers released their own incense into the warm air.

Tiriki turned and saw Deoris's large eyes full of tears.

'What is it? I must admit a hope that you are finally willing to fear what must come, if it will persuade you—'

Deoris shook her head, with a strange smile. 'Then I am sorry to disappoint you, my darling, but frankly the future has never had any real power to frighten me. No, Tiriki, I was only remembering . . . it hardly seems seventeen years ago that we were standing in this very spot – or no – it was up on the terrace. This garden was barely planted then. Now look at it! There are flowers here I still can't name. Really I don't know why anyone wants wine; I can grow quite drunken sometimes just on the perfumes here—'

'Seventeen years ago?' Tiriki prompted, a little too firmly.

'You and Micail were no more than children,' Deoris smiled, 'when Rajasta came. Do you remember?'

'Yes,' answered Tiriki, 'it was just before Domaris died.' For a moment she saw her own pain echoed in her mother's eyes. 'I still miss her.'

'She raised me, too, you know, with Rajasta, who was more of a father to me than my own,' Deoris said in a low voice. 'After my mother died, and my father was too busy running the Temple to pay attention to us. Rajasta helped take care of me, and Domaris was the only mother I knew.'

Although she had heard these very words a thousand times, Tiriki stretched out her hand in swift compassion. 'I have been fortunate, then, in having two!'

Deoris nodded. 'And I have been blessed in you, Daughter, late though I came to know you! And in Galara, of course,' she added, with a look almost of reproof.

The gap in their ages had given Tiriki and the daughter Deoris had by Reio-ta few opportunities to know each other. She knew much more about Nari, the son Deoris had borne to fulfill her obligation to bear a child of the priestly caste, who had become a priest in Lesser Tarisseda.

'Galara,' Tiriki mused. 'She is thirteen now?'

'Yes. Just the age you were when Rajasta brought me here. He was an eminent priest in the Ancient Land, perhaps our greatest authority on the meaning of the movements of the stars. He interpreted them to mean that we had seven years – but it was the date of his own death he foretold. We thought then that perhaps he had been completely mistaken. We hoped . . .' She plucked a sprig of lavender

51

and turned it in her fingers as they walked. The sharp, sweet scent filled the air. 'But I should not complain; I have had ten more years to love you and to enjoy this beautiful place. I should have died beside your father, many, many years ago!'

They had completed a circuit of the spiral path, and stood once more opposite the Mother's shrine.

Tiriki stopped, realizing that her mother was speaking not of Reio-ta, who had been a kind stepfather, but of her true father. 'Riveda,' she muttered, and in her mouth it was like a curse. 'But you were innocent. He used you!'

'Not entirely,' Deoris said simply, 'I – I loved him.' She looked around at her daughter, fixing her with those stormy eyes whose color could shift so swiftly from grey to blue. 'What do you know of Riveda – or rather, what do you think you know?'

Tiriki hid her frown behind a flower. 'He was a healer, whose treatises on medicine have become a standard for our training today – even though he was executed as a black sorcerer!' She lowered her voice. 'What else do I need to know?' she asked, forcing a smile. 'In every way that matters, Reio-ta has been my father.'

'Oh, Tiriki, Tiriki.' Deoris shook her head, her eyes filled with secret thoughts. 'It is true, Reio-ta was born to be a father, and a good one. But still there is a duty of blood that is different than the honor you owe the man who raised you. You need to understand what it was that Riveda was seeking – why it was that he fell.'

They had come to the center of the spiral, where the Goddess smiled serenely through her curtain of flowers. Deoris paused, bowing her head in reverence. Behind her was a garden seat carved of stone, inlaid with a golden pattern of turtles. She sank down upon it as if her legs did not have the strength to carry both her and the weight of her memories.

Tiriki nodded to the Power the image represented, then

leaned against a nearby olive tree and crossed her arms beneath her breasts, waiting. It was not the Great Mother, but the woman who had borne her whose words interested her now.

'Your father had the most brilliant mind of anyone I have ever known. And except perhaps for Micail's father, Micon, he had the strongest will. We never fell in love with ordinary men, Domaris and I,' Deoris added with a rueful smile. 'But what you must understand first of all is that Riveda was not a destroyer. Both black and white are mingled in the grey robes his order wore. He knew from his studies and the practice of medicine that any living thing that does not grow and change will die. Riveda tested the laws of the Temple because he desired to make it stronger, and ultimately he broke them for the same reason. He came to believe that the priesthood had become so locked into ancient dogmas that it could not adapt, no matter what disaster might occur.'

'That is *not* so,' Tiriki replied indignantly, defending the traditions and training that had shaped her life.

'I sincerely hope that it is not,' Deoris smiled tolerantly. 'But it is up to you and Micail to prove him wrong. And you will never have a better chance. You will lose much that is fair in this exile, but you will escape our old sins as well.'

'And so will you, Mother! You must agree to come away—'

'Hush,' said Deoris, 'I cannot. I will not. Riveda was tried and executed not only for his own deeds, but also for much that was done by others – the Black Robes, who were only caught and punished later. It was their work that broke the bonds Riveda had loosened. They sought power, but Riveda wanted knowledge. That was why I helped him. If Riveda deserved his fate – then my guilt is no less.'

'Mother—' Tiriki began, for still she did not entirely understand.

'Give my place to your sister,' Deoris said, resolutely changing the subject. 'I have already arranged for an escort to bring Galara and her baggage to your chambers the first thing in the morning, so you will have a hard time turning her away.'

'I assumed you would send her,' Tiriki said, exasperated.

'Then that's settled. And now,' said Deoris as she got to her feet, 'I think it's time we rejoined the men. I doubt that Chedan and Micail have had any more luck in persuading Reio-ta than you have had with me. But they are two against one, and my husband may be feeling in need of reinforcement by now.'

Defeated, Tiriki followed her mother back to the porch, where the men were sitting with goblets and two small jugs of Carian wine. But Micail looked thunderous, and Chedan was also glaring at his drink. Only Reio-ta showed any sign of serenity.

Tiriki shot Micail a glance, as if to say, *I take it he is also still determined to stay?*

Micail nodded faintly, and Tiriki turned to her stepfather, intending to beg him to go with them.

Instead, she pointed to Deoris, exclaiming, 'You would go fast enough if *she* decided on it! You are sacrificing each other, for no good reason. You must agree to come with us!'

Deoris and Reio-ta exchanged tired glances, and Tiriki felt a sudden chill, as if she were a novice priestess chancing upon forbidden mysteries.

'It is your destiny to carry the truth of the Guardians to a new land,' said Deoris gently, 'and it is our karma to remain. It is not sacrifice but an atonement, which we have owed since . . .'

Reio-ta completed her thought. 'Since before the . . . fall of the Ancient Land.'

Chedan had closed his eyes in pain. Micail looked from one to the other, brows knitting in sudden surmise.

'Atonement,' Micail echoed softly. 'Tell me, Uncle – what do you know about the *Man with Crossed Hands?*' His voice shook, and Tiriki also felt a tremor in the stone beneath her feet, as if something else had heard his words.

'What?' rasped Reio-ta, his dark face going ashen. 'He shows himself to you?'

'*Yes*,' whispered Tiriki, 'this morning, when the earth shook – he was trying to break his chains. And I – *I knew his name!* How can that be?'

Once more an odd look passed between Deoris and her husband, and he reached out to take her hand.

'Then you unwittingly bring the clearest proof,' said Deoris quietly, 'that it *is* our fate and our duty to stay. Sit,' she gestured imperiously. 'Tiriki, I see now that I must tell you and Micail the rest of the story, and even you, Chedan, old friend. Great adept though you are, your teachers could not give you the parts of the story that they did not know.'

Reio-ta took a deep breath. 'I . . . loved my brother.' His gaze flickered toward Micail in momentary appeal. 'Even in the Temple of Light . . . there have always been some who . . . served the darkness. We were . . . taken by the Black Robes who . . . sought for themselves the power of Ahtarrath. I agreed to let them use me . . . if they would spare him. They betrayed me, and tried to kill him. But Micon . . . forced himself to . . . live, long enough to sire you and pass to you his power.' He looked at Micail again, struggling for words.

Tiriki gazed at them with quick compassion, understanding now why it was Micail, not Reio-ta, who held the magical heritage of his royal line. If Micon had died before his son was born, the powers of Ahtarrath would have descended to Reio-ta, and thereby to the black sorcerers who then held him in thrall . . .

'They . . . broke . . . his body,' stammered Reio-ta. 'And . . . my mind. I did not know myself till . . . long after. Riveda took me in and I . . . helped him . . .'

Tiriki looked back at her mother. What did this have to do with the Man with Crossed Hands?

'Reio-ta helped Riveda as a dog will serve the one who feeds him,' Deoris said defensively, 'not understanding what he did. I assisted Riveda because I loved the spirit in him that yearned to bring new life into the world. In the crypt beneath the Temple of Light there was an . . . image, whose form seemed different to each one who beheld it. To me, it always appeared as a bound god, crossed arms straining against his chains. But the image was a prison that confined the forces of chaos. Together we worked the rite that would release that power because Riveda thought that by unleashing that force he could wield the energies that power the world. But my sister forced me to tell her what we had done. The wards were already unraveling when Domaris went down into that dark crypt alone, at risk of life and limb, to repair them—'

'All these things I knew,' Chedan put in quietly. 'The power of the Omphalos Stone can only slow the destructive forces unleashed by these rites long ago. The disintegration has been gradual, but it is still happening. We can only hope that when Atlantis falls, there will be an end.'

'Didn't Rajasta use to say, "To give in instead of fighting death is cowardice,"' Micail put in, tartly.

'But he would also say—' Deoris replied with painful sweetness, '"When you break something, it is your duty to mend it, or at least sweep up the debris." Although we meant no evil, we made the choices that brought it forth – we set in motion a chain of events that has doomed our way of life.'

A long moment passed in silence. The four of them sat as motionless as the carven friezes that framed the doorway.

'We must stay because there is one final ritual to perform.' By Reio-ta's steady speech, they recognized the depth of his emotion. 'When the Man with Crossed Hands breaks his chains, we who know him so well must confront him.'

'Spirit to spirit we will address him,' added Deoris, her

great eyes shining. 'There is no Power in the world without a purpose. The chaos that Dyaus brings shall be as a great wind that strips trees and scatters seeds far and wide. You are born to preserve those seeds, my children – glorious branches from the ageless tree of Atlantis, freed of its rot, free to take root in new lands. Perhaps the Maker will understand this, and be appeased.'

Was it truly so? At this moment, Tiriki knew only that this day offered her the last sight that she would ever have of her mother. Sobbing, she moved forward and folded the older woman in her arms.

FOUR

Although the long day had been unseasonably cool, the sunset brought winds that were warm and an ominously hot night. Most of those who actually tried to sleep tossed and turned in damp frustration. The city that had been so quiet by day became the opposite that night, as its people wandered the streets and parks. Perhaps surprisingly, few were actually looting the deserted houses and shops; the rest seemed to be searching, but for what, none seemed to know – a cooler place to rest. Perhaps the true goal was to achieve that exhaustion of the body that alone can give peace to the fevered brain.

In their rooms at the top of the palace, Tiriki sat watching her husband sleep. It was several hours after midnight, but rest eluded her. They had been up late making final preparations to sail in the morning. Then she had sung until Micail fell at last into an uneasy slumber, but there was no one to sing *her* to sleep. She wondered if her mother, who might have done so, was wakeful as well, waiting for what must come.

It does not matter, she told herself, looking around the room where she had known so much joy. *I will have the rest of my life to sleep . . . and weep.*

Beyond the open doors to the terrace the night sky was red. In that lurid light she could see the silhouette of Micail's feather tree, which she had rescued and repotted. It was foolish, she knew, to see in that small plant a symbol of all the beautiful and fragile things that must be abandoned. On a sudden impulse she rose, found a scarf to wrap around the pot and the slender branches, and tucked it into the top of her bag. It was an act of faith, she realized. If she could preserve this little life, then perhaps the gods would be equally merciful to her and those she loved.

Except for the light that burned before the image of the Great Mother in the corner of the bedchamber, all the lamps had gone out, but she could still see the disorder in the room. The bags they had filled to take with them stood next to the door, waiting for the last frantic farewell.

The fitful flicker behind the veil of the shrine focused her gaze. Ahtarra had many temples and priesthoods, but only in the House of Caratra were a high altar and sanctuary consecrated in the Mother's name. And yet, thought Tiriki with a faint smile, the Goddess received more worship than any of the gods. Even the humblest goatherd's hut or fisherman's cottage had a niche for Her image, and if there was no oil to spare for a lamp, one could always find a spray of flowers to offer Her.

She rose and drew aside the gauze that veiled the shrine. The lamp within was alabaster, and it burned only the most refined of oils, but the ivory image, only a handspan high, was yellowed and shapeless with age. Her aunt Domaris had brought it with her from the Ancient Land, and before that, it had belonged to *her* mother, the legacy of a lineage of foremothers whose origins predated even the records of the Temple.

From the lamp she lit a sliver of pine and held it to the charcoal that was always laid ready on a bed of sand in the dish beside the lamp.

'Be ye far from me, all that is profane.' As she murmured the ancient words, she felt the familiar dip of shifting consciousness. 'Be far from me, all that lives in evil. Stand afar from the print of Her footsteps and the shadow of Her veil.

Here I take refuge, beneath the curtain of the night and the circle of Her own white stars.'

She took a deep breath and let it out slowly. The charcoal had begun to glow. She picked up a few grains of incense and scattered them across it, feeling awareness shift further as the pungent sweet smoke spiraled into the air.

Bowing her head, she touched her fingers to her brow and her lips and breast. Then her hands lifted in a gesture of adoration so familiar it had become involuntary.

'Lady . . .' the word died on her lips. The time for asking that this fate should pass was gone. 'Mother . . .' she tried again, and whatever words might have followed were borne away by a tide of emotion.

And in that moment, she became aware that she was not alone.

'I am the earth beneath your feet . . .' The Goddess spoke within.

'But the island is being destroyed!' A panicked part of Tiriki's soul objected.

'I am the burning flame . . .'

'The flame will be drowned by the waves!'

'I am the surging sea . . .'

'Then you are chaos and destruction!' Tiriki's soul protested.

'I am the night and the circling stars . . .' came the calm reply, and Tiriki's soul clung to that certainty.

'I am all that is, that has been, that will be, and there is no power that can separate you from Me . . .'

And for a moment outside time, Tiriki knew that it was true.

When she returned to awareness of her surroundings, the incense had ceased to burn and the charcoal was grey. But as the lamp flickered, it seemed to her that the image of the Mother was smiling.

Tiriki took a deep breath and reached out to lift the image from its stand. 'I know that the symbol is nothing, and the reality is all,' she whispered, 'but nonetheless I will take you with me. Let the flame continue to burn until it becomes one with the mountain's fire.'

She had just finished wrapping the image and tucking it into her bag when the chimes at the doorway rang faintly. She ran to the entry, afraid Micail would wake. A few swift steps brought her to the door, where she waved the messenger back out into the hall with her finger at her lips.

'Beg pardon, Lady,' he began, red-faced.

'No,' she sighed as she cinctured her robe, remembering the orders she had left. 'I know you would not come without need. What brings you?'

'You must come to the House of the Twelve, Lady. There is trouble – they will listen to you!'

'What?' She blinked. 'Has something happened to Gremos, their guardian?' Tiriki frowned. 'It is her duty to—'

'Beg pardon, Lady, but it seems that the Guardian of the Twelve is – gone.'

'Very well. Wait a moment for me to dress, and I will come.'

'Be still—' Tiriki pitched her voice to carry over the babble of complaint and accusation. 'You are the hope of Atlantis! Remember your training! Surely it is not beyond you all to give me a coherent tale!'

She glared around the circle of flushed faces in the entryway to the House of the Falling Leaves and let her mantle slip from her shoulders as she sat down. Her gaze fixed on Damisa; red-faced, the girl came forward. 'Very well then. You say that Kalaran and Vialmar got some wine. How did that happen, and what did they do?'

'Kalaran said that wine would help him sleep.' Damisa paused, her eyes briefly flicking closed as she ordered her thoughts. 'He and the other boys went down to the taverna at the end of the road to get some. There was no one there, so they brought two whole amphorae back with them and drank all of it, as far as I can tell.'

Tiriki turned her gaze to the three young men sitting on a bench by the door. Kalaran's handsome face was marred by a graze on one cheek, and water dripped down his companions' necks from wet hair, as if someone had tried to sober them up by plunging their heads into the fountain.

'And did it put you to sleep?'

'For a while—' Vialmar said sullenly.

'He got sick and puked,' said Iriel brightly, then fell silent beneath Damisa's glare. At twelve, Iriel was the youngest of the Twelve, fair-haired and mischievous, even now.

'About an hour ago they woke up shouting,' Damisa went on, 'something about being stalked by half-human monsters with horns like bulls. That woke up Selast, who was already mad because they didn't get back here until all the wine was gone. They started yelling, and that got everyone else into it. Someone threw the wine jug and then they went crazy.'

'And you all agree that this is what happened?'

'All except for Cleta,' Iriel sneered. 'As usual, she slept through it all.'

'I would have calmed them down in another few minutes,' said Elara. 'There was no need to disturb the Lady.'

Damisa sniffed. 'We would have had to tell her in any case because Gremos was gone.'

Tiriki sighed. For the Guardian of the Acolytes to leave her post in normal times would have been cause for a city-wide search. But now – if the woman failed to take her place in the boat, it would go to someone more deserving, or luckier. She suspected that the events of the next few days would effect their own winnowing of the priesthood and test their character in ways none of them could have foreseen.

'Never mind Gremos,' she said tartly. 'She will have to take care of herself. Nor is there any point in casting blame for what happened. What matters now is how you behave during the next few hours, not how you spent the last.' She looked at the window, where the approach of dawn was bringing a deceptively delicate pallor to the lurid sky.

'I have called you the hope of Atlantis, and it is true.' Her clear gaze moved from one to another until their high color faded and they were ready to meet her eyes. 'Since you are awake, we may as well get a head start on the day. Each of you has tasks. What I want—'

The chair jerked suddenly beneath her. She threw out her hands, brushed Damisa's robe, and clutched instinctively as the floor rocked once more.

'Take cover!' cried Elara. Already the acolytes were diving for protection under the long, heavy table. Damisa pulled Tiriki to her feet, and they staggered toward the door, dodging the carved plaster moldings that adorned the upper walls as they cracked and fell to the ground.

Micail! With her inner senses Tiriki felt his shocked awakening. Every fiber of her being wanted the strength of his arms, but he was half a city away. As the earth moved again she sensed that even their united strength would not have been enough to stop the destruction a second time.

She clung to the doorpost, staring outside as trees tossed wildly in the garden, and a huge column of smoke rose above the mountain. The shape of a great pine tree made of ashes, from whose mighty trunk a canopy of curdled cloud was spreading across the sky. Again and again the ground heaved beneath her. The ash cloud above the mountain sparkled with points of brightness, and glowing cinders began to fall.

Chedan had told them how other lands had fallen into the sea, leaving only a few peaks to mark their former location. Ahtarrath, it was clear, would not disappear without a battle of titanic proportions. At the moment she could not decide whether to exult in that defiance or to whimper in fear.

A movement in the distance caught her eye – above the trees that surrounded the House of the Falling Leaves she saw one of the gleaming gold towers shiver, then topple. As it vanished from sight, a tremor like another earthquake shook the ground. She winced at the thought of the devastation that now lay beneath it. In the next moment the sound of a crash from the other side of the city reached their ears.

'The second tower . . .' whispered Damisa.

'The city is already half deserted. Perhaps there were not too many people there—'

'Perhaps they were the lucky ones,' Damisa replied, and Tiriki could not find words to disagree with her. But for the moment at least, it appeared that everything likely to fall was already on the ground.

'Someone get a broom,' muttered Aldel; 'we should get the rubble off of this floor—'

'And who will sweep the rubble from the streets of the city?' asked Iriel, her voice trembling on the edge of hysteria. 'The end is upon us! No one will ever live here again!'

'Control yourselves!' Tiriki pulled herself together with an effort. 'You have been told what to do when this moment arrived. Get dressed and put on your strongest shoes. Wear heavy cloaks even if it grows warm – they will protect you when ash and cinders fall. Take your bags and get down to the ships.'

'But not everything is loaded,' exclaimed Kalaran, trying to control his fear. 'We were not able to get half the things we were supposed to take. The shaking has stopped. Surely we have a little time—'

Tiriki could still feel tremors vibrating through the floor, but it was true that for the moment the violence had passed.

'Perhaps . . . but be careful. Some of you are assigned to carry messages for the priests. Do not enter any building that seems damaged – an aftershock might bring it down. And don't take too long. In two hours you should all be on board. Remember, what men have made they can make again – your lives are more valuable now than anything you might risk them for! Tell me again what you are to do—'

One by one they listed their duties, and she approved or gave them new instructions. Calmer now, the acolytes scattered to gather their things. The architects of the House of the Falling Leaves had built better than they knew – though ornamentation littered the floor, the structure of the house was still secure.

'I must return to the palace. Damisa, get your things and come with me—'

Tiriki waited at the door until her acolyte returned, watching the steady fall of cinders into the garden. Now and again a bit that was still glowing would set one of the plants to smoldering. New smoke was billowing from the city. Numbly she wondered how long before it was all afire.

'I thought the sun was rising,' said Damisa at her elbow, 'but the sky is dark.'

'The sun has risen, but I do not think that we will see it,' answered Tiriki, looking up at the dark pall rolling across the sky. 'This will be a day without a dawn.'

Cinders were still falling as Tiriki and Damisa set forth from the House of the Falling Leaves, adding danger from above to the hazards of navigating streets whose pavements were buckled by the earthquake and littered with fallen debris. When a particularly large piece of lava barely missed Tiriki, Damisa dashed into an abandoned inn and came back with two large pillows.

'Hold it over your head,' she said, handing one to Tiriki. 'It will look silly, but it may protect you if something larger falls.'

Tiriki caught the note of incipient hysteria in her own answering laughter and cut it short, but the thought of what they must look like, scuttling through the shadowed streets like mushrooms with legs, kept a weird smile on her lips as they picked their way toward the palace.

It was the only amusement she was to find during that journey. Shocking as the devastation from yesterday's quakes had been, she had at least been able to recognize the city. Today's jolts had transformed the skyline into a place she did not know. She told herself that this morning's tremor was only an aftershock, bringing down structures already weakened, but she knew that this time the earth had been wrenched in a different direction, and with every step she became more aware that what she felt beneath her feet now was not equilibrium, but rather a tenuous balance that at any moment might fail.

The chains that bind the Man with Crossed Hands are breaking . . . she thought, shivering despite the warmth in the air. *One more effort will snap the last of them and he will be free . . .*

The palace was deserted. When they reached her rooms, she saw that both Micail and his bag were gone. *He will be waiting for me at the docks,* she told herself. Snatching up her own satchel, she followed Damisa back out to the street and started down the hill.

The House of the Healers had collapsed, blocking the road. Tiriki paused, listening, but she heard nothing from within. She hoped that everyone had gotten out safely. Indeed, it was some time since she had seen anybody at all. Obviously, she told herself, the priests and city functionaries who lived and worked here had taken the warning to heart and were already seeking safety on the docks or the hills, but she could not quite suppress the fear that everyone was dead, and that when she and Micail sought Captain Reidel's ship at last they would find the harbor empty, and have only ghosts for company as they waited for the island to fall.

Guided by Damisa, whose experience as a messenger had taught her the back ways of the upper city, they retraced their steps, turning toward the House of the Priests just up the hill.

As they ascended the Processional Walk, littered with fallen statues and the ruins of archways, Tiriki caught sight of a hurrying figure in sea boots and a brown traveling cloak.

'Chedan!' she exclaimed. 'What are you doing here? Are the priests—'

'Those holy fools! They claim to command spirits, but they cannot control themselves. Your husband is there now, trying to talk some sense into those who remain. Some have gone down to the ships as they were bid, and others have fled, the gods alone know where. They're all half-mad, I think, begging him to use his powers to make it stop—' He shook his head in disgust.

'But Micail stretched himself to the utmost yesterday, and a little beyond. He can do no more. Can't they understand?'

'Can't, or won't—' Chedan shrugged. 'Frightened men are strangers to reason, but that husband of yours will sort them out. In the meantime, those of us who can still think straight have work to do. And who still survive—' he added grimly. 'The man who was to have led the team to load the Omphalos Stone was killed by a falling wall. I told Micail I'd take care of it, but there's no one left here, or no one that is of any use, anyhow.'

'There's us,' Damisa said stoutly, 'and the other acolytes will be all right if they have something definite to do!'

For the first time, Chedan smiled. 'Then lead us, if you can still find your way in this chaos, and let us find them!'

They met Aldel surveying the House of the Healers in disbelief, having found no one to whom he might deliver his message, and Kalaran beside him, clutching an empty sack. Speechless, Tiriki and Damisa returned to the House of the Falling Leaves. Elis and Selast were just inside, packing. Flakes of ash powdered their dark hair.

'Are you the only ones left here?' asked Tiriki.

Elis nodded. 'I hope the others reached the ships safely.'

'Aldel is waiting outside, and so is Kalaran, so at least you and your betrothed will be together,' said Tiriki bracingly. 'And Kalhan is a strong lad,' she added to Damisa. 'I'm sure that when we get to the docks he will be waiting for you.' *As Micail will be waiting for me*, she added silently.

'Kalhan? Oh, yes, I'm sure he will . . .' Damisa said flatly.

Tiriki looked at her curiously. This was not the first time

she had thought that Damisa's feelings about the boy to whom the Temple astrologers had mated her seemed tepid. Once more she realized how fortunate she and Micail had been when they were allowed to choose for themselves.

'Will they be enough?' asked Chedan as Tiriki shepherded the acolytes out the door.

'They will have to be,' she answered as a stronger tremor rocked the town. 'We must go, *now!*' As they started down the road two more jolts made them stagger, and behind them they heard a crash as the porch of the House of the Falling Leaves came down.

'That was a very heavy leaf that just fell!' said Kalaran, lips twisting as he attempted a smile.

'That was the whole *tree*,' corrected Damisa tartly, but there were tears in her eyes, and she did not look back.

Elis was weeping softly. Selast, who despised such feminine weakness, looked at her in scorn. But all of them kept moving, picking their way around debris, and passing with no more than a sign of blessing when they saw bodies on the road. It was as well that they found no one in need of assistance. That would have put their discipline to too great a test. Indeed, Tiriki thought that if they had found a hurt child she would not have been entirely sure of her own self-control.

That which we seek to save will preserve the lives of generations yet unborn, she told herself, but the old sayings seemed meaningless in the face of the kind of catastrophe they were enduring now. Cinders had begun to fall once more. She flinched and drew her mantle over her head – she had discarded the pillow some time ago – then drew first one deep breath and then another, invoking the trained reflexes that would bring calm. *There is no thought . . . there is no fear . . . there is only the right moment and the right deed.*

With relief, she caught sight of the entrance to the Temple. Only now did she allow herself to look beyond it to the mountain. The pyramid at its top and the priest who kept it had been engulfed long ago. The smoke that billowed from its summit swirled now in a shapeless cloud, but the side of the mountain had opened, and lava was inscribing its own deadly message down the slope in letters of fire.

For a moment she allowed herself to hope that the escape of lava from within the mountain, like the lancing of a boil, would ease the pressure within. But the vibration beneath her feet spoke of unresolved tensions underground that were greater still.

'Quickly—' Chedan gestured toward the portico. Its structure still seemed sound, although parts of the marble facings littered the road.

Inside things were less reassuring, but there was no time to wonder how deep the cracks in the walls might run. The cabinet built to carry the Omphalos was waiting in the alcove, and the lamp still swung on its chains. As soon as they had lit the torches they took up the box by the long handles that supported it from the front and back, and hurried the acolytes past the cracked wall of the entry toward the passageway.

To descend that passage in formal procession with the priests and priestesses of Ahtarrath had been an experience to strain the soul. To hasten toward those depths in the company of a gaggle of half-hysterical acolytes was almost more than Tiriki could bear. *They* feared the unknown, but it was the memory of what had happened here only a few days ago that made *her* afraid. Seeing her falter, Chedan grasped her arm, and she drew on his steady strength gratefully.

'Is that lava?' came a frightened whisper from Elis as they rounded the last turn.

'No. The Stone is glowing,' answered Damisa, but her voice was shaking. *As well it might*, thought Tiriki, following her into the chamber. Vivid illuminations like those the ritual had wakened in the Omphalos were already pulsing in the depths of the Stone. Eerie light and shadows chased each other around the chamber, and each time the earth moved, flashes bounced from wall to wall.

'How can we touch it without being blasted?' breathed Kalaran.

'That's why we have these wrappings,' said Chedan, lifting a mass of cloth out of the cabinet and dropping it on the floor. 'This is silk, and it will insulate the energies of the Stone.'

I hope, Tiriki added silently. But the Omphalos had been carried safely from the Ancient Land, so moving it must be possible.

With their hearts pounding, she and Chedan took the folds of silk and carried them toward the Stone. Closer, its power radiated like a fire, though she felt it neither as heat nor any other sensation for which she had a name. Then the silk fell across it, muting the pressure, and she released a breath she had not known she was holding. They veiled it a second time and she felt her fear ease.

'Bring the cabinet,' rasped Chedan. White-faced, Kalaran and Aldel dragged the box up until it was almost touching the Stone and raised the panel on its side. Taking a deep breath, the priest set his hands about the Stone and tipped it in.

Light exploded around them with a force that sent Tiriki sprawling. Damisa grabbed more of the silk wrappings and thrust them into the cabinet around the Stone.

'Cover it – cover it completely!' Tiriki struggled to her feet again. Chedan was handing the rest of the silk to Damisa, who rolled it up to push into the corners until the pulsing glow of the Omphalos could no longer be seen.

It could be felt still, but now it was a bearable agony. Unfortunately, without the distraction of the Stone, there was nothing to shield them from the groaning of the rock around them.

'Pick it up! Aldel and Kalaran, you're the strongest – take the front handles. Damisa and I will take the rear. The rest

70

of you can keep the way clear and carry the torches. When we get out of here you can take a turn on the handles, but we must go, *now!*'

As he spoke the floor of the chamber trembled ominously. Tiriki snatched up her torch and hurried after them, realizing that only the presence of the Omphalos had kept it stable for this long!

The bearers staggered and grunted as if their burden were not only immensely heavy, but unstable. Seeing their distress, Elis and Selast set their hands beneath the midpoint of the cabinet and helped to lift it. But as they got farther away from the hidden chamber, the weight seemed to grow less, which was just as well, for with every step their footing was growing more treacherous.

That last jolt had buckled the floor of the passage in several places. Great cracks now showed in the walls, and in places the ceiling was beginning to give way. As they toiled upward they heard the crash of falling rock behind them, a high, discordant keening that seemed to come from all around.

'My spirit is the spirit of Life; it cannot be destroyed . . .' Tiriki chanted, trying to make that awareness replace the dreadful singing of the stones. 'I am the child of Light, that transcends the Darkness . . .' The others joined her, but their words seemed thin and meaningless in this vortex of primordial energies.

'Hurry—' Damisa's voice seemed to come from far away, 'I can feel another quake coming!' They could see the pale light of the entryway before them now.

The earth jerked beneath them. With a crash that transcended all previous measures of sound, the left wall caved in.

The sounds of rockfall and the screams that followed now faded as dust billowed outward. Tiriki's torch had gone out. She coughed, shielding her eyes. When she could see again, the dim illumination from outside showed her the cabinet knocked onto its side and the acolytes climbing to their feet around it.

'Is everyone all right?'

One by one, voices answered her. The last to reply was Kalaran.

'A little grazed, but whole. I was on the other side of the cabinet, and its bulk protected me. Aldel—'

There was a shocked silence. Then one of the girls began to sob.

'Help me get the rubble off him—' Chedan dropped to his knees, pulling frantically at the lumps of stone and plaster.

'Damisa, Selast, Elis! Let's get the cabinet upright and pull it out of the way—' Tiriki took one handle and heaved. She felt the others take up the weight and they started forward.

'But Aldel—' whispered Elis.

'The others will bring him,' Tiriki said firmly. 'Let's get the cabinet outside.' The rock groaned and a little more dust sifted down as they dragged the Omphalos out through the portico. Tiriki looked back apprehensively, but in another moment she saw Chedan and Kalaran emerging from the gloom with the body of Aldel in their arms.

'He's knocked out, isn't he?' stammered Elis, looking from one to the other hopefully. 'Let me hold him until he revives.'

'No, Elis, he has been taken from us—' Chedan said compassionately as they laid the body down. Through the dust they could see the distorted shape of the boy's skull where the rock had crushed it. 'It was over in an instant, without pain.'

Elis shook her head, uncomprehending, then knelt, smoothing the dust from her betrothed's forehead and gazing into his empty eyes. 'Aldel . . . come back, beloved. We're going to escape together – we'll always be together. You promised me.'

'He has gone before us, Elis—' Damisa said with a compassion Tiriki would not have expected. 'Come now. Come with me.' She put her arm around the girl and drew her away.

Chedan bent over the still figure and closed Aldel's eyes,

then traced the sigil of unbinding upon his brow. 'Go in peace, my son,' he murmured. 'And in another life may this sacrifice be rewarded.' He stood and took Elis's arm.

'But we can't – just *leave* him there,' said Selast uncertainly.

'We must,' answered Tiriki. 'But the shrine will be a noble tomb.'

She was still speaking when the earth heaved once more and propelled them out through the portico. As they sprawled on the roadway a pillar of fire exploded upward from the mountain and the Shrine of the Omphalos collapsed with a rending roar.

Muscles and balance told Tiriki that they were going downhill as they struggled onward. But that was all she knew for sure. She jumped and nearly dropped the handle of the cabinet that held the Omphalos as the front wall of a house slammed into the street. Beyond it a second building was collapsing with gentle deliberation, as if it were falling asleep. A dark figure emerged from one of the homes, hesitated, and then dashed back into the falling building with a cry.

'I can smell the harbor,' gasped Damisa. 'We're almost there!'

A breath of moist air blessed Tiriki's cheeks and brow. Above the crackle of flames and the groans of dying buildings she could hear the almost reassuring sound of human shouts and screams. She had begun to fear they were the only ones left alive on the isle.

And now they could see the water and the masts that tossed in the harbor. Boats bounded across the dark waters, heading out to sea. Two wingbirds had collided and were sinking in a tangled mass while bobbing figures swam for the shore. As they hurried forward the ground shook as if to propel them on their way. Rocks tumbled from the cliffs and splashed into the bay.

'There's the *Crimson Serpent!*' cried Selast. The lines that

73

held it to the stanchions on the dock were still fast, and young Captain Reidel stood poised at the stern, shading his eyes with one hand.

Micail – where are you! Tiriki sent her spirit winging forward.

'My lady, thank the gods!' called Reidel. He jumped to the dock and caught her as she swayed. Before she could protest, strong arms were swinging her onto the deck. 'All of you get on board, fast as you can!'

'Someone, take the box,' Chedan commanded.

'Yes, yes, but hurry—' Reidel reached out to give Damisa a hand, but the girl pulled away.

'I'm supposed to be on Tjalan's ship!'

'It would seem not!' Reidel answered. 'The Alkonath fleet was anchored in the other harbor – and everything between here and there is in flames.' He gestured, and one of the sailors picked the girl up bodily and tossed her into his arms.

Tiriki struggled to her feet, trying to make sense of the confusion of people, bags, and boxes. She recognized the seeress Alyssa huddled in the healer Liala's arms, and Iriel.

'Where's Micail?'

'Haven't seen him,' answered Reidel, 'nor Galara. We can't wait for them, my lady. If the headland collapses we'll be trapped here!' He turned and began shouting commands. Sailors began to unwind the lines that held the ship to the harbor.

'Stop!' cried Tiriki. 'You can't leave yet – he will come!' She had been so certain he would be waiting for her, frantic at her delay, and now she was the one who must fear.

'There are forty souls on this ship whom I must save!' exclaimed Reidel. 'We've already delayed too long!' He grabbed a pole and pushed them away from the dock as the last sailor leaped on board.

The third great tower, the one that watched over the palace, was falling slowly, as if time itself were reluctant to let it go. Then, with a roar that obliterated all other sounds, it disappeared. Debris exploded into the sky and burst into flame.

Reidel's ship lifted and fell as the shock wave passed beneath it. Another craft, still tethered, crashed into the dock. The oarsmen heaved and struggled to pull the ship through the debris that bobbed on the dark waters.

Above, the sky boiled in a vortex of flame and shadow and fire fell back upon the already burning city in a hail of indescribable destruction. Damisa was weeping. One of the sailors swore in a murmur of meaningless sound. They had already come far enough that the figures who were casting themselves into the water were silhouettes without faces or names. Micail was not among them – Tiriki would have known if he were that near.

They were passing beneath the cliff now. A boulder splashed down before the bow and the deck canted over, sending Tiriki sprawling into Chedan. He hooked one arm around her and the other around the mast as the ship righted itself and leaped forward.

'Micail will be on one of the other ships,' murmured Chedan. 'He will survive – that too is part of the prophecy.'

Through eyes that blurred with tears Tiriki stared at the funeral pyre that had been her home. The motion of the ship grew more lively as the sails filled, carrying them out to sea.

Black smoke billowed up as the volcano spoke once more, blotting out the sky. In the moment before everything went dark, Tiriki saw the tremendous image of the Man with Crossed Hands, covering the sky.

And Dyaus laughed and stretched out his arms to engulf the world.

FIVE

Tiriki clawed her way out of a nightmare in which she was drowning. Reaching out to Micail for comfort in the dark, her fingers closed on cold wool. As she groped, the floor rolled and she tensed yet again, bracing herself for another earthquake; but no, this was too gentle, too regular a rocking to sustain her fear. Exhausted, she sank back limply upon the hard bed, thankful for woolen winter blankets, her eyes half closed again.

A dream, she assured herself, *brought on by the cool breeze through the window* . . .

For some reason, she had thought that it was spring already, and that the disaster had come – that somehow she and Micail had ended up on different boats. *But here we are side by side, as we should be.*

Smiling at the foolishness of dreams, she shifted position again, trying to stay comfortable despite a vaguely dizzy feeling and a persistent chill. Something hard through the blankets . . . And then, close by, someone began to weep.

Her own discomfort she could ignore, but not another's pain. Tiriki forced her eyes to open and sat up, blinking at the dim, recumbent shapes all around her. Beyond them she could see a narrow railing, and the darkly heaving sea.

She *was* on a boat. It had not been a dream.

As she looked about, someone out of sight, toward the bow, began to sing—

> *'Nar-Inabi, Star Shaper,*
> *Dispense tonight thy bounty—'*

As she listened, additional unseen voices joined the song.

> *'Illuminate our wingsails*
> *As we fly upon the waters.*
> *The winds here are all strangers*
> *And we are but sailors.*
> *Nar-Inabi, Star Shaper,*
> *This night reveal Thy glory . . .'*

For a moment the beauty of the song lifted her spirit. The stars were hidden, but no matter what happened here they remained in the heavens, afloat in the sea of space as their ship floated on the sea below. *Star father, Sea lord, protect us!* her spirit cried, trying to feel in the uneasy rocking of the ship the comfort of mighty arms.

But whether or not the god was listening, Tiriki could still hear someone crying. Carefully, she peeled away enough of the woolen blankets about the curled-up figure beside her to recognize the youthful face of Elis, fast asleep, her dark hair tangled, her eyes wet with unhappy dreams.

Poor child – we have both lost our mates – Tiriki choked back her own grief before it could overwhelm her. *No,* she told herself sternly, *though we shall surely never see Aldel again, Micail lives! I know it.*

Tenderly, she soothed Elis into deeper sleep, and only then withdrew enough to stand up. Shivering in the stiff breeze, trying not to let the continual gentle swaying underfoot disturb her stomach, Tiriki tried to will away the lingering tensions of her unrestful sleep and strained her eyes toward the foggy seascape beyond the railing. The wake of the ship glinted redly in the bloody glow that pulsed along the horizon, illuminating a vast cloud of smoke and cinders that roiled the heavens and hid the stars.

It was not the sunrise, she realized abruptly. The raging light was from another source – it came from Ahtarrath, even in its final death throes unwilling to submit to the sea.

As the lurid dawn light grew she recognized Damisa standing by the railing, staring forlornly at the distant flames. Tiriki started toward her but Damisa turned away, her shoulders hunching defensively. Tiriki wondered if Damisa was one of those people who preferred to suffer in privacy, and then she wondered whether she wanted Damisa's company for the girl's sake or for her own.

Most of the other people huddled on the deck were strangers, but she could see Selast and Iriel not far away, lying curled together like kittens as Kalaran snored protectively beside them.

From amidships came a quiet voice giving orders; then Reidel appeared carrying a lantern, his bare feet almost silent on the wooden deck. She nodded in automatic greeting. Since yesterday he seemed to have aged ten years. *For that matter*, she thought, *I wonder how much older I must look by now!*

Reidel returned her greeting, rather anxiously, but before they could exchange words, he was beset by a pair of red-faced merchants wanting something to eat.

A man whom she recognized as Reidel's sailor, Arcor, had been hovering nearby. 'My lady,' he said, as she finally turned to face him, 'we hoped not to trouble you while you slept, but the captain wishes you to know, there be comfortable beds for you and the young folk below. The honored ones, the adept Alyssa and the priestess Liala, rest there already.'

Tiriki shook her head. 'No – but I thank you—' she looked at him inquiringly and he murmured his name, once more touching his brow in a gesture of reverence. *Living at such close quarters during this voyage*, she mused, *how long will the old caste distinctions last?*

'I thank you, Arcor,' she repeated, in more pleasant tones,

'but so long as there is anything to see here—' She broke off. 'I must go,' she murmured, and quickly made her way amidships, where she noticed Chedan standing alone, gazing at the waves and the troubled sky.

'I am sorry. I meant to help keep watch over the Stone,' she said, as she reached Chedan's side. She intended to say more, but found herself coughing, and a sharp, growing ache in her chest reminded her that the very air they were breathing was poisoned with the ashes of Ahtarrath.

Chedan smiled at her fondly. 'You needed rest,' he said, 'and should feel no shame for taking it. In truth, there has been nothing to see. The Stone is at peace, even if we are not.' He gathered her against him, and for a moment she was content to rest within the steady support of his arms, but the mage's sparkling eyes and ash-whitened beard could not conceal his worried frown.

'No other ships?' Her voice was a rasping whisper.

'Earlier, I glimpsed a few sails, heading on other courses, but in this murk—' He waved at the smoke and fog. 'A hundred ships might pass unseen! Yet we can be confident that Micail will direct whatever boat he may be on toward the same destination as we—'

'Then you agree he is alive?' She gazed at him in appeal. 'That my hope is not just – a delusion of love?'

The mage's expression was solemn, but warm. 'Being who you are and what you are, Tiriki – bound to Micail by karma, and more – you would surely have felt him pass.' Chedan fell silent, then grimaced and let slip a muffled oath. Following his gaze, Tiriki saw the faraway glow of the dying land rapidly expanding in a swirl of flames.

'Hold on!' Reidel's voice rang out behind them. 'Everyone – grab something and hold on!' He already had one arm around the mainmast, but he and Chedan barely had time to clasp Tiriki between them as the ship's stern lifted, sending unsecured gear and sleepers sliding. With a scream, someone went over the side. The masts groaned, sails flapping desperately as the ship continued to lift until it hung poised on the very crest of the swell. Behind them a long slope of shining water stretched back toward the fires of Ahtarrath, perhaps ten miles away. Then the wave passed, and the stern tipped as the ship began a long slide back down. Further and further yet they plummeted until Tiriki thought the ravening sea meant to swallow them whole. The ship bucked, seeking balance on the water, but the overstressed mainmast cracked and came crashing down. The *Crimson Serpent* shuddered as waves whipped around it.

It seemed a long time before the ship came to rest again, rocking gently with the tide. Reidel's lantern was nowhere to be seen. The faint phosphorescence that danced along the wave crests was the only light. There were no stars above, and the fires of Ahtarrath had sunk, finally and forever, beneath the sea.

The next morning Chedan jerked upright with a snort and realized that against all expectation, he had been fast asleep. It was day, and that too, he supposed, was more than any of them should have dared to expect after the violence of the night before. It was a daylight, however, in which very little could be seen. He could hear quite clearly the omnipresent creaking of wood as the ship rolled on the swell, the gurgle of water beneath her bows, and the cries of seabirds as they bobbed like corks all around. A clammy grey fog rested between the sea and sky. It felt as if they were sailing through another world.

Although Chedan had often enough found danger in his wanderings, he could not remember ever having been quite so *uncomfortable*. His back ached from the odd posture he'd slept in, and there was, he perceived, a splinter in his elbow. *That's what I get for not going below*, he lectured himself as he plucked it out. He wished a lifetime of experience could help now to take him home.

With a sigh and a yawn, he drew in his feet as four sailors, sweating even in this chilly dawn, carried the top half of the mainmast past him. The sailors had unstepped the lower half of the mast from its base and cut chunks from both broken ends so that they could be fitted back together. Spliced and splinted with rope bindings the mast might be strong enough to support its sail.

If the winds stay moderate. If no natural disaster comes to finish what the magic of dead men started . . . Chedan sighed. *Bah! Gloomy thoughts for a gloomy day! At least Reidel has the sense to keep his men busy.* He hauled himself to a standing position, just long enough to sit down on one of the row of storage chests permanently bolted to the deck.

As he sat massaging his aching elbow, he saw Iriel moving with exaggerated caution through the broken crates and other odd items that littered the deck. Dark shadows beneath her eyes betrayed her strain, but she had put a brave face on. Indeed, her look of resolve warmed him more, he guessed, than would the bowl of steaming liquid that she carried so carefully in both hands.

She held it out to him, saying, 'They have a fire going in the galley, and I thought you might like some tea.'

'Dear girl, you are a lifesaver!' A poor choice of phrase, he thought as he saw her blanch.

'Are we lost?' Her hands shook with the effort she was making to remain calm. 'You can tell me the truth. Are we all going to die out here?'

'My child,' Chedan began, with a startled shake of his head.

'I am not a child,' Iriel interrupted, a little sharply, 'you can tell me the truth.'

'My dear – all here are like children to *me*,' Chedan reminded her, and sipped gratefully at the hot tea. 'More to the point, Iriel, you are asking the wrong question. We are all going to die – eventually. That is the meaning of mortality. But before that happens we must learn to live! So let's not gloom about. You have made a good beginning by helping me.' He looked around, and saw a torn meal sack lying on the deck, threatening to spill what remained of its contents.

'See if you can round up the acolytes. We'll make that meal into porridge and spare some sailor the trouble of cleaning it up.'

'What a good idea,' came a new voice. He turned and saw Tiriki shaking off the tangle of blankets in which she had passed the night. She rose and moved toward him, her steps somewhat uncertain on the gently rolling deck. 'Good morning, Master Chedan. Good morning, Iriel.'

'My lady.' Iriel bowed in the customary greeting, and then again to Chedan, before running off in search of the other acolytes.

'I don't know how she does it,' Tiriki commented, as they watched her go. 'I can hardly keep my knees from knocking.'

'Sit beside me,' Chedan invited; 'you look a bit green. Would you like some of this tea?'

'Thank you,' she said, and swiftly lowered herself onto the sea chest beside him. 'But I don't know about drinking anything. My stomach is uneasy this morning. It's not surprising. I . . . have never cared much for the sea.'

'The trick is not to focus on the horizon,' Chedan advised. 'Look beyond that – you just have to get used to it. Putting something in your belly will steady it, believe it or not.'

Her expression was dubious, but she accepted the tea bowl, and dutifully sipped. 'I heard you talking to Iriel,' she said, soberly. 'How many more of us *are* gone?'

'We have been lucky, all in all. Two or three persons went overboard when the wave hit, but only Alammos was not recovered. He was a warder in the library. I didn't really know him, but—' He forced his voice to steady. 'Five of the acolytes made it to this ship. We must hope that the others are with Micail. And there are a few others of the priests' caste – Liala has them all settled, or as well as can be expected. The crew is more of a problem. The greater number of them are from Alkonath and proud of it. In fact, Reidel had to break up a fistfight only a while ago.' Chedan glanced at her and, seeing that her face was troubled, watched her closely as he went on.

'Considering how difficult that broken mainmast will make everything, we must be thankful that the *Crimson Serpent* has a fully trained crew. When it comes to having little experience with the sea, well, that's one thing the priests' caste shares with the townsfolk – we are landlubbers all, although most, at least, are relatively young and strong. No, truly things could be much worse.'

Tiriki nodded, her features again almost as calm as Chedan hoped his were. Both of them might weep bitterly within, but for the sake of those who still depended on them, they must provide a steadfast appearance of hope.

Looking away, he caught sight of Reidel picking his way toward them through the debris on the deck.

'Why isn't this stowed away already?' Reidel was muttering, with the fiercest of frowns. 'The moment the mast is up – my apologies.'

'No need,' said Tiriki quickly. 'Your first duty is the sea-worthiness of the ship. We are comfortable enough—'

He gave her a startled look, and she thought again that he seemed overly stern for one so young. 'With respect, my lady, it was not *your* pardon I asked. To see my vessel so disarrayed – my father would say it is bad luck.'

Ashamed, Tiriki blushed, and seeing it, Reidel shook his head and laughed. 'Well, I've given offense again, I guess, which I didn't intend either time. We must still learn how to work together, it seems.'

'In regard to that—' Chedan spoke to distract the other two from their embarrassment. 'Can you tell us where we are?'

'Yes and no.' Reidel fumbled with a pouch at his belt and pulled out a rod of cloudy crystal about the thickness of his finger. 'This can catch the light of the sun even in the fog, so we know fairly well where it is above us – and can roughly

83

judge how far north or south we have sailed. But as for east and west – well, for that we await the pleasure of the Star Shaper, but he spurns us still.' He returned the crystal to its pouch. 'We set sail with provisions for a moon, and that should be enough, but still, if we have a chance to go ashore, it wouldn't hurt to take on fresh supplies. All assuming that the mast . . .' The words trailed off as he turned to watch his laboring crewmen.

'*Are* we on a course toward the Hesperides?' Tiriki blurted out. More calmly, she continued, 'I know that many refugees from the islands of Tarisseda and Mormallor have already gone to Khem, where the ancient wisdom has long been welcome. And others, I think, intended to seek the western lands across the greater sea. But – Micail and I planned to go north—'

'Yes, my lady, I know. The day before – before we left – I had a few minutes with the prince. With both of them, actually. Prince Tjalan told me—' He broke off, biting his lip. 'If all goes well—' Reidel paused again as one of the sailors approached, touching hand to forehead in salute. 'What is it, Cadis?'

'The lads are done binding the mast; they wait only thy word.'

'I will come – excuse me—' Reidel inclined his head respectfully to Chedan and Tiriki, but his eyes and his attention had already returned to his ship and his crew.

The wind never left their sails, which allowed the *Crimson Serpent* to make good time, and though the spliced mainmast creaked alarmingly, it held fast. But the wind also played in the overcast sky, shaping weird cloud-creatures from the curtaining mists. Ahtarrath might lie broken in the deeps, but the smoke of its destruction remained in the sky, dimming the sun by day and shrouding the stars at night.

As agreed, Reidel had set a northerly course, but many

days passed and they still had not seen land. They encountered no other ships either, but with the continual fog, it was possibly just as well. A collision would have been one disaster too many.

Tiriki made a point of spending a little while every day with the acolytes, particularly Damisa, who was still brooding over her failure to make it to the ship captained by Prince Tjalan; and Elis, whose grief for Aldel reminded Tiriki that at least she could hope that her own beloved survived. She could only counsel those who were still sunk in depression to follow the example of Kalaran and Selast, who were trying to make themselves useful, a suggestion often met with tears. Tiriki insisted, however, that they at least pursue their singing practice and other studies, even if they were not well enough to help with the chores.

She had hoped that Alyssa, as the next-most-senior priestess onboard, would be more helpful, but the seeress took full advantage of what was almost a private cabin to nurse her injured leg and meditate. Tiriki had begun to suspect her of malingering, but Liala assured her that the seeress's leg had indeed been badly sprained during the melee of their escape.

One afternoon, as Tiriki sat in the foredeck, wondering what, if anything, she ought to do about the lesser priest Rendano's repetitive, pointless quarreling with a small cheerful saji woman called Metia, the dreary skies darkened, and a storm whirled down upon them. If Tiriki had thought her first night at sea terrible, by the time the tempest had blotted out even the sight of the towering waves, she was actually wishing that she had stayed in the palace. There, at least, she might have drowned with dignity.

For an endless time of torment she clung to her bunk below deck, while the ship bucked and plunged. Selast, who had inherited at least the sea legs of the Cosarrath royal line, refilled her flask with fresh water. Mindful of Chedan's advice, Tiriki sipped at it in the occasional gaps between upheaving seas, and tried not to watch the others merrily downing cheesebread and the last of the fresh fruit.

Sometimes, between the almost endless sobbing of the elder priestess Malaera and the complaints of the acolytes, there came a respite long enough for her to hear the sailors shouting on the deck above, and Reidel's strong, clear voice responding; but always, just when she was beginning to hope the worst had passed, a rising wind would overwhelm every voice, and the ship would tilt until she expected they would go completely under. Reason told her that no vessel could survive such a battering. She did not know whether to pray that Micail's ship was faring better, or that he was already dead and awaiting her on the other side.

Her misery faded into a stupor of endurance in which her soul retreated into an inner fastness so remote that she did not notice that the gusts were growing gentler, as the roll and pitch of the ship eased almost to normal. Exhaustion became a long-awaited, dreamless sleep; nor did she wake until morning.

The mended mainmast had not survived the storm, but the other two remained still intact, though tall enough to support only small sails. Still, as the weather held fair and the breeze steady, they were able to move slowly forward. Yet at every dimming of the cloudy light, Tiriki stiffened, fearing disaster.

What has become of my discipline? she scolded herself, sharply. *I have been trained to face anything, even the very darkness beyond the reach of the gods, but here I sit frozen with terror while those children scuffle and chatter and hang off the railing.*

The creak of the ship's timbers, a sudden tilting of the deck, even the scent of burning charcoal from the galley, all had the power to set her heart pounding. Yet it was also a distraction from a deeper anxiety that had set in when the storm lifted and they found themselves the only ship on the calm blue sea. Chedan had said that the other boats, having departed earlier, could have used their sails to run ahead of the storm. Did he believe that? It did no good to tell herself that the acolytes would only be more frightened if their seniors let their own fears show. The fear was there, and it made her feel ashamed.

Tiriki took a deep breath and continued on toward the stern of the ship, where Chedan and the captain were taking sightings from the night sky. She was not alone, she reminded herself as she approached the two men. Reidel was an experienced sailor, and Chedan had traveled widely. Surely they would know how to find the way.

'But that is just what I am saying,' Reidel's finger stabbed upward. 'In the month of the Bull, the constellation of the Changer should have risen just after sunset. By this time, the pole star should be high.'

'You forget, we are much farther north than you have ever come.' Chedan lifted the scroll he held so that it caught the light. 'The horizon is different in many small ways . . . Well no wonder you can't find it, this is not the right scroll. Ardral prepared more recent charts for our use.'

'So Prince Tjalan said, but they never reached us.'

'What of the teaching scrolls?' said Tiriki as she joined them. 'I told Kalaran to fetch them from the chests—'

'Yes, and I thank you for remembering them,' said Chedan. 'The problem is they are very old. See for yourself.'

She peered at the scroll, which concerned the movement of the zodiac. Unhappily, it no longer seemed to her half as detailed as it had when she was a student trying to commit it to memory – and that was the last time she had given any serious thought to the stars.

It just isn't right, she thought angrily, as her stomach once more began to protest the unsteady movement of the sea. *Of all of us, Reio-ta was the sailor! He and Deoris took that trip to Oranderis alone, only five years ago. Either one of them would be more use here than me!*

Chedan drew a deep breath. 'The chief polar star is Eltanin, of course, as shown in all our charts. But for generations now, the configuration of the stars has been changing—'

'What?' Reidel exclaimed in shock. 'We know that land and sea can change their outlines, but the skies?'

The mage nodded solemnly. 'I have many times verified it with a nightglass, and it only became more obvious with every hour. The heavens change just as we do, only more slowly. But over the centuries, the differences become clear. You must know something of the wandering stars—'

'I know that they wander along a predictable path.'

'Only because they have been observed for so many years. When the pole star upon which so many of our calculations are based suddenly moves – well, such a tremendous change is regarded as foreboding some equally great shift in the affairs of men—'

'Yes. A disaster. As we have seen,' observed Reidel.

Shielding her eyes from the glowing lanterns, Tiriki gazed upward. Mists veiled the horizon, but the moon was very new and had already set. Directly overhead the darkness was studded with stars in such profusion, it would be a wonder if she could make out any constellations at all.

'Perhaps,' Chedan was saying, 'you may have heard old folks muttering that the days of spring and winter are not as they used to be. Well, they are not forgetful; they are right. Old Temple documents have proved it. The time of the planting season, the coming of the rains – all the cosmos is caught up in some unfathomable change – and we, too, must adapt, or perish.'

Tiriki wrenched her attention away from the confused splendor of the skies to try to make sense of his words. 'What do you mean?'

'Ever since the fall of the Ancient Land, the princes have ruled without restraint, forgetting their duty to serve as they pursued power. Perhaps we were saved so that we might revitalize the ancient wisdom in a new land. I am not speaking of Micail, of course, or Reio-ta. And Prince

Tjalan, too, is – was – a great man. Or would have been—'

Seeing Chedan's distress, she reached to comfort him.

'No doubt you are right,' Reidel said briskly, 'but at the moment it is getting us *to* the new land that must be my concern.'

'The stars may be unconstant,' Tiriki said, 'but nothing has happened to the sun and moon, has it? By them we can sail east until we find land. And if there is no land – we can take further counsel then.'

Chedan smiled at her approvingly and Reidel nodded, seeing the sense of what she said. She sat back and let her eyes drift up again toward the patch of stars. Cold and high, they mocked her and every mortal being. *Rely on nothing,* they seemed to say, *for your hard-won knowledge will do you little good where you are going now.*

Tiriki woke to the familiar sway of her hammock and groaned from the nausea that was becoming equally familiar within. It was the third day after the storm.

'Here—' said a quiet voice. 'Use the basin.'

Tiriki opened her eyes and saw Damisa holding a brass bowl, and the sight of it intensified her need. After several painful moments she lay back and wiped her face with the damp cloth Damisa offered her.

'Thank you. I have never been a good sailor, but I would have thought I'd be accustomed to the motion by now.' Tiriki could not tell whether duty or liking had prompted her assistance, but she needed Damisa's help too much to care. 'How goes it with the ship?'

The girl shrugged. 'The wind has come up, and every time the masts creak someone wonders whether they will crack, but without it we scarcely seem to move at all. If the wind blows contrary they complain that we're lost, and when it dies they wail that we'll all starve. Elis and I have cooked up a pot of gruel, by the way. You'll feel better for a little fresh air and a bit of breakfast.'

Tiriki shuddered. 'Not just yet, I think, but I will come on deck. I promised Chedan to help him work on revising the star maps, though the way I feel, I fear I'll be able to do little more than make approving noises and hold his hand.'

'He's not the only one who needs his hand held,' Damisa replied. 'I've tried to keep the others too busy to get into mischief, but the deck pitches too much for the meditation postures, and we can only debate the sayings of the mages for so long. They may be young,' she added from the vantage of her nineteen years, 'but they were selected for intelligence, and they can see our danger.'

'I suppose so,' Tiriki sighed. 'Very well. I will come.'

'If you spend the morning with the others, I can do a thorough inventory of the supplies. With your permission, of course—' she added reluctantly.

Tiriki realized just how much of an afterthought that request had been and suppressed a smile. She could remember feeling a similar disdain for the ignorance of her juniors and the weaknesses of her elders when she was that age.

'Of course,' she echoed blandly. 'And Damisa – I am grateful to you for taking on this responsibility while I've been ill.' In the dim light she could not see if the girl was blushing, but when Damisa replied her tone was calm.

'I was a princess of Alkonath before I was an acolyte. To lead is what I was brought up to do.'

Damisa had spoken with confidence, but by the time she finished her survey of the supplies stored in the *Crimson Serpent*, she was beginning to wish she had not claimed so much responsibility. But facing unpleasant truths was also part of the job. She could only hope that Captain Reidel, though he was only a commoner, would be able to do the same.

As expected, she found him with Chedan at the prow of the ship, calculating their position from the noon sighting of the sun.

'Damisa, my dear,' said the older man. 'You look grave. What is wrong?'

'I have grave news.' Her gaze moved from him to the captain. 'Our store of meal is going fast. At the rate we are using it,' she told them steadily, 'the open bag will be empty after the evening meal, and there is only one more. I can make a thinner porridge, but that is not much nourishment for working men.'

Reidel frowned. 'Once more I wish that our cook had made it on board. But I am sure that you are doing all you can. I would welcome any constructive suggestions. Are you telling me that we can feed ourselves for only two days more?'

'At this rate, more like one. I have noticed that *certain* people, and I don't mean just townsfolk—' Damisa felt herself flushing beneath the intensity of his dark eyes. Strongly built, with bronzed skin and dark hair, he was typical of the Atlantean middle class, but she realized now that he was much younger than he had seemed from a distance, with a mouth that seemed more used to smiling than its present grim line. 'Some people,' she repeated resolutely, 'have been putting food aside. I know where some of it is hidden – and if your sailors helped me take it away from them, we could distribute it properly, and get at least one more meal for everyone. Perhaps more.'

'Yes.' Reidel sighed.

Chedan muttered, his eyes still on the curious, delicate apparatus of crystal rods connecting to cones with which he was calculating the angle from the horizon to the sun.

'I have already discussed all this with the other acolytes,' Damisa said into the silence. 'We are accustomed to fasting,' she explained, and blushed again as both captain and mage turned to look at her. 'And we are not working very hard, really. It will do us no harm to go on meditation rations for a while.'

Reidel's eyes scanned her as if he were seeing her, as

someone distinct from the rest of the priests' caste, for the first time. Damisa felt herself blush beneath his scrutiny, but this time her eyes did not falter, and in the end it was he who looked away.

'We will come to land soon,' he murmured, staring at the horizon. 'We must. When you talk to your friends . . . tell them . . . thank you.'

'I will,' she said. She turned to Chedan. 'Come with me, Master. The acolytes are waiting in the stern of the ship. We can endure what we must, but we will do so with stronger hearts if you bring words of hope to us.'

The mage lifted an ironic eyebrow. 'My dear, I think you have words enough already. No, no, it is not a reproof,' he hastened to assure her, 'truly you bring me hope, in the form of the strength you have plainly won from these hardships. We are in your debt.'

In the middle part of the deck, some of the sailors were splicing ropes broken in the latest gale while others worked at mending a spare sail. Chedan could feel their eyes on his back as he followed Damisa toward the stern, but the rules of caste kept anyone from questioning him. The acolytes, and one or two others of the priests caste, sat clustered in an informal semicircle beneath an impromptu awning made from the remains of a sail too torn to be worth repairing. Their conversations came to a ragged stop as they recognized the renowned Master Chedan Arados, and he surveyed them with interest in return.

He had first met Damisa when she was a child on Alkonath. She had been outspoken then, and if she was introducing him now as if she had gone out and captured him, he supposed she was entitled to do so. He had been too busy struggling with his star charts to pay much attention to the acolytes, but with Tiriki so ill he supposed it was his duty.

As Damisa rather ostentatiously seated herself upon the

floor mat amid her fellows, the mage settled his aching bones upon a coil of rope, gazing from one youthful face to another with what he hoped was a reassuring smile.

'I regret that until now I have been too busy to visit you,' he began, 'but everything that I have heard in these last few days tells me that in these difficult circumstances you have made yourselves useful. Where guidance is not needed, I know better than to provide it. But I understand there are some here who feel that our situation is hopeless. Now, it is only reasonable to worry, indeed it is very sensible, placed as we are, but it would be wrong to despair.'

Little Iriel made a sound that could have been laughter or a stifled sob. 'Wrong? Master, much of our training is in reading signs. When the sun begins to set, we know the dark will fall. If the stars do not shine there may be rain. The signs I see now say we will die out here, for we have neither seen any other ship nor sighted land.'

A winged shadow crossed the deck and Chedan's gaze followed it, lifting until he saw the bird flash white against the azure sky.

'I do not dispute what you have seen.' He turned back to Iriel. 'Although I have traveled more widely than most, even I cannot be absolutely certain of our exact position. But you are drawing your conclusion before all the evidence has come in. Do not fall into the error of those who see change only as decline and say that in the end there will be darkness. In the end, too, is light – light that will show us at last the cosmos and our true place in it, the purpose of our hopes and our losses, our loves, our dreams—'

'Yes, Master, we do not doubt that our spirits will survive.' Kalaran's handsome face was contorted in a sneer. 'But if we are so important, why do the gods leave us suspended on the edge of the world?'

'Kalaran, Kalaran.' Chedan shut his eyes and shook his head. 'You come through fire and destruction almost unscathed, and now you complain about a little suspense?

No wonder the gods so rarely intervene! By their mercy we have been granted a path out of the devastation, but that is not enough? We must face rough conditions!' Chedan waggled his fingers, mock-horrified. 'All is surely lost.' He waited as a little ripple of nervous laughter passed around the circle.

'Children of bygone Atlantis,' he went on, more softly, 'we have lost all save one another, but when I say we should be thankful for our troubles I am not merely repeating worn-out philosophies. We would not *have* those troubles if we had not survived! Surely you do not think it is a mistake to survive, merely because things are changed.'

'But we *are* lost!' Kalaran objected, and a muttered agreement echoed him.

'It is worse than that,' young Selast exclaimed from her place at Damisa's side, her slight frame quivering with nervous energy. 'The sailors say we have sailed right off the world!'

'In my experience,' Chedan answered, glancing back down the ship, 'sailors will say a great many outrageous things to the young and innocent. I would advise you not to believe everything that you hear.

'But let us consider for a moment that these rumors are true, and we have sailed off the world. How do you know that we will not just as easily sail back onto it? The sea is vast and wild, but it is finite. We will find land, and sooner rather than later. But let me warn you in advance, my dear young friends, when we come again to the shore, we will probably *not* find warm halls or servants waiting with fine foods and tasty drinks.'

And just at that moment, as if the priest's words had been nothing less than prophecy, there came a squawk and then a shout from the sharp-sighted man Reidel had sent up to the masthead.

'Land! My captain, that be no cloud on the horizon! 'Tis land I see for sure!'

*   *   *

In the euphoria of discovery, they forgot that to catch sight of land was not the same as reaching it. As they drew closer, those who were farsighted described high cliffs of brownish stone, sculpted by wind and water into columns and towers. At their feet waves frothed in a vicious swirl.

'I think it is the Casseritides, the Isle of Tin, whose southern horn the traders call Beleri'in,' breathed Chedan. 'These must be the cliffs at the tip of the peninsula. On the south-western shore, there is a bay with an island where the traders put in.'

Reidel leaned into the tiller, and the sailors did their best, but the wind was from the east, and the most they could do without the midsail was to set the *Crimson Serpent* wallowing broadside toward the toothed cliffs. Swearing in defeat, Reidel turned his ship toward the relative safety of the open sea once more.

'Are there other harbors on the northern shore?' Tiriki asked softly, unable to tear her eyes from the dim coast until it had almost vanished in the evening fog.

'There are many ports here,' Chedan assured her, 'it is quite a big island. Many years ago our ships used to put in at a harbor farther up the coast. It was at the mouth of a stream they called Naradek after a river in the Ancient Land. There was a knoll like a pyramid, where they had built a Temple to the sun. But when the Ancient Land sank, contact was lost. I doubt there would be anything left now.'

Reidel managed a smile. 'At least we know where we are. Tomorrow, surely, we will come to shore.'

But the wind, it seemed, did not want them to do so. For three days more they fought their way along the craggy coast, battling hostile currents and contrary weather, and every day were less able to feed themselves with only the few fish they could snatch from the waves.

On the fourth day, the wind died. Dawn showed them a half circle of mountains that sheltered a broad estuary where earth and water mingled in countless streams. Small tree-clad islands ranged the marshes like the coils of a titanic serpent, winding inward toward a land whose contours the mists still veiled.

One by one, the refugees gathered on deck to gaze upon the unknown land, almost unable to believe that they had actually reached a destination. Tiriki stood alone in the prow of the ship, fighting tears as she realized that somehow she had expected Micail to be awaiting her when the journey was done.

They were still some leagues west of the trading station on the Naradek that Chedan had told them of. A trackless wilderness was not the landfall any of them had hoped for. But the tide was relentlessly pulling them landward, and their ship was too battered to tempt the sea again. With a sigh of half relief and half resignation, Reidel brought the tiller around and headed into the estuary.

'Here at last is the new land—' The voice was Chedan's, but unusually loud. A little startled, Tiriki turned to watch as he addressed the crowd. 'From now on, there will be no more time for mourning,' he was saying, 'for we will need all our energy to survive. Therefore let us now bid farewell to Ahtarrath the beautiful, and to Alkonath the mighty. Alas for the Bright Empire that was, and is no more.'

And then, with even greater poignancy, their grief for the Ten Kingdoms of Atlantis, whose mighty ships had ranged the world, subsided into silence. Their memories of all that they had lost were for a moment too clear; too vivid again was the vision of the Star Mountain as it exploded in fire and thunder and the last bastion of invincible Atlantis surrendered proudly to the sea.

SIX

'O beautiful upon the horizon of the East,
Lift up thy light unto day, O Eastern Star,
Day Star, awaken, arise!
Lord and giver of Life, awake—
Joy and giver of Light, arise—
O beautiful upon the horizon of the East,
Day Star, awaken, arise!'

Micail drifted toward consciousness upon the rise and fall of the verses that had begun his days for as long as he could remember. The voices had the purity of youth; was it the acolytes who were singing? He could not quite recall why they were with him, but their presence, and the life-affirming cadences of the song, were protection against the nightmares he had already begun to forget.

He tried to open his eyes, but cool grey cloth covered them. *Have I been ill?* There was an ache in his chest and behind his eyes . . . He would have lifted his hand and removed the damp cloth, but his arms felt weak and hot.

'Tiriki . . .' He had enough strength to whisper. 'Tiriki?' he tried again.

'Don't try to talk.' A deft hand smoothed the cloth back from his brow, then lifted his head. 'Here's something for you to drink. Easy now—' The hard rim of a cup touched his lips. Automatically he swallowed and the liquid, a tart

97

gruel almost leavened by the taste of honey, went down. Something in his chest eased, but the headache remained.

'There you are,' came the voice again, as the strong hands gently lowered Micail's head back to his pillow. 'That ought to calm you . . .'

He tried to focus on the speaker, but his eyes didn't want to stay open. The voice was tantalizingly familiar, with the accent of his own childhood home, but too low to be Tiriki's. *Why is she not* here, *if I am so ill?* He tried to summon the strength to call for her again, but whatever had been in the liquid was dragging him back down into warm darkness. He frowned, breathing in the fresh scent of rain and grassy earth as his confused awareness of the present was over-whelmed by memory.

> *'The balance is broken!'*
> *'The darkness rises! Dyaus is set free!'*
> *'It is the Cataclysm! Save us, Micail!'*
> *'Save us!'*

'Micail – can you hear me? Wake up, lad. You've lazed here too long!'

Sinewy hands with the dry skin of age grasped his, and the jolt of energy that passed through them shocked him to full consciousness. His eyes flicked open. The man bending over him was tall, with an expressive face and greying hair that fell like unruly feathers across his high brow.

'Ardral!' What came out was a croak, but Micail was too surprised to care. 'My lord Ardravanant,' he corrected himself, preferring the more correct form in addressing the Seventh Vested Guardian of the Temple of Light at Ahtarrath . . . In theory he and Micail were of equal rank, but the old adept had been a legend since Micail was a child, and to use the nickname seemed presumptuous.

'I like it better the way you said it the first time,' advised the Seventh Guardian. 'Lately I don't feel at *all* like a

"Knower of the Brightest." Besides, it begs the question, don't you think? It is bad enough in ceremonies. No, stick with Ardral. Do I go around calling you Osinarmen?'

'That *is* a point. But—' Micail shook his head and coughed. 'What are you doing here? For that matter—' he paused again, but didn't cough. 'Where are we?'

Ardral's grey eyes narrowed. 'You don't remember?'

I don't remember anything, Micail thought; but in the next moment, he *did*. 'We were in the library,' he gasped. 'You were trying to get a great wooden trunk down the stairs. My friend Jiri and I helped you, but then you ran back inside and—' His mind was overwhelmed by multiple images: the arguing priests, collapsing pillars, crumbling walls, scrolls scattering like windblown leaves, and the perpetual groaning of the earth, vibrating through stone and bone alike . . .

'You saved my life,' said the adept softly, and again his hands tightened upon Micail's, 'although as I recall, at the time I wasn't very thankful.'

'You practically broke my nose.'

'Yes . . . I'm sorry about that. I don't know what came over me. Didn't *I* make a lot of *very* fine speeches about accepting the inevitable? So naturally I was the one who couldn't resist the temptation to try and save one more thing – even if flying chunks of lava were setting the city afire! Well, I'm glad *you* could see it was time to get out.'

'How did we ever get to the harbor?' Micail whispered, his chest tightening. 'I remember the towers falling – blocking the way—' His memory overflowed with distorted pictures: people staggering as Darokha Plaza pitched, the ageless tiled stones suddenly rippling in a horrible wave – and an old woman falling, trampled by the mob, left lying in the middle of the street like a broken doll.

Micail's fists clenched helplessly as he saw again the red gleam on the roiling waters of the coastline, heard the clattering armor of the elite soldiers Prince Tjalan had sent to find him; and though he struggled not to, he could not keep from seeing, with unbearable clarity, the chaos of shattered cliffs where the harbor should have been – and where the *Crimson Serpent* had been moored.

And all the while the ash had been falling, coating land and sea with a foul grey powder, as if all life was dead and he no more than a ghost haunting a broken tomb, the tomb of . . .

'Tiriki!' His voice cracked and he fought for breath. '*Where is she?*' Coughs tore painfully at his lungs, but he arched upward, flailing. 'I must find her, before—'

But then he felt again the surprising strength in Ardral's hands as the adept murmured a Word of Power that sent Micail spiraling down into sodden dreams once more.

As he drifted in and out of consciousness, he was aware that a series of different hands tended him. Sometimes even the softest touch was intolerable. At other times his friend Jiritaren was with him, or someone else, talking rather urgently about some crisis, lung fever . . . Gradually Micail began to understand that he was in danger, but it did not matter. Tiriki was all that mattered. Micail could not remember how he had lost her, but her absence was a wound through which his life was draining away.

And then there came a moment when he felt her arms around him. *I am dying*, he thought, *and Tiriki has come to bear me home*. But she was swearing at him, yelling about a task he had left undone. He felt himself drowning in a mighty tide . . .

He woke to the drumbeat of a drenching rain. That seemed strange; the storm season was past. He took a deep breath and noted that though there was some congestion in his lungs, they no longer pained him.

The bed was unfamiliar, softer than he preferred. Raising his head from the downy pillow, he looked about at a warmly lit room with whitewashed walls and a narrow window. His heart pulsed as he saw a woman standing beside it, looking out at the sea and the storm, but it was not Tiriki. This woman had dark curls, edged with copper where they caught the light.

'Deoris?' he whispered, and as she turned he saw her golden skin, her huge dark eyes, the adolescent blemish on her nose . . . Of course it was not Deoris; this was her younger child, Tiriki's half-sister . . . 'Galara,' he said, more loudly. 'At least *you're* alive!'

'And so are you!' she exclaimed, leaning over him excitedly, 'and you are *yourself* again, aren't you? Thank the Maker! I'd better tell the prince, he'll want to know—'

Micail began to make sense of his memories. If Prince Tjalan was here, when they found the way to the main harbor blocked he must have taken Micail aboard the *Royal Emerald,* still safe in the cove, and brought him here . . . wherever *here* might be. He was about to ask, but could not get the words out before Galara had run from the room. He attempted to sit up, but the effort was too much, and he lay back on the soft bedding, trying a deeper breath.

The door banged against the wall as Prince Tjalan himself strode in. There were a few more strands of silver at his temples than Micail remembered, and a deep line or two around his eyes that had not been there before, but his green linen kilt was as finely pressed as ever, and seeing Micail, his face filled with delight.

'You *are* awake!' Tjalan threw off his woolen shortcape and sat down upon the stool by the bed, clasping Micail's hands briefly in his own.

'Yes . . . and glad I am to see you. I gather it was you who got me here in one piece?' Micail found it hard to feel thankful, but he had always had warm feelings for Tjalan, and that at least had not changed.

'I am commissioning myself a medal!' Tjalan chuckled. 'First I had to wrestle you onto the ship – no one else would dare! Then when we were about halfway out of the harbor you thought you saw Tiriki—' He stopped himself. 'You jumped overboard, and of course you went straight into a floating spar and got smacked on the head! Lucky you didn't drown, and your rescuer with you! That was me too, by the way. But they hauled us both back in somehow. Since then – between concussion from the head wound and lung fever from the foul water you swallowed, you have been a complete bore, unconscious or raving the entire time. But it was worth a little aggravation to keep you breathing.'

'Where is this place?' Micail asked.

'The Hesperides – the Isle of Tin – just as you and I intended.' Tjalan grinned again. 'We have made landfall here in Beleri'in to restock our larders and shake out the kinks, but as soon as you feel fit to travel again, we'll continue up the coast to Belsairath. It's nothing grand, just an old Alkonan trading station from my great-grandfather's time, but with all these refugees, it'll soon be a thriving town!'

'Refugees . . .' Micail shivered, despite the blankets and furs. 'So *other* ships have come in?'

'Oh yes. Not only from Ahtarrath, but there are some from the other islands as well. We saved more of your priesthood than I dared hope for in those last moments when the whole world seemed about to explode. When the road to the harbor was blocked, several of your acolytes made it to the cove. The *Royal Emerald* was packed full, but she's a good ship, and once we got out of the harbor we weathered the voyage well.'

'But there was no word—' He fought for breath.

'Calm yourself,' the prince urged, 'my dear friend! We've had no news of Tiriki, no. But ships are still arriving, and some have even sailed past us, no doubt headed to Belsairath as well. She may yet join us. But what good will that be, if you have torn yourself in pieces?'

In the days that followed, Micail began to fill in more gaps in his memory. The house in Beleri'in where they lodged him was one of several belonging to a native merchant who had grown rich on the tin trade. As his strength returned Micail walked in the spacious gardens, breathing in the clean wind that scoured the green foggy hills half visible beyond the garden wall. The sky looked immense, whether it showed itself as a tapestry of shapeless clouds or an expanse of radiant blue.

So this is the new world, he realized, and for a moment his grim mood almost lifted. *There is much beauty here . . . but it is cold, very cold. Father Sun, we sing your praises as we have always done, why will you not warm the earth here? Even the sea wind bears me nothing of you. Must I build your new Temple just to feel a moment's warmth?*

He watched constantly for ships, but not until they were leaving to go to Belsairath did he appreciate the beauty of the sea. The harbor was the same clear blue as the sky. In its midst was a small island that separated a cluster of wing-bird ships that bobbed in the tide. The largest was Tjalan's ship, the *Royal Emerald*, her green sails like bright leaves against the darker green of the island.

'The summit of that island is so pointed, it looks man-made,' Micail said to Galara, in an attempt to distract his mind from the rocking of the fish-smelling round coracle in which they were being ferried out to the *Emerald*.

'Maybe so,' said the native boy, as a skillful dip of his paddle sent them shooting forward. 'Has beacon up top. Light it when tin ships come. But now, no traders,' he added sadly.

'Take nothing for granted,' advised Micail, thinking of what Tjalan had told him of his plans for this new country. But did it really matter? Was there any point in trying to build a new Atlantis if Tiriki was lost?

He clutched the side of the coracle as the sea grew even more lively, astonished that the boy could govern the motion of so unlikely a craft. But as the oddly pointed islet drew nearer, Micail became aware of another sensation, a kind

103

of subaudible humming that he instinctively associated with the flow of power . . . He touched Galara's shoulder.

'Do you feel it?'

'I feel sick.' She looked pale and queasy. He remembered hearing her say that she did not like the sea. That must be why she did not notice the thrumming in the water.

Tiriki would have felt it. Awkwardly he patted Galara's arm and then closed his eyes, swamped by a new wave of sorrow. *Without her, I am crippled*, he thought. *The gods will not want me.*

When they came aboard at last, they found the deck of the *Royal Emerald* swarming with soldiers. Micail had not realized that Tjalan had brought not only his bodyguard, but a contingent of regular guards as well.

The soldiers remained on deck throughout the three days it took to sail north and east along the coast to Belsairath. The cabins below were reserved for noble and priestly passengers such as himself. That first night, however, he encountered only the acolyte Elara. He had been told that she had ended up on Prince Tjalan's ship, but had not seen her until now. Micail, glad to leave her with Galara, went in search of his cabin, where he fell into sleep as a rock into an abyss.

The second day was well advanced when he awoke to the discovery that he shared the cabin with Ardral, who had also let his friend Jiritaren into the room. Jiritaren was not about to allow Micail to wallow in self-pity in his bunk on such a beautiful day.

'You have to admit, Alkonans build good ships—' Jiritaren commented as they came on deck, running his hand along the polished wood of the rail. The wind put color into his sallow skin, and lifted locks of his lank black hair back from his brow.

'I suppose,' said Micail, gazing up at the bravely fluttering green banner whose ring of falcons seemed to flap their golden wings. 'After all, here we are.'

Jiritaren gave him a troubled look. They had been friends for a long time, and usually did not need to speak to know each other's hearts. After a moment, he put one arm around Micail's shoulder, and raised his other hand to point at the wingbirds that followed them, particularly one a little longer and leaner in construction, with an orange banner at its mast.

'That's the *Orange Swift*,' said Jiritaren, 'from Tarisseda! They arrived with a few empty cabins, so some of our people are with them. Good thing, too, or I'd probably be sleeping on deck with the spearmen.'

Micail managed something like a smile. 'What's that ship?' he pointed.

'Ah – that is the *Blue Dolphin*. An older ship but solid. There's a gaggle of folks on it, some from our Temple.'

'My fellow acolyte Cleta is on the *Dolphin*, my honored lords,' said Elara, moving forward to join them, 'with her brother Lanath and Vialmar as well.' She looked up at Micail with a smile that seemed rather too warm, considering that except for Damisa, whom he had often seen with Tiriki, he hardly knew the acolytes at all.

But few as they were, strangers or not, they would be the foundation of the new Temple, and they were his responsibility now. He managed to return Elara's smile. She was a pretty girl, old enough not to be flustered by the attention of two senior priests. She was only of middle height, but her features were good, and her curly black tresses, barely secured against the wind with a filigreed hairpin, had a glossy sheen like a raven's wing.

'You are promised to Lanath, are you not?' he murmured. 'I am sorry. It must be hard for you to be separated . . . At least Cleta and Vialmar are together.'

She lowered her eyes. 'All thought of marriage must wait, my lord,' she said. 'We are far from completing our training. I-I wanted to say, it is a great honor to be here, my lords, where I may hope to take instruction directly from *you*.'

*   *   *

To reach the trading port of Belsairath took two days. It lay on the southern coast of the land that the native inhabitants called the 'Isle of the Mighty.' It had been established when Alkonath first sought supremacy over the trade routes of the Sea Kingdoms, but since then had lingered in obscurity.

As at Beleri'in, a small islet stood a little way offshore from the port, surrounded not by ships at anchor, but by a line of long sandbanks that guarded the shore from storms. As the *Royal Emerald* headed past it, the soldiers rushed to the side to get a glimpse of their destination. Even Micail felt a faint stirring of curiosity.

He shivered and rewrapped himself in his newly acquired cape of Alkonan green. It was warmly lined, but it felt odd to him to replace his family's ceremonial crimson with this color. *But what does it matter?* he asked himself, *There is neither Ahtarra nor Alkona anymore. Even the gods seem far away . . .*

The clouds were drawing in again, foreshadowing rain, and the scene unfolding before him became a mural painted in greys and browns. The low delta at the back of the bay was dotted with pools and reed beds, as if the land had not entirely won its argument with the ocean . . . He guessed that storms might occasionally rearrange this landscape entirely. He hoped the Alkonans had built their port on solid ground.

Word of their arrival spread fast. He glanced about and saw that most if not all of the passengers had emerged onto the deck. Elara and Galara stood quite close to him, their attention focusing, it seemed, upon the soldiers rather than the view.

A feather floated landward past them, and Micail realized that the tide was on the flow. Straining his eyes, he looked further inland toward the rising mainland, a dim bulk of thickly forested hills. At their center he could see a single thin streamer of smoke, rising and curling in the wind. *Perhaps that is from the port,* he thought. *What do they call it? Belsairath? 'Point something port.' . . .*

Captain Dantu's voice rang out above the hubbub of passengers, calling out orders. The soldiers went to the other side of the ship to balance it, as the helmsman guided the wingbird's sharp prow through an inlet that opened into a foggy, quiet cove where the river at last made its peace with the sea. A bank of efficient-looking docks had been built out into the harbor, but Micail guessed that even so, at low tide the larger ships would all be aground.

This, then, is journey's end, he thought. *A fine place for dying.*

Close against the docks stood a palisaded enclosure. Behind it, a string of buildings, at first grey and indistinct, meandered away along the river bank. Masses of weathered wood, faded paint, and worn-out thatchings suddenly appeared in his vision, and he realized that each building in one way or another reflected the standard Atlantean forms: here an arch, there some balconies, and even, a little way uphill, a newer structure that looked like the beginning of a seven-walled courtyard. The outskirts of the old town were a sprawling expanse of new-looking villas, built in the aristocratic Alkonan style, with much of the building hidden underground. As elsewhere, wood seemed to be the primary material of construction, but the terraces and foundations at least were all stone, ornamented with the usual carvings and painted plaster. The alien mists made everything look vaguely ominous, but he smiled in spite of himself.

The fit of amusement did not last. Rajasta the Wise had said that the new Temple would be built in a new land, but Belsairath looked old, even neglected.

Prince Tjalan had arranged for Micail to stay in an inn on the water, as Micail wished to watch for ships arriving and any news of Tiriki.

Yet before he could rest, Prince Tjalan summoned Micail to a reception at his villa. As he stood in the midst of a brightly dressed throng, he found himself wishing that he had stayed in his bed at the inn.

'Prince Micail – you are most welcome!' A woman spoke behind him. 'I met you once, that year you spent with Tjalan in Alkona, but of course you would not remember me; I was the merest child then . . .'

Her voice had that throaty quality that so many found seductive, and her perfume, which Micail perceived even before he turned to see who had spoken, was blended from the most expensive spikenard. In truth, he needed no other senses to recognize Tjalan's wife, Princess Chaithala. Tjalan had told him that she had sailed from Alkonath well before the Sinking, bringing their three children here to safety. But he would have guessed that too, for her hazel eyes, artfully highlighted by kohl, were wholly unshadowed by the grim memories that haunted all who had watched the old world die.

Micail's royal upbringing had trained him in all the right responses. He bowed just so far and spoke softly of the impossibility of forgetting such beauty, but his mind and his heart were far away.

'You are too kind,' said Chaithala with equal compo-sure. 'I do the best I can. My lord says we must keep up our standards—' She glanced around to make sure that the servants were keeping every cup, goblet, and plate full.

'You have done very well,' he answered automatically. The constant clamor of conversation made his head ring. Worse, he had taken a polite drink with almost everyone so far and strongly suspected he would not remember anyone's name by morning.

'There is a great deal to do,' the princess said. 'But I wished to speak with you because, in a way, we are both faced with the same task.' She beckoned him to follow her into a long gallery that looked out on a pleasant courtyard open to the sky.

'Thank you,' he said gratefully. 'I am afraid I find these

underground rooms a little constricting, even with all the light-wells and ventilation shafts—'

'A style,' the princess observed softly, 'which shielded fair Alkonath from the fierce summer sun will serve well here to conserve heat.'

'No doubt you are right,' Micail demurred. The same tubes of polished bronze that brought in what sunlight there was would also keep out the winds that scourged these cold grey shores. 'But I am too much a son of the Sun,' Micail finished, with the necessary flourish, 'to thrive where its presence is seen less often than it is implied by shadow.'

'That may be so, but you will find no more sunlight in the windows of the port precinct than you do here.' Chaithala smiled. 'My lord has told me it is your wish to remain in Domazo's Inn, rather than to lodge with us here. It is your choice, of course, but still I hope you will visit often. I, too, have some need of your counsel.'

'So you said.' Micail tried to look attentive.

'It concerns the education of my children. My lord has so many responsibilities – their upbringing has been left to me.'

'Madam, forgive me, but I know nothing of teaching children,' Micail stammered, suppressing a pang of sorrow as he remembered the babies Tiriki had lost. *All my house is dead*, he thought, *what can I teach the living?*

'You misunderstand me, my lord. They already have a most satisfactory tutor, a learned and patient man. No, rather it is of the content of their education that I wished to consult you, for the acolytes are given into your training – is it not so?'

'I—' he paused and looked at her closely. 'You are entirely correct, madam, but I have had little chance to fulfill my duty to them. The House of the Twelve was moved to Ahtarrath only last year. And only four of them are with us now—' For a moment grief for all those lost closed his throat once more.

'Yes,' said Chaithala brightly. 'But at least those four are here. Do you think they might visit us from time to time? The gods know we shall have priests enough!' She gestured back toward the main hall with a rueful smile. 'But it seems to me that most of them have become far too holy to remember how to speak with children. With only their example, I fear that my three will grow up with no appreciation for the true meaning of our religion.'

'I will gladly ask if they are willing,' Micail said slowly, 'certainly I myself have not yet given them much to do.' His mind whirled with guilt and speculation. The princess had said before that they faced the same task, and he saw now that it was true. How could the acolytes preserve the wisdom of Atlantis if he did not instruct them? But without Tiriki it seemed that the only thing he could teach was failure and despair.

'That is all I ask, Sir Prince.' Chaithala favored him with another charming smile and laid her hand upon his arm, gently drawing him back toward the swirling crowd. In a moment, she let go of him in order to introduce the priestess Timul, who had served the High Priestess of the Temple of Ni-Terat in Alkonath, and was now the head of the Blue Order in Belsairath. Like the princess, Timul had come to the new land a little more than a year ago and seemed to have transplanted very well.

Tiriki would like her, Micail thought sadly.

Somehow he kept his eyes open and greeted everyone. Some were from Ahtarrath, among them his own older cousin Naranshada, the Fourth Vested Guardian. There was also old Metanor, who had been Fifth Vested Guardian in the Temple, and of course Ardral, whose position as Seventh Vested Guardian came nowhere near reflecting his actual prestige.

As the son of a royal house, Micail had been brought up to function in gatherings like this one. He knew that he ought to be moving around, establishing relationships, dis-

110

tinguishing the powerful from the merely influential, but he could not summon the energy. He had never realized how much he depended on Tiriki in situations like these. They had worked as a team, supporting each other.

A servant came by with a tray of *ila'anaat* liqueur in ceramic cups as fine as shell, and Micail grabbed two, downing the first in a single swallow. The stuff was tart and sweet and left a trail of fire from throat to belly.

'Yes, might as well enjoy that while we can,' said a wry voice. 'The *ila* berry can't be grown in this latitude.'

Through his watering eyes Micail recognized the bronzed and mustachioed face of Bennurajos, a muscular, middle-aged priest. Originally from Cosarrath, he had long served in Ahtarrath, and Micail remembered him as a strong singer and a specialist in the art of growing plants.

Micail took a smaller sip from his second cup and let the fire within build and diffuse through his limbs. 'Pity. But I suppose you would know.'

Bennurajos wobbled his head from side to side. 'There are some vines that look promising,' he said, 'but I won't be able to tell what they're good for until they ripen.'

'I'm not even sure what season it is,' Micail murmured.

'Yes, it makes an interesting problem. At home, the sun was constant and we prayed for rainfall. Here it must be sunshine men dream of, the gods know there's all the rain they need!'

Micail nodded. So far, it had rained every day. 'If this is springtime, I dread the winter.' He blinked, suddenly queasy, and shook his head sharply, but the odd feeling would not go away. *Is it the heat in the room, the noises, smells, liquors—?*

Bennurajos stepped back, sensing that Micail had lost interest in the conversation. Micail tried to say something courteous and friendly – he had always been fond of Bennurajos – but his self-control was eroding. He shook his head again, tears burning in his eyes.

'You must forgive him.' It was Jiritaren, appearing as if from nowhere, 'Lord Micail suffered a severe fever on the voyage here and is not yet entirely well.'

'Where were you? Were you watching me?' Micail accused.

'Come away, Micail,' Jiri said softly, 'there are too many people here. It will be cooler in the garden. Come outside with me.'

They pushed past a cluster of priests from Alkonath. He ought to know them – memory supplied the names of First Guardian Haladris, a rather proud and pompous man, and the famous singer Ocathrel, who held the rank of Fifth Guardian. And there were survivors from the Temple on Tarisseda – the priestesses Mahadalku and Stathalkha the psychic. A gaggle of lesser priests and priestesses moved about on the fringes. More than a few seemed familiar to him but that, he decided, was only because they looked so obviously to be priests of Light. But none of them interested Micail. There could never be a big enough crowd until it included the one person he wished for so desperately.

SEVEN

'How could I possibly know whether I like it here?' Grimacing, Damisa swatted a midge from her arm. 'Ask me tomorrow!'

'Will your opinion have changed?' Iriel's words came muffled through the veils she had swathed around her face and throat to protect herself from the midges and other insects that seemed to swarm everywhere along the river. Reeds edged the shore and willows hung over the brown waters of the channel that the *Crimson Serpent* was following. Yesterday they had seen the sun and felt a promise of warmth in the air. But today the sky was as gloomy as their spirits, and mists hid the line of hills they had glimpsed from offshore.

'Not at all,' Damisa denied, with an envious eye for Iriel's veils, 'but I can't help thinking, if you had asked me yesterday whether it wouldn't be better to go back out to sea, I would have called you an idiot—'

'You're the idiot,' said Iriel automatically, her own eyes still fixed upon the lush riverbank that was slowly passing beyond the railing. Damisa shook her head, suspecting she was not seeing whatever it was the younger girl was staring at.

To Damisa one meandering stretch of marshland was quite indistinguishable from another. If tangled willow trees weren't overhanging a stretch of murky water, there were tall spiky reeds or thorny stunted shrubs. Either way, they couldn't get anywhere near the solid ground. *The interior is probably all just foggy undergrowth anyway*, she thought. For three days, they had been misled by the numerous rivers that fed into the estuary, each broad and promising at its mouth, but becoming too choked with half-submerged oaks, willows, and vines for the ship to do anything but retreat. She hoped someone was making a map.

'Look!' said Iriel excitedly, as a flock of birds rose noisily from the reeds and scattered like a handful of stones flung across the pale sky.

'Enchanting,' Damisa said dully, not so easily shaken from her gloom. She was beginning to suspect that the hills they had seen from the sea were no more than a vision sent by mischievous sprites to entice them into this wilderness in which the *Crimson Serpent* was doomed to wander until they all sank into the muck and mire below.

Or is the rotten smell I've been noticing all day something recently half-eaten by something waiting to eat us?

The river had in fact become much more brackish as they moved inland, but its level was still determined by the sea. Yesterday the men Captain Reidel sent ashore as scouts stayed out too long and were stranded in the marshes until ebb tide. By the time they could get aboard, they were covered to their necks in mud that was full of leeches and . . . Damisa shuddered and swatted another tiny-winged predator from her eyebrow, swearing, and Iriel snorted with laughter behind her veils.

'Oh shut up,' Damisa warned, watching Arcor, the grizzled old Ahtarran sailor, taking soundings from the ship's bow. *How does he stand it?* she wondered. His knotted muscles flexed and released beneath the short sleeves of his tunic as he swung out the line and the lead splashed into the water, again and again. Midges clouded around him, but he never once paused to swat them. Even a few moments' inattention could leave them stranded on a mudbank until the evening tide.

By sheer force of will, Damisa ignored the little insect

now walking on her elbow. *I should not complain*, she told herself, thinking that even Arcor had an easier job than the men who rowed the small boat that was laboriously towing this one upriver . . . She hoped Reidel knew what he was doing. The only thing worse than being eaten alive as they floated through the wilderness would be to get stuck here, unable to move at all.

Suddenly Arcor stood up, peering ahead.

'What is it?' came Reidel's calm voice, 'What do you see?'

'Sorry, Cap'n, thought 'twas a helmet,' Arcor joked. ''Tis only Teiron's bald pate! And there's our Cadis wit' him, keepin' the magpies off!'

The captain's broad shoulders relaxed in a light laugh, and Damisa, watching, felt her own tension easing as well. Reidel was only a shipmaster, and a lot younger than he looked, but in the past weeks they had all come to depend on his quick mind and ever-ready strength. Even Master Chedan, to say nothing of Tiriki, seemed to defer to him, which seemed vaguely *wrong* to Damisa. Abruptly she realized that she had been assuming that their journeys would lead them to a new civilization and Temple in the new land. She and the other acolytes had spent quite a lot of time speculating about what the people here would look like and, to a lesser degree, how they lived, or where; but so far it seemed that there simply *were* no inhabitants.

Which, she frowned, *might be better*. At the moment they were quite simply castaways. Reidel had done well enough at sea – maybe even remarkably well – but how would he fare against angry savages?

Lost in thought, Damisa jumped when the undergrowth shivered and two men suddenly pushed into view, muddy to their calves and perspiring freely. But she saw their teeth flash in fierce grins and recognized them as Teiron and Cadis, who had been sent out to explore earlier. Arcor tossed a rope over the side and they scrambled aboard to the welcoming jokes and laughter of the other sailors.

Tiriki and Chedan emerged from below, accompanied by Selast and Kalaran. It occurred to Damisa that she had not seen Elis since morning. Was she still trapped below deck, assigned to cheer up the priestess Malaera, who was still weeping for all they had lost? Damisa shuddered . . . *That's right, she drew today's duty with the Stone. Ugh. Even with it in its box, just sitting outside the cabin door, it makes me uncomfortable. Better the bog-rats! Or even Malaera's endless tears . . .*

'Good news, gentles,' the shaved-head Alkonan sailor Teiron was saying, 'there be someone in these parts! Where 'e live I don't know, but someone made that trackway in the marsh!'

'Trackway?' Chedan repeated. 'What do you mean?'

Teiron moved his hands tentatively, sketching on air. 'It's – a raised pathway, over the muck. Too weak to take a chariot I guess, but still good an' solid. Made from split planks – laid across logs – everything pegged into place. An' since some logs are old and some are new. Someone must keep 'em repaired.'

'But where does the path go?' Iriel wondered out loud. 'Didn't you even look? Are there lions?'

'No, no lions, little mistress,' the Alkonan said mildly, 'at least I didn't see any. But we were under orders to return quickly—'

'*I'd* guess the plank road leads there,' said Cadis, pointing past the trees that lined the shore. The mist had begun to fade away. Before them they could see the spreading blue waters of the lake that fed the stream. Beyond it, thin spring sunlight glistened on the green protruding tip of a hillside perhaps a thousand ells farther in.

Tiriki gripped Chedan's arm as they advanced across the muddy trackway. The carefully cut planks seemed to sway alarmingly underfoot, but after so many days on shipboard, she suspected she would have felt unsteady walking on the smooth granite stones of the Processional Way in Ahtarrah. She swallowed, fighting back the familiar nausea. She no longer felt as wretched as she had at sea, but she was far from her usual self, and she felt bloated, even though she could see that her wrists were growing thin.

On the high ground just ahead, a group of marsh dwellers in leather kilts awaited them with faces that were impassive but not, she hoped, implacable. They were small in stature, but wiry and well muscled, and pale where the sun had not browned them. Their dark hair glinted with rusty highlights in the sun.

Tiriki focused on her feet. It would not befit the dignity of a priestess of Light to arrive with her backside smeared with mud, even if the hems of her robes were stained already. *If I slip now, likely I will drag down Chedan with me, and maybe Damisa and old Liala as well.* Taking a deep breath, she kept her steps as measured and solemn as if she walked not amid a ragtag of sailors and refugees, but at the head of the Great Procession to the Star Mountain.

I should have worn my cloak, she told herself as the sweat cooled on her brow. The sun was finally shining, but the sky remained cloudy, and the air held a chilling dampness. Why that should surprise her she did not know. Chedan had said often enough that the weather here was peculiar. *But I haven't been truly warm since last Micail held me . . .* Ruthlessly, she put the thought away.

Only the faint cries of birds disturbed the silence, as the natives continued to stare. Their black eyes seemed to examine every detail as they approached – from the elaborate priestly costumes and the glittering metal that gilded Chedan's ceremonial dagger to Reidel's shortsword and the short pikes of the sailors. Some of the natives carried cudgels or spears, but most were armed with bows of finely worked, polished yew, the arrows flint-pointed. The sailors noticed that the marsh folk did not seem to even have bronze and took heart. A little swagger even came back into their steps.

Tiriki took a breath and stopped a few feet away from the natives. Chedan halted just behind her, and then Reidel. The sailors took up positions on the plankway, ready to cover a quick retreat. The silence became absolute.

Raising her open palms to the sky, Tiriki trilled the lilting formal phrase: 'Gods, look kindly upon this meeting.' Only then did she remember that these people almost certainly would not understand the Atlantean tongue. She tried to smile, wondering if it would help to bow again . . . but the marsh folk were no longer looking at her. Their eyes had returned to the foreign silhouette that had drawn them here – the high-prowed wingbird just visible through the willows that hid the river.

'Yes,' said Tiriki, still smiling tightly, 'that is our ship.'

Perhaps in response to her words or her gestures, a thickset man with heron plumes waving from his headband stepped forward, showed his palms, and made a series of rippling gutteral sounds. Helplessly, Tiriki turned to Chedan, and after a moment the mage replied, rather slowly, in the same sort of speech. Tiriki blessed again the fate that had sent Chedan to these isles once before. She sensed it was going to be hard enough to reach an understanding with these people even *with* the help of words.

The headman's scowls melted away, and he spoke again. Chedan's eyes widened in surprise.

'Tell me what you're saying,' Tiriki whispered.

Chedan blinked at her. 'Oh. Sorry. This fellow is the chieftain. His name is Heron. He says our arrival is fortunate, or fated. If I understand correctly, these people spend winter in the hills, and have only now returned here for the hunting season – and to celebrate some kind of festival.'

As Tiriki nodded thoughtfully, Chedan turned again toward Heron, and initiated another complicated exchange . . . Tiriki bit her lip and tried to look patient and wise.

'He says,' Chedan interpreted at last, 'their priestess – a wise-woman of the tribe – has invited you to visit her.

118

Apparently she dreamed about our ship. He says all may come and receive her blessing, but the men must wait apart while she speaks with you—'

'What? Lady, you must not go alone!' Reidel interrupted, with a protective glare that, Tiriki thought, was really meant for Damisa. She had observed such glances often lately and wondered if the girl herself had noticed them.

'Tell him we will come,' said Tiriki suddenly, and catching Heron's gaze, gave him a smile and a nod of her head. 'I think that Liala and Damisa and I can handle one old woman by ourselves, no matter how wise she may be.'

Reidel muttered and cast a dark look around, but Chedan turned and indicated to the chieftain that he should lead the way. To Tiriki, however, the mage said softly, 'Do not underestimate these people. There are some in this land who wield great power. I do not know if that is the case with this wisewoman, but . . .' He shrugged, and said again, 'Do not underestimate her.'

With Reidel and Cadis at their back to guard against treachery, Tiriki, Damisa, and Liala followed the trackway across the marsh and through a dense stand of beeches and alders to a wide, raised platform made of broad planks. At its center were a number of huts and lowwalled buildings, some weathered or even roofless, but several had been freshly daubed with mud and thatched with green reeds.

The inhabitants emerged to greet them – a mixed group, old and young. Although the women were no taller than an Atlantean child, many of them clasped even smaller children, who stared at the newcomers out of huge dark eyes. Tiriki wanted to spend some time there, but the chieftain hurried them on into the marsh again, along yet another wooden trackway, until they reached the banks of an island of solid ground. The distinctive point of the hill they had seen earlier loomed up ahead, between the trees and the clouds.

Until now, the marsh folk had behaved almost casually,

laughing and talking among themselves, with many a side-long glance at the strangers. Now they all fell silent, and began to move with exaggerated care, as if the spot was somehow as unfamiliar to them as to the Atlanteans. The wooden planks went no further, but there was a path, old and well trodden, and edged with small rounded stones.

Tiriki knew immediately that this was holy ground. The rustle in the leaves made it clear, as did the subtle shift in pressure in the air. It was not only because the path was so level that she found herself straightening and striding more freely. She began to draw strength from the earth and the air. More than relief, she felt a surge of actual hope, and a quick glance showed her that Liala felt the same wonder at the unusual energy here.

The path wound gently upward along a wooded slope, curving only occasionally to accommodate a particularly venerable tree. From time to time the smooth green rise of the Tor could be seen between the leaves, and this, she realized, was because the trees were thinning.

Before them lay a small meadow. To the left, a tangle of hawthorns formed an enclosure. From an arched opening in the bushes emerged a small stream, edged by rusty red stones. On the right, farther up the hill, white stones jutted from the ground, half hidden by trees. From among them, a second stream coursed down to join the first. On a knoll just above the point where the rivers joined nestled a small round hut, its faded close-packed thatching extending almost to the ground. Unlike the simple shelters in the village, this building had clearly been there for a very long time.

They had not quite reached the edge of the rushing waters when a figure emerged from the hut, leaning on a short staff. To the Atlanteans, her stature seemed that of a girl of ten, but as she raised her head to survey them Tiriki saw a face webbed with wrinkles and knew that this was the oldest person she had ever seen.

Heron held out his palms and greeted the wisewoman in

his throaty speech, then turned to Chedan and spoke again.

'This is their priestess. Her name is Taret,' Chedan interpreted. Tiriki nodded, unable to look away. Though the wisewoman's flesh was ancient, surely no one had ever had such lively and penetrating black eyes.

As the Atlanteans made their various bows, Taret took another step forward.

'Welcome,' said the wisewoman in the tongue of the Sea Kingdoms. 'I wait for you.' Her words were heavily accented but otherwise entirely understandable. Observing their surprise, she grinned merrily. 'Come *now*.'

With hardly a pause, the priestesses set out across four great stepping stones that bridged the turbulent waters. But when Reidel sought to follow, the chieftain stepped in front of him. Immediately, the sailors rallied to their leader and the scene grew tense, but Chedan put his hand on Reidel's shoulder and drew him gently back.

Taret, standing at the edge of the water, stared at the mage for a long moment, but his only response was to make an odd kind of salute to the sun.

'*Ah!* You, then,' said Taret – it was clear to whom she spoke – 'you shall walk here.'

Chedan looked startled, but Heron appeared even more surprised. He looked from Taret to Chedan and back again several times before, with a conflicted expression, he moved aside, allowing the mage to tread the stepping stones.

Chuckling softly, the wisewoman settled herself on a sturdy three-legged stool just outside of the doorway of the hut, and motioned to the others to take their ease on a bench carved from a felled tree trunk.

Taret's bright black eyes darted over each person in turn, and came to rest on Tiriki's headdress and the wisps of golden hair that were visible beneath it. The wisewoman smiled again, but more gently.

'Sun people,' she said, with evident satisfaction. 'Yes. Children of red snake that I saw in dreams.'

121

'We are very thankful to have found this place,' answered Tiriki, and though her words were formal, they were enlivened by genuine emotion. 'I am Tiriki, a Guardian of the Light. This is Chedan, Guardian and mage—'

'Yes. Man of power,' said Taret. 'Most men, I don't ask to come here.' Chedan was flustered at the compliment and made another little bow, but the wisewoman's gaze moved inquisitively to the others.

'Liala is a priestess of the healers and kinswoman to me,' said Tiriki, not quite realizing how slowly and carefully she was enunciating the words. 'And Damisa is my chela.'

Taret inclined her head. 'Welcome. But there is another.' Again her ageless eyes probed at them. 'With you in my dream . . . one who sees into closed places. Perhaps—' She gazed curiously at Liala, then shook her head. 'No. But you are friend to her, maybe?'

Tiriki and Chedan exchanged glances as Liala replied, a little nervously, 'We do have a seeress. Her name is Alyssa. She injured her knee during the journey, and I have tended her, but she is . . . unready to leave the ship.'

'If you wish,' Tiriki offered, 'we will bring her to you when we can.'

'Good. I like to ask her, did she see what is here? Did she see *me*?' The old woman chuckled again.

'We come here not by intention,' Chedan said earnestly, 'but by a turn of fate. We ask only to be friends with you and your people. Our home has been destroyed, and we must seek refuge here.'

Taret shook her head. 'You lose more than old home. And you come here because Shining Ones want you. You feel their power.'

'Yes,' said Tiriki fervently. 'But we did not know—'

'The gods knew,' Chedan interrupted. 'Indeed, I saw it myself in the stars! But I did not understand until now. We thought we were sent here to build a Temple, but it may be that the sanctuary is already here.'

Taret grinned. 'Not Temple like Sea Kings make, but holy place of safeness, true.'

'We don't want to disturb your sacred place—' Chedan said swiftly.

This time Taret's wizened shoulders shook with what they soon realized was not a spasm of pain, but uncontrollable laughter. 'Fear not!' she gasped at last. 'Shining Ones not disturbed!' Her wrinkled face could not contain her smiles. 'In dreams I see. I know you belong. And dreams be true, or you not be here. Anyway, sacred place not belong me.' She gestured toward the Tor. 'I show some things. Then, if Shining Ones wish, *they* show more.'

'The Shining Ones,' Chedan repeated, as if not certain he had heard her correctly. 'You will introduce us to them?'

'What?' Taret bobbed her head and almost laughed again. 'No, no. I just say – you people live here. New home. Shining Ones – find *you*.'

Chedan grew thoughtful, then said, 'Wise one, your generosity is far greater than we could have hoped. We sought this place because it is well above the flood line. But I was beginning to get the impression that building here would not be allowed.'

Taret nodded. 'For *my* people, no. All this valley a spirit place, but the Tor – special. A gate. Only wisefolk live here.' She sat back for a moment, seeming to look within, and then pointed a bony finger at the mage. 'So now you know. And you go now, yes?' She smiled, almost coquettishly. 'Tell others, all is well. But priestess and priestess must speak – of other things.'

Chedan clasped his hands and bowed his head. 'I think I understand. Thank you once more, wise Taret. You greatly honor me.' The mage stood and gave her the salute that one adept accords to another who stands high in the Mysteries. Then he made his way back to Reidel and the sailors, who looked relieved to have at least one of their charges safely back in their care.

'Tiriki,' the old woman said when he had gone, 'little singer . . . You serve the Sun but, for true, you are priestess of the Mother.' Her fingers curved in a sign that Tiriki had thought unknown to anyone but an initiate of Ni-Terat and Caratra. Even as her fingers moved reflexively in the answering sign, Tiriki's eyes widened at a sudden, clear memory of the vow her mother Deoris had made before she was born. Tiriki's work in the temple had followed other paths, but always that primal allegiance was there, the foundation of her soul.

'You think us wild folk.' Taret's youthful laughter cackled anew. 'But we know Mysteries. In this land, nine wise-women serve Her . . . Sometimes, we meet priestess from other lands. So I learn your talk, long ago.'

'You speak our language very well,' Damisa complimented.

'Not be so kind.' Taret gave the girl a smile. 'But, know enough to teach the maiden Mysteries of red and white.' Damisa frowned in confusion, and Taret went on, 'Soon you see. Rocks white where one stream comes – white rocks, white cave. Other spring leaves red stain, like moon blood. And you will go there.'

'You offer initiation into your Mysteries?' Tiriki asked doubtfully. 'It is a great honor, but none of us can submit to any rite that may conflict with oaths we have already sworn—'

'*We call on Thee, O Mother, Woman Eternal.*' Taret tilted her head like some bright-eyed bird. 'No conflict *that* oath – Eilantha.'

Hearing her sacred name, Tiriki felt the blood leave her face. What the old woman had said was the very oath that Tiriki's aunt and mother had sworn for themselves and their offspring before her birth. 'How—?' For a moment, her voice would not obey her. She had come to this new land to preserve the high magic of Atlantis, but this was something far more profound. On Ahtarrath the worship of Ni-Terat had been a minor cult, honored, but not particularly important; yet Taret plainly welcomed Tiriki not as a Guardian of the Light, but as a priestess of the Great Mother, as if that was a higher distinction. *'How can you know?'*

Taret only smiled. 'Mysteries, Mysteries. Everywhere the same. Now you believe me? The Mother welcomes you . . . and your child . . .'

Tiriki swayed. Damisa reached out to support her, brows lifting in surprise.

'What?' Taret laughed, tipping her head to one side like some ancient bird. 'You do not know?'

'I thought I was seasick,' she whispered, mind whirling back to her symptoms. She had never suspected. In sorrow for the children she had lost, she had repressed the very memory of what pregnancy was like. Without volition her hands moved to protect her belly, which was now no longer empty, if what the wisewoman said was true.

Tiriki shook her head. 'How could I still be carrying a child, after what we have gone through? All the healers of Atlantis could not keep me from losing my babes before!'

'How you come here to Hidden Isle?' Taret laughed once more. '*She* wants you here – you and your kin!'

Tiriki curled forward, cradling her womb, remembering that last night when she had lain with Micail. Had his seed taken root in that moment of ecstasy? And if so, was it that part of him that lived within her that she was sensing, when she felt so certain he survived . . . ? Tiriki blinked, and then found herself weeping openly in Damisa's arms, not knowing if it was joy or grief in her tears.

The news of Tiriki's pregnancy spread like wildfire and was a ray of hope in a situation that seemed bleak despite the marsh dwellers' welcome. The Atlanteans first needed housing, and in the days that followed, Tiriki was not the only one who found herself doing work she had not been trained for. Even if they had not all been heartily tired of life on shipboard, the *Crimson Serpent* could not serve as a long-term shelter. In fact, the vessel herself was in need of protection while undergoing repair.

Chedan had in his day supervised the construction of more than one Temple – and not all of them had been built from stone – but his expertise was limited to the esoteric requirements for sacred space, and the aesthetics of design. And though he understood the magic by which song might be used to move stone, without enough trained bass and baritone voices to make up even a single stand of singers, there was little they could do. And the actual cutting of stone was the guarded specialty of the guild of stonemasons, none of whose members had ended up on the *Crimson Serpent*.

The marsh folk built with wood, a craft with which the priesthood was not familiar. But in the more rural communities of the Sea Kingdoms, where most if not all of the sailors had been raised, the peasants lived in huts that were not too different from those they saw here. Moreover, shipbuilding itself required a woodworker's skills, and Reidel, the son of a shipmaster, had learned quite a lot about the craft.

Once again, Damisa found herself grumbling, *our bold captain takes charge*. She had to admit he was doing a good job. In next to no time, he had set the seamen to the work of construction, but Damisa had to wonder how they would take to it. Sailors from Ahtarrath or elsewhere might not mind, but on Alkonath the men of the sea were a privileged caste. Damisa had grown up near the Great Harbor, and remembered all too well their scorn of landsmen's tasks.

Now, pausing at the edge of the woods with an armload of willow branches, she heard raised voices and detoured around a hawthorn bush to see what was happening.

'Not another log will I lift, an' I dare ye give me reason why I should!' From the thick Alkonan accent, Damisa identified the speaker as the sailor Aven, threatening Chedan with balled fists and a ferocious frown.

'You'll need a roof to sleep under, will you not? Surely that should be ample reason.' Chedan's tone was perfectly level.

Who can argue with that? Damisa thought, as she pulled up her hood. The blue skies that greeted the morning had already disappeared behind grey clouds that seemed ready to dissolve into rain.

'Our tents serve well enough!' Aven argued. 'If all of us get back t' work on the *Crimson Serpent*—' The Alkonan had already lowered his hands. Now his manner eased even more. 'In a week we could be away from this benighted foul backwater! 'Tis no place for the likes of us, holy one! Let us be off t' some civilized land!'

'I have told you that this place is our destiny.' Chedan's voice was stern. 'Do you question the wisdom of the priests' caste?'

'Not I!' Aven answered with a smirk. 'All I know o' destiny is, I'm no tree-grubber! And beggin' your flippin' pardon, but I'm not your slave neither.'

'Well then, my good man,' said Chedan in a controlled tone, 'if your destiny is so different, we must not detain you here. Can we assume that you will not be attempting to claim any further share of *our* food and drink?'

'What?' Once more Aven's stance became threatening – and that was enough for Damisa. She dropped her load of branches and began to run down the path to the shore.

As she had hoped, the captain was close by the ship, planing down a piece of wood to replace a plank that had been cracked by a sunken rock. The day was chilly, but the work had made him warm enough to be comfortable, and he was stripped to his clout. In Ahtarrah, that would not have been worth noting, but here, the cold made most of the exiles go about layered in every garment they owned. To see his muscular bronze body flexing in easy motion as the plane rasped down the plank was . . . a surprise.

She had no time to analyze her reaction, for at the sound

of her swift footsteps Reidel had straightened, eyes widening in alarm.

'What is it? Are you – no, I see you are unhurt. What has happened?'

'It's what's going to happen!' she replied. 'Aven is close to mutiny. Says we should be working on the ship instead of—'

'Damned fool!' A dangerous glow lit Reidel's eyes. He snatched up his tunic and strode off so swiftly that Damisa had to run to catch up with him.

In moments they had reached the clearing. She had not been gone long, and Aven apparently had not progressed beyond insulting words and postures, but the air had a charged tingle that she did not like. Chedan stood immobile as a pillar of stone, but his hair was bristling and the pupils of his eyes expanded with the focus of the force within. The air was becoming super heated. Everyone could feel it, especially Aven, though he tried to seem unaffected as sweat began to pour from his face and shoulders.

'Oww – at last!' he croaked defiantly, 'a warm breeze. The wind gods do confirm me words to yez!' With uncommon impudence he reached toward Chedan, but his nerve failed as the cuff of his shirt caught fire, and he withdrew his hand with a gasp.

'Master, please!' Damisa shrieked, 'He's just an ignorant man—'

'No, *don't* stop!' Reidel's voice cracked like a whip.

'But Cap'n,' Aven wailed, childlike, 'this be no work for honest sailors! Just le' me return to the ship. I'll blister me fingers for ye, only we leave these marshes and get back where we belong!'

'Oh?' asked Reidel very softly. 'And where might that be?'

'Back on Al – on—' Aven's voice faltered.

'Indeed,' Reidel nodded, 'that's just where you would be, were it not for Master Chedan – on Alkonath, or Ahtarrath – at the bottom of the sea!'

Damisa released her breath in a long sigh as the last of the defiance went out of her countryman.

'Truth, I grant,' said Aven desperately, 'but *why here?*'

Reidel's gaze flicked to Chedan, who appeared quite relaxed, though his voice was edged with strain.

'The error is mine,' said the mage, 'for while this *is* the haven which the gods have vouchsafed us, I forget sometimes that not all of us have sworn the vows of a servant of Light. Why were *we* saved when so many died? Precisely so that we might come here. Though you see it not, there is power here enough to make this place a beacon for all the world. And in this life and beyond, I am bound to do all that I may to further that possibility. Will you not consider, at least, that you also may have been brought here for a purpose, and lend us what help you can?'

Aven stared at the ground, as sulky as a boy. Chedan yawned and declared his intention to go and have a drink from the White Spring while Reidel, hands on his hips, shook his head.

'Master Chedan is too kind,' he observed. 'When this community is secure, Aven, you shall go where you will, but until that day comes, we will all work together – and you will obey Master Chedan as you would a prince of the blood!'

After that, there was no further defiance and surprisingly little grumbling. A week of hard work got them all under some sort of shelter. The construction was simple enough – following the example of the villagers, they had made walls by weaving slender branches of willow between log posts driven into the soil and thatched the roofs with bundles of reeds. Plastering the walls with mud to make them wind and watertight would take longer, but at least they were out of the rain.

Alyssa had finally been carried up from the ship to share a large round hut with the Blue Robes, Liala and Malaera. Close by was a small enclosure in which the Omphalos Stone waited, still in its cabinet, wrapped with silks. Nearby, two more huts, small but private, had been erected for Tiriki and Chedan. Around these were three larger dwellings. The female acolytes were lodged in one; the saji Metia and her sisters occupied another. Kalaran had a bed in a third, which he shared with a white-robed priest named Rendano. Reidel and the crew, along with the merchant Jarata, and a few other surviving Ahtarran townsfolk, had built another scatter of shelters for themselves near the place where the wing-bird had come to ground.

It was well on the way to becoming a community. But though the results of their work were good enough to keep them dry, by Atlantean standards none of it could be called homelike, or even warm. Huddling over a peat fire in her drafty hut, Tiriki shivered and sniffled and wondered if she was coming down with a premonition of disaster or only a cold. She cast a beseeching glance at the image of the Mother she had set up in a little alcove of stones, but in the flickering firelight even the Goddess seemed to be shivering. The ache and tingle of her breasts supported the mysterious Taret's diagnosis, but what hope had she of carrying a child to term in this wilderness? Had the refugees survived the fall of Atlantis and the voyage only to be defeated by the climate of this new land?

Even allowing for a certain amount of exaggeration, Damisa's account of the confrontation between Aven and Chedan left Tiriki's belly clenching with a pain quite different from the pregnancy-induced nausea that had finally begun to subside. It did not help that she understood, as her acolyte had not, that Aven had challenged not merely the mage's authority but that of all the priesthood. And Chedan was of the Old Temple. There was no real choice for him but to defend his caste.

He does not do this for his own glory, she had reminded Damisa. *What he does, he does for you and for me. And there is no way of judging how the confrontation would have turned out without your interference.*

Damisa had gone away suitably chastened, but the tale continued to haunt Tiriki, as palpable a presence in the drafty hut as a bowl of spoiled milk. Tiriki did not doubt that he was capable of it, but could not quite accept the notion that Chedan, whom she knew to be gentle and reasonable, would actually have burned an Alkonan sailor to ash. But that did not prevent her thanking the gods and goddesses that Reidel *had* put a stop to it, even though the real problem had only been suppressed, not resolved.

Aven was not the problem. He had only been the first to say out loud what she had already heard others mutter when they thought no one was listening.

'Micail, Micail,' she whispered, 'why did we even try? It would have been better to meet fate with our own people, hand in hand. By now the pain would be ended, and we would be at peace.'

You know why, the voice of her spirit answered. *You are sworn to the Light and the prophecy.*

A sudden shift in the wind sent the billowing smoke into her eyes. By the time she had stopped coughing she was weeping in earnest.

'Damn the prophecy!' Roughly she thrust aside the deer-skin tacked across her doorway and went outside. The air was fresh and sweet with the scent of greenery, a powerful reminder of her mother's garden, and of Galara, who should also have been at her side. She blinked away tears and only then realized that the clouds had gone. The sun shone full and bright overhead, and she raised her arms, exultantly voicing the ageless hymn of greeting—

> *'Lift up thy light unto day, O eastern star,*
> *Joy and giver of Light, awake!'*

She let her arms lower slowly, eyes half closed, luxuriating in the benign radiance that shone on every land. What month was it now? The moon had shown full and the Dark

Sisters dimmed since the equinox. *Even in these misty hills, summer should have begun some time ago* . . . Chedan's theory about the gradual slowing of seasons came to mind.

Sun Children, Taret called us . . . *Of course!* Tiriki's hands fell at last to her sides. *Atlanteans do not like to huddle in the dark! No wonder everything seems so grim and gloomy. I've got to get away from here.*

Aware that the others might be watching, she found herself moving quickly through the trees. Without any clear idea of where she was going, her feet found a pathway. In moments she was alone, beyond sight and sound of the settlement.

Instinctively Tiriki chose the way that led upward. The path disappeared; not even a deer run or rabbit track marked the ascent. She felt strongly that she must get away from the encampment and the marshes, and respond to the whisper of the breeze and the clarion call of the sun. Since their arrival she had wondered what lay at the top of the Tor, and so she was not surprised to realize that every footstep was taking her closer to it, though the undergrowth forced her to double back upon her tracks in order to find a way through, so that she ended up tracing her way back and forth around the Tor.

Soon, perspiring, she pulled off her mantle and looked about. She was high enough up that the trees had mostly given way to scattered shrubs and bracken, but between them stretched grass – brilliant with the sun, more vibrantly green than anything she had ever seen. Once more, tears sprang to her eyes, but they were tears of joy. *Silly girl*, she told herself, *did you actually think there could be no beauty in the new land?*

A last scramble brought her to the summit – a gently rounded oval expanse with a coverlet of the same richly green turf. Even in that first moment, half-blinded by glorious sunlight, she was aware of it, like another kind of radiance . . .

Her eyes adjusted quickly. From here, high above the primeval forest that girdled the Tor, even the marshes below revealed to her a strange, wild beauty, for the vast fields of green spring reeds were spangled and veined with pale blue whenever the water reflected the sun.

Magnificent, she told herself, but her sigh of appreciation at once gave way to a sudden stab of nostalgia. In Ahtarrath she and Micail had often greeted the day from the summit of the Star Mountain, where the blazing sun above the diamond sea had revealed each and every feature of the countryside and glittered on a thousand decorated rooftops with breathtaking clarity. Here, even on a cloudless day, the view fell away into a misty shadow of rolling hills backed by a foreign sea.

In Ahtarrath she had always known who and where she was. Here she had no such clarity. Instead, what she saw in the subtly veiled landscape before her was . . . possibility.

Slowly she turned, noting how the long ridge to the south and the higher hills to the north sheltered the levels between. To the east, the mist was turning to a brown haze, but Tiriki scarcely noticed. Before her, at the summit of the Tor, was a circle of standing stones.

Compared to the massive edifices of Atlantis it was not particularly impressive. For one thing, these stones still were shaped as the gods of earth had made them, the tallest scarcely breast-high. But the very fact that such a thing could exist here forced her to a sudden reassessment of the skills, or perhaps the will, of the people who had made it.

The real question, she thought then, *is why?* She straightened and took a deep breath, remembering her own skills. Near the center of the stone circle she could see a darkened area and the remains of a fire. Moving sunwise around the perimeter of the circle, she entered through a slightly wider gap on the eastern side. With the first step, she knew she had been right about the power here; as she continued inward, her awareness of the energy in the earth grew even stronger, increasing yet again as she reached the circle's center. Only her training enabled her to stay upright.

Closing her eyes, she let her senses seep into the earth, rooting herself ever more deeply, and feeling the swirling currents of power as they rayed out in every direction, but most powerfully to the southwest and northeast. Yet more strongly still she felt the vitality that surged in the ground beneath her, flowing upward through her body until her arms again rose by themselves and stretched toward the heavens, making herself a living conduit between earth and sky.

Tiriki had thought to use this moment to lay claim to the new land, but instead she found herself surrendering.

'Here I am . . . Here I am!' she cried. 'What would you have me do?'

Keen as the wind, radiant as the sun, steady as all the earth below, the answer came.

'Live, love . . . laugh . . . and know that you are welcome here . . .'

Tiriki's eyes flew open in shock, for the voice was not that of her spirit. She was hearing it with her physical ears. For a brief and angry moment she thought that someone had followed her uphill from the encampment, but the woman before her, clad in garments of sunlight and spiderweb, was no one she had ever seen before.

Noting the slender limbs and cloud of dark hair, she thought this must be another of the marsh folk. But there was something in the line of the cheek and brow, and even more in the way the slanting light played about the figure – at times shining on her, and at other moments glowing through her – that proclaimed this was no being of the mortal world.

Tiriki bowed her head in instinctive reverence.

'That is well,' said the woman, with a wry but gentle smile, 'yet I am not one of your gods, either. I am . . . what I am.'

'And that is—' Tiriki's mind raced, her heart pounding so that she could hardly speak. In the Temple they had called such beings *devas*, but here it seemed more natural to echo Taret's words – 'You are one of the Shining Ones . . . ?'

The woman's strange eyes widened, and she seemed to dance a little above the ground. 'So some say,' she allowed, still with that faint air of amusement.

'But what shall I call you?' There was a pause, and Tiriki felt a tingle as if a delicate hand had brushed her soul.

'If a name is so important, you may call me – the Queen.' She lifted a hand to her hair and Tiriki realized that the Lady's brows were crowned with a wreath of white hawthorn bloom. 'Yes,' she added with a hint of laughter, 'thus I may be sure you will respect me!'

'Assuredly!' Tiriki breathed, kneeling; spirit though the woman might be, she had the stature of the Lake dwellers, and it seemed discourteous to look down at her. 'But what should I offer you?'

'An offering?' The Queen frowned, and for a moment Tiriki felt that glancing touch upon her soul once more. 'Do you think I am one of your . . . merchants . . . requiring payment for the gifts I bring? You have already offered yourself to this land,' she said more kindly. 'What else could I ask of you? What do *you* desire?'

Tiriki felt herself flushing. 'Your blessing . . .' she said, her hand over her womb. Surely the best safeguard she could have would be the favor of the power in this land. 'I ask your blessing on my child.'

'You have it—' the answer came soft as the fragrance of flowers. 'And so long as they shall remain true to the hallows here, I promise you also that your line shall never fail.'

'This hill?' Tiriki asked.

'The Tor is only the outward semblance, as your womb is the shelter for your child. In time you will learn to know the Mysteries that lie within – the Red Spring and the White, and the Crystal Cave.'

Tiriki's eyes widened. 'How shall I learn about these things?'

The Queen lifted one dark eyebrow. 'You have met the wisewoman. She will teach you. You have been a servant of the sun, but now you shall learn the moon's secrets as well. You . . . and your daughters . . . and those who come after . . .'

She smiled, and the radiance around her intensified until Tiriki could see nothing but light.

EIGHT

The days since Micail's arrival in Belsairath stretched into
weeks, and still Tiriki did not come. He had always thought
of himself as the strong one, but he was beginning to realize
that despite her apparent fragility, her bright spirit had supported his. By day, he participated in rituals and attended
meetings, hoping to hear some word of her or persuade the
Alkonans to mount a search, though he had no idea where
the other refugees might be found. Every night in his dreams
he retraced the bygone streets of Ahtarra, searching for
Tiriki as the light went out of every shop and home and
temple.

Sometimes, for a moment, she seemed so close he thought
he touched her. And then he would wake and realize that
she never drew away because she was always gone.

The days were almost as depressing. The existence of
Belsairath proved that Atlanteans could indeed survive, even
thrive in a new land, but somehow the number of new buildings going up, with their grandiose imitations of antique
architectures, only contributed to Micail's deepening gloom.

Tjalan would have installed Micail in his villa, indeed in
his own suite, but Micail protested in the strongest terms.
Belsairath was noisy and less than sanitary, and the inn was
at the center of it, but he *needed* to be able to see the harbor.

'Tiriki might come. If I were somewhere I could not see
her ship, then—' he shook his head. 'She might leave. Some

of the ships that come here do not stay. No, I need to be here.'

After that, Micail was exempt from the council meetings at Tjalan's villa. Of course he was glad enough to miss the unending scholarly debates over astral influences and power flows in the land. It was certainly not difficult to enjoy the regular temptation of the finest foods, spiced with loore, marinated in raf ni'iri . . . Still, Micail would have preferred more solitude. Continually, it seemed, there was a soldier nearby to protect him, a Blue Robe or other healer looking after him, Jiritaren or even Bennurajos visiting, offering heady liqueurs and a steady stream of quips and diversions.

Stoically, Micail had tolerated the special treatment and endless interruptions, for at some level he knew he walked close to madness . . . Perhaps most difficult of all were the bracing visits from Tjalan, who repeatedly made it known that he was prepared to provide *anything* that might break through Micail's lethargy, up to and including fetching young women for his diversion.

His cousin Naranshada came once or twice, but Micail could never decide whether Ansha's visits brought comfort or more pain. When they had been junior priests he and Ansha had been close, but as Ansha moved more deeply into the engineering studies that were his specialty they had grown apart again. Now what they had in common was their loss, for in the chaos of the escape from Ahtarrath, Ansha's wife and children had drowned. The *Royal Emerald*, searching for survivors, had found him clinging to a spar, half-mad with grief.

At times Micail envied his cousin, who could put aside the vain torment of waiting for news and move on. But then he would see again the mute pain in Ansha's eyes and realize that the slightest hope was better than a certainty of despair. If he had seen Tiriki sink beneath the waves, he would not have survived.

* * *

Late one afternoon, Ardral came unexpectedly to call on Micail, offering a jar of honey wine from Forrelaro's cellars and a platter of succulent roast pig direct from Tjalan's personal chef. The day was warm, but less than sunny, so they dragged a low table and a pair of benches closer to the open balcony and attacked the repast fiercely.

Some little while later, mere appetite sated, they began to speak of plans for the new Temple.

'You ought to attend some of those meetings, my boy. Haladris and Mahadalku make a formidable team, and you're the only priest with the rank to challenge them,' said Ardral, seriously. 'If they have their way, the new Temple will faithfully reproduce all the flaws of the old.'

'Isn't it a little soon to be worrying about who will be in charge of the new Temple? After all, we can hardly decide without Tiriki and Chedan—'

'And in which lifetime will *they* rejoin the debate?' Ardral's dry response shocked Micail upright. 'Ah, lad, I'm sorry,' said the adept more gently, 'but you have met every ship, boat, and seal that comes into this cove since we got here, and for three new moons now there has been no sign nor word. There comes a time—'

'I know!' Micail shook his head. 'I know. It is foolish of me, and stubborn. But still – how can *this* be all of us? I cannot believe it, that would be too cruel a jest. I will not believe that my dearest – that they are *all* gone, the best of us – leaving only a handful of obscure priests and a lot of prideful nobles, a gaggle of scribes and chelas, and all too many soldiers! And so many of them hardly more than children.'

'Listen, Micail.' Ardral's voice grew softer, his tone almost comforting. 'You are not wrong to keep hoping. I often heard Reio-ta say the two of you were as one soul – and he understood such things. If you believe she lives – then I believe it, too. But remember – all will be as it is meant to be. Perhaps Tiriki's work and yours, so long performed in parallel, must for a while run in separate courses.' The adept paused, measuring his words. 'And when it comes to establishing a worthy Temple, consider this – it is not for our talents or our numbers that we will be held accountable. Only one righteous spirit is needed to preserve all the ways of Light.'

'So I have heard,' Micail rejoined, 'but to preserve the priestly skills we need more, and the simple fact remains, of the Chosen Twelve, we have saved only four. *Four.*'

Ardral nodded. 'More?' he asked, and sighing, Micail allowed his goblet to be refilled. Again the wood-aged liqueur of the Ancient Land rippled over his palate, leaving a delicately dusty savor.

'Yes, we have left much behind,' Ardral murmured. 'Of course I don't know precisely what you expected—'

'Expected?' Micail's laughter rang with a tinge of hysteria. 'I can't even remember what I expected! Though I know Rajasta always seemed to be describing – something more primitive than – this.' He waved one arm toward the crumbling buildings of Belsairath.

'A savage land *would* be easier,' Ardral agreed, as he sliced off another hunk of ham. 'The uncivilized are usually willing to be taught.'

The four survivors of the Chosen Twelve often found themselves dependent on their own resources. The acolytes were not even lodged together, but lived in various places in and around Belsairath. Princess Chaithala's villa, well heated and spacious, had rapidly become the favored gathering point for all of the younger Atlanteans. The acolytes themselves, of course, should have been occupied with meditation and study. There were a few elder priests who could have taken them in charge, but those priests were the ones most deeply involved in disputes and studies of their own. Time dragged on, and though Micail had not formally set aside his responsibility to supervise their training, he never seemed willing to begin. Elara, who had once wondered if she might be reassigned as his acolyte when they reached the new land, thought they might be better off without him. She had seen enough of him on the journey from Beleri'in to Belsairath to question whether he could manage his own life right now, much less theirs.

'It's a pity, really,' she said to Lirini, the great singer Ocathrel's middle daughter, who at seventeen was the closest to herself in age. 'I would enjoy learning from him. When my lord is himself, he's a charming man.'

'Charming! I think he's the handsomest of all the priests. Do you suppose he will ever marry again?'

Elara raised one well-shaped eyebrow. Lirini did not seem to be mourning her betrothed, who had not escaped the Sinking, but then Elara doubted that she herself would have been devastated had Lanath not survived. At the moment, he seemed to be undergoing complete devastation in the game of Feathers he was playing with Vialmar, but that was not unusual. Lanath looked even pudgier than usual as he frowned at the pattern the tiles made on the board, while Vialmar, tall and lanky, with unruly black hair, drummed his fingers impatiently on the curving arm of his chair.

'Surely it is a little premature to think of such things,' Elara said repressively, though she had wondered herself what would happen if Tiriki never arrived. But what right had Lirini to gossip? She was only a chela, and even more neglected by her master, the priest Haladris, than the acolytes were by Micail.

Hearing footsteps and shrieks, Elara reached swiftly to rescue her bowl of tea as Prince Baradel raced by, hotly pursued by Princess Cyrena, whose scarf he waved above him like a captured prize. The nine-year-old princess was the last survivor of the royal family of Tarisseda, and tended to hide her sorrows by bullying her betrothed, two years younger.

'What a little brat,' sniffed Lirini, 'thinks he's High Prince already. But he has two sisters and a baby brother, and then there's Galara, from your island,' whispered Lirini. 'She's

Lord Micail's cousin twice over. It seems to me there's plenty of royalty here, and precious little for them to rule over.'

'Even more priests and priestesses,' Elara sighed, 'and no temples for them to serve.'

'There's Timul—' Lirini reminded her.

'That's true,' Elara frowned, remembering the strong-bodied, strong-willed woman she had met shortly after arriving. 'I'm an initiate of Ni-Terat – well, a novice,' she blushed. 'At home, I was apprenticed to Liala—' She paused a moment, remembering the Blue Robe with regret, for Liala, though firm, had always been kind to her. 'The Mother smile on her. But doesn't Timul seem to you – a little over-whelming?'

Lirini shrugged. 'She doesn't have any use for men, but she has endless patience for women. She has some kind of chapel set up. A lot of women from the town go there.'

'Perhaps I should pay her a visit,' Elara said thoughtfully. *It might be well to expand my options*, she decided, silently, *but not, of course, if it means giving up men . . . At least not before I find someone worth giving up!*

She suppressed a grin. Lanath, as her future husband, wasn't available to her yet. Again she looked speculatively at Vialmar, who had just won the game of Feathers and was cracking jokes as he tried to persuade Karagon, a quiet young man who was chela to the Grey Adept Valadur, into a game . . . Either one might be glad of a dalliance with someone less sober than Cleta. For that matter, Karagon had already attempted a flirtation, although she hadn't realized it at the time. She smiled again. Life might become quite interesting, even on this desolate shore.

There was a stir at the doorway, and everyone rose as Princess Chaithala swept into the room.

'No, no,' the princess said graciously. 'Do not disturb your games for me.' Pale green draperies floating behind her, she moved about the room, chatting with the young people. Elara noticed that she had approached first Cleta, then Lanath and Vialmar, so she was not surprised when the princess began to waft her way.

Elara turned toward Lirini, saying, 'I suspect that duty is about to call me. I'm glad we had the chance to talk like this.' Before the chela could reply, Elara detached herself and was joining the other acolytes in Chaithala's train.

'I have been thinking about your situation,' said the princess, 'and wondering if we might invite Prince Micail to join you, and see if we can resolve the question of your boredom and idleness. But we may need a pretext. What do you think? Perhaps a small dinner party? Nothing formal, of course – but it might make it easier for him to recognize, without embarrassment, that he has been neglecting your training . . .'

And how much of that training would just happen to involve giving some special lessons to your children? Elara wondered. Still, it might not be too high a price to pay, if participating in Chaithala's machinations brought about the resumption of a proper regime of studies. It was fine to sit about, talking and playing games, but Elara feared that the acolytes were becoming like overripe apples, beginning to spoil from within.

'Micail! I am so glad you could join us! You are looking much better than when I saw you last.'

Micail winced as Tjalan laid a brawny arm across his shoulders and squeezed. The receiving room of Tjalan's villa was crowded with priests and priestesses. The light from myriad hanging lamps set their shadows to leaping against the frescoed walls. Micail allowed himself to be shepherded to a bench beside Haladris and Mahadalku.

'You are all aware of the efforts which Naranshada and Ardral have been making to identify the ideal site for our new Temple,' said Tjalan. 'We have called this meeting because it has been finally demonstrated that an energy flow does indeed run up from Beleri'in and continue across the main part of this land. Is that correct?' The prince looked to Naranshada.

'Good enough for our purposes,' Ansha said with a smile. 'The theory of such forces is well known to most of us, but even on the larger islands, we were only able to identify a few very localized examples. Here it would appear that the networks are much more extensive and may provide a power source we can use. But – there are some unanticipated problems.'

A faint muttering swept through the room.

'Nothing we cannot handle,' Ansha continued, 'but we will have to gain a more precise fix – preferably a site where two major pathways cross.'

'Are you saying that there is such a place?' Haladris, already one of the taller men in the room, drew himself up straight, his hooded eyes widening.

Prince Tjalan stepped forward again.

'Perhaps. A trader called Heshoth has recently arrived in Belsairath with a small party of traders in raw stuffs such as grain and hides. This Heshoth comes from a tribe called the Ai-Zir, which apparently dominates the plain that lies beyond the coastal downs north of here. At the center of their territory is a sanctuary. According to Heshoth, it is a place of great power. Their name for it means "a meeting of the godways."'

'Are you certain you have understood him correctly?' asked Mahadalku. She was a powerful woman whose strong frame belied her years.

'Can he be trusted?' Metanor wanted to know.

'The merchants here consider him dependable,' Tjalan answered. 'More to the point, he speaks our language. The first task, Lord Guardian, will be yours—' the prince addressed Haladris. 'Use your skills to determine the potential of the site. The second component is military, and that responsibility, of course, is mine. I will be sending a patrol out to investigate the territory. We need to know if the population is numerous enough to supply us with a labor force that can support our projects.'

Is there any reason they would want *to?* wondered Micail, but Haladris and Mahadalku were nodding a grudging approval, and the others also seemed willing to go along. Perhaps they hadn't considered that the natives here might not wish to become the foundation for a new Atlantean empire, or maybe they did not care. But if Atlantis was fated to rise anew in this wintry land, then Micail supposed it would do so, whatever anyone might say.

By local standards, Belsairath might be a metropolis, but it was in fact smaller than the least precinct of Ahtarra, Alkona, or even Taris. Elara and Cleta certainly had no difficulty in finding the Temple that Timul had built here for the Great Mother. Compared to the marble columns, spires, and gilded tiles that had adorned such temples in the Sea Kingdoms, this low, thatch-roofed building was less than imposing, but the wooden uprights of the portico were properly rounded and whitewashed, and the sigil of the Goddess was painted in blue on the pediment above the door.

'It would have been more sensible to build this in the hills, where the villas are,' said Cleta. Her round face brightened as the sun peeked through the clouds that had covered the sky all day. Almost as one, the two girls turned like flowers toward the summery light, welcoming its blaze through closed eyelids.

'There probably weren't so many of them here then,' Elara murmured. 'Oh Day Star! It seems an aeon since I felt Manoah's warmth—' But even as she spoke she felt the brightness fade, and opening her eyes, watched the clouds close in once more.

'I shouldn't have spoken. I frightened Him away . . .' She smiled, then sighed as she saw Cleta looking at her in confusion. 'It was a *joke*, Cleta. Never mind. Now that we've found the place, we may as well go in.'

There were more surprises inside. As the door opened, they found themselves in a long room with tinted walls and three inner doors. One of them opened and a priestess emerged, her face placid and unemotional, but as she recognized the white robes of the acolytes, the Blue Robe began to smile.

'Lodreimi! What are you doing here?' exclaimed Elara, recognizing her in turn. Apart from Timul herself, and Marona, whom Elara did not know well, the young Alkonan woman seemed to be the only other Atlantean-born initiate of Ni-Terat, or Caratra, in Belsairath. Elara had wanted to find her but no one had been able to tell her where Lodreimi was staying.

'Serving the Goddess . . .' The Alkonan's usual gravity dissolved into another smile. 'When I arrived here I felt so lost . . . until I met Timul I didn't know what to do! I just know you will gain from her wisdom, too. Wait here and I will call her!'

From somewhere deeper within they could hear the repetitive sound of singing or, rather, of girls learning a song. From another direction came the scent of herbs and a faint suggestion of incense. The noise of the muddy but busy thoroughfare just outside was no more than a distant hum. Elara felt her eyes pricking with reminiscent tears as the peace of the place enveloped her. The Temple of the Healers in Ahtarra had felt just the same.

When she could see again, the archpriestess herself stood before them, a comfortably rounded woman with auburn hair braided into a crown around her head, who radiated her own subtle authority. 'Elara, Cleta, we have been hoping that you would come to see us. Lodreimi has told us so much about you. Are you chilled? Come into the kitchen and you shall have hot tea, and then I will show you what we are doing here . . .'

The right-hand door led down a hall. More doors opened off of it – they led to sleeping rooms, Timul told them, some used by the priestesses, and others reserved for women who might come to them needing refuge.

'It is hard here for some,' said the archpriestess. 'Among the tribes here, women are respected, as a rule, but when they come to the town there is no clan structure to protect them.'

'You give them medicines?' asked Cleta as they passed into the kitchen.

'We give them whatever we can,' said Timul primly. 'Food or refuge or healing, according to their need.'

'It was intended that I should become an herbalist,' Cleta said then, 'but I have not been able to begin the training.'

'You may begin here whenever you like.' Timul nodded toward a saffron-robed woman who was squatting by the hearth, stirring a cauldron that hung above the fire. 'Sadhisebo would welcome your assistance.'

'A *saji?*' Cleta said doubtfully, as the woman rose with a peculiar fluid grace and turned to greet them warmly. Elara shrank away. She had heard too many tales of the saji women who had served in the temples of the Grey Order in the old days. The Grey Robes studied magic, and magic was a power that might be put to many uses, not all of them approved by the Servants of Light. The mere sight of the diminutive, small-boned saji woman was disturbing in a way that she could not quite identify.

Timul smiled gently. 'Did you think them mindless Temple whores? The arts of love are one path to the divine realm, to be sure, but Sadhisebo and Saiyano, her sister, are highly skilled in herbal lore.'

'Herbs to cast forth a child?' Cleta wondered.

'Those too, if necessary,' Timul said austerely, 'along with those to keep it safely in the womb. We serve life here, you must understand, and the greater good sometimes requires harsh deeds. In order to save, the Goddess must sometimes slay.'

'I do know that.' Elara bowed her head, smiling tentatively as the saji woman placed bowls of tea upon the low table before them. 'Even before I was chosen as one of the Twelve I was consecrated to Ni-Terat. In Ahtarra I was the chela of the priestess Liala in the Blue Robe Temple.'

'So I had heard, and that is one reason why you are doubly welcome here . . . But this Temple is not dedicated to Ni-Terat, but to Caratra.'

Elara looked up in surprise. 'But – are they not the same?'

'Are you the same child who was taken into that Temple?' Timul asked lightly.

'Of course,' Elara began, and then shook her head. 'Oh. The answer, I suppose, is both yes and no. I remember being that child, but I am very different now . . .'

'And the Goddess changes too.' The hard features of the archpriestess grew softly radiant as she continued. 'Only to men does she always appear as Ni-Terat, the Veiled One, for to men her clearest truths remain mysterious. But within the Temple, those mysteries are revealed, and so we call her always Caratra, the Nurturer.'

'But I was taught that Caratra was the daughter of Ni-Terat and Manoah—' said Cleta. 'How can she be a mother as well?'

Elara lifted one eyebrow. 'I suppose, in the usual way! How do you think that *you* came into the world?' she grinned.

'I know where babies come from, thank you!' Cleta flushed. 'I am *trying* to understand the theology!'

'Of course you are,' put in Timul, though she, too, had to suppress a smile. 'Drink your tea and I will try to explain it, but do not be surprised if this is not quite the way you have heard the story before. When we travel, we often arrive at new points of view as well as at new lands. But in ancient times the Queen of the Earth was called the Phoenix, because with the turning of time, she fades and is renewed.'

'Like the double-faced statue in the great square in Ahtarra?' asked Cleta.

'Exactly—' Timul agreed.

Elara grinned. 'But is the statue of Ni-Terat or Banur?'

She paused. 'What, did you never hear *that* old joke?' she went on as Cleta stared at her in incomprehension. 'Cleta, you are impossible!'

'But what is the answer?' the younger girl asked.

Timul was smiling broadly now. 'The answer, my child, is "Yes." That is the Mystery. All the gods are one god, and all the goddesses are one goddess, and there is one initiator. Surely, even in the Temple of Light, they taught you *that* . . .'

'Of course!' said Elara. 'But – I was always given to understand that it meant we should seek past forms and images to that which lies beyond them all.'

'The essence of the gods is beyond our comprehension, except for those moments when the spirit takes wings—' Timul looked from one girl to the other.

Elara bowed her head, remembering a moment in her childhood when she had stood watching the sun sink into the sea, straining for something she felt just beyond her grasp. And then, at the moment of greatest splendor, the door had suddenly opened, and for a moment she had felt as though she were one with the sky and the earth. Cleta also nodded, and Elara wondered what memory had come into her mind.

'But we still make statues—' Cleta brought them back to awareness of the present once more.

'We do, because we are in mortal bodies surrounded by physical forms. The Deep Mind speaks a language that uses symbols, not words. No amount of *talking* about the Goddess can communicate as much as one lovely image.'

'That still does not answer my question about Caratra,' Cleta said stubbornly.

'I was wandering, wasn't I?' Timul shook her head. 'Forgive me. The women here are true daughters of the Goddess, but except for Lodreimi, they do not have the training to discuss theology.'

'Caratra—' Elara repeated, with a sidelong grin for Cleta.

'It is all a matter of levels, you see,' Timul replied. 'At the highest level, there is only One, unmanifest, ungendered, all-encompassing, self-sufficient. But when there is only Being, there is no action.'

'And that is why we speak of God and Goddess,' said Cleta. 'That much I know. The One becomes Two, and the Two interact to bring spirit into manifestation. The female force awakens the male, he impregnates her, and she gives birth to the world . . .'

'In each land the gods are different. Some peoples have only a few gods while others worship many. In the Sea Kingdoms, we worshipped four,' continued Timul.

'Nar-Inabi, Lord of the Sea and the Stars, to whom we prayed to bring us through the dark night when Ahtarrath fell,' whispered Elara.

'And Manoah, Lord of Day, whom we honor in the Temple of Light,' Cleta agreed.

'But also Four-Faced Banur, who both preserves and destroys, and Ni-Terat, who is the earth and the Dark Mother of All,' Elara said.

'In Atlantis all we saw of the earth were islands, and so Ni-Terat remained veiled.' Timul reached down to touch the packed earth floor in reverence. 'Here,' she said, straightening, 'it is otherwise. This place is also an island, but so great that if you go inland you can travel for days with neither sight nor sound of the sea. And so we remember another story. In the Temple of the Goddess it is said that the Age of the Goddess is coming, but this is not something we speak of with outsiders, for too many of them would see any diminution of the primacy of Manoah as a rebellion against the Light itself . . .'

'What does that have to do with the Temple that the priests are going to build?' asked Cleta, setting down her tea.

Timul's face grew darker. 'I hope, very little. The Goddess needs no temples of stone. Indeed, She may be honored *more* fitly in a garden or a holy grove. The cult of the Great Mother flourished in this land long ago, and there are still some among the natives who can rightly be called priestesses. It is

my hope to find them and build on that ancient allegiance
. . . It will not matter what the priesthood does then.'

Elara lowered her eyes to her bowl and took another sip
of tea. *And if it does come to a serious conflict of interest*,
she asked herself, *where will my loyalties lie?*

Still deep in thought, she followed the archpriestess
through the door that led into the shrine.

The space was all in darkness, save for a single lamp
flickering upon the altar. When her eyes became accustomed
to the masses of shadow, Elara observed that the walls were
frescoed with images that seemed to move in the subtly
shifting light.

'The four powers we honor are a little different here—'
whispered Timul. 'Behold—'

On the eastern wall the Goddess was pictured as a maiden
dancing among flowers. The southern wall bore a mural of
Caratra as Mother, enthroned with a laughing child upon
her knee and all the fruits of the earth around her. In the
west was the familiar representation of Ni-Terat, veiled with
grey mystery, crowned with stars; but the north wall set
Elara's heart to pounding, for there the Goddess was shown
standing with sword in hand, and her face was a skull.

Elara shut her eyes, unable to bear that implacable regard.

'The Maiden, the Mother, and the Wisewoman are the
faces of the Goddess that all women know,' said Timul
quietly. 'We honor Caratra as the source of life, but we who
are priestesses must accept and revere both of Ni-Terat's
faces as well, for it is through Her judgment that we will
pass in order to be reborn.'

It is true, thought Elara, eyes still closed. *I can still feel
the goddess looking at me.* But even as that awareness passed
through her mind she felt the power that surrounded her
changing, warming, holding her like the arms of her mother.

'*Now you understand*,' came a thought that was not her
own. '*But do not be afraid, for in darkness and in light, I
am here.*'

151

NINE

To those who had relished the sultry noontides of an Ahtarran summer, the light of the new land seemed always less gold than silver, just as, for a true Atlantean, the warmest of these northern waters would always evoke a shiver. But none could have denied that a change had come, bringing the marshlands to ever more vibrant life. The refugees welcomed every lengthening minute of light. Even if the sky would never achieve the deep turquoise blue that had crowned Atlantis, still no meadow of the old world could have matched the vivid green of these hills.

For Tiriki, the luxuriant growth seemed one with her own fertility. As the hawthorn bloomed in the copses and primroses opened their glowing petals beneath the trees, her own body rounded and her face grew rosy in the sun. With the fruits of the woodland she ripened, the child within her growing with a vigor unknown in her previous pregnancies, and she gave thanks to Caratra the Nurturer.

The coming of Micail's child renewed her hope, and new hopes were sparked in the acolytes as well. Tiriki's child became their link to the future, their talisman of survival. They found excuses to visit her, and gossiped among themselves over every tiny change. Iriel bubbled and cooed and fretted; Elis cooked and cleaned for Tiriki at the slightest opportunity; and Damisa became like a solicitous shadow, except when she was annoyed. Tiriki accepted it all with good grace – indeed, she would have been completely happy – only sometimes in the night she woke weeping, because Micail, who should have shared her joy, was lost, and she knew she must bear and raise the child alone.

There was a spot on the bank where willow trees made a whispering enclosure by the rushing river. It had become a retreat where the senior clergy could gather; warm sunlight still fell dappled through the leaves, strong enough to sparkle in Alyssa's grizzled hair.

'One is lost . . . one is found . . . many tread the sacred round . . . from the hill unto the plain . . . and two will be one once again . . .' The seeress's voice trailed to silence, and she smiled, eyes focused on nothing. Chedan watched her, wondering whether this time there would be some significance to her meanderings.

With an effort, he kept his features serene as he gestured to Liala to fill the seeress's bowl with tea. Oracles, the mage reminded himself, were problematic enough when delivered in a properly prepared setting, in response to specific questions. But although in the months since their arrival, the Omphalos Stone, wrapped in silk and enclosed in its own shelter of stone near the hut Alyssa and Liala shared, had been quiescent, Alyssa had begun to drift in and out of the prophetic state without warning, as if she had been uprooted not only from Ahtarrath but from ordinary reality.

The scent of mint and lemongrass filled the air as Liala poured tea from an earthenware beaker into four carven beechwood bowls.

'It is just as I was saying . . .' Tiriki paused to accept a bowl of her own. 'We must never forget that our lives are not only our own. Before, there were always the rules of the Temple to guide us. Now it is our own feet that create the path, and we must be prepared to see them falter from time to time.' She paused again, and Chedan knew she was thinking about Maleara, the older Blue Robe priestess,

153

who had attempted to hang herself the night before.

'I believe Malaera has not completely lost her way,' Tiriki continued, 'although we will have to keep watch on her for a while. She is confused and heartsick, and who among us has not felt something similar? Worse, she suffers from aching joints, so there is little for her to do that does not cause her actual pain.'

'I don't like to say it,' Liala muttered, 'but the biggest actual pain around here is her. We've all lost our friends and family! Does she have to gloom about it *all* the time?'

'Evidently so,' said Chedan calmly. 'Perhaps she is moved by the gods, to remind us that not everyone will easily let go of their lost loves and hopes. I am told Malaera is one who has never concealed her emotions. Who are we to require that she do so now?'

'I think her despair will pass,' Tiriki repeated. 'More than most, maybe, she seems to understand that our mission here demands more of us than simple survival . . .' She cast an uneasy glance at Alyssa, but the seeress seemed absorbed in savoring the pleasant scent of her tea.

'If we are to establish the new Temple, it must be *soon*,' Tiriki continued, 'or in a generation, two at most, our children will be absorbed into the local population, and our purpose lost. I have not become an oracle, but I have read enough history to know that it has happened before.'

Chedan nodded. 'The first generation of shipwreck survivors remember that their ancestors came from beyond the ocean; a century on, their grandchildren often say the *ocean* is their ancestor, and make offerings to it.'

'Hah,' snorted Liala. 'I'm less concerned about the future than what is going on right now. I am grateful that so many of us were saved, but I could wish male and female priests had arrived in more equal numbers. There's you and all of us, and Kalaran and all those girls. Don't you think we are more than a little out of balance here?'

'What you say is so.' Tiriki sounded faintly surprised. 'I

really had not felt it as a problem before now. The energy of the Tor itself is so very balanced—'

'A single rising peak,' Alyssa crooned, her face half-turned from them, 'an earthly spark, guarding three springs and six caves, and so many more hearts. Shining, shining, shining, shining. Never mind the dark.'

Wind ruffled the willows; branches lashed for a moment, then settled. No one spoke. The mage stared at his tea bowl, fingering the tiny seashell carvings that banded its sides. *Liala is right again*, he thought. *Tiriki has simply not allowed herself to consider the problem, because then she would have to think about Micail. She and I may work as high priest and priestess, but we cannot generate the kind of energy that she and Micail— Or maybe it is not her preoccupation but my own that is at fault?*

A sharp sound on the edge of hearing caught his attention. Framed by willow leaves, a merlin hung in the silvery air . . . There had long been a rage for falcons among the noble houses, but Chedan had never particularly noticed them. Now he seemed always to know when a hawk or an owl was nearby. Perhaps it was a promise, a reminder of what was beyond.

Liala was still speaking. 'If our priestesses are to have mates and continue our tradition, we may have to recruit priests from among the others. For instance, there's Reidel – I think he has potential—'

'Especially with Damisa!' Alyssa, suddenly quite normal again, loosed an unappealing snort of laughter. 'You've seen how he looks at her?'

'And how she does *not* look at him in response?' Tiriki interjected briskly. 'I agree that we will need to do something eventually, but . . .'

'I'm a priestess of the Mother, not one of you adepts. We Blue Robes seek to celebrate the body, not transcend it!' Liala grinned. 'I don't like the sailors much, but I'm getting a lot less picky. I've even started eyeing the marsh folk men.'

Chedan looked at her, suddenly aware that there was a womanly body inside that blue robe. There was a time when he would not have been this surprised at her comment. Had the struggle to survive distracted him, or was he simply getting old?

'I understand what you are saying—' Tiriki continued, 'and I agree, but mating between cultures or castes can be risky.'

'They cannot be too different,' said Liala. 'Taret is a priestess of the Great Mother, even as we are.'

'They do not seem to have many ceremonies,' Chedan interjected. 'These people live lightly on the land, and they have been at peace for some time. Those the gods have satisfied,' he concluded, 'often seem to want little else.'

'Do *not* ask the wrong question,' Alyssa interrupted, her strange eyes gone colorless and flat.

Chedan turned, wondering what byway of the mind she had strayed into now.

Alyssa continued, 'You build channels for raindrops but make no provision for the sea. There are powers here that must be addressed. There are names to learn. And what of the other power, the one you claim to serve and preserve? *What of the Omphalos Stone?*'

Into the shocked silence came the cry of a falcon, darting and twisting through the air, bent on unseen prey.

Chedan grimaced. It had been the worst of errors to think the Grey Robe useless. Her control over her gift might be degenerating, but even in madness, Alyssa could still remind them of truths they ignored at their peril.

As the nights became colder and longer, the last of the shelters was finished, and though the dwellings were something less than grand, they were no longer damp or drafty. An enthusiastic start was even made on a proper meeting hall, but little work could be done in the cold rain. It was a hard life. Yet if sometimes the freezing mist never seemed to lift, their summer's foraging had left them with sufficient, if not very interesting, stores of food.

On the eve of the winter solstice, with a fresh storm front blowing in from the sea, Tiriki was in her hut, putting on another tunic to counter the chill, when she heard a sharp outcry.

'Damisa? What is it?' she called out. 'Is something wrong?'

'Not wrong,' came the answer, 'wonderful!'

Tiriki wrapped another shawl around her shoulders, then moved to the doorway, unwinding the thongs that held its hide curtain tightly closed.

'Oh, just look!' Damisa whispered, and Tiriki caught her breath.

A brisk wind was blowing, and the dark trees tossed a ragged net of branches toward charcoal and pearl-grey clouds layered with every astonishing combination of lavender and pink and rose. She had seen such a riot of colors in her mother's garden, but only in this strange new land were the heavens filled with such heart-stopping magnificence . . . 'Wings of storm,' she murmured, half-aloud, 'wings of marvel.'

Moment by moment the sky-blaze deepened, until every cloud was a scarlet shimmering of phantom fire . . . and for a moment, Tiriki thought she saw the final flames of Ahtarrath rising again from the sea. She drew closer to Damisa, whose fair skin seemed to have borrowed some new radiance from the dying of the sun.

The Sun only lends stewardship to Lord Nar-Inabi, Shaper of the Sea and the Stars of the Night, Tiriki told herself, reprising the catechism she had learned as a child, *and though in winter Banur the Destroyer briefly takes the throne, the Four-Faced One is also the Preserver, and his wintry reign prepares the path for the miracle of Ni-Terat, Dark Mother of All, who brings forth Caratra the Nurturer, ever and ever again.*

Still shivering, but curiously heartened, Tiriki tucked in

the ends of her shawl and watched the sunset colors darken until the merest traces of purple remained. The last banner of the light diminished to a sword-point of incandescent orange, then faded to crimson, dimmed, and disappeared.

'The Lord of the Day has turned His face from the earth,' Tiriki announced to the group that had gathered alongside her. 'Have ye put out every hearth fire?' At home, on the eve of the winter solstice all fires would have been extinguished at noon, but here common sense had prevailed, and Chedan determined that tradition actually forbade flames upon the hearths only during the ceremony itself.

The Atlanteans shuffled and stamped their feet uneasily. Tonight would be cold and dark beyond anything they had known; not even Chedan Arados had ever wintered in these northerly isles. Worse, the storm clouds cut them off from the stars. Even Manoah's messenger, the moon, would not appear. Only the star of Caratra, glowing on the horizon, gave hope that life and light might remain in the world.

The winter solstice ritual they were about to celebrate had never before seemed so necessary. In this bleak environment, it was hard to trust the ancient certainties; and while reason and tradition both told Tiriki that even when she could not see them, the constellations never ceased shining, in her heart, some atavistic spirit trembled, whispering that if her prayers failed, this night would never end.

At the center of the stone circle atop the Tor, Chedan was making his own preparations for the solstice ritual. Since their arrival, every member of the priests' caste had, of course, maintained the daily disciplines of salutation and meditation. But in all that time, this was the first true Working that they had attempted.

Since midmorning he and Kalaran had labored to build a small square altar and consecrate it with water and with oil and, after that, to gather kindling for the sacred fire. Throughout this time of preparation, Chedan had been troubled by memories that disturbed his concentration.

With his aching back turned toward the east, the mage donned the glittering wide-eyed mask of Nar-Inabi and intoned the Opening, unheard by any but his acolyte and the gods. In the same moment there arose from the Tor's lower slopes the holy music of flutes and drums, as the priests and priestesses began to climb the path newly cut through the woods. Many voices rang out, mingling in the dark—

> *'The sky is cold, the year is old,*
> *As the Wheel turns.*
> *The Earth is bare which once bloomed fair,*
> *And the Wheel turns.'*

Tiriki was first to enter the sacred space, the golden cap of her guardianship gleaming above her brow; even more remarkable was the bulge of her belly as her pregnancy neared its term. Her pregnancy, Chedan knew, had actually increased her power, but in her condition it would have been dangerous to allow her to take the role of the priestess in this ceremony.

He fixed his eyes upon the next entrant, Liala, in the grizzled mask of Ni-Terat. Chedan smiled beneath his own mask. She was an experienced priestess, solid, dependable. Chedan trusted that she would be able to handle an erratic influx of power.

> *'By frozen streams we harbor dreams,*
> *While the Wheel turns.*
> *One tiny spark defies the dark . . .*
> *And the Wheel turns.'*

For this ceremony, as tradition required, everyone was wearing the simple robe of the Temple of Light; but, truth to tell, hardly any scrap of that gleaming white cloth could be seen beneath the coarse wrappings that the climate required.

Chedan smiled wryly behind his mask. *We shall have to fashion warmer vestments if we are to maintain our ritual splendor*, he thought.

With a wrench, he brought himself back into focus, and added his voice to the song—

> *'Darkness falls, yet moonlight calls,*
> *And the Wheel turns.*
> *The starry night may grant delight . . .*
> *Till the Wheel turns.'*

With the last word, the singers, flutes, and drums stilled. A moment passed.

'Who comes here at the halted year?' Chedan sang, 'where Banur, four-faced king, holds sway? Why do you tarry, as the world sinks into darkness?'

'We are the children of Light,' the chorus answered. 'We do not fear the shadows. We rise to build beacons that will grant light to all!'

'Yet in this kingdom of the frozen moons,' Liala's warm voice soared, 'beyond wisdom and faith, what power can sustain you?'

'The power of Life! The circle of Love . . .'

'Come then,' Chedan and Liala sang together, 'let this warmth into our hearts—'

All the voices united. 'Father Light, return unto the world!'

Garments rustled and all too many joints creaked as the celebrants settled into the form of meditation. The ground was surely very cold, but not too damp, or not at first.

'Now does the longest night fall,' Chedan intoned, 'Now Banur holds all earth in thrall . . .' He paused, trying to calculate just how much time remained before the celestial nodes intersected the northern point of the ecliptic. He had labored long to identify the precise instant when the hidden sun would pass from the realm of the Sea Goat into that of the Water Bearer.

'From the earliest days of the Temple,' he continued, 'we have celebrated this moment before the sun begins to wax once more. We gather, therefore, not only to reconsecrate ourselves to the great work, but to affirm that our powers *are* worthy to be allied to those that rule all that there is.

'Fire is an earthly manifestation of that Light. Thus we honor it, knowing as ever that the Symbol is nothing, but the Reality of which the Symbol is born, is everything. Tonight, we ally our energies with those of earth to invoke heaven. Are you prepared to join your powers now, that the Light may be reborn?'

From the circle came a murmur of assent.

'Lead us from the unreal,' Chedan sang, 'unto the Real—'

'Lead us out of darkness,' Liala sang, 'into the Light—'

'Lead us from the fear of death,' the acolytes sang in reedy chorus, 'to the knowledge of Eternity—

> *'Champions of Light, arise!*
> *Awake, alive in the mortal sphere,*
> *And as the moon, reflect Manoah,*
> *In His refulgence ever near—'*

Chedan did not see the celebrants join hands, but he felt the shift in pressure as the circle closed. Liala stood on the other side of the altar, her hands extended, palms out. He mirrored the movement, and the first tendrils of power sparked between them.

Together they sounded the first of the sacred syllables, bringing up the power from the earth on which they stood to the base of the spine. Chedan sustained the note as Liala drew breath, then breathed in himself as she recommenced, and so all around the circle so that the sound was almost seamless. The Word of Power began to surge through the circle and build in force, until the Tor beneath their feet seemed to hum.

Chedan drew another breath, and let the power rise to

161

his belly, and began the Second Word. As the circle rein-forced it, his manhood stiffened with the raw power spiraling through his abdomen, but even as he recognized his arousal he was refocusing the energy . . . It was not usually so difficult. Sweat beaded on his brow.

The circle made a smooth transition into the Third Word, but Chedan could not help twitching spasmodically as fires flared in his solar plexus, implosions of energy that sparked in every nerve. When the tremors eased, he saw that Liala had become a glowing golden figure flecked with topaz lightnings. But her power was wavering. As her difficulty began to resonate back to him, Chedan fought panic.

But it was too late for second-guessing. Chedan took another deep breath and voiced the Third Word again, this time directing the full force of it at the figure in the Mask of Ni-Terat. Her limbs shook, cascading bands of blue and violet rippled around her like a feeding serpent, and with a shock the barrier gave way. The circle gasped and swayed in the sudden surge of energy.

Trembling with relief, Chedan modulated the lingering resonances into the higher note that carried the Fourth Word . . . hearts opened, they were filled with waves of love. With the Fifth Word came a wind of energy, a sound of beauty so intense it became unbearable. It was a deliv-erance to move onward to the point of power in the third eye.

The utterance of the Sixth Word, reflecting and recurring in visible waves of sound, resolved the conflict of percep-tion and illusion. Even Chedan could not tell if the auras of the others had grown brighter or if it was his own vision that had changed; yet he could see each member of the circle plainly – and not only their physical features. Chedan knew that he was looking into their very spirits. The merest glance at Liala revealed her dedication and her pride, and the need for love that yearned within her soul; but then all was sub-sumed as the greater power flowed, a great pillar of light, arcing between earth and heaven.

Little by little it steadied, and Chedan began to draw the energy downward and out along his shoulders to his hands.

Suddenly, out of the kindling piled upon the altar stone, a pale thread of smoke spiraled upward.

Lines of gold sparked in the wood, and then the flames rose. The scent of sweet oils filled the air.

'Blessed be Light!' they chorused, 'Blessed the Light at our inner dawn, showing the way to wake, to warm. Blessed the Light that lives in every pulsing heart. Blessed the Light of which we each and all are made.'

The flames leaped higher, gilding the faces of the worshippers as they began to dance sunwise around them, and glowing upon the weathered contours of the ancient stone circle. Chedan stepped backward as the eternal power of the earth swelled to a steady flow of energy that radiated out from the altar, burning away the fog that had cloaked the Tor.

Chedan gestured, and the celebrants unclasped their hands, raising their arms. 'Come, Light's children, Light's champions,' he sang, 'Bathe your worldly torches in the fire of the spirit. Bear new light to hearth and to home!'

One by one, each of the celebrants approached the altar, lit his or her torch from the sacred fire, and then continued round the circle to begin the journey downhill. Chedan watched with a tired smile as the line of torches bobbed away, garlanding the path with light. The singers continued,

> *'A spark to make the sunfire blaze,*
> *And flame-lit visions fill our gaze,*
> *Yet Love endures; we know its ways,*
> *As the Wheel turns.'*

In years to come, the mage mused, things would have to change. There had been an uncommon roughness to the power, and though all had come out well in the end, the strangeness troubled him. What could the explanation be? *Was my uncle Ardral right?* he asked himself, with a pang of loss. *Do we stand at the verge of a new age?*

> *'The Mother rests, but soon will wake,*
> *Her herbs to gather, bread to bake,*
> *From Earth's womb, new life we take,*
> *And the Wheel turns.'*

Chedan frowned, then smiled more broadly than before. The old song seemed newly appropriate. *But then the seeds of the future are always found in the past*, he reminded himself. *The father is not dead if his wisdom survives . . .*

'Are you all right? Shall I lend you my cloak? Do you need to lean on me on the way down?' Damisa's words were kind, but underneath them Tiriki could hear exasperation mingled with concern.

She shook her head. It had been embarrassing enough to lumber through the ritual dance like a foundered pony! Next someone would be offering to carry her around in a sedan chair . . .

'My lady?' Damisa pressed. 'Shall I—?'

'I'm fine!' Tiriki snapped.

'I'm sure you are!' The girl's tone sharpened as well. 'I was only trying to help!'

Tiriki sighed. She was growing tired of Damisa's erratic alternation between leisurely distraction and solicitous concern, but she knew that expending energy as they had done in the ritual often left tempers thin. She took a deep breath, gasped at the icy quality of the air, and tightened her hold on her own composure.

'I thank you,' said Tiriki courteously. 'I'll come down in my own time, and meet you there. Go on – the feast that Reidel and the sailors promised will probably be ready by now!' She lifted her torch, which flared wildly in the fierce wind that had begun to blow as soon as the ritual ended.

'Oh, Reidel!' Damisa tossed her head. 'I suppose sailors must learn to do for themselves at sea, but I haven't found their cooking to be anything worth hurrying for . . .'

'Perhaps not,' Tiriki said dryly, 'but I am sure you are hungry, so run along.'

Damisa looked taken aback, but if she was insulted it was not enough to prevent her from taking Tiriki at her word. As the girl proceeded down the path, Tiriki sighed and, much more carefully, followed. At least going downhill she would have her torch to light the way.

The next step went wrong, and her foot came down strangely across a little hollow in the rocky ground. Her breath caught, the muscles of her belly cramped, and she stopped again, leaning on her staff, remembering once more the babes she had been unable to bring to term. With this thought a little fear came, a horror that perhaps she had harmed the child . . .

Nearby, a boulder poked out from the turf. She considered sitting down, but her instinct was to keep in motion. *Surely*, she told herself, *it is not so serious. Once I have warmed up a little, the ache will go away.*

Taking another deep breath, Tiriki started out again. She could hear happy laughter from below, and one or two voices still above, but for the moment she was quite alone on the path. As she angled toward the lower slope, the shrubbery on each side grew thicker. Soon she would be among the trees. *And not too soon – it's coming on to rain*, she thought as a hint of dampness kissed her cheek.

Once again, dense clouds obscured the stars. A fine mist was falling, laying a veil of crystals across the rough weave of her shawls. She tried to hurry her pace, but the ache in her back had become a beating pulse of pain.

The imperceptible condensation of the mist became a steady patter as the rain began in earnest. Her torch hissed as heavy droplets filtered through the leaves, soaking her clothing and making the path treacherous. She would have to move even more slowly to avoid a fall. *If only I had not sent Damisa away*, she thought. *I might be willing to accept a little assistance now . . .*

Sighing, she told herself to breathe carefully and, for a little while, it helped to manage the pain. Then another loose stone turned beneath her foot and sent her reeling, torch and staff alike flying from her flailing hands. Icy water splashed her face and arms as she struck the ground, and in the same moment she felt a gush of warmth between her thighs. Her breath burst from her in a sob as her belly clenched harder.

The child! she thought in panicked understanding. *The child is coming . . . now . . .* She should have taken more care, so close to her time. In such bitter cold, she had been mad even to climb the hill for the ritual.

She reached for the fallen torch, still dimly glowing; but before her fingers could close on the stock, it sputtered and went out. She could not restrain a curse. Faint as that light had been, without it the darkness seemed impenetrable.

'Liala!' she breathed, for though there was no House of Caratra here, the blue-robed priestess had promised to see her through her labor. 'Someone! *Help me!*'

She took another breath, teeth chattering, and fought for control. She had a little time – the tales she had heard of childbirth said that a first babe always took many hours. The thought offered little consolation. Shivering, she heaved herself up onto hands and knees, wondering if she could make it to her feet, and whether it would be safe to walk if she could. *Crawling is better*, she told herself. *At least this way I can feel my way along the path*. It was a painful mode of progression, however, and before she had gone very far she wanted nothing more than to curl into a moaning ball of pain.

Tiriki forced herself to keep moving. 'D-darling child! I me-me-mean to see you *alive!*' Strangely, her resolve made her feel a great deal warmer. *I'll be fine. And if all else fails, Chedan and Liala will surely find me when they come downhill . . .*

The rigorous disciplines of the Temple had made her certain she would have the strength to endure whatever might come, but she had never before realized how much she had depended on the army of servants ever present in Ahtarrath. In the world of the spirit she could face all dangers, but this was a challenge of the flesh, and she found herself unexpectedly weak, alone, and in pain.

And worst of all, she realized, as she came up against a sodden tree in the middle of what she had thought was the path, she was lost.

Clinging to the tree trunk, she hauled herself upright. 'Halloo!' she yelled, but the wind tore her breath away. It seemed to her that she could hear someone else shouting from higher on the hill. Were they looking for her? Surely by now someone must have noticed that she was missing. She tried to call again, but her shrieks were muffled by the drumbeat of wind-driven rain.

This child was a miracle, she thought numbly, *surely the Powers that sent me this joy will not allow it to be destroyed . . . not in this senseless way!* She rested on hands and knees, breathing cautiously as the pain rolled through her body again.

I am a Guardian, said that part of her mind that was still capable of thought, *surely I can summon someone, even if my body is trapped here . . . The Lady! The Queen! She gave me her blessing!* But when she gathered her forces to focus the call, another contraction scattered her concentration and forced her back into her body again.

In the end, all she could do was seize the moments between the pangs and continue dragging herself slowly downhill.

'Get up.'

The simple animal awareness of pain to which Tiriki's

consciousness had retreated took in the words without understanding them. Half-conscious, she had continued to crawl. Now small hands were gripping her arms with surprising power, pulling her to her feet.

'That's it – you can walk! I will show you the way.'

'*Who are you?*' Tiriki moaned, as warm energy flowed into her through those small, strong hands.

'Keep your mind on your feet!' came the terse reply, as Tiriki stopped to let another contraction pass.

'Good!' said her helper. 'Now breathe into the pain!' It was a woman's voice, and from the size of her hands, probably one of the marsh people. Perhaps, Tiriki thought dimly, one who had come to the Tor to observe the lighting of the solstice fire . . . She had no idea where they were going in that wilderness of whipping branches and showering rain, nor how long they made their way through the forest. But presently her mysterious companion led her into a clearing beyond the trees. Tiriki's feet felt level ground. She could smell woodsmoke, and sensed rather than saw the bulk of a dwelling.

Her guide called out then, in a string of liquid notes like a birdcall, but Tiriki realized they were actually words.

Flickering light spilled out as a leather door flap whipped open. The stranger's hands released her, and Tiriki fell forward into the wisewoman Taret's arms.

Perhaps mercifully, the next few hours would remain forever unclear in Tiriki's memory, but interspersed with bouts of shocking pain was an awareness of warmth, and the brightness of Taret's wise old eyes, and the comfort of her hands. Later, Liala's face was there also, but she knew that it was Taret whose strength was supporting her.

As the pangs peaked, she lost awareness of her surroundings entirely. It seemed to her that she was back in her bed in the palace of Ahtarra, cradled in Micail's arms. She knew that it could only be a dream within a dream, for according to the traditions of the Temple no male, not even the father of the child, would have been allowed anywhere near a birthing chamber, nor would he even know if mother and child had survived until his wife was able to bring the babe herself from the House of Caratra.

But perhaps in the Otherworld the rules were different, for surely he was with her, murmuring encouragement as her flesh was wracked by pain after pain. And she remembered being lifted, and another woman's soft breasts and belly bracing her back as strong hands bent and parted her thighs.

'One more push—' Did the words come from Taret or Micail? 'Draw strength from the earth . . . Scream! Shout! Push the baby into the world!'

Of course. She must call on the power of the land. For a moment Tiriki was in clear control. She remembered how the forces at the Tor had fountained through her, and she drew upon them anew, until she felt as though she *was* the earth. With a shout that seemed to reverberate in every land she pushed her child into the world of humankind.

The leather door flap was wide open, making a bright triangle against the darkness.

Consciousness, awakening gradually, recognized it as a pale sky, tinted with all the pearly hues of a winter dawn. Tiriki realized with surprise that although she was weak, she was not in pain. Indeed, her dominant sensation was of radiant contentment, and as she realized that a small life lay nestled in the crook of her arm, gurgling and burrowing against her, she understood why.

In wonder she examined the smooth curve of the head, crowned with a wisp of fiery hair, and then, as the baby moved, she saw the tiny features, closed in sleep like the bud of a rose.

A shadow fell across her field of vision. Looking up, she met Liala's smile. 'He is whole?' Tiriki whispered.

'*She* is perfect,' came the voice of Taret from her other side.

Tiriki's gaze returned to her child. Not a son, then, to inherit Micail's powers – if indeed those powers meant anything in this new land. A daughter, then, to inherit – what? Silently, unable to voice the questions that whirled through her, she looked up at Taret.

'Daughter of holy place,' said the wisewoman cheerfully. 'She be priestess here, some day.'

Tiriki nodded, only half hearing, yet feeling all the scattered pieces of her soul slip back into place. But it was not quite the same configuration. There was a part which linked her to the child at her side, and another that touched the earth on which she lay, and something else that she could not have defined or named. She knew only that with this birth, the process that had begun with the ritual on the top of the Tor was complete. Now she would always belong to this land.

With that thought came another. 'Thank you,' she said to Taret, 'and you must take my thanks to the woman who brought me here. Without her help I would have died. Was it you, Liala? Or Metia? Or—?'

'What?' Liala's brows wrinkled with confusion. 'I did little enough. It was Damisa who grew worried when you did not join us at the feast, and then could not be found. So I came to Taret, hoping she might be able to help. I had only just gone inside when we heard your cries and let you in – but I thought you came alone!'

Taret's smile had become a grin. 'The Queen of the Shining Ones, it was,' she said proudly. 'She takes care of her own.'

TEN

Micail sighed in his sleep, reaching out to Tiriki with an instinct that even the loneliness of the last nine months had not been able to destroy. And this time it seemed to him that his arms closed around her. He felt the hard round of her belly contract, and with the certainty of dream knew that she was giving birth to his child.

She moaned in pain and he held her more tightly, murmuring encouragement, and then, abruptly, they were on a grassy plain in the grey hour before dawn. As his wife's belly heaved, the earth was also heaving, but not with the fires of destruction. Everywhere new life was springing from the soil. Tiriki's struggles grew harder until, with a cry, she pushed the child into the world. As she lay back, gasping, he reached down to take the babe and saw that it was a girl, perfectly formed, with an unruly wisp of hair like a new flame.

Laughing, he held her high. 'Behold the child of the prophecy, my pledge to this new land!' As all the beings gathered on that plain, both human and other, shouted in enthusiastic welcome, waves of contentment lifted him and carried him away.

Micail fought free from his blankets, blinking as he realized that he was still hearing cheering and the sound of voices raised in song.

Was it a dream, he wondered, *or is all I remember of*

171

the past year only a nightmare? But the dim outlines of the room around him were only too familiar, and they belonged to no memories that included Tiriki or a child.

It was a dream, then – a lie. But strangely that realization did not fill him with the despair he usually felt when the bright promises of the night were snatched away. If it had been an illusion, at least it was a good one.

The tumult outside was getting louder. He lurched out of bed, stumbled across the woven mat, and fumbled open the shutters that kept out some of the damp night air. To the west a new stormfront was rolling in, trailing streamers of rain behind it, but the new moon, Manoah's messenger, slid among the streamers of clouds, seeking rest beneath the horizon, and the stars shone cold and dim.

All the world was at rest, dark and silent – except for Belsairath. The muddy crossroads outside the inn were alive with torches, and in the square an immense bonfire blazed. People were dancing around it, shouting.

Has another ship come in? He strained to see the harbor, but the docks were dark and still. He rubbed his eyes, unable at that moment to imagine what other reason people might have for such frenzied celebration.

The door to his chamber opened and he saw Jiritaren's angular shape against the light of the lamp that was always left burning in the hall.

'You *are* awake! I thought you must be, with all the racket outside!' As usual, Jiritaren sounded as if he were on the brink of laughter.

'Did I have a choice?' Micail gestured toward the window. 'What in the name of all the gods is that commotion about?'

'Didn't anyone tell you? This is how they celebrate midwinter here!'

'Oh.' Micail shrugged and pulled the shutters closed, which dulled the noise slightly. He *had* known it was the winter solstice and had chosen not to attend the ritual of the New Fire at Prince Tjalan's villa . . . 'I haven't been myself lately.'

'You *sound* a lot better than you have in some time. Let's have a little light!' Jiritaren thrust a splinter into the flame and brought it back to kindle the lamp in Micail's room.

'Ye-e-s,' he said then, as he looked into Micail's ear. 'Someone home there, all right, and just in time.'

'Oh stop!' Micail aimed a mock punch at his friend and turned, looking for his cup and the water he hoped was still in it. 'But I am glad you're here. I'm even glad for the damned festival! It's high time something cheerful happened around here.' He stopped, peering at Jiritaren. 'In time for *what?*'

'Haladris and Mahadalku have called a special meeting – relax, they won't actually start until after dawn prayers. But since I just got back from the ritual and happen to know you're often up late, I thought you'd like to know—'

'Indeed I would,' Micail growled, 'if you'd be so kind as to *tell* me anything!'

Jiritaren's dark eyes glowed. 'What I was *about* to say is that the Tarissedan psychics that Stathalka has been working with have found the place, and it's not too far away.'

'The place?'

'The power source we need to build our Temple! Naranshada has been able to confirm that the energies probably coordinate, too. It's in the place Prince Tjalan was talking about, the Ai-Zir lands.'

Micail frowned, his mind beginning to engage as it had not for many moons. 'If Ansha agrees it's the right place, then we should start planning—' He stopped short at Jiritaren's laughter.

'No, no, go on – it's just that you sound more like yourself than you have in, oh, far too long.'

'I suppose you're right.' Even if his dream were only illusion, Micail blessed the gods for sending it to give him the strength to fulfill his responsibilities. If Tiriki should sail into the harbor today, he thought, he would be almost too ashamed to face her. *I have done nothing*, he told himself sternly, *but that will end now.*

Jiritaren nodded, sober again. 'They want you to lead the expedition. Tjalan says he means to go with you, but he will almost certainly have to return here, just to keep an eye on things. You are the only one with both the rank to command a detachment of soldiers *and* the status to control the priests they will guard.'

Micail shook his head in wonder. What Jiri was saying surprised him less than the fact that for the first time since the Sinking he found himself genuinely interested.

Micail lay awake for what seemed a long time after his friend had left, listening to the noise of the revelers outside. The rain that presently began to rattle against the tiles of the roof dampened their spirits not at all. It reminded him of waves on the shore of Ahtarrath, and he found himself smiling.

He closed his eyes at last, going over the bright images of his dream once more. And just as the first birds were beginning to herald the day, the vision changed. He heard a voice proclaiming, '*The Daughter of Manoah brings life back into the world!*' and from the babe he held grew a blaze of light as the midwinter sun began to rise.

As the first anniversary of their arrival in Belsairath came and went, even the dead winter foliage seemed to celebrate, giving way to brilliant green, filling the world with a sweetness that seemed to linger in the air. The cycles of the sun, which at home had been measured and perceptible only to priests, were the very heart of the native religion in this northern land. Certainly Micail had never before been so aware of the lengthening days. Caught up in preparations for the expedition to the country of the Ai-Zir, he found himself too busy for much brooding, but that was not the only reason.

His grief was not gone, but it had grown distant. He was beginning to accept that Tiriki was lost to him. He had spoken to traders who came to the town, and even persuaded Prince

Tjalan to send a ship around Beleri'in to check the more likely landfalls, but there had been no word. Though Micail mourned for the form of flesh in which he had loved her, he told himself that in another life they would come together again. And sometimes he even believed it.

The day of departure came, and Micail stood on the docks with his white robes girdled up for walking, stout sandals on his feet, and a staff in his hand that could be used for more than magic. Behind him he could hear a confusion of voices as the column formed, the white robes of the acolytes who had been selected to go with them pale against the green tunics the soldiers wore. The waves were blue today, with sparkles of foam. His gaze caught a gleam of reddish gold and he stiffened for a moment, sure that he saw a wingbird rounding the point, heading in . . . But the wind shifted, flattening the waves. It had only been a trick of the sunlight.

Do not mistake the signpost for the destination, old Rajasta murmured in his memory.

'Micail! Come on, man, we can't leave without you!' The voice of Jiritaren roused him.

'Farewell,' he whispered, lifting his hands in salute to the glimmer of light on the waves. Then he turned and strode away from the harbor to take his place in the column beside Prince Tjalan.

For the first hour of that first day's journey the rutted road was all Micail saw, and he paid little heed to anything he heard until someone behind him exclaimed in surprise. Micail looked up to see a turf-covered embankment along the side of a hill to the left of the road.

'The natives here built that?' he asked Tjalan. 'I would not have thought them capable of it.'

'They built it,' responded Tjalan, 'or rather their ancestors did. And they lived in it, until we came. My great-grandfather established the port—' He gestured, thumb over his shoulder. 'My father regarded the Tin Isle ports as a total loss, but in local terms, they've done well. In fact, Domazo, who runs that inn you like so well, is the direct descendant of that chief. I wouldn't be surprised if he doesn't have as much real authority there as I do! Anyway, as you can see, nobody lives here now. It gives us plenty of space for expansion . . .'

'Impressive,' Micail said at last.

'Yes, it is. We should not forget that when properly led and motivated, these people can accomplish a great deal.'

Micail looked at him sharply but Tjalan only walked on, scanning the horizon. Surely Tjalan did not mean what he seemed to be suggesting, that the native people wanted only for a strong leader. Himself, perhaps? In their planning, they had only discussed scouting the Ai-Zir lands and *asking* the native king for permission to build there. Micail did not recall an Atlantean empire built on the labor of subject peoples as being part of Rajasta's prophecies.

On the morning of the second day, Micail dropped back far enough to join the younger members of the expedition. He was far from sure what kind of welcome to expect – they were often rather stiff and uncomfortable in his presence – but today all seemed glad to see him.

After his recent exposure to the prickly vanities of his fellow priests, he was glad to see that the acolytes were making no attempt to lord it over the chelas who served the other priests and priestesses. Li'ija and Karagon were not being treated as anything less than equals, and neither Galara's semiroyal status nor the fact that she was Micail's sister-in-law won her any favors. But the boy, Lanath, worried him. He continually lagged a little behind the rest, his eyes vague, as if remembering some evil dream. Micail stepped off the rutted road and bent, pretending to retie his sandals.

'You look tired,' he said, straightening as Lanath started to pass him. 'Did you not sleep well?'

Startled, Lanath peered up at him. 'W-well enough,' he

stammered, hand going to his chin in the nervous habit he had developed since his beard had finally started to come in. 'Last night, anyway . . .'

Micail nodded. 'We all dream of what we have lost. But we have to go on,' he said, knowing he was speaking to himself as well. 'I dream of my lost wife. Last night I saw her as if she were here before me.'

'When I'm not having nightmares, and I can never remember them, thank the gods!' said Lanath haltingly, 'I dream of Kanar – the Temple astrologer on Ahtarrath. *You* know.'

'Yes?' said Micail, with an encouraging lift of his eyebrows.

'Well, I had just been apprenticed to him – I've always been good at numbers. But in the dreams, I – it's nothing too strange at first, I mean I just see him in his observatory or walking on the beach. But then he gets – it's like he's trying to tell me something, but I can't quite seem to understand . . .'

'Yes, but aren't the stars usually counted among the things no one can really understand?' Micail replied. Suddenly *his* mind was whirling with a hundred self-doubts that were not his own. Lanath was broadcasting his feelings. No wonder the others seemed uncomfortable when he was around.

The boy needed training. Micail cleared his throat. 'Well, Lanath, if you are called to the star lore, you really ought to talk to Ardral – or Jiritaren,' he went on, as Lanath flinched. 'You should not fear the Seventh Guardian. His jokes can teach you more than the sober wisdom of many, but I imagine you'll find Jiri more approachable. But right now, there is another thing you need to learn. Your voice has finally finished changing, is it not so?'

'Yes – I'm going to be a tenor, they say,' Lanath flushed, 'like you.'

'Very good,' said Micail, 'and that is no mere polite encouragement. When it comes time to build the new Temple, we will need trained singers – so I think you ought to begin working with me now. What do you say?'

'Right now? I mean, I have a lot of trouble concentrating,' Lanath reddened again, 'especially in public like this. But – but I would be happy to try!'

Micail nodded. 'That is all I ask. Let's start with a basic centering exercise. Can you intone the fifth note and hold it? Yes, yes, that's good, but now listen, *very* carefully—'

'It's so beautiful!' exclaimed Elara. The road along which the native trader Heshoth led them wound northeastward. To their left rose a line of low, tree-covered hills. Even the turf between the deeply cut wheel ruts was brilliantly green, starred with spring flowers. 'Our journey must have been blessed by the gods!'

'Which gods?' muttered Lanath, 'ours or theirs? I still hurt from yesterday's walking!' Galara and Li'ija groaned agreement.

'If you had got off your rear end more often when we were in Belsairath you would be in better shape now,' snapped Elara, surveying him with disfavor.

Almost without warning, Lanath had grown taller than she, but what muscle he had was still overlaid with a layer of what she could only describe as 'pudge.' His dark brown hair still flopped over his eyes like a child's, but he had the beginnings, finally, of a beard. Elara was resigned to their betrothal, but in no hurry for marriage, not when there were so many other interesting men around.

'Lord Ardravanant kept me more than busy enough,' Lanath was saying, self-righteously, 'Studying the stars mostly *requires* you to sit still.'

'And to sleep late,' added Cleta rather wistfully. She was sturdily built, and sober and smart, and when she had had a full night's sleep, she was good-tempered, too . . .

'I expect the journey will toughen us all,' said Li'ija brightly.

Karagon, who had joined the expedition with his master Valadur, snorted disdainfully. 'Just a pleasant stroll to you, is it?'

'Absolutely. If we were not tied to the pace of those Ai-Zir ox carts,' Li'ija persisted, with a smile that suggested she might not be entirely serious, 'then we could go twice as fast!'

Lanath groaned at the thought, but the others laughed. Ardral was riding in one of those ox carts with their supplies and baggage, and Valadur to keep him company. Everyone else walked, as in fact they would have done at home, where only the powerful, or the aged and feeble, rode in sedan chairs.

Considering the state of the road, she wondered how long it would be before the Seventh Guardian was walking along with the rest of them, despite his advanced years . . . however many they might be.

She had inquired more than once, but no one seemed to know how old Ardral was. 'Old enough to know better – and how I wish I did!' was his usual answer to anyone bold enough to ask. And there were other, darker, rumors about him. Some said that in his younger days Ardral had used his powers to kill. He himself denied it, or rather, he would say no, his enemies only went mad and ran away . . . which was not exactly reassuring. Still, the densely forested hills they were passing through might conceal any number of dangers, from wild animals to bandits. She was glad to be traveling with any sort of mage.

Of course there were the soldiers, too. Half of them brought up the rear, while the others formed a protective vanguard around Heshoth, a pair of native guides, and Prince Tjalan. Micail walked sometimes with the prince and his bodyguards, but no less often with the other priests. There were the engineers, Naranshada and Ocathrel, and Jiritaren, whose job, Elara suspected, was partly to nursemaid Micail, but mostly to assist Ardral with his astronomical calculations . . .

Elara was much less sure what the priestess Kyrrdis was doing there. *If they wanted a singer, she's good, but Mahadalku is better; and if they just wanted a woman along they could have brought one of the sajis . . .* She blushed.

Then there was Valadur. She was entirely mystified as to his function. The Grey Order had a very mixed reputation . . . *Ardral will keep him in line*, she decided. *That leaves . . . Valorin. Of course.*

She slowed her steps, looking about, but still did not see Valorin anywhere. A priest from Alkonath who had been selected because of his vast knowledge of growing things, Valorin was continually leaving the beaten path to investigate some unfamiliar shrub or flower.

'Look – is that a *village* over there?' Galara exclaimed, pointing toward an irregular collection of carefully laid-out plots radiating out from a round hut with a roof of green turf. At one end of the field a long green mound seemed to stand guard.

'A farm, at least,' Cleta ventured, 'though it does not look like the ones at home.'

'Several farms,' observed Karagon as they crested the road and more fields and buildings came into view. The plots were small, divided by hedges or ditches, and as they drew closer they saw the dirty brown backs of a flock of sheep being driven along by a small boy in a brown tunic with a stick and a yapping dog.

'There's water in those ditches!' Lanath said in surprise. 'Just lying there.'

As they drew closer, a man hoeing between rows of young grain called out a greeting in the local tongue and Greha, one of the ferocious-looking native guides, replied. Both natives had the curly brown hair and grey eyes typical of these people, though Greha was both exceptionally broad and tall.

'You've learned a few words of the local patois, haven't you, Cleta?' Galara asked, 'What are they saying?'

'Something about shepherds and sheep. I think they are talking about us!' Cleta's round face grew slightly pink. 'Oh my. I hope the prince didn't hear that!'

With his bodyguard prowling around him, Prince Tjalan strode forward as boldly as the falcons that fluttered on his banners.

Behold the great lord of Atlantis, taking possession of the new land, Elara thought, *but what will the new land take from him?*

The journey took on a rhythm of its own as the days passed. They rose early and walked, with occasional pauses, until the middle of the afternoon, when the vanguard would seek out a campsite with good water. One night they were troubled by the howling of wolves, and more than once Lanath woke them with his nightmares, but otherwise all seemed peaceful. The acolytes and chelas soon grew accustomed to the exercise, and once they lost their fear of the unknown terrain, they were eager to go exploring.

Micail had not wanted them to go off on their own, but the trader Heshoth assured them that the folk here were not only peaceful but timid. When the natives saw the Atlanteans coming, with their brilliant white tunics and brightly colored mantles, not to mention the banners, spears, and swords, the pigherds and woodcutters of the forest ran away even faster than had the lads tending sheep or cattle in the meadows.

The next day the expedition turned gradually northward, tediously following the road around the end of a line of densely wooded hills. By late afternoon, the travelers approached a solitary hill with the oblong hump of an old barrow on its top, commanding the countryside.

'We should probably stop here—' Heshoth pointed to a broad clearing between the road and the stream. 'Once people came to this hill for the summer's-end ceremony, but then there was a war. No one left to come here now but us.'

The day had been fair, and the long afternoon gave way to a lingering sunset as Prince Tjalan's servants prepared the pavilions, and gathered wood to cook the evening meal. Until they had finished, there would be little for the acolytes and chelas to do. Meanwhile the hill beckoned, with its leafy slopes and dark hints of ancient tragedies.

'Let's climb it,' Karagon suggested. 'From the top we should get a fine view of the countryside.'

'Haven't you had enough walking today?' Elara grumbled; but except for Lanath, who was muttering something about ghosts, the others seemed eager for the adventure. Li'ija and Karagon soon found a path that led almost directly up the hillside to the summit, and they made good progress. Presently they came to a ditch and a low bank, both quite overgrown. Oddly enough, the ditch had been dug in segments, with a walkway of solid ground left between them.

'Neither ditch nor bank seems very defensible,' Karagon observed, 'there must be another purpose here than fortification.'

On the north face they found the timber posts of a gatehouse, still leaning against each other although the roof must have fallen in long ago.

'If it's not a fort,' asked Li'ija, 'what was this for?'

'It feels . . . odd . . .' Lanath shivered, then hastened to add, 'Not unfriendly-odd, just very ancient. There's an echo of many voices—'

'Yes,' agreed Li'ija, 'I can hear them too—'

'It's wind. But something has been digging in one of those pits,' said Cleta. She moved closer and squatted down, brushing away the soil. 'There's a quern here, like the ones the native women use for grinding grain. But it's broken.'

'Smashed,' volunteered Elara.

'Sacrificed,' Karagon whispered dramatically.

'Is that a pot?' Galara leaned over to see.

'It's a skull,' Elara answered. 'Maybe the woman who used the quern.'

'Let's see what's inside,' suggested Karagon, picking his way through the ruins of the gatehouse. Lanath and Galara protested again, then shrugged and followed the others.

'It's a stone circle!' said Elara, and stopped only a few steps inside, testing that expectant stillness as she had been trained to do, but there was no altar, only grasses waving in the twilit breeze and a few sapling hazel trees.

'I think,' said Galara tremulously, 'we've found their cemetery.'

'Then why wasn't that body buried?' Li'ija pointed to the interior of the circle, where bleached bones lay scattered on the grass.

'Could have been burned,' Cleta mused. That was done in Atlantis, in hope of loosening the ties of karma that bound the spirit and freeing it to seek a higher path; but there were no marks of charring on these bones.

'They laid the bodies out here so the birds and beasts could receive the flesh,' Lanath said then, in a strange still voice. 'The skull was placed in the family's pit with the offerings.'

Elara looked at her betrothed in surprise. Lanath had never been able to read the history of a place this way before. She glanced at Li'ija as if to say, *I thought this kind of thing was* your *talent?*

Ocathrel's daughter shrugged and turned away.

'It's getting really late,' said Galara with an exaggerated shiver, 'Shouldn't we be going back? That slope will be harder going down.'

Once outside the gatehouse, they all felt better, but the path that they took down the hill did not lead back to the encampment. Instead they found themselves entering what was obviously another enclosure, much more extensive than the first. Tangled vegetation covered fallen house-posts, and a series of overgrown hedges marked out paddocks for animals, and plots where a few sparse stalks of native wheat still grew.

'This one only seems deserted,' Lanath said, 'like somebody's about to come back. But at the same time – it's like it was never really lived in.'

'Perhaps they *were* temporary dwellings,' Elara suggested, 'the guide said people came here for a festival . . .'

'They should have stayed away, if they wanted to live,' said Li'ija in an odd voice. Elara turned and saw her standing very still, staring at something in her hand.

'You found an arrowhead!' exclaimed Karagon. 'Say, I didn't know you were a sensitive. What else do you pick up from it?'

'Blood,' the girl said, 'and hate. Cattle. A raid . . . men running . . . walls of flames . . .'

'These house-posts do look – charred,' said Galara uneasily.

'And that,' Cleta pointed out, 'is not an old woodpile. Those are bones—'

Elara put her arms around Li'ija and gently turned the chela's hand so that the bit of flint fell to the ground. The Alkonan girl shuddered and relaxed against her with a sigh.

'Are you all right?'

'I will be.' Li'ija shivered again. 'That was strange.' She straightened, moving a little away from Elara. 'I remembered my father telling me that there was a place near Belsairath that used to be a famous mine for flint, and I thought about the road we've been on, and that arrowhead – it was like it appeared out of the ground, winking at me. So I picked it up, and it just—'

'It was calling you. There are a lot of spirits here.' Lanath looked around uneasily. 'Their skulls were not buried. No one made the offerings. They're still waiting.'

Everyone had moved closer together. The setting sun crowned the trees with fire, and bars of bloody light slanted across the ground, making wavering lines in the dim air.

'Yes,' said Cleta, unexpectedly, 'even I can feel that. Ugh! I hate this kind of thing. Let's get out of here!' she exclaimed, taking Li'ija by the hand.

184

By the time everyone had made it out of the enclosure, the first stars were beginning to appear. Li'ija seemed to recover quickly, but Cleta and Lanath continued to mutter about spirits. Everyone else seemed to expect Elara to know what to do. Grounding their energies might not be the best remedy – it was from the earth, after all, that the trouble came. *Caratra's other face*, she thought, and shuddered again.

The obvious solution was to get completely off the hill, but that proved to be more difficult than expected. Though the sky was fairly clear, there was no moon. Beneath the trees it was darker still, while every possible path turned and twisted as if trying to lead them astray. In the end, all they could do was to force their way downward through thorny shrubs and tangled saplings until they smelled woodsmoke and heard Tjalan's servants chattering as they cooked the evening meal.

Most of the explorers stumbled the rest of the way down into the camp as fast as they were able, but Lanath tarried, and after a moment, Elara climbed back up to rejoin him. 'Come along,' she said softly, 'it's over.'

'No. We have not escaped . . .' Lanath whispered. 'The one in the barrow on the hill. She is very old, the Mother of all her tribe. And she doesn't want anyone here . . .'

And no wonder, thought Elara, *after the way we went blundering about among the bones!* She gave Lanath a gentle push toward the campfire. 'It's going to be all right,' she said again. When he had gone, she turned back toward the woods, lifting her hands in salutation.

'Grandmother, our apologies. We mean only good to you and your people, honor to the dead and the living alike. Let me set out an offering for you in the forest, and in the morning we will depart from here. This one night I ask for your protection. Send us no evil dreams!'

Throughout the following day the acolytes and chelas remained unusually close together, but walked mostly in silence. The next day, the travelers turned to the east once more. Micail found himself oddly reluctant to head in that direction, for that night in the camp beneath the barrow-crowned hill, Micail had dreamed of Tiriki as she might have become if she had reached this chilly land. For the first time in a year he had awakened smiling. So clear had the image been that he almost seemed to see her still, crowned with hawthorn bloom, framed by lush green hills . . .

But as they moved toward the rising sun, that awareness of Tiriki began to fade. *What do you expect? It was just a dream*, he told himself sternly.

They camped that night at the edge of the hills. Before them lay a new countryside whose gentle undulations flattened into a broad plain that rolled away to a misty horizon. The countryside here seemed more thickly settled than any they had yet seen, but the same hedge and ditch system defined the fields where new wheat stood thick and green. Beyond that lay more open pastures where little brown sheep or wide-horned cattle grazed. The round farmhouses were much larger than the ones they had seen near the coast and were roofed with straw thatch instead of grassy turves.

'This is Azan – the Bull-pen – where King Khattar rules!' Heshoth proclaimed. Clearly the trader was proud of his ruler. 'At the noon meal we will stop, and you may put on festival clothing to honor him.'

Tjalan caught Micail's eye with an amused smile, but plainly he found the counsel good. 'We begin,' the prince murmured, 'by impressing this native chieftain, but soon, I think, he will honor *us* the more.'

'Do you know anything of this king?' Micail asked, just as softly.

'From what Heshoth has said, Khattar is lord over the many chieftains whose holdings ring this plain. They war with one another over grazing rights, then gather at a central shrine for their great festivals – over which the king presides. They say that he carried off and married the woman who is now high priestess for all the people of the Bull. His reputation as a warrior was apparently great enough to discourage retribution.' He shrugged. 'But Heshoth tells me that it's not his wife but his sister who is called queen. Her name is Khayan-e-Durr, and her son will be his heir. It's all rather complex and primitive, and as I say, I don't fully understand it. But you know what they say, when in Khem, walk sideways.'

'How will he receive us, do you think?' Micail cast a quizzical look at his old friend. 'As allies, or as a threat to his supremacy?'

'Ah, well, that will depend on how we handle this embassy,' Tjalan answered with a laugh. 'I hope you brought your best bracelets.'

They came to Azan-Ylir, the home and stronghold of the high king, at the time when the cookfires had been lit and the savor of roast meat was beginning to scent the air. The village was set on a rise above willow-clad banks where the river Aman flowed gently down from the north. The afternoon sunlight shone sweetly through the new leaves. Heshoth's ferocious bodyguard, Greha, had disappeared during the noon rest, so Micail was not surprised to find that they were expected.

Greha was waiting, with a line of warriors dressed as he was, in tanned leathers and furs, and armed with bronze weapons. They stood in two groups on each side of gateposts made out of gigantic tree trunks that towered above the logs of the palisade, twice the height of a man. As the Atlanteans marched through the gate, the guards fell in behind them.

Are they threat or protection? Micail wondered. And then, remembering his conversation with Tjalan, *Which are we?*

The village consisted of a collection of roundhouses whose conical roofs were thatched with straw, interspersed with storage structures and pens for valued livestock. But a single

187

central building dominated – a great roundhouse whose roof was built in two sections, the inner cone lifted on pillars above the outer ring so that smoke could filter out beneath it. Inside, light filtering down from above added to the illumination of the central fire.

The hall was filled with people, but in that first moment, Micail saw only the man who lounged on a high seat placed between the tallest posts and closest to the fire. He was as broad as a barrel, but the shape of his shoulders suggested that most of his girth was muscle as well. His neck needed to be strong as well to support his headdress, crowned by the horns of a bull. But the man's grey eyes were clear and intelligent.

As the newcomers came to a halt before the hearth, the king said something in the gutteral tongue of the tribes.

'Khattar, son of Sayet, heir of heroes, Great Bull of Azan, and King of Kings, bids you welcome to his hall—' translated Heshoth.

Tjalan was murmuring a polite thanks, introducing himself and his company to the trader, who translated it in turn. It was a courteous way to let the rest of them know what was being said. Tjalan had been studying the native language since his first voyage to this land, several years before. *I have wasted my time*, Micail realized. *I ought to have spent the past year learning the native ways as well.* But what he did know of native manners suggested that it would not be until much later that they would get down to discussion of the Atlanteans' purpose here.

There was another interchange and Heshoth motioned the men in the group to benches set before trestle tables on the southern side of the hall. Only then did Micail realize that, except for Tjalan's faithful shadow Antar, their military escort had been kept outside.

The Atlantean women were gently escorted to a separate section in the east, near a sort of lesser throne, where a woman draped in a shawl sewn with small bits of gold sat facing the king. Now that he had leisure to look about, Micail saw a golden lozenge sewn to the front of the king's sleeveless tunic and bracelets of gold that flashed on his arms. A few of the native men who sat at the other benches also wore gold or bronze, but mostly their ornaments were of jet or finely worked antler or bone. Micail understood then why Tjalan had insisted that he have a new set of royal dragon bracelets and headband made for him in Belsairath. It was still not as grand as his own regalia, of course, but that had perished with Ahtarrath . . .

More compliments were exchanged, and great slabs and joints of smoking beef and mutton were brought in, arranged on beds of boiled grain on wooden trays. There was drink as well, a yeasty brew with a hint of honey, served in finely made pottery beakers. King Khattar, he noticed, drank from a beaker made of gold.

The king's bards sang of his victories in battle, and a leather-robed man called Droshrad, whom Micail recognized as some kind of priest, boasted of how the gods had given Khattar power.

By the time darkness had fallen, Micail was beginning to suspect the king's plan was to stupefy them with food and drink. Their situation did not seem certain enough to allow him to comfortably take more than a few polite sips of the brew, but the demands of courtesy required him to eat more meat than he was accustomed to tasting in a month. Tjalan, however, was in fine form, joking with Heshoth and commiserating with the king on difficulties with crops or neighbors, just the kind of conversation that had bored Micail to madness in Ahtarrath, and which he found no more interesting in translation . . . But the ordeal did at last seem to draw to an end. Singly and in groups, the feasters took leave of the court.

The king and queen themselves, however, remained in their places with a few attendants around them. The shaman

Droshrad and his fellows stayed behind as well. Micail caught Ardral's eye and found the old man observing the situation with his usual sardonic smile.

'Yes, of course we have the manpower to build barrows for our honored chieftains,' Heshoth translated the king's most recent words, 'but in the old days many tribes came together to make greater monuments. To build a new one with mighty stones would surely prove my power!'

'There were many such monuments in my country,' answered Tjalan, 'and they have uses that you have never dreamed . . .'

'Maybe so,' the king grinned back, 'but your laborers lie under the sea, and with them, your power.'

'No, my lord, the men who have the magic to raise the stones for you are here . . .' Tjalan spoke very softly, holding Khattar's gaze with his own.

Micail came to full attention, eyeing his cousin narrowly. They had discussed asking this king for permission to investigate the site identified by their calculations, and then perhaps to build there. What game was Tjalan playing?

'The men of my race have many powers,' the prince continued, 'but as you have said, our people are, at the moment, few. Yours are many, and if we work together, you will become – greater. The People of the Bull will rule this land forever.'

Khattar pulled at his beard, eyes narrowing, as the shaman whispered in his ear. Micail watched them, and realized how hard he had been gripping his beaker only when he let go and saw the corded pattern imprinted upon his hand.

'What advantage for you is in this offer?' Khattar asked at last.

Tjalan gazed back at him with grave sincerity. When he and Micail were boys playing at the game of Feathers, that look usually meant that the Alkonan was about to make some decisive, or possibly deceptive, move.

'The Sea Kingdoms are no more. We need a place where our arts can flourish. We need a homeland . . .'

'Droshrad can call spirits and compel the hearts of men,' Khattar said obliquely, 'but only the sweat of men can move stone.'

'Or their song . . .' Tjalan said softly. He turned toward Ardral and Micail. 'To move large things requires a full stand of singers, but the great among our priests can work alone. Will you show them, my friends, what the power of Atlantis can do?'

Now that winning smile was turned on them. Micail glared, but Ardral's dry chuckle defused his anger.

'Why not?' said the Seventh Guardian, lifting his cup in salute to the king and then draining it. He turned to Micail and whispered, 'The old Bull should toast us in return, don't you think?' He cast a meaningful look at the golden beaker, and then, without waiting for Micail's answer, began to sing.

Ardral's baritone was both deep and resonant, whatever his age. The note he produced was wordless, but focused very precisely. Khattar set the golden cup down rather hastily as it began to vibrate in his hand. A sidelong look from Ardral invited Micail to join the game.

Why shouldn't I? he thought suddenly. *Who are these barbarians to sneer at the son of a hundred kings?* He took a deep breath, and with equal precision, produced a second note, a half-tone higher than Ardral's, directed to the same target. The beaker rattled and danced on the wood of the table – then rose and for a long moment hovered in midair, slowly turning on its own axis, until finally, with equal deliberation, it sank back down to rest beside the high king's trembling hand.

For a moment Khattar simply stared. Then he slapped his hand down upon the table. As the beaker fell over, he began to laugh in a booming voice that seemed to grow louder and louder, until Micail's ears could hardly bear the sound.

ELEVEN

When the archpriest Bevor first told me I was to be an acolyte, the year before the Sinking,' Selast observed – 'can you believe that was three years ago? Anyway, he *said* I would be required to discipline mind and body beyond anything I had ever known ... But I thought the fasting was supposed to be voluntary!'

Damisa nodded, but kept her eyes on the three Lake women she and Selast were following down the narrow path edged with spiky weeds. 'Willed hunger is only a discomfort of the flesh,' she quoted, without sarcasm. Damisa really thought she was becoming almost accustomed to the empty feeling in her belly, and the way her clothing hung loosely on her once-sturdy frame ... 'To discipline the spirit against the body's demands,' she finished the quote, 'is the only surety against the illusions of wealth and security.'

'Uh-huh, lovely,' Selast muttered, 'but it's one thing to understand how the marsh folk live, never knowing if their supplies will be sufficient, trusting in the gods—' She glanced at Damisa and forced a laugh. 'But I thought we'd *done that* on the ship! Besides, we did a lot better than this last year. We did better than this the year we got here! Plenty of food then.'

'Hush,' Damisa advised, 'you're getting yourself worked up for nothing. Anyway, this year is always harder than last year – haven't you noticed? And *you're* always hungry, every year.'

The other girl grimaced, but did not deny it. Even in her homeland of Cosarrath, where she had been allowed to eat whenever and whatever she wanted, there had never been an ounce of fat on Selast. Prowling along the path in a short blue tunic, she looked every inch a creature of the wilderness, ever wary, muscles rippling beneath the taut brown flesh.

Yet just the other day she heard one of the boys say she looked about as cuddly as a skinned rabbit, Damisa reflected with a shake of her head. *That can't be right.*

In the old days, or so she had heard, even a betrothed acolyte had been free to take a lover, sometimes even more than one. Here, apparently, no one had done so. But it didn't help that there were hardly any men around, at least not men of the priests' caste. *There's Kalaran, who just doesn't seem all that appealing, and Rendano, who obviously isn't interested, and of course Master Chedan, but, well—*

Unbidden, an image of Reidel came to mind, his deep warm eyes, his strong shoulders . . . Damisa banished the thought with a shake of her head. In Atlantis, the genealogists of the Temple would have been horrified at the very idea of such a connection, and she agreed. But lately Tiriki had mentioned the possibility of inviting someone from among the sailors or merchants into the priesthood. Of course, Damisa knew that in the troubled times before the rise of the Sea Kings, a fair number from the other castes had been taken in. She herself came of the royalty of Alkonath, and Selast was of the pure noble stock as well, but the majority of the acolytes had ancestors of more humble origins.

Not that it mattered anymore. Damisa sighed. *We girls will just have to lie down with one another, as they say the warrior women do on the plains of the Ancient Land* . . . She stifled a snort of laughter, but her gaze returned speculatively to Selast. Almost unconsciously, she began to copy the Cosarran's stealthy gait . . . until she caught herself doing it, blushed, and tripped over her own sandals.

Just around the turn in the path, the marsh women had paused to make an offering at one of their forest shrines, a primitive affair of braided straw and feathers set in the hollow of an oak tree. Damisa felt a renewed pang of hunger as she glimpsed the tubers of wild onion laid there. How strange to realize that here a few roots were a sacrifice more precious than incense . . . But if the way-shrines were more modest than the pyramids and towers of Atlantis, she had to admit the powers here were well served, for they seemed to reward such simplicity.

As far as Damisa could tell – although all the hunting and foraging severely limited the time available for theological analysis – the spirits of this land were much more approachable than the gods of Atlantis, who were in essence nonhuman forces who dwelt beyond the mortal sphere. For all their legendary quirks and feuds, Manoah or Ni-Terat seemed less like individuals than signifiers, representatives of the immeasurable powers that moved the sun and the stars.

Although sailors prayed to the Star Shaper because he was the Lord of the Sea, and children prayed to the Great Maker because it helped them to sleep at night, not even Ni-Terat, the Dark Mother of All, had interceded to save a single human life. Only Caratra, the Nurturer, the Child Who Becomes the Mother, was traditionally believed to demonstrate a genuine interest in ordinary people, and that was only a few times a year.

In contrast, the Lake folk honored the simple spirits of field and forest. But they did not treat them as great gods; they were not magnificent beings who might eventually grant a favor, but . . . *The Lake gods seem more like good neighbors*, Damisa decided, *inclined to be helpful whether they notice you or not . . .*

She shivered a little as she approached the tree, wondering as always if what she felt at such rustic shrines was an illusion somehow created by the beliefs of the marsh folk or something more genuine – the actual presence of a real spirit.

'Shining One, accept my offering,' she muttered as she tucked a spray of white hawthorn blooms into the straw. 'Help us find food for our people.' She stood back to let Selast kneel and add some primroses. As they gazed up into the branches where the new leaves filtered the sunlight to lucent pale green, all the air seemed to shimmer and dance.

For a moment, then, Damisa seemed to feel the touch of a presence on her soul – curious, a little amused, but not unfriendly. Instinctively she sank to her knees, resting her hands upon the damp soil. *Someone* was listening, and that was more than she had ever felt in any of the splendid temples of Alkona or Ahtarra.

'Bright One! Help me! I am so hungry here!' her heart cried, and in that moment she realized that her emptiness was not that of the body, but of the soul.

Selast had already gone after the Lake women. Damisa got to her feet, glad that the other girl had not seen her moment of weakness. Her business just now was to find food for their bodies, and until they did her spirit would just have to fend for itself.

In the first year, the refugees had cleared ground near the springs and planted the seeds they had brought with them, but perhaps they had not done so at the right time, for their first harvest had failed entirely. Without the nut flour the saji women made, the preserves of fruits, the good fortune of the sailors in their incessant hunting, and the hearty cooperation of one and all, the refugees might have fought a hunger more gnawing than they had ever known.

They did better in some ways the following year, but the amount of food ripe enough to be harvested had been small indeed. If Elis had not had a real talent for growing things, their survival would have been even more doubtful. Although she could hardly 'make a rock bear fruit,' as Liala often said, nevertheless, every seed Elis had personally planted took root and lived. She had even been able to persuade the battered feather tree that had once belonged to Lord Micail to thrive.

According to the marsh folk, there were tribes further inland who sowed grain and kept cattle. The marsh folk lived by the fruits of the earth because the land was unsuitable for farming. Yet the natives had never hesitated to share what they had, and were always willing to take the Atlanteans with them to hunt or forage for edible plants and water-fowl, fish and shellfish, and a wealth of other resources for those who knew where to find them. That was, after all, why Heron's tribe came here.

But life by the lake is not so bountiful when the warm season ends! They probably think we're all idiots because we stay, Damisa laughed, then quickened her pace to catch up with the others. She grimaced, envying the efficient way Selast had of loping along. Perhaps she could catch up if she took a shortcut across the meadow . . . but the ground beneath the soft grass was part bog. With the next step, her foot went through the soft surface and with a cry she went down. She had just managed to get free, leg muddy to the knee, when Selast ran back to her.

'Don't try to sit up!' the younger girl snapped. 'Where does it hurt? Let me see!' Her clever fingers probed Damisa's ankle and then her knee.

'I'm fine, really, just muddy—' Damisa insisted, though in truth, it was rather pleasant to feel those warm fingers on her skin. She plucked a handful of grass and tried to wipe her leg clean.

With a sigh of relief, Selast sat down beside her.

'Thank you!' Sudden warmth filled Damisa and she reached out to give the other girl a hug of gratitude. Selast was all muscle and bone; it was like holding some supple wild thing. For a moment everything was very still, but then Selast hugged back, hard, but not roughly . . .

'We had better rest until we can be sure that foot will bear you,' Selast said a few moments later. But Damisa, astonished by how pleasant it felt to hold the other girl in her arms, did not let go.

'Do you remember the shop in Ahtarra,' she asked wistfully, 'just by the pylon, where they sold those delicious little cakes dribbled with honey?' She eased back upon the soft grass and Selast went with her, nestling into the curve of her arm.

'Oh yes,' Selast was saying, with her eyes half-closed. 'I'd die for just one! This year the stupid emmer and barley seeds had better figure out how to grow! Nuts make good flour in a pinch I guess, but – it's not the same.'

Damisa sighed, half-consciously stroking Selast's strong shoulders. 'When I was a little girl in Alkona, they would bring in cartloads of grapes and ila berries from the vineyards in the hills at summer's end, so many they didn't even care if they spilled over the wagonsides. And more and more of them fell off, getting crushed on the cobbles, until the gutters looked as if they were running with wine.'

'Never be able to grow good grapes here. Not enough sun . . .' But there was light enough to turn Selast's skin to gold, glowing warm against the wind-ruffled meadow grass.

Damisa pushed herself up on one arm and looked down at her. 'Your lips are just the color of those grapes,' she whispered.

Selast stared up at her, her face filled with light. 'Taste them,' she dared, and smiled.

By the time they caught up with the others, it was past midday. The marsh women clustered, softly gossiping as they poked into the dense reeds around the lakeside. Hearing Damisa and Selast approach, one of the women gabbled excitedly and pointed; then, as the two girls clearly did not understand, the woman flapped her hands, and cupped them, as if she were cradling something between her palms.

'Eggs?' asked Damisa. After two years, all of the acolytes had made some progress in learning the Lake folk tongue, but Iriel and Kalaran were the only ones who could actually speak it. Damisa herself had not yet progressed beyond a limited vocabulary. The small woman grinned and simply crooked her hand in a summoning gesture.

As she followed, Damisa took the precaution of kirtling up her skirts, and she was glad she had: their destination was the nest of some strange duck, which had evidently thought itself well hidden among the reeds.

It would have been hard to say who was less happy with the encounter, the duck or the acolyte, as it degenerated into a furious mix of swearwords and squawking. She left each mother duck at least one egg to hatch, but that didn't seem to soothe them. Damisa would not have thought a duck could bite, but she had nicks and scratches on both hands before they moved off toward higher ground to search for spring greens.

The tender new leaves of chickweed and goosefoot and mustard could be eaten raw, and there were lilies whose bulbs would provide more solid fare. Nettles were edible too, stewed as greens or steeped to make tea, but the native women always laughed when the acolytes tried to harvest them, for there was no way not to get stung, which made the girls curse in a manner most unbecoming to future priestesses.

Selast sucked her sore fingers and sulked, even after they turned toward home. 'It could be worse,' Damisa said, taking the other girl's hand and kissing the reddened stings, 'Kalaran had to go out with the hunters. Nettles sting, but you don't have to chase them. And they don't sneak up on you. *And* they don't have claws and big teeth!'

'I'd rather be hunting,' Selast growled, 'except then I'd have to be with Kalaran.'

Damisa sighed, wracked with conflicting emotions. She had long ago come to terms with the fact that what she felt about having lost her own destined husband was mainly relief. But Selast and Kalaran were still officially betrothed and would be expected to marry some day, even though they had about as much interest in one another as a couple of rocks. *Why is it,* she thought, *that however often somebody tells us the rules have changed, that things are different here* – she felt her face warm as she remembered the events of the afternoon – *why is it we still have to keep doing pretty much whatever we would have done in Atlantis?* If they could have kept the splendid ways of old Atlantis she would not have minded, but it was the rules, not the rewards that seemed to have survived.

'But there are so few of us,' she said finally. 'Can you honestly say you wouldn't care if something happened to him?'

'He's got the luck of a drunk!' Selast scoffed. 'He never gets hurt – except for his feelings. Besides, animal attacks have not been our worry.'

Damisa frowned, but she knew what the other girl meant. Early last summer, two sailors had gone missing. The marsh folk sent out trackers, but found no sign of them. The straggling scatter of huts where the sailors who had taken native wives lived with the merchants and others who were not of the priesthood was full of stories. Some thought that the missing seamen had grown tired of waiting for the *Crimson Serpent* to head out to sea again, and had gone back to the coast, where they had been picked up by a passing ship, but few took the tale seriously. Whether they said so or not, most believed that the sailors had simply fallen into a bog and been sucked down.

There was less ambiguity about Malaera's death. Morose from the beginning, the elderly Blue Robe priestess had finally succeeded in drowning herself in the lake. Damisa suspected that Liala blamed her personally for allowing the older woman to die. *It wasn't even my turn to sit with her*, she told herself, with a pang of guilt, though it was true that she had been the one most often assigned to help.

'That's cruel,' Damisa said suddenly. 'You really wouldn't miss Kalaran at all, would you!'

'Depends,' said Selast darkly. 'Will I get his dinner?'

'You're terrible,' Damisa said, not even noticing the tear in her own eye. 'You wouldn't even miss *me*, I guess!'

'What? Oh, *don't* be stupid,' Selast began, but before she could say more, they emerged from the woods and found the settlement buzzing like a hive.

'A ship is coming!' Iriel was running toward them. 'Reidel and his men sailed out to guide them in!'

'They left hours ago,' Elis added, approaching them. 'We shouldn't have to wait much longer.'

Everyone turned as Tiriki came out of her hut, waving cooing farewells to her baby, although little Domara seemed quite oblivious in the saji woman Metia's arms. The birth and healthy growth of the child seemed to have made the high priestess into a far more cheerful person, but as Tiriki turned toward them and smiled in greeting, Damisa saw that the old familiar haunted pain had returned to Tiriki's eyes.

'She's hoping they bring news of Micail,' said Elis in a low voice.

'After all this time? Not too likely,' Selast scoffed.

'It's all very well for you to sneer!' Elis snapped. 'Your betrothed is still alive and well. And at least I *know* what happened to Aldel – I can mourn him properly. But not knowing . . .' She shook her head, eyes wet with compassion. 'That must be the worst of all.'

Damisa grimaced, but she and her betrothed had only known each other for a year. She could hardly even remember what Kalhan looked like after all this time.

From the lake came the watchman's high, clear, call.

'Finally!' Iriel shouted and started running down the path

that led to the river. Laughing, the others followed her.

They arrived just in time to watch the *Crimson Serpent* dropping anchor alongside another, smaller craft, not a warship but a midsize fishing boat, with only one mast and what looked like a crude shelter inside the ship. Her once-bright blue-and-copper paint had been worn away by wind and wave. Next to Reidel's wingbird, she looked like a mule beside a racehorse; but mules are sturdy beasts. This craft had not only survived the Sinking but made it here . . . 'How many of them, I wonder,' Damisa muttered.

Selast said, 'I hope they brought something good to eat.'

'There you go again,' Elis reproved. 'Just as likely, they're hungrier than we are, and we'll have to cast lots for every bite.'

'Good,' Selast growled. 'I'm feeling lucky!'

By now, everyone for acres around must have heard about the arrival. At every moment someone else joined the crowd until the muddy shore was three-deep with marsh folk and Atlanteans, jostling one another and chattering excitedly.

As Reidel's ship settled into place beside the other craft, some men on the shore swung planed logs to her side, and then two groups of sailors leaped lightly down to finish the job of securing the ships to the tree stump that served as a mooring post. Damisa found herself holding her breath as the huddle of shapes on deck separated enough for them to see the first passenger, a strongly built man with a grizzled black beard. Cautiously, he made his way across the plank, carrying a little girl who looked to be about five years old. As he stepped onto the narrow promenade, the child at last loosened her grip on the man's neck and shoulders and looked about, allowing Damisa a quick glimpse of her face – well-shaped eyebrows, a noble nose, and a heart-shaped mouth.

The big man turned and watched anxiously as the sailors helped a slender woman step off the plank. She gazed at the watching crowd, and then, weeping gratefully, ran into the bearded man's embrace.

'A family!' Iriel whispered. 'A real family!'

'As opposed to a false one?' Selast scoffed.

But Damisa understood, or thought she did. Married or not, the priesthood did not always choose to live together in family units; among those who had escaped on the *Crimson Serpent*, there had been no such couples. There were, of course, many families of Lake folk, but these were Atlanteans, and possibly even of the priests' caste . . . Damisa realized that the stinging in her eyes came from tears. Furtively she dashed them away as Tiriki hurried toward the newcomers, holding out her hands.

Damisa started after her with a spurt of resentment. The high priestess had apparently forgotten how to form a proper escort . . . But would these people even realize that Tiriki *was* a priestess? Damisa blinked, trying to reconcile her memory of the ethereal figure who had welcomed the Prince of Alkonath to Ahtarra so long ago, with this woman whose wispy fair hair was already coming free from a simple braid. Yet if Tiriki's coarse robe was badly woven, ragged at the hem and stained with mud, still she addressed the strangers with all the gravity and formal poise of a Guardian of Light.

Chedan had by now also joined the escort. Damisa noted with pride that he was at least wearing the golden cord of the Robe of Ceremony, although it was cinctured around a faded tunic . . . *Of course*, she thought, *these new people look pretty shabby too. But they have an excuse, they've been at sea!*

Somehow, without ever quite letting go of the woman or the little girl, the bearded man bowed. 'Honored Ones!' he said, in a warm voice that could be heard to the back of the crowd, 'I am Forolin, merchant of the city of Ahtarra. And this is Adeyna, my beloved wife, who also greets you in great respect – and my daughter, Kestil. We – there was another, born just after the Sinking, but—' Realizing he was babbling, Forolin stopped. His chin twitched briefly. 'We give thanks to the gods!' He touched his heart and extended the hand skyward. 'For we have found you!'

'And you are most welcome here!' said Tiriki again, as she offered further blessings to the trio. 'Forolin, Adeyna – and let this welcome be a personal one, for I have a little daughter of my own, just over a year old. Perhaps Kestil will like to play with Domara?'

'Indeed you *are* welcome,' Chedan said to Forolin. 'But may I inquire, where you have come from? Please tell me you have not spent two years upon the sea in that little boat!'

'No! No, indeed—' Forolin's face grew grim again, as he delivered his daughter into his wife's waiting arms. 'We sought refuge on the mainland, in Olbairos, where my merchant house once maintained a trading station. We found it deserted, mostly, but we hoped to make a new start there. But there were so few of us – and then the plague came. We are the only ones who survived.'

'But how did you know where to look for us?' asked Chedan.

'I told you – Olbairos used to be a well-known trading station. The merchant fleet is long gone, of course, but natives still pass through there from time to time – even some from these isles. We had more than one report of others of our kind settling hereabouts.'

'More than one?' Tiriki turned toward him with a new sharpness in her voice. 'You know of others?'

'Well, my lady, I have not seen them myself. And of course my informants mostly did their trading with the coastal settlements. The tribes that dwell inland are said to be strong and fierce. But it was said that several wingbirds had been sighted at Beleri'in, so we went there; it looked quite deserted, which is why we did not fight very hard when the storm drove us back out to sea. We were forced to turn west and northward, and when at last we were able to come to shore, we encountered a group of native hunters who told us you were here. As we were seeking you, your captain came to guide us in his ship. Please thank him for me! We are eternally in his debt, and yours.'

'It was storm winds that drove us here as well,' Chedan mused. 'Maybe none can find this place, except they are called by the gods . . .'

'What we may offer you is little enough,' said Tiriki, 'but we had some warning of your arrival, and so a hot meal awaits you, and dry, warm dwellings for you to rest in. Come now, let us begin to be friends.' She drew the merchant and his family toward the wooden trackway that led to the settlement below the Tor . . .

'I suppose,' Selast grumbled, 'this means *we* will have to go to bed hungry—'

But no one was listening. Iriel clutched Damisa's arm and pointed at a strange figure just crossing the plank from the fishing boat. 'Who is *that*?'

Tall, rather gaunt, the stranger wore a dingy white robe that, after a moment's examination, identified him as a priest of the Temple of Light. In each hand, he clutched a large leather satchel. Frowning, he stopped at the center of the plank, peering nervously at the curious crowd, but his face brightened as he recognized Chedan.

'Wise One!' He bowed as well as he could without dropping his bags in the mud of the wharf. 'I am Dannetrasa of Caris. I doubt that you will remember me, but in Ahtarra I served with the Guardian Ardravanant in the Hall of Records—'

'Ardral!' Chedan explained. 'Have you news of him? Did he escape?'

'Ah, if I only knew,' said Dannetrasa apologetically, 'but if you knew *him*—'

'He was my uncle.'

'Then you know there is *no* reason to believe he would

not escape! He was prepared, if any man ever was . . .'
Dannetrasa paused again, and then hefted his satchels. 'Of
course you know, it was our duty to preserve what we could.
And I have with me still a number of maps and several treatises about the stars – and some other things that may be
useful—' Dannetrasa broke off again, as some sad memory
seemed to pass before his eyes.

Chedan's expression grew concerned. 'Come with me,
friend. I can see you have had a bitter time – let us make
you welcome. You shall join the feast, such as it is, and then
you will show me what treasures you bring in these sacks
of yours!'

'Many things,' Dannetrasa repeated, with a grimace, 'but
no texts on healing, alas . . . Still, maybe they would not
have helped. The sickness that drove us from Olbairos was
unlike anything we had known.'

Despite the still-bright sunlight, Damisa shuddered, just
as glad she could not hear the further details of their conversation as the two men moved away. Reidel, she observed,
had taken it upon himself to arrange a proper welcome for
the crew of the fishing craft. It was strange how relieved
she felt at seeing him safely returned.

'A whole family of survivors!' Iriel was bubbling. 'And
the man said there were others, too. Maybe we will *not*
always be so isolated here! But did you *see* that little girl?
What incredible sparkly eyes! I hope—'

'It's not like we don't already *have* a family,' Damisa said
suddenly, but only realized she had spoken aloud when the
other two turned to her, Selast frowning, Iriel curious. 'In
a way we do,' Damisa insisted. 'Chedan is our father, and
Tiriki our mother. And aren't they *always* saying we are all
sisters and brothers here?'

'Then come, sisters,' said Iriel with a grin, as she linked
their arms in her own. 'The headman's son Otter promised
me some cuts from that deer he killed yesterday, and I will
gladly share them with you . . .'

'Sweet Iriel!' said Selast merrily. 'Why couldn't I be betrothed to *you*?'

On the day after the new ship came to the Tor, Chedan met with the priestesses beneath the willow tree by the stream to discuss the implications of the recent arrivals. It was one of those spring days in which sun and cloud become intermingled, at one moment almost as warm as summer, at another threatening rain. At first the conversation focused on food and housing, but in the mage's midnight ponderings, other issues had occurred to him.

'Let us leave such considerations for a moment,' he said finally. 'They are obviously important, and for that very reason, unlikely to be ignored. We spend so much of our energy worrying about physical survival that we forget the reason that we dared the seas instead of staying to die with our land.'

'We were sent to save the ancient wisdom,' Tiriki said slowly, as if she were repeating an almost forgotten lesson. 'We were to establish a Temple of Light in new soil.' As if in answer, light broke through the clouds and gleamed from her bright hair.

'And we haven't done a very good job of it, have we?' Liala sighed.

'How could we, when it has taken most of our time and energy just to survive?' Tiriki exclaimed. 'But I cannot imagine building the kind of Temple we had on Ahtarrath here. Even if we had the resources, it would be . . . wrong.' Tiriki sighed, and whispered, 'There is so much we do not know, that I did not trouble myself to learn. How can we build a new Temple out of golden memories, when memory itself is failed and scattered across the seas?'

Chedan nodded. 'This place has power of its own, and that is what makes the situation so complicated. These new faces have reminded me of matters we should have been dealing with all along. Tiriki at least knows the story of what happened when Reio-ta and his brother, Micail's father, were captured by the Black Robes. Micon could not allow himself to die under their torture, because he had not yet begotten a son to inherit the power of the storm. He could not allow that power to pass to one of the Black Robes who happened to be his kinsman. And yet, Micail's was not the only power that may stray from its hereditary holder.'

Alyssa, playing with a pinecone, suddenly giggled. 'The sun is unrisen, the son is not born. The power is hidden, the Sea King forlorn.' Over the past few months, the mental state of the seeress had become increasingly unstable.

They frowned at her, wondering if there would be more, but the seeress only went on toying with the pinecone. Liala turned back to Chedan, saying, 'What do you mean?'

The mage hesitated before he spoke. 'What I fear is that latent abilities in us, in our acolytes, even in the sailors or merchants, may be awakened by the powers in this land.'

'Not evil!' Liala exclaimed.

'Very few powers are evil in themselves,' the mage reminded her. 'But an untrained psychic is a danger to himself and everyone around him.'

'We must complete the acolytes' initiations,' Tiriki said slowly. 'They will be better able to deal with such energies when they have been taught the advanced practices and received the sigils, and when they have been sealed to the rulers of their proper degrees.'

'The initiations themselves could threaten to unleash evil forces,' observed Liala. 'But I agree that we have to try. Damisa's progress is – adequate. But she is Tiriki's acolyte. We should be giving each of them individual training.'

The mage smiled at her. 'You are quite correct, Lady Atlialmaris,' he said then, using her full, formal name. 'We have delayed long enough, hoping others would arrive and lift some of these burdens from us. But it is clear that no others of the priesthood will arrive. I suppose that Kalaran should be apprenticed to me. I have reviewed his astrology and his personal history, and I believe the lad is up to the challenge.

'He has learned some useful skills, too, and the discipline to apply them. I think he now knows himself well enough that he will welcome more knowledge. I only fear—' He stopped, and the two women looked at him inquiringly.

'I'm afraid he will look at me and see an old man, a ghost of the past – unable to tell him what he most wants to know, which is how to make a future out of so much uncertainty.'

'Do any of us know how to teach that?' said Tiriki, touching his hand.

'Well—' Chedan cleared his throat. 'Just so. I shall speak to him tomorrow, and set up a schedule. And if he has the potential I suspect, I will also show him how to keep watch for signs that one of the sailors, or anyone, may be awakening to spiritual power.'

'Do you think that will happen?'

'It may have happened already,' Tiriki observed. 'We all know that Reidel is interested in Damisa. She ignores him, but I have seen that he has a gift for anticipating – not only Damisa's needs, which might be the result of love, but also mine, or Domara's, or anyone he is around. When something falls, he is there to catch it, and when no action is needed, he knows how to be still.'

'That's so,' said Chedan, 'I observed it on the voyage. I will speak with him. For them to study together might be good for Kalaran as well.'

'That leaves the girls for us, then,' Liala said briskly. She looked over at Alyssa, but the seeress was leaning against the willow trunk with her eyes closed, apparently asleep.

Liala continued, 'Elis is ready to be inducted as a priestess of Caratra. She has the touch for growing things, and you've seen how good she is with Domara, or any child. *And she's a singer*. I mean, she could be a *real* singer. The Temple had planned to apprentice her to the singer Kyrrdis, before. I'm no great singer, I say; but I know enough to set Elis on that path. If she's willing to walk it.'

'That at least is very good news,' said Tiriki. 'Damisa and I have tried to ensure that they keep up with their basic exercises.'

'One thing at a time,' Liala said. 'First she'll have to find her inner pitch. But as for Iriel and Selast – well, I just don't know. Selast doesn't really *talk* to me, not if she can possibly avoid it, and Iriel, well, *she* says so much sometimes I can hardly follow her!'

'I often have the same feeling,' Chedan nodded. 'They still seem so very young sometimes, even after all they have been through.'

'Young,' Tiriki echoed, 'but not foolish. Iriel is a very canny judge of people and only rarely abuses her sensitivity to them. Perhaps we might simply team her *with* Selast more than we have. Selast is small for her age, but she's as strong as a little horse, and generally shows good sense—'

'It would not prosper them—' Alyssa's eyes opened suddenly, and for that moment she was back with them, fully awake and aware. 'Their spirits sing from different cores. Selast will follow only Damisa, until blood calls her to her man . . . Let Iriel sit with Taret for a time, less to study than to learn that patience is not only for the children of Atlantis, and that to be wise is not to depart from joy, but to see instead its many sides.'

The newcomers had in fact brought a little food with them, but it became clear that they had made another contribution, which proved far less welcome, and put their physical survival in jeopardy. Within days of their arrival, Heron, the village headman, came to Chedan complaining of aching muscles and a headache. The marsh folk might be impervious to the weather here, but they had no resistance to the invisible spirits of disease that the ship had brought from the continent.

An ague, Chedan called it, and said he had encountered such fevers more than once in his travels. Before anyone could even ask her, Metia had gone to confer with Taret concerning the brewing of healing herbs.

It was odd, thought Chedan as he watched her go with Iriel chattering along beside her, how they had all without even noticing gradually come to accept the saji women as part of their community. At home the sajis would never have been allowed to speak to a priestess of the Light, but Metia had been a devoted nurse to little Domara, and her sisters had quite naturally taken over as Alyssa's caretakers. In the Sea Kingdoms, the scions of the priests' caste saw the temple girls only from a distance, darting through some courtyard or passage like a flock of bright-winged birds.

Rumor had held that they were at best licentious and unclean, that they were recruited exclusively from outcastes – the unclaimed babes of the trade towns or worse. And that was partly true. But even after the Grey Temple had been dissolved it was popularly believed that the sajis were used for the most outrageous of semilicit rituals. And that was bigotry of the worst sort.

It was only after he had observed how patiently the sajis had endured the voyage on the *Crimson Serpent* that Chedan had given them any thought at all, and he dredged up from his memory a story that long ago their ancestors had been devotees of a discipline no less respected than his own. The very word *saji* was nothing more than a contraction of a very archaic word for 'displaced foreigner.'

But wherever they came from, he was glad indeed that the saji women were with them now, as they were experts in the mixing of natural remedies.

The illness brought by the refugees had spread quickly though the marsh folk and the sailors alike. Damisa and Selast were sent out often to gather not food but herbs, while the sajis, or Liala and Elis, were kept busy moving from one sickbed to another. Faces veiled against sneezes, they patiently pressed cold compresses against burning brows and dosed them with tea made from willow bark and other things. Yet the sickness continued to spread.

One grey morning, Chedan emerged from the headman's hut to find Tiriki waiting for him, with her daughter in her arms. Mist lay low across the Tor, veiling the treetops, but somewhere above the clouds there was sunshine, for in the distance he could hear a falcon's hunting cry.

'Heron is recovering,' Chedan said, in answer to the question in Tiriki's eyes, 'as are many of the others. But his son Otter has been hard hit by the disease.'

'Why should he be so vulnerable?' Tiriki's face creased in a worried frown. 'Otter is the strongest boy here.'

Chedan sighed. 'The young and strong, if they succumb at all, sometimes prove to have less resistance than those who are more accustomed to illness.'

'But he will live?' She shifted the restless red-headed child from her arms to her hip. For a moment the sight of the toddler's face eased Chedan's heart, but he shook his head.

'Only the gods know how this will end. In any case, I don't want you and Domara – or Kestil, for that matter – anywhere near the sick.'

'As healing is part of your duty, so it is mine!' Tiriki spoke softly so as not to disturb her daughter, but there was no concealing her mutinous glare. For a moment the mage regarded her. To ordinary sight she was no more than a slender young woman, yet there was a new maturity in her now, a radiance that had come with the birth of the child. *Indeed*, he thought with a smile, *it seems to me the air of this northern land suits her – though I suspect she would not appreciate my saying it.*

'What of Domara?' he said aloud, and grimly. 'Would you risk her as well?'

Tiriki's arms tightened around her daughter. '*You* have not taken the sickness,' she observed.

'Not yet at least,' said the mage, more gently. 'I suspect

this may be a new form of an illness to which, in my travels, I may have gained some resistance, but perhaps not. Now let me add, there is good reason to be hopeful! I am glad Dannetrasa was on that ship – he and the sajis have proven invaluable! And Alyssa was certainly right about Iriel and Taret. No, I do not think we will suffer the fate of Olbairos. But really, only one thing can be said with certainty. *Everything that can be done is being done.* You will help us best by keeping the children and yourself well away from danger. I know you are used to having Metia's help, but I think you are doing perfectly well without her. Is it not so?'

Conflicting emotions warred in Tiriki's face, but at last, however reluctantly, she nodded. 'May the gods be with you,' she whispered, and gave him the salutation of his grade, as if they were completing some ritual.

'Blessings upon you, daughters,' he said in a low voice, saluting her and the child in reply. As he lowered his hands, they brushed across a hard shape in the pouch that hung at his waist.

'Wait! Here I am determined to send you away – but it just so happens I have something here I've meant to give you.' He pulled out the small cedar box and offered it to her.

'But . . . that's mine!' Tiriki exclaimed, her luminous eyes moving from the box to his face. 'How did you come by it?'

'I was rummaging through one of my travel sacks, looking for a packet of herbs, and there it was. Micail gave it to me. It was on the day before . . .' He left the sentence unfinished, knowing she would understand. 'With all the excitement, I lost track of it. We had been snatching a bite as we went over the lists, and suddenly Micail just handed the box to me, saying – what was it he said?'

Chedan shook his head a little, forcing back the accompanying memory of hot, bright air and the taste of fear. 'Micail said you ought to have it, but you were packing so efficiently you would only say it would be better left behind.

212

He—' Chedan smiled raggedly, 'he said he was fairly sure you wouldn't let *him* keep it, either.'

'It sounds just like him,' Tiriki laughed, 'We argued several times about what to take, what to leave.' Her eyes misted, and seeking to cover her emotions, she flicked the box's catch and looked inside. It was crammed full of various small items, a jumble of earrings, pendants on chains, odd rings. 'Princes have strange priorities.' She started to close up the box again, and then her eyes abruptly focused.

'Mother of Night,' she breathed, 'bless you, Chedan. Bless you both.'

The mage craned his neck, trying to see. 'What is it?'

She opened her hand and he saw the glint of a ring, a little thing of improbably numerous surfaces, scaly and smooth, intaglio and cameo in one, a filigree of shadows and gleamings . . . 'We were little more than children when he gave this to me. Probably it was an heirloom bauble, appropriated from his grandmother's regalia.'

Chedan nodded, recognizing the representation of the Imperial dragons, red and white locked in their perpetual wrestling match of good against better. But he could also see that to Tiriki it was not an emblem of the Sea Kingdoms, but the first, best token of Micail's love.

'Will it still fit, I wonder?' she murmured shakily, 'It has been so long . . .' She slid it along her finger, grimaced as it stuck on the knuckle, then forced it past.

'You see—' Chedan said gently, 'No matter what happens, Micail's love still holds you.'

Her startled gaze flew to his before he could hide the thought that had come to him, that she would need any comfort she could find if the plague got worse, and he did not survive . . .

A shadow flickered across the grass. He looked up, his heart lifting despite his anxiety as he glimpsed the graceful shape of a falcon against the sun.

TWELVE

The falcon floated above the plain, a speck of life against the grey immensity of sky. To the falcon's eye, there was no difference between priest and ploughman, between the humans who hoed the fields and those who toiled to move the great sarsen stones out on the plain. The falcon viewed all the activities of men with the same lordly detachment. Micail, striving to weld seven singers into an instrument able to levitate stone, wished he could feel the same.

Last night he had dreamed that he sat with Chedan in a little taverna in Ahtarra just below the library, sipping raf ni'iri and letting their conversation range as it sometimes did with Ardral. In fact he was rather surprised that it had not *been* Ardral, and he wondered if for some reason he were projecting one man's face onto the other; though he had respected the Alkonan mage, he had never seen enough of him for them to become close friends. But no doubt this was merely some scenario born of his current preoccupation, of no significance. They had been discussing the training of chelas, as he remembered, and the various uses of song.

'All right, then—' Wrenching his thoughts back to the present, he pointed toward a rock he had placed on a stump about ten feet away. 'Give me your notes, softly first, and at my signal, focus the vibration upon the stone . . .'

He had brought his untried stand of singers to a bit of

woodland that lay between the plain and the cluster of huts the Ai-Zir had built to house their guests. They had now been here for over a year already, and if he could not yet call this place home, at least it was a refuge.

'That's fine,' Micail said, as the voices quavered and veered into disharmony. 'Best to begin with the more experienced singers.' He gestured to the Alkonan priest Ocathrel, who had until yesterday been out on the plain with Naranshada and the trainee engineers, selecting and splitting sarsen stones to make the great ring formation. Sarsen rock was a kind of sandstone, but forces which even Ardral could not entirely explain had in some distant eon compressed it so that it was both harder and more dense that any natural rock the Atlanteans had ever seen. If it had not been formed between bands of lighter stone it would not have been possible to crack such large slabs loose at all. But that same compression had aligned the crystalline particles mixed into the stone, and the hammering had awakened them.

This was not the promised Temple, but the means to build it, a construct that would not only allow them to calculate the movements of the heavens, but to raise and focus power.

Only this morning, Ocathrel had volunteered to help teach the acolytes, partly because he had three daughters of his own and felt he might know better how to motivate them. Micail had been dubious at first, but it was soon apparent that the older priest had spoken nothing less than the truth.

Ocathrel smiled, smoothed his thinning hair, and filled his lungs. He then released a note so deep, so resonant, Micail could feel its vibration coursing slowly through his own bones. He himself was a tenor, but he could handle the baritone range, and came in on the next note, four steps up.

Lanath was already sweating with strain, his tone wavering, but Micail commanded him with a glance, and after that the boy's quaver resolved and held true. In the same moment Kyrrdis brought Elara in, four notes up in the contralto range, and then in turn Cleta and Galara, who both had proven rather unexpectedly to have fine, if not particularly powerful, soprano voices.

Brows furrowed in concentration, the singers kept the sound going through circular breathing until the seven tones united into a simple chord; and though it grew no louder, the vibrations perceptibly shifted in quality. Micail damped his excitement and redirected their focus to the piece of stone waiting on the stump. The harmonics rose and fell slightly, making a unity that thrummed through the shady grove, one with the wind . . . until the rock began slowly to rise, higher and then . . . *higher* . . . With a gasp, Lanath lost his place in the rhythm. The chorus turned ragged, and the rock teetered and fell to the ground.

'When one fails, all fail!' Micail snapped. 'Now pull in your energies and *ground!*' The seven closed their eyes, consciously regularizing their breathing.

'I'm sorry!' whispered Lanath, his face red with embarrassment. 'I can do it just fine when I'm alone . . .'

'I know, lad. And you did very well, until the end.' Micail forced himself to speak with kindness. The glares the girls were giving the boy were enough reproof for now. 'You just lost your concentration; that is not a fatal flaw. But from now on I want you to practice when you're in company until you can hold that note, no matter *what* is going on!' He turned to the others. 'Ocathrel, Kyrrdis – thank you for your help. I know you have other tasks to perform. As do we all—' He frowned at the others. 'Go on then. Wait, Galara – Ardral wants you to copy a text. Come with me.'

'But why do we need another copy of *The Struggle of Ardath?*' Galara muttered as they walked back through the woods. 'It might as well have happened a million years ago—'

'More like eight hundred. And I warrant you will find it is something more than just an old legend,' Micail replied with hard-learned patience. At first he had feared that working with Tiriki's half-sister would only remind them both too painfully of all that they had lost. Instead, they seemed to find a strange comfort together.

Galara proved to have very little in common with Tiriki, who to his certain knowledge had never, even at age fifteen, exhibited anything like this girl's mercurial moods that so self-indulgently veered between sullen poses and outright rebellion. He had to remind himself how much younger the girl was. They had not been raised as sisters, so why should they be alike?

'I *mean*, what does *any* of it matter?' Galara raged. 'I *mean* – what did you tell me, practically the first thing? When you first said we'd have to leave? That there would be very limited resources in the new land! And you were right! So why is it the first thing everyone wants to do is build another Temple to the same gods who did nothing for us when we needed them most?'

Micail stopped in his tracks, glaring. 'Hush, now, Gallie,' he muttered, with a quick glance about to see if anyone had heard her. Keeping up morale among the Atlanteans was almost as important as presenting a united face to the Ai-Zir. 'Who but the gods preserved us? They did not need to send any messenger to warn us, but in fact they sent many – to whom we did not even truly listen. They saved us to reestablish our Temple—'

'Do you really believe that?' Galara laid a hand on his arm, gazing up at him intensely. 'I can't – not when you have to do it with lackwits like Lanath and that sourpuss Cleta! If the gods really wanted the Temple rebuilt, why didn't they save Tiriki instead of them?'

'Don't say it! Don't ever say that to me!' Sudden rage surged through him and he thrust her away.

Galara took a quick step to regain her balance, her face suddenly pale. 'I'm sorry – I didn't mean—'

'You didn't think!' Micail got out through clenched teeth. He had believed his sorrow healed. He could go for weeks, even months at a time now, without dreaming of Tiriki – and then some memory would tear the wound open again.

'Go! You know the way. Leave me be. Plague Ardral with your endless questions, if you dare,' he managed at last. 'I don't know why the gods chose *us* to live. I no longer even know if saving anything of Atlantis is the right thing to do! But the prophecy did *not* say that you or I would rule the new land – only that I would found the new Temple here. And that, by all the gods, is what I shall do!'

'The lord Micail – say you he *too* was a royal prince?' Khayan-e-Durr, Queen of the Ai-Zir, inclined her head as Micail passed by the sunshade beneath which the women sat spinning. 'Uneasy the land with so many rulers,' said the queen, speculatively, 'yet he has some appeal . . .'

Elara traded glances with Cleta and suppressed a smile. It had taken some months for them to learn the language well enough to be accepted, and only now was real communication beginning to be possible. *Micail is indeed a man whom women's eyes follow*, she thought, as he slowed for a moment and bowed in return. She doubted, though, that he had really been aware of the queen's salutation. It was an automatic response, trained into him at the court of Mikantor in Ahtarrath.

'He was the heir of the eldest son, yes,' Elara answered at last. 'In the Ten Kingdoms, and the Ancient Land before them, there were powers that descended mostly through the male line of the royal house. But my lord's preference has always been for the priesthood. It was his uncle, Reio-ta, who actually ruled.'

'So the prince did not take his throne, and the land was lost,' the queen replied. 'We have a similar story that the people sometimes tell. Still, the blood of kings is always worth something. A pity the man has sired no child. Our shaman, Droshrad, says you outlanders came with the wind and will soon go, but I am not so sure.' She paused, considering, and Elara raised an eyebrow at this hint of conflict between the shamans and the women of the tribe.

Cleta was frowning. 'I had heard that Droshrad opposed your decision to welcome us,' she said guardedly, 'but I thought he had come to appreciate the knowledge we bring – at least there has been no difficulty in recent moons.'

'Fear the wolf that prowls, not the one that howls,' the queen answered. 'That old man goes into the woods to lay plots and mutter spells. It would be better if your people made blood-bond with our tribe. Perhaps outbreeding will improve Prince Micail's fertility, as it does among the herds. Yes,' Khayan-e-Durr chuckled softly, 'we shall have to find your unripe lord a wife of good family, from a royal clan.'

Elara schooled her face to hide her shock, both at the content and the calculation in those words. Almost equally appalling was the flare of possessive fury that heated her cheeks. The queen had a point – it would be a pity to lose Micail's bloodline. But his seed belonged to the sacred lineage of the Temple. If a mate who was unrelated must be found, there were others who qualified – Cleta, or – her pulse quickened unexpectedly – she herself could certainly bear him a child.

But she controlled her reaction and looked at the queen with a sigh. 'My lord still mourns his wife, who was lost in the escape,' the acolyte said solemnly. 'I do not think he is ready to think of such things.'

But I am, she could not help thinking, *and not with Lanath!* She cast another swift glance at Cleta and realized that she, too, was watching Micail as he finally disappeared in a crowd of Ai-Zir. It was strange. Elara had always thought of Micail as the husband of the high priestess. It was strange to view him suddenly as . . . a man, and an available one, at that.

'Well, there is no urgency yet,' the queen said comfortably, as she set her spindle turning, 'but the alliance between our peoples would be strengthened by a marriage.'

Elara had been in Azan-Ylir long enough to understand that according to tradition, almost all matings were arranged by the matriarchs of the clan. She eyed the queen again, uncertainly. In the warm sunlight she had taken off her royal cape of finely tanned doeskin painted with the symbols of her rank and tribe. The elbow-length sleeves and hem of her upper garment of pale grey-green wool was edged in a patterned braid sewn with discs of bone, straining a little over an ample bosom on which lay necklaces of amber and jet. A voluminous skirt with interwoven woolen stripes of different colors fell in folds about her feet. Khayan-e-Durr's brown hair, bundled into a net of twisted cord, was threaded with grey, but the queen had a majesty about her that did not depend on fine attire.

Over the preceding months it had become clear that the Women's Side held a very real, if different, kind of power. According to custom, the queen was not Khattar's wife, but his elder sister, and at times seemed to view him as hardly grown. It was her son Khensu, not his, who would be Khattar's heir; moreover, she and the clan mothers had the right of final decision to go to war.

They recorded the matings of the beasts as well as men, and before the men could make war, the women must agree they had the resources to do so. In the priestly caste of Atlantis, certain powers were inherited by the men or the women, but nevertheless, in Temple or palace, gender was no barrier to leadership. The soul, after all, changed sex from one lifetime to another. But one did not expect to find that knowledge among unschooled primitives.

'The king has a daughter called Anet,' Khayan was saying now. 'She is ripe for the marriage bed. She has been at the sanctuary of the Goddess at Carn Ava with her mother, but she will return before winter. We will see how she likes him, yes . . . that mating might well serve . . .'

Cleta bent her head to whisper, 'But will Micail like *her*? And what will Tjalan say?'

Khayan was clearly concerned with the welfare of her people, but did she support the king's dream of making his tribe supreme? During the past months she had made something of a pet of Elara, and Tjalan, on his most recent visit to Azan, had urged her to gain the queen's confidence . . . yet Elara felt she was no closer than ever to learning Khayan's true mind.

'And you young ones,' the Queen said suddenly, 'you too must think of your husbands to be.'

'Oh, Cleta has a betrothed who is still in Belsairath. And I am betrothed to Lanath,' Elara said, a trifle bitterly.

'You said that you were not married.'

Elara shrugged. 'There is – much to do first. We must complete our studies—'

'Huh!' the queen grinned. 'Maidens think to be young forever. But it is true, the priestess-born are different.' There was a brief pause, but before anyone else could speak, Khayan resumed. 'Your Lady Timul is far away, but you are here. Maybe I should send you to Ayo.'

Cleta frowned, trying to understand. 'Ayo? The king's wife?'

'But also the Sacred Sister, who dwells at the Sanctuary,' Khayan nodded, smiling. 'The women of the tribes share information that sometimes the men do not know. One has come to us from your village by the shore. She says that the Blue Robe priestesses who build the Mother's Temple there know something of our Mysteries. And this – this is no business for the shamans. Yes, I think the sisterhood will wish to speak with you.'

I must tell Ardral – Elara stared at the queen, her mind whirling. *Or should I?* Khayan was only an Ai-Zir, maybe, but she was right. These were women's mysteries, not to be shared with any man. Somehow she would have to get a message to Timul . . .

She found her voice at last. 'I would be most interested in meeting them.'

*   *   *

221

Micail took a long, deep breath of the fair wind that caressed the plain. He had walked out to the site where the henge of stones would be built early that morning, when the rising sun had just begun to promise a blazing day. Now, at its closing, the scent of ripe grass was like incense – an incense of the earth, flavored with the warmer odors of the cattle who ate the grass. In the middle distance one of the small herds kept on the plain for milking in summer was following the lead cow homeward, their brown hides glowing like copper in the slanting twilight.

Slowly he was coming to understand their importance to the people here. An ordinary Atlantean meal had consisted of fruit, vegetables, and boiled grains, with perhaps a few small fish for flavoring.

In Azan, cattle were the life of the nation, their health and numbers the gauge of a tribe's power, their leather and their bones worn as clothing and decoration, or used for myriad other purposes. Grains were eaten as porridge or flatbread, and wild greens in season, but at every season of the year, the people fed by preference upon the meat and milk of their cows.

At first, most of the Atlanteans had found it difficult to digest the high-protein diet, and even when they grew accustomed, found it even harder to metabolize efficiently. *All of us*, he thought ruefully as he patted his middle, *have become more substantial . . . except for Ardral*. The old guardian appeared to survive on air and native beer, though he continually pronounced the latter a poor substitute for proper liquors. Still, whatever Ardral was or wasn't eating, it gave him plenty of energy. He never seemed to cease moving from one part of the work site to another, observing, ordering, correcting, his robes flapping around him like the wings of one of the great cranes that stalked the river and the ruins.

Outside the line of sticks that had been stuck in the ground to mark the circle, men were shaping two great sarsen blocks with round mauls of the same hard stone. The song of the singers had succeeded in cracking the great slabs free from larger pieces of rock that lay scattered everywhere across the plain, but the fine shaping had to be done by human hands. The pounding of the mauls made a dull music in the cooling air.

'Come here, will you?' Ardral's call roused Micail from his abstraction. 'Bring Lanath. I need a second check on this alignment.'

Micail looked around and saw his acolyte standing next to one of the holes left by an uprooted bluestone, gazing across the plain toward the slow fading of the light.

'Lanath, we're wanted,' he said softly. 'Come, lad, there's nothing out there to see.'

'Only the Heralding Stars,' Lanath responded dully. 'But anything could be creeping unseen in the darkness. This whole countryside is ghost-ridden—' and he motioned toward the rounded humps of barrows on the plain. 'When night falls it all belongs to them. Maybe that's what Kanar's telling me.'

'Kanar!' exclaimed Micail, 'Your former master? Is this another of your dreams?'

'He talks to me,' Lanath replied in that same strange small voice.

'Ghosts are notoriously untrustworthy messengers, especially when you don't know the right questions to ask,' Micail replied more roughly than he intended. 'Let's have no more about it now; the shamans' tales have made the men nervous enough without adding to their fancies! We need their labor, lad – we cannot do all the work with song!' He grasped Lanath's shoulder and hauled him back to the center of the circle, where Ardral was gazing at the wooden poles that were set to mark the rising and setting of the midsummer sun.

'Look there—' he commanded, pointing westward. 'There is the light!'

Clouds were blowing in from the distant sea, touched

now to flame by the descending sun. As he watched, a long beam flared across the sky, tracing a path of gold across the darkling plain. Ardral muttered some words and swiftly incised a string of hieroglyphs onto his wax tablet.

Micail closed his eyes against the glare and felt as if the sunlight was becoming a current of energy – as if he stood in a flowing stream, or at the crux of many streams. There was one that flowed from the west, where the sun set at equinox, and another whose origin was farther south. The new ring of stones would center on a northeast to southwest alignment, so as to catch the midsummer sunrise, amplifying the flow of energy.

'You have not been out here at end of day before, have you?' he heard Ardral say to him. 'When the sun is rising or setting you can feel the currents quite strongly. It is why the sensitives directed us here. If we angle the stones correctly, this place will be an enormous focus of power.'

Micail opened his eyes and realized that the masons had fallen silent.

'If the Omphalos Stone had been saved, Tjalan would have installed it here,' Ardral added. 'Perhaps it is just as well that—' Whatever else he might have been about to say was lost as someone cried out in terror.

Lanath stood staring at the barrows again. The workmen were watching him.

'Look, something *has* come out of the barrow!' Their mutterings became louder. 'The young priest sees it! The old priest is angered because we moved the stones! Droshrad was right! We should not be here!'

Micail squinted into the shadowy middle distance, and seeing a large horned head, began to laugh. 'Are you children, to let an old cow frighten you?' There ensued a moment of tense silence, broken by a mournful moo.

'She could take the shape of a cow,' someone whispered, but then everyone was laughing.

'And if there *were* a demon here—' Ardral's voice

commanded their attention. 'Do you think I could not protect you?' In the dimming light, all could see the shimmer of radiance that swirled about him.

It was only a magician's trick, Micail knew, and the kind of display that the initiates and adepts who had taught him had considered beneath them . . . but not beyond them. Taking a deep breath, Micail allowed his own awareness to shift, transferring energy to his aura until he also glowed.

Can Droshrad do that? he wondered, with a flare of pride which as swiftly turned to shame as the workmen backed away, making protective signs. The prophecy had said that by his efforts he would found the new Temple, but was this structure they were building a place to serve the powers of Light, or for some more earthly ambition?

Winter was when the Atlanteans longed most deeply for their lost home. After almost three years, Micail's bones still ached when the north winds brought snow. *God of Winter*, he would often swear, *in this cold, Four-Faced Banur Himself would put more logs on the fire!* But for the moment, the roaring fire in the center of the royal roundhouse and the sheer body heat of the people gathered in it for the midwinter feast had made the temperature rise high enough so that Micail was almost willing to remove his sheepskin cape.

To Khattar's left sat Droshrad and the shamans of the other tribes, and to his right the Atlantean priests, in an uneasy symmetry. On the other side of the fire, the chieftains of the five tribes had shed their capes and round hats long ago and lounged on their benches in tunics of patterned wool. Droshrad was still swathed in his deerhide vestments, painted and sewn with many clattering bits of bone.

Micail wondered if he should have sent Jiritaren and Naranshada and the acolytes back to Belsairath for the winter along with Ardral and the others, but the social life of Tjalan's new capital seemed to him a harder exile than this life among savages. Last fall, staying here had proved wise enough. He and Lanath had been able to fine tune the calibrations used in placing the stones. But this year, Droshrad seemed to be eyeing them with more than his usual disturbing disdain.

'Not much like the formal celebration of the Passing of the Stewardship of Nar-Inabi – is it?' Jiritaren asked, in the language of the Temple of Light. The formal words sounded oddly incongruous as Jiri cracked open a roasted rack of rib bones. Among the tribes, acorn-fattened pig was the favored food for feasts held in winter; the fatty meat staved off the chill. So did the beer. Micail lifted his beaker and took another swallow.

Naranshada frowned, and scratching his beard, said in a less refined form of the temple language, 'I must admit I am not charmed. I look forward to the day when this work will be done and we no longer have to live here. But I have just heard that we will not have a labor force for the other stones until after sowing is done in the spring.'

'What?' said Jiritaren. 'Is this true, Micail?'

'So – you like our feast?' interrupted King Khattar in badly accented but quite serviceable standard Atlantean.

He learns fast, thought Micail, with a reflexive smile. *A good reminder that even though we may use the most arcane Temple dialects, we must be more careful what we say.*

'The meat is fat and the beer is strong, Great King,' Naranshada answered politely. Micail echoed him, observing that the carved circles and lozenges on the houseposts were already beginning to twist and blur. Perhaps he had better go easy on the drink for a while.

'It has been a good harvest!' The king's glare dared anyone to disagree. 'The Old Ones are pleased. Soon they have their new Temple!'

'We are fortunate that the ancestors have the patience of eternity. But the work progresses well.' Not for the first time, Micail wondered how well Khattar actually understood their explanations of the purpose to be served by the alignment of stones.

And what, he asked himself, *do the stones mean to me? The first step in creating the Temple I was destined to build, or simply a reason to live another day?*

'Good,' the king approved. 'How long?'

'The sarsens for the trilithons in the inner court have been transported to the site,' said Naranshada, ticking them off on his fingers. 'That's fifteen stones. Most of them have yet to be shaped, but one crew can work on that until more stones arrive. Just over ten sarsens have been cut for the outer ring – that leaves another forty uprights to find – we could make do with less, I suppose, but we underestimated before and we may have to reject some of the new ones too. I'd rather err on the inclusive side. And of course that doesn't include the lintels to conjoin them.'

Khatar frowned. 'It will take many men to move so many.'

'Yes,' agreed Jiritaren, 'but if everything goes according to plan, we should be able to raise the trilithons—' He looked to Naranshada.

'Oh, certainly by next year,' Ansha smiled, a little tipsily. 'But when does anything ever go according to plan?'

'*That* is why farmers belong in fields, not pulling stones.' Droshrad's gutteral speech issued from somewhere behind the king. 'Gods hold back grain harvest when they are not enough served. I warn you before, King Khattar – people mutter too loud.'

Micail glanced toward the king's nephew Khensu, who sat with the young warriors on the northern side of the hall and saw a similar calculation in the eyes that leaped to meet his own. As in the Sea Kingdoms, a prince was the soul of his land. Micail's father chose to endure torture rather than betray that sacred trust. But here, Micail was beginning to realize, the relationship between king and country was even more basic. The queen served the nameless goddess of the land, who was eternal, but the god who made her fertile was represented by the king. If the crops failed too often, a more virile man must be chosen, and the old king must die.

Ignoring the shaman, Khattar held up one hand, fingers splayed. 'You make five big stones for the five mother-tribes, and the outside circle for the clans.'

'Well, that's not exactly—' Naranshada began, but Jiritaren poked him hard.

Droshrad's scowl deepened.

'You bring sun-power into the circle—' Khattar began, but the rest of his speech was drowned out by cheers, and the first staccato bursts of drumming were heard.

At the beginning of the feast, the bonfire had been so hot that a wide space had been left around it. But as the hours passed, the logs had burned down to a gentle glow, their residual heat enough to maintain a comfortable warmth in the hall. Now the drummers were convening around the fire, some still angling their drums toward the heat to tighten the skins, while the others began to build the soft rhythmic patterings that compelled attention. All conversations stilled as the drumming commenced.

The king's nephew stood up, beckoning to his friends, and those who were sober enough joined him beside the fire. With their hands on each others' shoulders, they danced around it, bending and leaping in perfect rhythm. As they picked up the pace, they added more and more complex kicks, until first one and then another stumbled, and ducked out of the line laughing. Micail was not surprised to see that the last man to remain dancing was Khensu. He moved with more power than grace, but his energy was impressive. With curling brown hair and a muscular frame, he suggested what King Khattar must have looked like in youth. Either of them would be formidable in a fight, Micail thought, and wondered why a dance should remind him of war. Then Khensu too halted, lifting his hands to accept the people's acclaim as the king watched with an expression that suggested he might have preferred his successor to be received a little less enthusiastically.

'You raise stones quick – mine first,' Khattar muttered. 'Then ancestors give me power.' He held out his beaker to be refilled.

Micail sighed and said nothing, hoping the interrogation would end there. It came down to a question of power, but for what purpose and for whom? Khattar wanted the stones in order to make himself preeminent among the local tribes. Tjalan wanted them as a focal point around which he might restore the Sea Kingdoms, or even the empire. Naranshada and Ocathrel and most of the other priests wanted them, if at all, as an opportunity to demonstrate their skills, proof that there had been some purpose in their survival . . . *I felt that way at first*, thought Micail, *and maybe I still do. What did Ardral say the other day? It's like sculptors making a statue of a god – just to see if it can be done.*

And what do I want the new Temple for? It was a question he had never thought to ask himself until very recently; and now it had become a constant itch in his awareness.

'Ah!' Khattar breathed hoarsely, laying his fat-smeared, beer-sticky hand on Micail's shoulder. 'This, you will like! Watch!'

There were rustlings and murmurs from the Women's Side as several of its benches emptied. The young men began whistling as a line of girls moved into the firelight, shawled and skirted in wool and leather with long fringes that swung as their bodies swayed. Necklaces of carved wood and bone, of jet and of amber, shifted gently upon young breasts. With downcast eyes and linked hands they circled, feet treading a pattern as complex as the beat of the drums, while a bone flute twittered and sang. Their slender bodies curved and straightened like young birches at the edge of the forest, like willows beside a rippling stream. Even Micail could not help smiling.

229

'You like our girls, yes!' The king wiped beer from his mustache and grinned.

'They are as beautiful as young heifers in a green field—' Micail replied, and the king shook with deep laughter.

'We make a bull of you yet, outland man!'

The servants circulated through the crowd with baskets of nuts and dried berries, the last of the autumn's bounty, and many hard rounds of cheese. Micail wiped his greasy hands on his tunic and took a handful of nuts, and then several berries, ruefully remembering the countless filigreed bowls filled with scented waters that would, at home, have been circulating for guests to cleanse their fingers. He also missed the exquisite glasses brimming with the most fragrant of wines. Instead, he would obviously have to drink still more of the native beer that was already making him feel off-balance. But that seemed to be the custom here – the men on the outer benches were plainly drunk already – and when the next serving girl came to fill his beaker, Micail did not object.

The dancing maidens undulated back to their sector of the hall, but the drums did not cease their throbbing beat. The crowd, instead of relaxing into the banter that would signal an end to a formal ceremony, sat up even straighter on their benches and waited in excited silence.

Finally the drumming did stop and the broad doorway opened, its creaking terribly audible in the stillness, and someone entered. No one noticed the doorway closing as a slim figure moved forward into the firelight – a girl wrapped in a bearskin cloak, her dun-colored hair knotted high on her head, with the ends falling down her back in a glossy tail.

The king stepped forward and gazed at her with an unreadable expression.

'My father, I salute you.' The girl's slim arm, braceleted in amber, emerged from the folds of fur to touch her brow, lips, and breast.

'My daughter, I welcome you,' the king replied. 'Do you

bring your mother's blessing to our festival?'

'I do – and that of the Mother!' she answered, stepping forward with a centered grace that Micail recognized with some surprise as the mark of a spiritual discipline. This must be Anet, the royal daughter of whom Elara had told him, then, whose mother was high priestess here.

King Khattar sat back. 'Then bestow it,' he said softly.

The girl smiled again, and turning to the drummers, loosed her grip on the glossy fur of her cloak and let it fall. Micail's eyes widened, for beneath it the girl wore only a quantity of jet and amber jewelry, and a brief skirt of twisted strands of wool bound at top and bottom with woven bands. But the whisper that swept the hall was one of satisfaction. Obviously this was expected, a part of the ceremony; and why should that surprise Micail, who had seen the saji girls of the Ancient Land dance clad only in their saffron veils?

The tightest drums spoke sharply, once, twice, and again, as Anet moved into the clear space before the fire, her shapely arms raised high. Then the other drums broke in with their own exclamations, a wordless interplay of question and answer that set Micail's pulse beating a hot response in his veins – and still the dancer had not even moved. Only when the figure of polished amber that lay between her young breasts flared with light did he realize that every inch of her flesh was – *shimmering*, in controlled tremors that swept from knee to breast and back again.

'She channels power,' said Naranshada in a low, awed voice, and Jiritaren nodded drunkenly.

'If this is what they teach them at the sanctuary at Carn Ava, we should send our girls there!' replied Jiritaren.

Micail heard them, but could not speak. It was too hard to breathe, and his skin tingled. He was aware of every hair at the back of his neck – the very air seemed to crackle with tension. This girl was nothing like his beloved, and yet there was a focus, a grace in her poise, that reminded him oddly of Tiriki at prayer.

Almost imperceptibly she had begun to bend her knees, arms gradually coiling down, around, up again, a continuing sinuous motion that carried her forward to spiral around the tall posts holding up the roofs. The firelight brightened her brown hair so that it became the same patchy gold as the dry grass on the hills when touched by the sun. To Micail's eyes it was as if she glowed with the very radiance of Manoah, and he thought, *She is dancing Light back into the world* . . .

Four times around she passed, weaving in and out among the circle of houseposts. Each time she paused, faced a different direction, sank to her knees and arched backward, then straightened both legs and arms, as her back bent like a bow, until with a sudden twist she came upright, arms raised, to begin again. With a twirling, sidewise step, she then made one final circle, scooped up her bearskin cloak and flung it about her. It was as if the light had vanished from the room. She stood unmoving, smiling faintly as her audience let out its breath in a collective sigh, then she turned and swept through the crowd toward the open door.

Briefly, as she passed, her gaze met Micail's. She had green eyes.

'What an astonishing girl!' said Jiritaren, a little too fervently.

'Aye. Like her mother when she was young, and I first ran off with her.' The king grinned reminiscently, bad teeth showing through his grizzled beard. 'Got to find Anet a good husband before some hot-blood with more balls than sense decides to copy me!' His shrewd gaze caught Micail's. 'Khayan-e-Durr says I should marry her to you, outland holy man. What do *you* say?'

Micail stared up at him in shock. *But I am married to Tiriki*, he thought, and at the same time, realized that he did not dare to answer at all. It was Naranshada who rescued him.

'Great King, we appreciate the honor you do us, but I

beg you to remember, my Lord Micail is royal among our people – and can make no alliance with – without consulting with Prince Tjalan,' Ansha finished, almost as smoothly as if he had known what he was going to say.

Beyond Khattar's burly shoulder Micail could see Droshrad scowling, if possible, more deeply than he had before. This proposal had come as a shock to the shaman, too. The realization that there might be more reasons than his own confusion to avoid an immediate answer washed over Micail with cold clarity.

'It is so—' he stammered, and watched the king's face darken.

'Then take counsel to your other prince, from me,' Khattar snarled, in his badly accented Atlantean. 'You Sea People say you wish to serve me, make me great among tribes. But without the Royal Woman, I have no power! Consider your answer how you like, but do not take long. Without blood-bond, you will lose your labor force, your stones, and everything else that is here.'

THIRTEEN

'Mama! Pretty! See?' Domara danced forward, pointing at the blackbirds that dotted the grass, their sleek feathers iridescent in the sun. The night before it had rained heavily and the birds were feasting on earthworms flooded out of the ground. Tiriki tried to grab the child, and failing, straightened with a smile. Domara had celebrated her third birthday last spring and was constantly moving, her bright hair flickering about the Tor like a tiny flame.

Forolin's daughter Kestil walked with the dignity due her seven years. 'Why do you chase them? They only fly away—'

Domara glanced back over her shoulder. 'Pretty!' she said again, flapping sturdy arms. Laughing, Tiriki scooped her up and held her high.

'Fly, little bird!' she sang, 'But never so high you forget the nest . . . Your friends, Mudlark and Turtle and Linnet are waiting to play with you, you know.' She settled the child on her hip and started along the plank walkway that led to the old summer village which, for over a year now, the marsh folk had been rebuilding into a permanent home. She felt again a small thrill of pride, as she thought about their first year in this land, when it had been so clear that the natives thought the Atlanteans were mad to attempt to live in the marshes year round . . .

Yet at the same time she knew that if they honored her,

they revered Chedan, who had personally nursed so many of them through the plague. When he walked through the village, they brought their children for his blessing, and they had been collecting the feathers of hawks to make him a cloak of ceremony. It was for him, not for Tiriki, that they had agreed to live here through the winter, and also to dig out and drag into place the rocks that the mage was using to build the community's first stone hall.

Tiriki sighed and decided that she was not jealous, but simply a little – conservative. The concept of a male healer was disturbing to her, as strange to her as the idea of a woman, even herself, leading the formal ceremonies. And yet in the Ancient Land, her own father had been a healer whose writings on the subject might even be considered by the Lords of Karma a sufficient atonement for his sins.

'New customs for new lands,' her old teacher Rajasta the Wise used to say. Tiriki let her thoughts wander. *Maybe if I'd paid more attention to his prophecies, I would find it easier to make adjustments. But perhaps it is not supposed to be easy.*

Overhead, the sun was burning through the clouds and the marsh mists, leaving only the merest veil of vapor across the sky. She and Domara walked in a circle of clarity whose edges blurred into uncertainty. From a distance the village seemed to shimmer in and out of vision, yet when they neared, they saw women grinding seeds, snapping beans, or cutting up tubers outside their doors, and men mending nets or fletching arrows.

Many villagers lifted a hand in greeting, and Domara chattered back at them happily. Tiriki often left her to play with the village children, and as a result, Domara echoed the gutteral local dialect as often as she did the lilting subtle grammar of the Sea Kings.

'Mor-gan, you late. Glad you are good,' said Heron's wife, a cheerful woman with the incongruous name of Nettle.

The natives had made much better progress in learning

foreign tongues than Tiriki, but she could usually puzzle out the meaning of most of the Lake folk names. *Morgan*, she repeated silently. Chedan had told her the word described a sea spirit in several very old Lerandian legends, but then he had laughed and said no more about it.

Now what is it they call him? She tried to remember. *Sky-Crier? Light-Wing?*

'Sun Hawk!' she exclaimed. 'Have you seen Sun Hawk today?'

'He go to new spirit house.' Nettle snapped another handful of longbeans. 'They argue about *stones*. Men,' she shrugged.

Tiriki nodded agreeably, but was distracted by the same little stir of excitement she always felt whenever she thought of the new Temple – at once a restoration of traditional splendor and a commitment to the new land. Forolin had proved especially helpful, for he came from a family that had produced more builders than merchants. His practical experience complemented Chedan's grasp of theory so well that Tiriki was beginning to believe that the project might actually succeed.

And why not? she asked herself. *We have accomplished a great deal else*. In the four years since their arrival, the first rude huts had been replaced by solid log structures, caulked and plastered against the weather. Beyond the thatched roofs of the village, Tiriki could see sheep grazing in the water meadows, and on higher ground, fields of emmer wheat and barley rippling green and silver beneath the breeze.

She supposed that not only the buildings but the people themselves had changed, though the transformation had been gradual. A few of the glorious and shining robes of Atlantis still remained, but they were rarely worn anymore; and as their ordinary linen garb fell to rags, many of the refugees had begun to go about in simple garments of deerskin, like the people of the marsh.

But that may not last, she told herself, catching sight of one of the village women clumsily carding wool. Now that the priest Dannetrasa's maps had allowed Reidel's sailors to find more sheep to import, spun cloth was beginning to gain in popularity, and Liala and the saji women had begun to process the local wild flax, dyeing it with a native herb that made a lovely blue.

And if we're not very careful, men will end up wearing blue, too, she thought with an involuntary shudder of revulsion. To her, blue would always be Caratra's color, sacred to her priestesses.

As they neared the end of the village, a flock of children came pelting out of one of the houses, their sweet voices piping like birds. Domara answered in the same language, and Tiriki released her daughter to join them. A slender dark woman followed, and Tiriki saluted her.

'Day's blessing on you, Redfern. May I leave Domara with you again? I will be teaching on the little island today, but at sunset I will return.'

Redfern nodded, smiling. 'We watch. Kestil,' she added, turning to Forolin's daughter, 'you help? Keep Domara from water, she don't fall in?'

'Yes!' Kestil piped happily in the marsh folk language, before she went back to chasing after Nettle's children, Mudlark and Linnet.

At least, thought Tiriki in resignation, *Domara knows how to swim.*

The rocky hillock at the far end of the trackway was surrounded by water so frequently that it was more often called an island. Tiriki had come to realize that in this unknown wilderness, land and air and water did not have the same clear identities she had known on Ahtarrath. In the mists, they all tended to blur together, just as the caste distinctions between priest and sailor and native had begun to fade.

The acolytes and others who were her students were waiting in the clearing that they had carved out of the tangled ferns and alders in the midst of the isle. The energy in this spot had a certain youthful quality that made it appropriate for teaching the young. Not that her students were that youthful. In the interests of evening the ratio of priests to priestesses, they had adopted Reidel into the ranks of the junior priesthood, and after long debate, the sailor Cadis, as well.

Tiriki did not doubt that they had been right to adopt Reidel. The sea had taught him how to anticipate the currents of power, and any captain must learn to command himself before he can command men. Already his steady support was proving its value in the rituals. Reidel's own reasons for agreeing to the training were less clear, though Tiriki suspected that Damisa was one of them. She nodded a greeting, and seeing a smile soften his strong features, observed that Reidel was really a very handsome man.

'Today, our topic is the Otherworld,' she began. 'Our traditions teach that there are many planes of existence, of which the physical plane is only the most obvious. Adepts have ventured into the worlds of the spirit and mapped them, but are those maps always the same?'

She let her gaze travel around the circle. For once, wiry Selast, who seemed to quiver with energy even when she was still, was sitting next to her betrothed, Kalaran. Since he had begun to work regularly with Chedan, the scowl that had once marred his fine-boned features had eased, but she suspected that he probably found it harder to accept Cadis and Reidel because he still missed his old companions, the male acolytes who had been lost . . . Beside him, Elis was meditatively running her fingers through the dark soil. But neither Damisa nor Iriel was there.

Damisa's absence was not intentional. Really, it was all Iriel's fault. If Liala had not asked Damisa to take Iriel a message, Damisa would have gone straight to class and never needed to bother with the younger girl at all. But when Damisa finally reached the bower that Iriel had made for herself among the willows, the girl gave her no more than a quick glance before returning her gaze to the tangle of blackberry bushes that she had been staring at before.

'Liala says that Alyssa is still feeling ill,' Damisa said briskly, 'so she wishes you to fetch her some more of the dried yarrow blossoms the next time you come up the hill.'

Iriel neither spoke nor stirred.

'You can take it to her after class, which is where you should be, by the way . . . What *are* you doing? It's not the season for berries—'

'Hush.' However softly voiced, it was a command, and Damisa found herself obeying before she had time to question it. Instinctively she sank to her knees beside the younger girl. A moment passed . . . and another. There was no sound but the wind that whispered in the willows and the gurgling of the stream trickling past. She could see nothing to explain Iriel's transfixed stare.

'You're spending entirely too much time with Taret – you're seeing things!' Damisa muttered, 'Now look. It's lovely here, but we have to—'

'*Hush.*' This time there was a clear hint of fear in the word, and catching it, Damisa's tongue stilled again. Shaken, she started to withdraw from Iriel, more than half-expecting that the other girl would suddenly grab her and laugh.

'Please!' insisted Iriel, 'Don't move!' There was no sound in the words, only the movement of the girl's lips, and all the while Iriel never blinked, never glanced away from whatever she had been so fixedly staring at – a deeper darkness in the underbrush that Damisa had not yet noticed.

And then there was a noise, a wet kind of ripping, and a rustling in the brambles. Unexpectedly, Iriel relaxed.

'What is it?' Damisa could not keep from saying.

'A spirit of the forest,' Iriel whispered with an odd smile, 'but it has stopped listening now. If you move very softly and very slowly, you can see it too.'

Damisa unfroze a little, but before she could so much

as twitch her shoulder, Iriel hissed again, 'Slowly, I said! It's almost finished. When it *does* finish it will go. Then *we* can go.'

Neck-hair prickling, Damisa shifted by inches until she could focus on the shadow in the brambles. At first it looked exactly like a hundred other places in the marshy woods, but as the wind shifted she could smell blood, and something else: a rank, wild smell.

Either we've both gone competely crazy, Damisa decided, *or something is out there.*

She scanned the quiet scene again, focusing fiercely on every mushroom, every patch of grass, until she noticed a thick brown branch at the edge of the darkness – a furry branch that ended in a black, shiny, cloven hoof. She had skinned enough deer by now to recognize that is what it was, but why was it lying there like that?

The dead deer's leg twitched spasmodically, and she heard again the odd tearing, crunching sound.

Perhaps in her shock she made some noise, for the brambles shifted and suddenly she saw clearly a massive, heavy-jawed head, muzzle dripping with blood, and the glow of dark amber eyes. The brambles heaved again as the creature lurched to its feet, jaws still clamped around the deer's haunch, and began to drag it away.

For a moment Damisa saw the animal in its entirety, a dark silhouette against the daylight, its shape like that of a man clad in thick dark brown fur. A strong instinct that owed nothing to her temple training held her utterly still, in awe of a power more ancient than Atlantis itself.

'A she-bear!' Iriel exclaimed, as the crackle of breaking branches faded. 'Did you see her swollen dugs? She must have cubs hidden nearby!'

'A bear . . .' That seemed a small word to contain such power. Damisa had seen a bear once, in Alkonath's Great Zoo of Wonders, but it had been considerably smaller, and differently colored, and she had been assured that it only ate vegetables. But then, there had been very few animals in the Sea Kingdoms, other than those that served men.

'That is *all* we need.' Damisa tried to pull herself together. 'But didn't Otter say there are no dangerous animals in this valley?'

'There aren't – usually. That is why this is so wonderful,' said Iriel, her face alight with enthusiasm. 'Taret says that Bear Mother is the oldest spirit, mother of all the animal powers. It's good luck to see her!'

Damisa wasn't sure about luck, but she did not doubt the power. Looking into those golden eyes, she had felt a frisson of awe in the depths of her spirit unlike anything raised by ritual.

Iriel continued, 'Taret says the Old Ones who lived here worshipped her. They had caves where they worked magic. Some of them might still survive! Not the Old Ones, the caves. Maybe the she-bear has found one and lives there now! It would be a place of great power—'

'This is a *marsh*, Iriel!' Damisa gritted, exasperated. 'How could there be caves here?'

Iriel turned, eyes narrowing. 'There are caves in the Tor,' she said, as if it settled the matter. 'Come on,' she added, getting up at last, 'didn't you say they were waiting for us?'

One custom of Atlantis that the immigrants had been able to recreate was that of coming together for the evening meal. On Ahtarrath, the acolytes had dined in a square chamber lit by hanging lamps and frescoed with interlacing images of the octopi whose tender flesh was a basic part of Atlantean cuisine.

Unlike the native dwellings, the dining hall the Atlanteans had built at the Tor was rectangular, with doors set along the woven walls that could be opened when the weather allowed. Here, the whole community – except for a few sailors who had married native women and lived with them in the village, gathered around a long central hearth whose smoke spiraled upward through the thatch of the peaked roof.

241

At one end, the little statue of Caratra stood upon a plinth made from a stout log. Tiriki noticed with a smile that someone had already laid a spray or two of purple asters before the goddess. She wondered who it had been, and what words, if any, had been used.

The refugees still often spoke of Caratra as Ni-Terat, while the natives called Her Hearthmother, but all drew comfort from Her sweet regard. Today, though, Tiriki found herself suddenly feeling a little more out of place than usual. At home, she had served Light in the form of mighty but distant Manoah, whose presence was experienced only in the most rarified ecstasies of trance. But at the Tor they lived close to the earth and it seemed more fitting that the Mother who never abandons Her children should have Her home here at the center of the community.

Tiriki looked again about the crowded dining hall and smiled, remembering her teacher Rajasta's words, *'But it is man, not Manoah, who needs testimonials in stone. He can never be forgotten. The Sun is His own monument . . .'* And *besides*, she realized, *this* is *a place of Light*.

And so it was. In summer, as if to make up for its lack of strength by length of light, the sun lingered into the evening, its long rays slanting through the western doors, filling the space with a golden glow. The honeyed light veiled the deficiencies of their clothing, turning the countless stains and patches into subtle decorations. Tiriki felt an unexpected rush of pride. Although she could still recognize the same proud priesthood that had ruled the Ancient Land, the faces that now turned to welcome her were marked by lines of endurance and lit with a radiance she had never seen in the Temple at Ahtarrath, and it seemed to her that a new wisdom glowed even in wise old Chedan's eyes.

As Tiriki took her seat at the head of one of the long tables, Domara close beside her, she began a mental roll call. Reidel and the unmarried sailors sat together at one table, even now maintaining shipboard discipline. Chedan headed another group, with Forolin and his family on one side and the priests Rendano and Dannetrasa on the other. The saji women were not present – they generally took their meals privately with Liala and Alyssa – but Tiriki's table was far from quiet because the acolytes sat there.

Damisa and Selast sat together as they usually did these days, and Elis was arguing with Kalaran, also a common occurrence. Even now, Kalaran did not seem to get on well with any of the others, as if grief for the companions he had lost still prevented him from taking joy in those who remained. Tiriki frowned, noticing that the place next to him was empty.

'Where,' she asked aloud, 'is Iriel?'

The acolytes looked at her and then at each other.

'I haven't seen her since class this afternoon,' said Elis. 'You never told us why the two of you were so late, Damisa. Was she working on some project that she might have returned to and forgotten the time again?'

Damisa shook back her auburn head, brows creasing in thought. 'Not a project,' she said at last. 'But – I meant to tell you – we were late because we saw a bear.' Her voice had risen, and folk from the other tables turned to see.

'A *what?*' exclaimed Reidel. '*Are* there bears here?'

'I gather there haven't been for a long time,' Damisa answered. 'Iriel was ecstatic. Apparently Bear Mother is a great power here, and the marsh folk used to do rituals for her in sacred caves.' She rolled her eyes, still unconvinced about the last part.

'She wouldn't have gone looking for the bear?' Elis voiced the thought that was in everyone's mind. Tiriki's eyes met Chedan's in alarm.

'We must find her!' Reidel pushed back his bench and stood up, reassuming the authority of command. 'The marshes can be treacherous, and we don't want to lose anyone else. We will form teams to search – Tiriki and Chedan can coordinate from here, and Elis should stay too, in case you need a messenger. Cadis, I want you to look around the settlement; make sure she isn't here. Teiron, search the area around the lake, and then run down to the village and ask Heron to send hunters to track the bear. Otter will want to help. He seems to have a fondness for Iriel. Damisa, you and Selast and Kalaran – come with me. We must search the Tor, and the villagers do not go there . . .'

Damisa clutched at another branch as her foot slipped again, and clung, catching her breath in hoarse gasps. Above her the slope of the Tor bulked like the Star Mountain against the night. She let out a little shriek as hard fingers closed on her arm.

'It's just me,' Reidel murmured in her ear. She relaxed against his strong arm with a sigh, a little surprised at the sense of security his support gave her. Their torches had failed some time ago, and the world had relapsed into a jumble of shadows. Reidel's arm was one point of certainty in all the wild world.

'Has the Tor gotten bigger, or are we covering the same ground over and over again?' she asked, when she could speak again.

'It does seem that way,' Reidel said ruefully. 'All these trees – they make me nervous. Almost makes me wish I were back at sea!'

'At least we can see the stars.' She could feel no wavering in his arm. 'Will they not guide you as well on land as on sea?'

'That's true—' He tipped his head skyward, where an interlace of branches seemed to net the gleaming Wheel. 'And in truth . . .' He paused for a moment, and when he spoke again there was a constraint in his voice that had not been there before. 'In truth, I do not wish myself anywhere but here.' Very gently he released her. 'I hope Selast and Kalaran have fared better than we,' he added, and looked upward once more, not giving Damisa a chance to reply.

What should I have said? she wondered. *How can I ask him what he means when I already know?* In the old world, even if she had not been destined for the Temple of Light, a girl of her rank might never have spoken to someone like Reidel, much less wondered what it might be like to lie encircled by those strong arms. She felt his warmth again, as he stopped to help her cross a fallen tree. She dreaded the necessity of mating, but for the first time it occurred to her that it might not be so terrible after all. Smiling in the darkness, she followed Reidel uphill.

'Poor old Alyssa . . . Yes, I know what you're thinking!' The seeress parted the frizz of unkempt hair that veiled her face and peered at Tiriki with a skewed smile. 'If I am crazy, though, why ask *me* if you've lost another acolyte? And if I am sane – why wait until midnight to ask me?'

Tiriki could find no answer. Her startled gaze sought Liala, who only shrugged and shook her head. The seeress was usually washed and combed whenever Liala brought her to any event, but apparently Liala's control did not extend to Alyssa's own dwelling, which was a mess of half-eaten foodstuffs, with bits and pieces of strange keepsakes from the Ancient Land lying alongside oddly shaped rocks and strange constructions of twigs and pinecones . . .

'Sanity is not the issue here – I need your vision!' Tiriki stopped short, realizing how anxiety had betrayed her. Ordinarily, she weighed her words more carefully. She relaxed a little as Alyssa began to laugh.

'Oh yes. Madness sees clearest when fate costs dearest. And since the Omphalos Stone never stops speaking to me—' She gestured toward the wall beyond which the Stone rested, swathed in silks in its wooden cabinet in the hut built to house it.

That was another thing, Tiriki realized with a shudder, that she had not thought about for far too long. She held Alyssa's gaze with her own, waiting.

Alyssa closed her eyes and looked away. 'The girl is unhurt. I cannot say if she is safe.'

'What? Where?'

'Seek the heart of the hill. You will learn your fill.' Her hair swung forward over her face once more as she resumed slowly rocking back and forth on her stool.

'What do you mean? What do you see?' Tiriki demanded, but Alyssa's only answer was a wordless crooning.

'I hope that was helpful,' said Liala with a sigh, 'because you will get no more from her tonight.'

'It gives me an idea,' said Tiriki after a moment. 'Others have searched the caves, but perhaps I will see signs they could not . . .' She gasped as her eye was drawn again to the strange assembly of stones, twigs, and oddments on Alyssa's floor. They were, she suddenly understood, a model of the Tor as it must look from high above . . . 'If someone has not already seen them,' she added, with new confidence.

'I will go with you.' Liala arose and reached for her shawl. 'Happily Teviri the saji is here, and can keep watch. Ordinarily, Alyssa passes from this state into deep sleep and will not wake till after noon.'

As Tiriki and Liala approached, torch flames wavered sharply in the chill current of air from the mouth of the cave. Taret had told her many things about this place, but Tiriki had always found herself too busy to take time to explore. Or perhaps she had been afraid. She peered with mingled excitement and apprehension into the darkness.

'Perhaps we should leave this for one of the younger folk.' Liala eyed the uneven footing dubiously.

'You have grown soft! Besides,' Tiriki added more soberly, 'if Iriel needs us, she cannot wait for us to find them.' Not waiting to see if Liala followed, she started forward along the edge of the stream.

The stones, whitened by the lime-rich waters, glistened in the torchlight. In some places the minerals had crystallized in midflow and hung from the ceiling of the tunnel in an irregular series of upside-down pyramids. At their tips, drops of water formed and fell. When she reached out to steady herself against the sloping wall, the rock was cold and damp beneath her hand.

Was this passage natural, or had it been shaped by men? In most spots the stone had been worn smooth by water, but there were places overhead that seemed to have been chipped away. Curious, Tiriki quickened her pace, somehow keeping her footing on the slick stones. It was not until a sudden turning stopped her that she realized that Liala was no longer behind her. Softly she called the woman's name, but the sound was soon swallowed in the whisper of water over stone.

For a moment she stood, considering. There had been no divergence in the passageways, so Liala could not have gotten lost – and she would have heard the splash if she had fallen from the slippery rocks. More likely, the older priestess had simply given up and turned back again. Pulling her shawl more tightly around her, Tiriki started forward once more. She was no more alone than she had been before, of course, but after a few steps she realized that knowing Liala was not behind her had made her more wary. She noticed that there was a secondary passageway on the far side of the stream, leading off to her left. As she raised the torch, she could see the sensuous curves of a running spiral pecked into the stone around the opening. Damisa had said that Iriel might be looking for a temple hidden in an ancient cave. With her lips tightening in decision, Tiriki bent and drew a leftward pointing arrow in the mud to show where she was going, and then stepped across the glittering stream.

To the eye, there was little difference between this passage and the one she had been following, but she could sense a definite change. Frowning a little, she put a fingertip to the carving and began to trace the spiral inward to the center and then out again.

She stood, transfixed by the pattern, until suddenly she realized that her arm had dropped to her side and the torch was flaring dangerously near to her skirts. Startled, she jerked it away, peering around her.

How long had the pattern held her in trance? How far had she come? Tiriki shook her head; she ought to have known better than to touch the spiral. Taret had warned her that there was, somewhere on the island, a maze which would lead to the Otherworld if one trod it to the end.

The curved passage before her seemed less shadowed, but she could see neither very far ahead, nor back the way she had come. *I am not lost*, she told herself firmly. She had only to follow the spiral back to find the stream. And with that self-assurance, she set her hand to the stone and went forward once more . . .

In the next turning she found herself under open sky.

The torchlight seemed suddenly pale and she blinked at the light around her. Could it be morning already? The sky had all the silver pallor of dawn, but mists swathed the base of the Tor, and its slope hid the horizon.

Tiriki continued climbing, but when she reached what appeared to be the top she saw only the ring of stones, taller than she remembered, and glowing as if with their own light. The sun was not the source of that illumination, for the eastern sky was no brighter than the west. The air was not cold, but a shiver passed through her as she scanned the horizon. *I am no longer in the world I know . . .*

Shifting veils of mist drifted across the land, but not the smoke from the settlement's morning cookfires; indeed there was no sign of any habitation whatsoever . . . and yet the mists themselves were luminous, as if whatever they concealed was lit from within. Holding her breath, Tiriki strained to focus her eyes.

'You strive too hard,' said a soft, amused voice behind her. 'Have you forgotten your training? *Eilantha* . . . breathe out . . . and in . . . open your inner vision, and see . . .'

Not since childhood had anyone had the power to command her perceptions, but before Tiriki could think to resist, she responded, and instead of trees and meadows saw glimmering lattices of radiance. Dazzled, she turned and perceived the Tor itself as a single crystalline structure through which currents of energy, spiraling around the peak of the Tor, formed a dazzling circle ascending to the sky. Tiriki lifted her hand and saw instead of a human arm, a dragon-dance of radiance that refracted and interacted with all the rest in turn, as intricately interconnected as the serpents on her ring.

'*Why are you surprised?*' She could no longer tell if the thought came from without or within. '*Did you not know that you are also a part of this world?*'

The truth of it was evident. Tiriki was simultaneously aware of her own being and of a myriad of interlocking lattices of light, layered from one dimension to the next, and containing every entity from pure spirit to stone and dust. She was aware of Alyssa's disorderly spirit as a scatter of sparks, Chedan's steady glow of faith and power, and the bright flicker that was Iriel, her soul-spark so close to that of Otter that they were nearly one. The power of the Tor rippled through the landscape in rivers of light. Her excitement rose as she extended her perceptions, for here, where all planes of existence were one, was where she might surely find Micail . . .

And for a moment, then, she touched his spirit. But the surge of emotion was too great, and Tiriki plunged dizzily back into her body – or rather, to whatever form her body had here, for her own flesh glowed like that of the woman whom she saw standing before her, robed in light, crowned with stars.

'Micail lives!' Tiriki exclaimed.

'*All things live,*' came the answer, '*past, present, future, each in its own plane.*'

Beneath the leathery leaves of unknown plants, monstrous forms moved; but also ice covered the world, and nothing grew. She saw the Tor at once tree-clad and cleared, a slope of close-cropped grass crowned with standing stones, and also a strange stone building which in the same moment fell, leaving only a tower. She saw people dressed in skins, in blue robes, in garments of many colors, and buildings, fields, and pasture over-laying the marshes that she knew . . . Her perceptions overwhelmed her, and she felt as though she knew nothing at all.

'*All of them are real,*' the voice in her mind explained. '*Each time you make a choice, the world changes, and another level is revealed.*'

'How shall I find Micail?' Tiriki's spirit cried, 'How shall I find *you?*'

'*Only follow the Spiral, up or down . . .*'

'My lady, are you all right?' a man's voice inquired.

'Tiriki! What are you doing here?'

The voices converged, distinct, but with an underlying harmony. Tiriki opened her eyes and realized that she was lying on the grass just inside the circle of stones at the top of the Tor. She struggled to sit up, squinting against the light of the rising sun.

'Were you out wandering all night too?' A sturdy figure she recognized as Reidel reached out to help her to stand.

'Wandering indeed,' said Tiriki giddily, 'but where?'

'My lady?'

'Never mind . . .' She was stiff in every joint, but though the thick grasses were damp with dew, her clothing was almost entirely dry. Blinking, she looked about again, comparing what she saw with her memories.

'She seems dazed,' Damisa said with an undertone of exasperation. 'Best get her downhill as soon as we can.'

'Come then, my lady,' said Reidel softly, 'you can lean on me. We may not have located Iriel, but at least we have found *you.*'

'Iriel is safe . . .' Tiriki's voice was a croak and she tried again. 'Take me to Chedan. What I have seen . . . he needs to know.'

FOURTEEN

A pillar of dust was moving across the plain, marking the progress of yet another mighty piece of stone. Micail climbed up on the embankment that circled the henge and gazed northward across the ditch, shading his eyes with his hand to make out the line of sweating men who hauled it. Others ran ahead, ready to dart in and replace anyone whose strength failed, clearing the track ahead for the rounded wooden runners that carried the load.

A stand of singers could lift such a stone for a short time; seven times that number might even transport it overland if the distance was not too great, but there were no longer enough singers left in all the world to levitate one of the great sarsens all the way across the plain. And to raise the stones once they had been brought to the circle would require the talents of all the trained singers who remained.

They had tried moving the stones with oxen, but men worked harder and longer, and they were easier to train. King Khattar seemed unable to comprehend why Micail thought that a problem. For generations, once the emmer wheat and barley were well up and the cattle had been driven to the hill pastures in the care of girls and young men, the king would call out the levy. One able-bodied man from each farmstead or hamlet was expected to report for community labor. That was how the great ditched enclosures had been made, and the barrows, the wooden henges, and probably the older circles of standing stones as well.

There is still so much that we do not know, thought Micail, *I only hope we do not come to rue the gaps in our knowledge.* Turning, he surveyed the five pairs of sarsen stones that already stood within the circle. Despite his misgivings, he felt a thrill of satisfaction at the sight of those sharply hewn shapes against the sky. Atlantean magic could not do all the work, but it had certainly helped speed it. It was beginning to seem as if a task that would have taken the entire labor force of all the tribes dominated by King Khattar nearly ten years to accomplish was going to be finished in less than three. In a single year they had prepared five pairs of monoliths for the inner semicircle. The great lintels too were ready, and lay waiting.

When the rest of the singers arrived from Belsairath, and the lintels were raised to their places on wings of sound, then the shamans would understand the need to work with, rather than against, this new power. *And after that, we will be able to complete the new Temple without further interference.* It occurred to Micail that he had been so focused on the construction of the stone circle for the last two and a half years that he was finding it difficult to envision the work that would follow.

'My lord?' A touch on his elbow roused him from his reverie and he saw Lanath waiting there.

'What is it?'

'Will it please you to inspect the third stone now?' The acolyte's bronze skin had a healthy glow in the summer sunlight, and the rigorous work had made the boy a man. It had been quite some time, Micail reflected, as he followed Lanath back into the semicircle of stones, since he had to rouse the lad from a nightmare.

The third stone was surrounded by a timber framework, from whose top a native workman was grinning down.

'Is like the other side, aye? You look and see—'

Micail walked around the stone once, then again,

comparing its sides with each other and with the second stone as well. All of the monoliths had been roughly dressed before being erected, and each had one side that had been made particularly smooth, and slightly concave. But not until such a stone had been raised could the narrowing of top and bottom which made the sides appear straight be adjusted to perfection.

'Yes, it is good. You may come down now. Tell them I said to give you an extra ration of beer.' He smiled genially.

Micail laid a hand against the rough surface. Whenever he touched a dressed sarsen he could feel the subtle thrum of energy within it. When the construction was complete, he suspected, he would be able to sense its power without touching it.

Common people might think of stones as lifeless things, but within these stones he sensed a potential for far greater cumulative power. Already it could be perceived somewhat at dawn and sunset. Many of the native workers refused to come into the site at those times. They said the stones had begun to talk to each other, and Micail half believed it.

'Soon all shall hear you,' he murmured to the monolith. 'When you are joined to your brother and the others stand beside you, we will invoke your spirit, and all will under-stand . . .' And for a moment, the subliminal vibration became an audible hum. He started, and noticed that Lanath had heard it too.

'It is easy in this savage place to forget all the glories that are gone,' he told the boy, 'but our true treasure was always the wisdom of the stars. We shall make in this place a monu-ment that will, when the very name of Atlantis is forgotten, still proclaim that we were here.'

'There it is!' Elara pointed past the line of trees that marked the river Aman's winding course. 'You can see the timbers of the palisade.'

Timul shaded her eyes with her hand. 'Ah, yes. At first

I thought those posts were more trees . . . What's that atop them? Bull's horns? Ah. Barbaric, but effective.'

The others, too, were chattering with relief and curiosity as the rest of the Ai-Zir village came into view. Micail had sent word that work on the circle of stones was reaching a stage where everyone would be needed, and even those who until now had remained in Belsairath had answered his call.

Elara glanced back down the line. Ocathrel had returned, this time with all three of his daughters and Micail's cousin Galara as well. There were the great singers Sahurusartha and her husband Reualen, along with Aderanthis and Kyrrdis and Valadur and Valorin with their various chelas, most of whom had been here at least once before. But now the senior Guardians were with them – grim Haladris and stern Mahadalku, and even, riding in sedan chairs, frail Stathalkha and old Metanor – and *there* was Vialmar, almost at the end of the line, looking about nervously as if he expected at any moment to be attacked by something, despite the presence of Tjalan's men-at-arms.

Almost every priest and priestess who had sailed to Belsairath was present – at least those who had also survived last winter's coughing sickness. Prince Tjalan's wife and two of his children were among those who died. Elara had been in Belsairath when the epidemic began, and Timul had immediately pressed her into service as a healer. For so long, it seemed, the acolyte had been facing misery and death; she found herself surprisingly eager to see the village of Azan again. *Poor Lanath, he must have been bored to tears. I wonder if he ever convinced Micail to learn how to play Feathers.*

'I know it looks small compared to Belsairath,' said Elara, 'but the other tribal centers are no more than a few houses near the barrows, although tents and reed huts spring up all over the hillside during the festivals. Azan is the only place here that could even qualify as a village.'

'Quit babbling, girl, I understand.' Timul's dark eyes continued to flick alertly over the scene.

Micail's letter had summoned all the singers to help him complete, consecrate, and activate the Sun Wheel. It had apparently become an event of some importance for the tribe as well. She wondered if the queen would be there. At the time Elara left, Micail had been putting off all talk of marriage by protesting that he must remain celibate in order to work with the stones. She wondered if anyone would ever manage to get into Micail's bed.

Micail surveyed the assembled priests and priestesses who sat waiting beneath the willow trees by the river. *How is it that we have become so strange to one another?* he sighed. *Or is it only I who have changed?*

Once, presiding over such meetings had been part of his daily routine. He found himself mentally rehearsing the traditional salutations, the little compliments and discreet formalities that had been his best tools in administering the Temple and the city of Ahtarrath, then winced, as if the memories were muscles gone stiff from disuse. These days he was more accustomed to the rough courtesies of the Ai-Zir, or the easy cameraderie of Jiri and Ansha.

He took another breath and began, 'I thank all of you for answering my call. In truth I did not know how many of you would be able to make this journey, but it is most important that we successfully demonstrate our power to move the stones.' He turned to Ardral. 'My lord, is there anything you would like to add?'

The old adept arched one eyebrow and shook his head. 'No indeed, dear boy. Now that we are at the stage of physical manipulations, I am happy to defer to you.'

Micail suppressed another sigh. The other thing that he had not really considered when he had sent his message was that, in general, Guardians did not attain their rank until middle life. Most of the men and women who sat with him here were *old*. Fortunately, the Temple disciplines had kept them relatively healthy, and a good night's rest had eased some of their fatigue. Ardral, of course, was evidently ageless, but old Metanor was looking more than ordinarily grey – they would have to watch out for his heart if the work grew heavy. Stathalkha too seemed halfway to the Otherworld, but then she was a farseer.

Haladris of Alkonath and Makadalku of Tarisseda, on the other hand, presented a curiously solid front that reminded him of the sarsen stones, though why that simile should occur to him he did not know, since they had not shown themselves to be particularly stubborn, obstinate, or inflexible . . . *There is so much that I do not know*, he repeated to himself with a wry smile. But even great guardians did not always guard their tongues around the junior priesthood. He made a mental note to ask Elara what she had heard; or Vialmar, who had been in Belsairath since their arrival in the new land . . .

'Of course we had to come,' Mahadalku was saying now, her demeanor as majestic as if she addressed them from beneath the portico of the Temple of Light on Tarisseda, not a thatched sunshade in Azan. 'The trade town offers only . . . survival. Here is where you are building our future. We would not wish to be elsewhere.'

Most of the crowd murmured polite agreement.

'Yes, well—' Micail struggled to recollect the high temple formula for what he wanted to say, but could not. He bit his lip and settled for a gesture that signified a lack of time for a more exacting presentation. It would open the subject for general discussion, but he had expected that anyway.

'If we all come together, along with the acolytes and chelas, we should be able to raise three stands of singers – which should be more than enough to lift the lintels for the trilithons. My lord Haladris will act as director.'

'Oh, Haladris could probably lift the stone all by himself,' Ardral interjected.

256

Haladris shook his head, his eyes hooding as he frowned. 'No – I can fully levitate a boulder the weight of a small woman, no more, and I must confess I am exhausted thereafter. I will be very glad of the help, I assure you.'

Micail pursed his lips, thoughtful. He had remembered the Alkonan First Guardian's talent for telekinesis. What he had forgotten was that the man had no sense of humor at all.

'We will first complete the tallest trilithon, which represents King Khattar's tribe,' Micail continued.

'Which the king *believes* to represent his tribe,' Mahadalku corrected, in a voice like silk.

'Which does not affect the outcome,' Micail interrupted. 'I pray thee forgive my impertinence, Most Honored Lady, but it would serve us well to remember how *they* will think. We are no longer in the Sea Kingdoms—'

'As if anyone could forget,' Mahadalku exclaimed, and turned to glare across the river, where the grasslands rolled away to disappear in a golden haze . . . *'But the Wheel turns.'*

There was a little silence then, broken only by a rueful cough from Ardral.

'I do agree that what Khattar believes should not be discounted,' Naranshada said at last. 'We are few and they are many. It is their land, and we build using their labor, their stones . . .'

'Technically, yes, of course,' Haladris answered coolly. 'I am not suggesting that we cast him aside. He seems a useful ally – there is no need to insult him. But surely these barbarian warriors would be no match for Tjalan's spearmen. However, you are correct, my lord Micail. Whatever the native folk *think* the stones mean, the circle will still be a device to amplify and direct the vibrations of sound. Once the Sun Wheel is completed, we will be able to use its power – howsoever we will.'

Haladris had spoken as if there could be no possible objection to his assessment of the situation. Micail caught Ardral's eye, pleading for further intervention, but the adept shook his head.

In any case, Micail sighed, *we need Haladris to move the stones. No one can match his focus.* The question of who was using whom, and for what purpose, could wait until after the work was done.

'How long do we have,' Mahadalku asked quietly, 'until this . . . king's festival . . . when you intend to raise the stones?'

'I rely on my lord Adravanant's figures, which I have always found to be precise. The festival will begin in half a moon, when the herds will be driven back down from the hills. It is the custom of the tribes to gather at the henges at that time. There is a cattle fair and races, and offerings are made to the ancestors. All their shamans will be there—' *And the Sacred Sisters from Carn Ava as well*, Micail thought uneasily. He had met Anet's mother on more than one occasion, but so far had avoided more than superficial conversation. Since the dinner where Micail first laid eyes on Anet she made him uneasy.

'So, we will not only raise the stone, we will be seen to do so—' There was no warmth in Mahadalku's smile. 'I like that,' she said. 'It should serve us very well.'

Timul gazed with interest at the people who thronged the great fair that was held here at the end of summer every year. 'I think I understand the folk who visit the Temple in Belsairath a little better,' she said, 'now that I see them in their native habitat, as it were.'

Elara smiled dutifully, thinking that she had always rather enjoyed the various tribal celebrations even though the noise and bustle made her homesick for Ahtarra on market day. For all of them, she supposed, the inevitable memories of the Sea Kingdoms were becoming less poignant. A sudden scent or sight still had the power to pierce her heart with its deceptive familiarity, but such moments came less often. And today there were many sights, sounds, and smells the like of which she was sure she had never encountered before.

The lonely plain beyond the henge had been transformed by the influx of people. The five tribes had raised their circles of skin tents and made booths of woven branches, each marked by a pole topped with the horned skull of a bull, and painted in the colors of the tribe: red, blue, black, yellow-ochre, or white, which had seemed redundant until she had seen it. King Khattar's people followed the red bull, and his standard, like the pillars of his chosen trilithon, stood the highest.

'Where are we going?' Timul asked, as Elara led her through the chattering hordes that were gathering where the craftsmen displayed their wares: pottery cups and bowls and beakers, fine leatherwork and wood carving, fleeces and bundles of carded wool, stone axes and arrow-heads and blades for plows. But there was no bronze. The highly prized metal weapons were owned and distributed solely by kings.

'To the Blue Bull—' Elara pointed toward the woad-stained skull just visible over the heads of the crowd. Hanks of blue-dyed wool hung from its base, lifting gently in the breeze. The horns were twined with summer flowers. 'They are the northernmost tribe of the Ai-Zir. Their sacred center is Carn Ava.'

'Ah. Where the priestess lives.' Timul nodded, with barely suppressed excitement. 'I had hoped she would be here. Lead on.'

Ayo's tent was easy to find – it was as large as a chieftain's. The posts were richly carved, and the hide cover was painted with sacred signs in blue woad. The eyes of the Goddess above the entrance watched as they drew closer. A young woman who had been grinding grain in a quern by the doorway rose.

'Enter, honored ones. My lady expects you.'

The day was warm and the sides of the tent had been tied up to let in light and air. The girl who had welcomed them now motioned for them to sit on leather cushions stuffed with grass, and she offered them cool water in clay cups imprinted with cord marks that made them easy to hold. As she eased back out again, the curtain that separated the front part of the tent from the private area was pulled aside and Ayo herself appeared.

Like her attendant, the priestess wore a simple sleeveless garment of blue fastened at the shoulders with pins of bone. Her hair was coiled in a net held across the forehead by a band. Unlike every other woman of rank Elara had seen, Ayo wore no necklaces. She hardly needed them – she bore a mantle of power that reminded Elara of Mahadalku or even Timul. Micail's wife, Tiriki, had looked that way when she was leading a ritual, Elara remembered sadly.

Timul offered the other woman the salutation due a high priestess of Caratra and, smiling, Ayo made the appropriate response.

'It is true what they say. You are of the sisterhood of the far lands.' Ayo was older than she had at first seemed, but she took her seat with a supple grace that reminded Elara of her daughter Anet.

'But our land is no more,' Timul answered flatly. 'We must learn which face the Lady wears in this one or She may overlook us.'

'That is good,' Ayo smiled. 'You speak our language well, but with the accent of the Black Bull tribe. I had heard that someone was offering service to our sisters when they visit the strange stone houses by the sea. It is a pleasure to meet you. But I wonder, why do you come here?'

'The priests of my people will perform a great magic tomorrow. I was called to attend.'

'And you, child? You are skilled in healing, I understand.' Ayo's grey gaze had shifted and Elara found it hard to look away.

'I am also a singer,' she answered. 'And I will be helping build the stone circle.'

'Ah. And this magic will serve what ends?'

260

Elara bit her lip, uncertain how to answer. The acolytes and chelas had not been told everything, but she had heard enough to know that the Guardians did not believe that King Khattar understood the purpose of the circle and that they preferred that things remain that way. And this was Khattar's wife, however independent of him she might be. Elara did not like to lie, so she was going to have to choose her words carefully.

'I am a servant of the Light,' she said slowly, 'and I believe that when the circle is completed, the stones will bring light into the land.'

'Light is in the land already. It runs like a river. The souls of the ancestors ride its currents to the Otherworld and then return to the wombs of our women once more.' Ayo frowned thoughtfully.

'I have heard that the shamans are not happy with what we do,' Timul said suddenly, 'and they would stop the work except that our priests are supported by the king. Do you too think we are – wrong?'

'Perhaps. Perhaps not. But you are few,' said Ayo, 'and there are many things you do not understand.'

'What do you mean?' Elara eyed her uncertainly.

'If I *could* tell you, I would not need to.' Ayo smiled. 'But we will all become one people in time.'

'Are you speaking of a marriage between your daughter and Lord Micail?'

Ayo laughed. 'It is Khattar and Queen Khayan who want *that* mating. But my daughter is not destined for the hearth of any man. She will give herself as the Goddess bids, not the king. Is it not so with you?'

Timul nodded. 'In my order, yes, we are free.'

'Khattar wishes only to bind your people to him,' said Ayo. 'If not through the marriage bed, he will seek his goal by other means. His hopes may be too high, but look you to your own,' she said, grinning.

Is that a threat or a warning? thought Elara, shocked.

At that moment, the attendant came in with a basket of flat cakes glazed with honey and the conversation became self-consciously social. But afterward, as Elara escorted Timul back to the Atlantean encampment, both were still puzzling over the meaning of Ayo's enigmatic smile.

On the day chosen to raise the stones, the people gathered outside the ditch that encircled the village, humming like a gigantic beehive. Facing the entrance, a bench had been set for King Khattar.

For Micail, it was wrenching to see and greet the singers who awaited within the circle like so many ghosts of his past life, their fine white garments still redolent of the distinctively Atlantean spices in which they had been packed. His own garb, a very beautifully made but rather large robe borrowed from Ocathrel, drew exclamations of admiration from the others and even a number of reminiscent tears. But soon most of the singers settled back into their places, ranked according to voice range.

When the silence was complete, Micail nodded and cast a handful of frankincense into each of the three incense pots on tripods at the place of Nar-Inabi, in the eastern quarter. The hot coals blinked like red stars as the resin began to melt, releasing the fragrant smoke to billow upward into the air. The familiar heavy sweetness caught in his throat, and for a moment, Micail was again in the Temple of Light on Ahtarrath; but at the same moment Jiritaren, standing in the south, whispered the other Word of Fire and his black torch burst into light.

Sahurusartha knelt before a small marble bowl set on a low altar in the west, and intoned the Alkonan form of the Hymn of Placation to Four-Faced Banur, Destroyer and Preserver, God of Winter and of Water; while the Tarissedan priest Delengirol twice raised and then lowered a filigreed platter of salt to the north, for Ni-Terat was honored without words.

Micail strode to the southern edge of the embankment, his staff held high. The orichalcum knob on its head blazed like a star in the noonday sun.

'By the power of Holy Light let this place be purified!' he cried. 'By the wisdom of Holy Light let it be warded! By the strength of Holy Light let it be secure!'

He turned to his right and slowly began to pace around the circle as the other three followed, purifying each quarter with the four sacred elements. As they did so, the other priests and priestesses softly sang—

> *'Manoah's rising frees the world*
> *From darkest night;*
> *From age to age we are reborn,*
> *And greet the Light!'*

Micail could feel the familiar slip and shift of gravity that told him the warding was rising around them. It was not only the copious incense smoke that caused everything beyond the circle to waver as if seen through water. The singers were separating the stones from the ordinary world . . .

> *'Within this holy fane we see*
> *With spirit sight—*
> *Ye Lords of Faith and Wisdom come*
> *And bless our rite!'*

He completed the circuit as the chant ended and stood for a moment, listening. They had shaped the stones well to contain both sound and energy. Whatever noise the Ai-Zir might be making outside the circle was less than the whisper of wind in the trees. He let out his breath in relief. Speaking with the native workers, he had grown accustomed to thinking of the stones as a Sun Wheel, but what they had designed was intended to function as a resonator, amplifying soundwaves into a force that could be directed along the lines of energy that flowed through the land. With that power at their command they could build a new Temple to rival the old. Strictly speaking, so powerful a warding should not be necessary for this sort of Working, but he had enough respect for the power of Droshrad's shamans to take precautions against any chance of magical interference.

Once the sacred elements had been returned to their altars, Micail and the other hierarchs removed their masks and joined the ranks of the singers. He took a moment to examine each one as he passed by – the more experienced priests were already expressionless with concentration, the younger ones wide-eyed with last-minute nerves.

Haladris had taken up his position and now addressed them all. 'You know what you are to do—' He fixed each stand-leader in turn with his hooded glare. 'I will give you the keynotes, and then the bass singers will project the sound toward the stone. As the chord builds, it will rise, and I will direct it. Remember! It is focus, not volume, that is needed here. Let us begin.' Very softly, he hummed the short and innocuous-seeming sequence of notes that they had been practicing for the last few days.

Haladris lifted his hand, and the three bassos, Delengirol, Immamiri, and Ocathrel, emitted a wordless hum so deep it seemed to vibrate out of the earth itself. The stone did not move yet, of course, but the first, responsive stirring of the particles within were apparent to Micail's inner eye.

The baritones came in, Ardral and Haladris dominating until they modulated their voices, blending with Metanor, Reualen, and the others in that range until all their throats were producing the same rich note. The shimmering energy about the target stone became almost perceptible to ordinary vision as Micail and the other tenors eased into the growing resonance, balancing the middle range.

The sarsen was shaking, its concave face glittering weirdly with inner light. Now was the time when care was needed, lest they shatter the stone instead of raising it.

The contraltos joined the developing harmony, and then the sopranos came in, doubling the volume, and the song became a rainbow of overwhelming sound. The stone moved – empty space could be seen beneath it.

Smoothly, the singers modulated the great chord upward. The sarsen lifted past their knees, and then waist-high, moving upward with the music until it was even with their shoulders . . . and had passed them. Micail could feel the massive power flowing around and through Haladris, even as he used his own gift to augment and refine it.

The uprights of the trilithon were three times the height of a man. As the sarsen lintel floated toward its destination, the heads of the singers tipped back to keep it in view.

Once more Micail's stern will controlled his emotions as the slowly rising arms of the archpriest lifted their voices and with them, the great sarsen stone. Watching it riding the tide of sound, Micail felt his spirit expanding with a joy that was entirely pure. *This* – the thought flitted through his awareness – *this is what we are seeking. Not power, but harmony . . .*

The stone hesitated, hovering alongside the tops of the uprights. Haladris nudged it a fraction higher so that it would clear the bumps of the tenons in the center of each, then eased it forward until the hollows on the underside of the lintel were just above them; and lowering his hands a little, modulated the volume of the singing and allowed the stone to settle into place.

Micail straightened and let out his breath in a long sigh. They had done it! He nodded to the singers, whose faces glowed with quiet pride. But their shoulders sagged and he knew they shared his exhaustion as well. Once more he could hear the murmur of the crowd outside, shrill now with wonder. King Khattar was grinning as though he had won a battle. Already the drums were booming. Micail winced with each beat as if the blows fell upon his very flesh, but he knew that they would not cease. *As well ask wild geese not to fly.*

King Khattar, ecstatic at the success of the Working, was as determined to celebrate as if he himself had raised the stone. The other priests and priestesses had been allowed to retire to their dwellings, but the king had insisted that Micail stay to represent them at the feast. He yawned and tried to focus his bleary eyes. The night was fair and almost windless, and the fires at which each clan and tribal chieftain feasted glowed like scattered stars. King Khattar's tents were closest to the henge. He was enthroned now on an oddly shaped bench over which his men had thrown a red cowhide. His nephew and heir, Khensu, sat upon a stool at his feet. For the important guests there were other benches, but the king's warriors lounged at their ease on hides laid upon the ground. Tjalan and Antar and their officers squatted somewhat farther off, beside the sons of the chiefs of other tribes.

Torches had been raised in front of the completed trilithon so that the king could continue to gaze raptly upon it. Red light played on the two massive uprights and the heavy lintel that crowned them, stark against the crisp stars, and Micail suddenly had the odd fancy that it had become a gigantic doorway to the Otherworld. *And what would I find if I passed between them? Does Tiriki await me on the other side?*

Holding out his beaker to be refilled, he realized too late that the graceful maiden carrying the jar was Anet.

'Your magic is indeed great,' she said as she bent closer than was necessary merely to pour the beer. At least she was fully clad this time, but still Micail drew back a little, dizzied by the scent of her hair. At that, she laughed softly and, handing off her jar to one of the other girls, slid onto the bench beside him.

'Now that the stone is up, you need sleep alone no longer, yes?'

'You know my prince will not allow me to marry—'

She shook her head, eyes flashing. 'I laugh! Those are words for you to say to my father, not to me. I know, in rank, you are equal. But you need not fear. Marriage was my father's idea, not mine.' She leaned against him with an alluring smile, her flesh warm even through his rough tunic.

Micail lifted a hand to push her away, but somehow it settled instead upon her silky hair. His brows bent in confusion. 'Then why—? Why are you—' *What are you doing?* was what he meant to say, but his tongue would not obey him.

'You serve the truth,' she said then. 'Can you truly say you do not want me?'

He felt the blood rush to his face, and elsewhere as well, and without a conscious decision he pulled her closer and his lips met hers. Her mouth was very sweet, and he was painfully aware of how long it had been since he had held a woman in his arms.

'You have answered me,' she said when he let her go at last. 'Now I will answer you. I do not wish to be your wife, O prince from the far lands. But I want to bear your child.'

Her hand drifted lower. He certainly could not deny that he wanted her now. 'Not here, not yet,' he said hoarsely. 'Your father is watching . . .' And, indeed, within the moment he heard King Khattar call his name.

Micail jerked around. The king was smiling. Had he seen?

'Now the stones *are* up, eh? Now all the world sees my power!' The royal laughter echoed from the walls. 'Now comes time to use it!'

Micail stiffened in alarm.

Khattar leaned forward, his breath reeking of wine and meat. 'We show them, aye! All people who do not follow the Bull! The People of the Hare, the Ai-Akhsi who live in the land you call Beleri'in – they defy us. And the Ai-Ilf, the Boar Tribe to the north, they steal our cows! We will

267

attack them now, not to raid but to conquer, for we will have swords that do not bend or break in battle! Swords that cut through wood and leather and bone!'

Micail shook his head, trying to clear it of the double effect of arousal and alcohol, as Anet slid away from his side and slipped off into the crowd. Prince Tjalan was sitting up now as well, eyes narrowing as he tried to hear what was happening on the other side of the fire.

'You have good blades of strong bronze,' Micail began, but the king pounded his knee.

'No! I have seen your blades with the white edges cut wood as readily as our knives cut grass!' Khattar clapped his hand to the sheathed dagger that hung around his neck by a braided thong, making the tiny golden nails that studded its grip flash in the firelight. Khensu had risen and now loomed behind his uncle, hand on the hilt of his own blade.

Micail stifled a groan. He had counseled Tjalan against allowing his men to demonstrate the sharpness of those blades so casually. 'We do not have enough of them to arm your warriors,' he began, but Khattar wouldn't stop bellowing.

'But *you* are the great shamans foretold in our tales! We have seen it! You will make more.'

Micail shook his head, wondering if he dared admit they *could not* do so even if they willed. In time, even the orichalcum that edged the swords they had would begin to flake away, until at last it dissolved into its component minerals; and among all the priests and mages who had escaped the Sinking, there was not one – so far as he knew – who had the talent needed to forge the sacred metal anew.

'You will give your oath to do this—' Khensu's hoarse whisper sounded in his ear, as one strong arm clamped both his own to his sides and he felt the cold kiss of metal at his throat. 'Or you taste *this*.'

Micail cast a frantic glance toward Tjalan, but the Alkonan prince was nowhere to be seen. If Tjalan could reach his men, at least they would be able to protect the others. He took a deep breath, and then another, and as his pounding pulse grew calmer he thought he heard shouting from beyond the fire. *Great Maker*, he prayed fervently, *don't let them catch Tjalan!*

A crowd of men pushed forward and Micail recognized two chieftains from other tribes, with warriors behind them.

'Why does King Khattar wish to kill the stranger shaman before he has finished raising the stones?' came a girl's voice, teasingly familiar. Was it Anet? He strained to see her, struggling to understand.

'You are high king, Red Bull, but you are not alone!' called the man who ruled the land where Carn Ava lay. 'Let the outland priest go.'

Khensu's arm tightened, muscles rope-hard beneath the skin, and Micail felt a warm trickle of blood run down his neck. The younger man smelled of woodsmoke and fear.

'If you wish to be king after your father, you should obey them now,' said Micail, but Khensu was not listening. Even through the tumult and uproar, the regular tramping of feet could be heard. Tjalan had returned with his soldiers.

Micail did not know whether to be glad or sorry, but he had no time to wonder. In a disciplined rush, the spearmen forced a wedge through friend and foe – and a single javelin arced through the air.

Later, Micail thought the guardsman's throw had been meant only to frighten the king. But Khattar, rising from his seat like an enraged bear, was caught full in the right shoulder. With a dull cry, he spun around and fell. Khensu's grip loosened, the knife dropping away from Micail's throat. Seizing the chance, Micail grabbed his captor's knife hand and twisted it away, leaping free – suddenly the soldiers were all around him.

A careful swallow reassured Micail that his throat had not been cut. He saw Khensu struggling with one of the soldiers, while Khattar lay curled up on the ground, cursing and gripping his pierced shoulder. Micail broke through the protective circle of soldiers and knelt at the king's side, prying up the man's bloody fingers to examine the damage. Khattar gazed up at him with uncomprehending fury as Micail drove the heel of his own hand hard against the wound to control the bleeding. Turning, he drew a deep breath.

'Be still!' It was the voice that had helped raise the stone, and it shocked the crowd to silence. 'King Khattar lives!'

'Return to your firesides! We will hold council in the morning—' Tjalan's voice echoed his, and if it held no compulsion, still everyone recognized the note of command. Slowly the crowd began to disperse. Tjalan bent over and placed his hand upon Micail's shoulder.

'Are you all right?'

'I'll live,' said Micail tightly, 'and so will he. Fetch me a strap and a pad of cloth!' Not until Micail had finished binding Khattar's wound did he look up at his cousin. 'This was an evil deed.'

Tjalan only grinned. 'What, are you sorry I rescued you?'

'The boy was already panicking. In another moment I would have talked myself free.'

'Perhaps—' The prince's hawklike gaze rested for a moment upon his guards, who had taken up position around them. 'But this moment was bound to come. As well now as later, wouldn't you say?'

No, thought Micail with a grimace, *better never. Rajasta's prophecy did not predict this day* . . . but some inner warning kept him silent.

FIFTEEN

During high summer in the marshes, the skies sometimes stayed clear for as long as a week. Standing in full sunlight with closed eyes, Damisa could almost imagine herself basking in the radiant heat of Ahtarrath. Even in the shade of the enclosure they had built for Selast to dwell in during the month of seclusion that preceded marriage, it was warm.

Too warm, she thought, fanning her cheeks with her hand. *I have grown used to living in the mists*, and then, *I have been in this land too long.* And yet if they had been in the Sea Kingdoms, she still would not have had Selast to herself forever.

As Iriel and Elis stripped off the robe Selast had worn to her ritual bath in the Red Spring, sunlight falling through the branches that thatched the enclosure dappled her skin like the hide of a fawn. Five years in the fogs of the new land had faded her bronze skin to gold, and constant physical labor had given her angular limbs a wiry strength and a grace in movement that reminded Damisa once more of some creature more graceful than humankind. But Selast was not a fawn, she thought with a sudden pang; she was a young mare with a thick mane of wavy black hair and fire in her dark eyes.

'And now for the robe—' said Iriel, lifting the folds of blue linen in her arms, 'and then we will crown you with flowers!' She looked around her, frowning as she realized the basket was empty. 'Kestil and the other children were to have gathered them this morning! If they have forgotten . . .'

'I'll run down to the village,' said Elis, starting for the door.

'If both of you go, you can cover the ground more quickly,' put in Damisa. 'I will stay to watch over our bride.'

When they had gone, Selast paced about the enclosure. She picked up the white linen shift, and then the blue gown – made of linen from flax they had grown themselves and dyed with native woad. It was not quite the blue worn by the priestesses of Caratra at home, but close enough to make Damisa uncomfortable. To don that blue was to offer oneself to the service of the Mother. Damisa felt a little ill at the thought of Selast's slender body swollen with child.

'Are you nervous?'

'Nervous?' Selast answered with the quick turn of the head that Damisa had learned to love. 'A little, I suppose. What if I forget my lines?'

Damisa did not think it very likely. They had been trained in memorization since they were chosen for the Temple as children.

'Nervous about being married, I mean.'

'To Kalaran?' Selast laughed. 'I have known him since I was nine years old, even before we were chosen as acolytes, though I have to admit I didn't think much about him until that night last year when we were looking for Iriel. He always seemed so angry with everyone. It wasn't until then that I realized how guilty he still feels for surviving when Kalhan and Lanath and the others were lost. That's why he's so . . . sarcastic sometimes. He's trying to hide his pain.'

'Oh, is that the reason?' Damisa heard the sarcasm in her own voice and tried to smile. 'Are you marrying him from pity, then, instead of duty?'

Selast stood still finally, staring at her with a frown. 'Perhaps a little of both. And at least we are friends. Does it matter? This day had to come.'

'In Ahtarrath, yes, but here?' Damisa rose suddenly and gripped Selast's slim shoulders. 'We have no Temple, and little remains of our priesthood. Why should we ruin our lives in order to breed up more?'

Selast's eyes widened, and she lifted her own hand to touch Damisa's hair. 'Are you jealous of Kalaran? It won't change anything between you and me . . .'

But it already has, thought Damisa, staring down at her friend, wild-eyed. 'You will sleep by his side and care for his home and bear his children, and you think you will not change?' She realized that she was shouting as Selast recoiled. 'You don't have to do this!' she pleaded, 'Remember Taret's tales of the island to the north where the warrior women train? We could go there and be together—'

Selast shook her head sharply, and with an abrupt movement slipped from Damisa's grasp. 'And to think that I was always the rebel, and you the proper priestess with her nose in the air! You don't mean what you're saying, Damisa – you are Tiriki's acolyte!

'Kalaran needs me,' Selast continued. 'That night on the mountain he told me that after the Sinking he lost all faith – he could no longer feel the unseen powers. But when we clung together, lost and shivering, he realized that he was not alone.'

'*I* need you!' Damisa exclaimed, but Selast shook her head.

'You *want* me, but you are strong enough to live without me. Do you think it was so we might seek our own pleasure that we were spared when so many others died?'

'Damn those who died, and damn Tiriki, too!' muttered Damisa. 'Selast – I love you—' she reached out to take the other girl in her arms again, her heart full of everything she couldn't say. She let go quickly as the gate swung open and Iriel and Elis pushed through, their arms filled with flowers. Face flaming, tongue-tied, Damisa fled the bride-house, and only the sound of laughter followed her.

* * *

273

The wedding procession was coming, curving around through the forest and starting up the path that led up the eastern slope of the Tor. Tiriki glimpsed their bright robes through the trees as the chime of bells was carried through the wind. Carefully, Chedan lit a waxed splinter from the lamp and thrust it into the kindling laid on the altar stone.

The wind whipped the spark into flame and fluttered the draperies of the priests and priestesses who waited within the circle of stones. The weight of necklet and diadem felt strange to Tiriki, who for so long had worn no ornament at all, and the silken draperies oddly smooth to one who had become accustomed to leather and coarse wool.

I will remember, thought Tiriki as the wedding party crested the rim of the hill, *but I will not weep. I will cast no shadow on Selast and Kalaran's day.*

Tiriki and Micail had been married in the temple that crowned the Star Mountain – the most sacred precinct of Ahtarrath. Their union was witnessed by Deoris and Reio-ta and the senior clergy of the Temple, and blessed by the old Guardian Rajasta in one of the last rites he had performed before he died.

Now it was Chedan who stood to welcome the bridal pair with the sacred symbols that adorned his tabard gleaming in the sun. Instead of the Star Mountain, their temple was this rough circle of stones atop the Tor. But though this sanctuary in the marsh lacked Ahtarrath's majesty, Tiriki had learned enough in the past five years to suspect it might be a match in power.

Micail had been resplendent in white, the band of gold across his brow no brighter than his hair, and she had for the first time donned the blue robe and fillet of Caratra, though she herself had been little more than a child. *Did I seek to begin bearing too young?* she wondered then. *Was that why I could never birth a living child? Until we came here*, she added as Kestil and Domara came dancing ahead of the procession, strewing the path with flowers. But Selast had reached her twentieth year, and life in this wilderness had made her healthy and strong. Her babes would thrive.

Domara emptied her basket of flowers and came running to her mother's side. Tiriki gathered her up gratefully, delighting in the child's warm weight and the wildflower scent of her red hair. *Micail is lost to me, but in his daughter, a part of him lives still . . .*

Her preoccupation had kept her from hearing Chedan's words of welcome. She had been so excited at her own wedding, so completely focused on Micail, that she had scarcely heard them that first time, either. Already the mage was binding Kalaran's right wrist to Selast's left and passing them, still linked, over the flickering flame. Then, still bound together, the couple processed sunwise around the altar stone.

Chedan led them through the formal oaths in which they promised to bring up their children in the service of Light, and act as priest and priestess to each other. There were no words of love, Tiriki noticed now, but for herself and Micail the love had been there already.

The stars themselves foretold our union! her heart cried, released by the stress of the moment from the control that had enabled her to survive. *So why were we torn apart so soon?*

Kalaran's voice wavered, but Selast's responses were loud and firm. They had respect for each other, and perhaps in time the love would grow. As the lengthy oaths were finished, Chedan lifted his hands in benediction and faced them across the fire.

'To this woman and this man grant wisdom and courage, O Great Unknown! Grant them peace and understanding! Grant purity of purpose and true knowledge to the two souls who stand here before you. Give unto them growth according to their needs, and the fortitude to do their duty in the fullest measure. O Thou Who Art, both female and male and more than either, let these two live in Thee, and for Thee.'

This part, Tiriki remembered. Bound wrist to wrist, she

had felt Micail's warmth as her own, and in the invocation, something further, a third essence that enfolded them both in a power that united them even as it transcended. She could sense that sphere of energy now, even though she stood on its fringes, aware for a moment not only of the link between Selast and Kalaran, but of the web of energy that connected everyone in the circle, and beyond that, the land around them, resonating into realms she now knew existed within and beyond it, but could not see.

'*O Thou Who art,*' Tiriki's heart cried, still thinking of Micail. '*Let us all live in Thee!*

It was strange, thought Chedan as he set down the deer rib he had been gnawing, how scarcity changed one's attitude to food. Watching Tiriki and the others tuck into the feast which the folk of the Lake Village had created to honor the newlyweds, he remembered how, in the Ancient Land, the priesthood had seen food as a distraction from the cultivation of the soul. But in the Sea Kingdoms, whatever land and sea might lack, the trading ships could supply. In Alkonath, not so many years ago, Chedan had been on the verge of becoming portly. He could count his own ribs now.

There had been times, particularly during the winter months when the only thing left to eat was millet gruel, when Chedan had wondered why he fought so hard to keep the body alive. But even the Temple had recognized that the pleasures of the table and the marriage-bed helped reconcile men to incarnation in physical bodies, whose lessons were necessary to the evolution of the soul. And so he chewed slowly, savoring the interplay of salt and fat and the flavors of the herbs with which the roast had been rubbed, and the juicy red meat of the deer.

'That was a beautiful ceremony,' Liala commented. 'And the power in the Tor is – even more than we had thought. Is it not?' She had been ill for much of the spring, but she had refused to miss this celebration.

'I suppose someone must have known that, even here, because they built the circle of stones to focus the power,' observed Rendano, who was sitting on the other side of the table. He frowned as if doubting that these primitives could manage such a feat.

'We are not the first of our kind to come here,' said Alyssa in a flat voice. 'The Temple of the Sun that stood beside the river Naradek on the coast of this land is in ruins now, but the wisewoman of these people is an initiate of sorts.'

'Of sorts!' Rendano said disdainfully. 'Is that all we will leave behind us? What will *her* children know of the greatness of Atlantis?' He gestured toward Selast, who was attempting to feed a piece of bannock to a laughing Kalaran.

'Atlantis is lost,' Chedan said quietly, 'but the Mysteries remain. There is much for us to do here.'

'Yes . . . Do you remember the maze below the temple on the Star Mountain?' Tiriki asked then. 'Was it not intended to teach the way to pass between the worlds?'

'Only in legends,' Rendano scoffed, 'such devices are a training for the soul.'

'That night when Iriel was lost . . .' she struggled to find the right words. 'I walked the maze in the heart of the hill and came to a place that was not this world.'

'You wandered in the spirit while you slept on the mountainside,' Rendano said with a thin smile.

'No, I believe her,' objected Liala. 'I followed her into the passage made by the waters of the White Spring and went back to the entrance to wait for her when my hip pained me. She did not emerge that way, and we found her on top of the Tor.'

'Then there was another exit—'

'The acolytes have scoured that hill by daylight and found none,' observed Chedan. 'I have myself explored the passage to the spring, without finding the tunnel – I believe it is there, though I find no rationale for it.

'You have spoken much with Taret, lately . . .' Chedan

turned to Alyssa. 'What does she say?' Washed, combed, and dressed in her ceremonial garments, the seeress seemed to have recovered some degree of mental and emotional stability. They might as well take advantage of her fleeting moments of clarity.

'Much that I may not tell,' answered Alyssa with a smile that reminded them of the woman they had known in Ahtarrath. 'But I have *seen*—' her voice wavered, and Liala put out a hand to steady her. 'I have seen a crystal hill with the pattern of the maze gleaming with light.' She shuddered and looked around as if wondering what she was doing there.

Liala cast an accusing glance at Chedan and then handed Alyssa an earthen mug of water.

'Thank you, Alyssa,' Tiriki said softly, patting her shoulder. 'That is what I was trying to say.' She turned to the others. 'Perhaps it was some rare conjunction of the stars that opened the way, or perhaps it was only meant for me. But I wonder – if we were to cut the pattern of the maze upon the outside of the hill, somehow I feel – that we might learn how to reach the Otherworld by walking it. And who knows what we might learn then?'

'Fancies and notions,' Rendano muttered, not so softly.

But Chedan frowned thoughtfully. 'For so long, our work here has been directed toward mere survival. Is it time now to build on that foundation, to gather our singers together and create something new?'

'Do you mean we should raise stones and build a great city around the Tor? I do not think the marsh folk would be very comfortable there . . .' Liala said dubiously.

'No,' Chedan murmured. 'Cities arise for a reason. I think this place will never be able to support such a population, nor should it. I am beginning to glimpse something different. Perhaps . . . Let us begin by simply tracing the maze upon the surface of the hill and learning to walk that spiral path . . . I think that what we have been granted is an opportunity to create in this place the kind of spiritual harmony that once existed on the Star Mountain.'

'A new Temple?' asked Rendano doubtfully.

'Yes, but it will be unlike anything that has gone before.'

> 'Young Otter is a furry snake—
> Ai, ya, ai ya ya!
> What a hunter he will make,
> Ai, ya, ya . . .'

A dozen voices joined in as Otter rose from his bench and gyrated around the circle, pretending to pounce on one or another feaster as he passed.

In honor of the wedding, the marsh folk had brewed a quantity of something they called heather beer. It was only moderately alcoholic, but as the Atlanteans usually abstained from alcohol, and the natives drank only at festivals, even a little went a long way. Though she had at first grimaced at the mix of herbal flavors only slightly lightened by a hint of honey, Damisa had progressed to an expansive enjoyment that kept her going back to the skin that hung from the oak tree for more. After cup number four she had stopped counting.

> 'Elis digging in the mud—
> Ai ya, ai, ya, ya!
> Tell us if you find some food!
> Ai, ya, ya . . .'

She noted without surprise that the singers had run out of villagers to tease and were starting on the Atlanteans. Such foolishness would never have been tolerated at home. Nor would there have been so public a celebration after a mere wedding. It was a measure of the degree to which the new and the old inhabitants of the Tor had become one community that the villagers had offered to prepare a feast for the newly-weds in the broad meadow by the shore. Tiriki and Chedan had accepted only after some serious debate with the others. In Atlantis, the matings of the priestly class had been occasions of high ceremony, not of bad jokes and strong drink.

But why should I care? Damisa asked herself as the buzz in her ears grew louder. *Neither by the old custom nor the new will there be a mate for me . . .*

> *'Liala in your gown of blue—*
> *Ai ya, ai ya, ya!*
> *Won't you tell us what to do?*
> *Ai, ya, ya . . .'*

The game required that the person being 'honored' get up and dance around the circle. Liala, her cheeks flushed and her eyes bright, made a slow circle and then, to the accompaniment of enthusiastic cheering, bestowed a hearty kiss on the leader of the singers, a grey-bearded elder who was the closest thing the villagers had to a bard.

> *'Selast, like the wind you run—*
> *Ai, ya, ai ya, ya!*
> *Won't you stop and have some fun?*
> *Ai, ya, ya . . .'*

Not anymore . . . thought Damisa, glumly. *She'll be hobbled now, at Kalaran's beck and call . . .*

The brilliance of the long summer's day was softening now to a luminous twilight. Treetops edged the clearing with an interlace of branches, black against the shell pink of the western sky, but eastward, the long slope of the Tor still caught the light. For a moment it seemed to Damisa that the glow came from within. Or perhaps it was only the drink, she told herself then, for when she blinked and looked again, all she could see was a dim bulk above the trees.

> *'Kalaran taught us how to row—*
> *Ai ya, ai ya, ya!*
> *Teach him how to tup his doe!*
> *Ai, ya, ya . . .'*

Someone called out in the marsh folk tongue and was answered by cheers and laughter. It took Damisa a few moments to realize they were calling for volunteers to escort the bridal couple to their bedding. She allowed herself one look at her beloved. Selast's flower crown was askew, her eyes bright with mingled excitement and apprehension.

'Go with your *husband* . . .' she muttered, lifting her cup in ironic salutation, 'and when you lie in his arms, may you wish that you were still in mine.'

The escort returned and the dancing started up once more. Reidel had taken over one of the drums. His teeth flashed white in his dark face as he grinned, his fingers flickering above the taut skin. She observed a little resentfully that he seemed to be having a good time. Some of the sailors whirled by hand in hand with village girls. Iriel was sitting with Elis on a log at the edge of the clearing. Otter stood by them, and as Damisa watched, Iriel laughed at something he said and allowed him to lead her into the dance.

As Damisa got up to refill her cup, she encountered Tiriki, who was getting ready to leave the celebration, holding a sleepy Domara by the hand. Chedan and the other senior clergy had already gone.

'It is well past her bedtime,' said Tiriki with a smile, 'but she did want to see the dancing.'

'It certainly is different from the way we celebrated things in the Temple,' Damisa answered sourly, remembering the exquisitely prepared meals and the stately dances.

'But you can see why. Survival is so uncertain here. It's no wonder that when people have food and fire in abundance they revel in it. It's an affirmation of life for them,

281

and for us, as well. But now it's time for sleep, isn't it, my darling?' Tiriki added as Domara yawned. 'Will you walk with us back to the Tor?'

Damisa shook her head. 'I'm not ready to seek my bed.'

Tiriki eyed the cup in Damisa's hand and frowned, as if considering whether or not to exert her authority. 'Don't stay here and brood. I know that you and Selast were close, but—'

'But it is possible to live unmated, you would say? Like you?' Even as Damisa spoke she knew the beer had betrayed her.

Tiriki straightened, eyes flashing, and Damisa took an involuntary step backward.

'Like me?' Tiriki spoke with quiet intensity. 'Pray to the gods that you never know the joy I had, lest you also one day feel my pain.' She turned abruptly and strode away, leaving Damisa staring stupidly.

Events after that became a little hazy. At one point she looked up to see Otter and Iriel heading for the bushes, arms entwined. She got to her feet, blinking. Only a few people were left beside the fire. Reidel was one of them.

'My lady, are you well?' He came quickly toward her. 'Can I help you back to the House of Maidens?'

'Well? Very well . . .' Damisa giggled and steadied herself against his shoulder. He smelled of heather beer and sweat. 'But I'm . . . a little drunk.' She hiccuped and laughed again. 'P'raps we'd better wait . . . a while.'

'Walking will help,' he said firmly, tucking her arm in his. 'We'll take the path that circles the Tor.'

Damisa was not entirely sure that she wanted to lose the warm buzz of the beer. But she had noticed before that Reidel's arm was strong and comforting. Holding on to him did make her feel better, and when they sat down to rest on a grassy bank with a view of moonlight on the water, it seemed natural to rest her head against his shoulder. Gradually her dizziness began to ease.

It took a little while for her to notice that fine tremors were shaking the hard muscle beneath her cheek. She straightened, shaking her head.

'You are trembling – are you cold, or was I too heavy for you?'

'No . . .' His voice, too, seemed strained. 'Never. I was foolish to think I could . . . that you would not know . . .'

'Know what?'

He released her abruptly and turned away, his body a dark shape against the stars. 'How hard it is for me to hold you and do no more . . .'

That heather beer has loosened your control too, she thought then, *or you would not dare to say so!* But why should she deny him, she wondered then, since Selast was lost to her?

'Then do it—' she said, grasping his arm and drawing him back to face her.

Reidel came closer in a single smooth movement that took her by surprise, one arm tightening around her waist while the other lifted to tangle in her hair. In another moment he had pulled her against him and his lips sought hers, at first tentative, then hard as her own need responded to his. The stars whirled overhead as he bore her down upon the grass, his hands first questioning, then demanding, as lacings and pins gave way.

Her breath came faster as a slow fire that owed nothing to the heather beer began to burn beneath her skin. In those moments when his lips were not otherwise busied, Reidel's voice was a whispered accompaniment of wonder and adoration.

This is not right, thought Damisa in a moment of clear thought as he released her in order to pull off his tunic. *I am only driven by lust, and he by love . . .*

But then Reidel rolled back and his wandering hand found the sanctuary between her thighs. Desire descended upon Damisa like the coming of a goddess, melting all her thoughts of restraint, and she welcomed his hard strength as his body covered hers.

Tiriki lay wakeful upon her narrow bed, but sleep would not come. She could hear the drumming from the fire circle like the throbbing pulse of a man and woman in the throes of love. Her lips twitched with wry amusement. There had been gasps and laughter from among the bushes as she carried Domara back to bed, and she had been grateful the child was not awake to ask her what was making the noise. Weddings were celebrated at times propitious for matings, so it was no wonder if others found themselves stirred by the same energies.

Unfortunately she could feel that yearning as well as anyone else, and she was alone. She could imagine herself in Micail's arms, but the stimulation of memory was no substitute for the exchange of magnetism that took place with a physical partner.

Oh my beloved . . . it is not only my body that longs for yours . . . when our spirits touched, we remade the world.

From beyond the curtain Tiriki could hear Domara's regular breathing, and an occasional snore from Metia, who still served as the child's nursemaid. Moving softly so as not to wake them, Tiriki got up and pulled a shawl over the shift in which she slept.

She would go and see if Taret, who customarily kept late hours, was also wakeful. The older woman's wisdom had supported her through many crises – perhaps Taret could teach her how to survive the endless loneliness of the coming years.

'Will it be permitted . . . do you think they will they let us marry?'

Damisa came back to full awareness with a start as she realized that Reidel was talking to her. He had been speaking for quite some time, actually, words of love which she had ignored as she tried to understand just what had happened between them and why.

'Marriage?' she looked at him in surprise. Reidel had always seemed so self-contained. Who would have suspected he had so much passion dammed up inside?

'Did you think I would have dared to touch you if my intent had been dishonorable?' He sat up, shocked.

Do you think that if mine had been honorable I would have let you? Damisa bit back the bitter words, remembering that she had wanted this as much as he, if for different reasons. She sat up in turn, reaching for her gown.

'The matings of acolytes are ordained by the stars . . .'

'But I am of the priesthood now, so surely—'

'Nothing is sure!' snapped Damisa, driven beyond patience suddenly. 'Least of all me! Do you consider what we just did a commitment? I descend from the princes of Alkonath and may not mingle my blood with any lesser breed!'

'But you lay with me . . .' he repeated, uncomprehending.

'Yes. I did. I have needs, just like you—'

'Not like me . . .' Reidel drew a long, shuddering breath. She felt a twinge of compunction as she realized he understood her at last. '*I* love you.'

'Well . . .' she said when the silence had gone on too long. 'I am sorry.'

Reidel grabbed his tunic and belt and got to his feet, slinging them over his shoulder as if disdaining to hide his nakedness. 'Sorry! I could find a cruder word.' But he did not say it, and by that she understood that what he felt for her was indeed love. For a moment she saw the graceful line of muscled shoulder and tapering hips stark against the stars, then he turned and strode down the path, leaving her alone.

I spoke truth, she told herself. *I don't love him!* So why, she wondered, was her last sight of that departing figure suddenly blurred by tears?

SIXTEEN

The evening is cold and the wind plucks at hair and garments like a mischievous child, but Chedan's travel cloak
keeps him warm. His body is young again, responding to
every command of his will. Grinning, he lurches through
rough-leafed high hedges, following a deer path downhill.

The sudden cry of a bird of prey rips through the silence
– 'Skiriiiii!' – the falcon is at once behind him and above
him. Instinctively Chedan ducks, but there is no attack.

After a moment, he moves forward toward the glowing
ring of standing stones. Five great trilithons loom through
the mist, and in their shaping he recognizes the touch of
Atlantis. But the statue of a dragon stands between him and
the stones. He pauses, listening, as a voice thinned by pain
but oddly familiar keens, 'Tiriki, Tiriki.'

'Are you there?' Chedan sings. 'Micail? Is it you?'

But the dragon has become a falcon with Micail's face,
beating against the grey mist with shining dark wings.

'Osinarmen? You would disguise yourself? Here?'

'Skiriiiii!' The same savage cry is his only answer.

'Wait!' Chedan calls, but Micail's spirit has flown into a
darker dreamland, and though Chedan is mage, and great
in power, he dares not follow.

'This is why you have failed to find him.'

Chedan turns but sees only the glowing ring of stones.

'He will not recognize you. Though he needs your counsel

as never before, you can no longer guide him. Least of all here! He believes you are dead. He fears you bear a message that he does not wish to receive. But it does not matter – the test is for Micail. By his own deeds, he must endure or fall. You cannot prevent him from fulfilling his fate.'

'Who are you?' Chedan sings, commanding. 'Reveal thy truth!'

'Alas, I cannot be revealed to one who will not see. When you can see,' the voice murmurs, 'you shall. But men are never so entangled in the past as when they glimpse the future . . .' The voice becomes a hurricane, hurling him head over heels away from the ring of stones.

'Go back, Chedan,' the voice commands. 'When the time comes for you to pass on your legacy, the way will open. You will not wonder who or when or why – you will know. But until then – go back. Complete the work that you must do.'

Chedan woke sweating in his rough blankets, his mind still reeling from images of standing stones dancing wildly, whirling away in the mist.

Micail! his spirit cried. *Where are you?*

Since coming to the Tor he had dreamed of Micail often. At times they were back in Ahtarrath or even in the Ancient Land. They would be walking together or sitting over a carafe of Hellenic wine, indulging in the kind of far-ranging conversations both men loved. Chedan was half aware that the talks were a kind of teaching, as if in sleep he was trying to pass on all the wisdom he had not been given time to impart in the waking world.

Where, he wondered, was all that information going? He knew that Tiriki, in her secret heart, believed her beloved was still alive somewhere in this world. But Chedan knew that it was equally possible he had been meeting with Micail in his dreams to prepare Micail's spirit for rebirth in this new land . . . Yet this last vision, if that was what it had been, was different. He felt the same sense of release that

287

always followed trance. And though Micail had fled from him, Chedan had been able to contact him.

But I was young again. The memory of that vigor still filled his awareness – and yet with every moment, his body reminded him more painfully that it had served his soul for over seventy years. And the five years that had passed since they arrived at the Tor had been hard ones. He would not be sorry to lay down this aching flesh and fare to the Halls of Karma, even though it meant he must face judgment.

He shook his head ruefully. '*Complete the work that you must do,*' the voice had said. At this moment Chedan would be doing well to get out of bed. *Perhaps it was a promise,* he thought hopefully.

A brisk wind stroked across the plain, flattening the new grass beneath the stalks bleached by winter, then letting the blades spring back one by one – green, silver, and green again.

The afternoon sun had warmed the air, but the day was fading, and the hope that had lifted Micail's heart contracted like some winterchilled bloom. A memory of the dream that work had driven from his head returned – he had been a dragon, or a hawk – some creature fierce and wild – struggling wildly to escape the stones. And once more, Chedan had been there.

Micail eyed the men working before him ruefully. Tjalan's dream was, he now realized, simply to create something that would outlast them all; but there were times when the five great trilithons seemed to project an arrogance beyond even the imaginings of a prince . . .

The unfinished sarsen ring was less daunting, at least to Micail, perhaps because it was incomplete. Twenty-four uprights had been raised around the trilithons, including one shorter stone that allowed even casual users to sight down the Avenue to the point of the midsummer sunrise . . . The six missing stones would be hauled in next summer, by levies which would probably be drawn from the Blue Bull tribe.

Six more lintels had already been brought in, and two of them raised to better suggest the final effect – a Sun Wheel a hundred feet across. Finding and transporting the remaining twenty-four stones to complete the pattern might take another year of labor.

Thanks largely to the efforts of Timul and Elara, the king had survived the wound's fever, but the javelin blow had permanently ruined his shoulder. Khattar would never again wield any battle-ax, of bronze or of orichalcum. There was talk, mostly from the younger warriors, that he ought to abdicate as high king and allow Khensu to take his place. But only the matriarchs could make that decision, and the Women's Side had conspicuously refused to decide.

Did they too fear Prince Tjalan's spearmen? There were times when Micail himself felt uneasy with the continual display of Alkonan potency, yet he had to admit that Tjalan's show of strength might be necessary. Until Khattar's ability to rule was proven, the Red Bull tribe had declared they would provide no further assistance. So far the other tribes had not joined the rebellion, but Micail knew that they could not rely on their full support.

They think we have only a hundred swords to defend ourselves, and it is true – for now. Luckily for us, the tribes want to see the henge completed too. When the last stone is set in place, they will make their move – but it will be the worst time for them to do so! They cannot begin to imagine what powers we will be able to draw on once the circuit of force is closed.

'Lord Prince, dark is coming,' said the old man who acted as foreman for the White Bull work gang. 'We go back to our fires?'

'Yes, it is time,' Micail nodded.

He sat down against one of the half-polished stones and watched the men walk away one by one toward their camp by the river. He would not have had to go far, either, to find food and shelter and the company of his own kind, but he found himself reluctant to move. Too much speech – that was the problem – the petty bickering, the constant maneuvering for status, was driving him mad.

He continued to sit, half watching the cryptic play of twilight and clouds, thinking that if he came in late enough, he might persuade Cleta or Elara to bring him some food in his hut, away from the others. It occurred to him that he rarely felt any need to be on his guard against the acolytes – not even after Elara had told him that if the king became too insistent that he take a mate, she herself was willing to bear him a child. But she had not pressed him, and now as he sat alone in the sunset he found himself beginning to actually consider her offer, if only because it distracted him from the disturbing memory of how Anet had felt in his arms.

Just thinking about her lithe dancer's body lit a fire in his flesh. He frowned, the half-illicit visions washed away by the sudden memory of a native legend that he had recently heard, in which the stones in some of the older circles were said to wake with the darkness, and even dance at the times of the great festivals. The stones here were already moving toward awareness, the whispers ran.

The original ring of stones had obviously been part of a simple cremation cemetery, like the earthwork that had so frightened the acolytes on their journey here. Most of the other circles had apparently been built for that purpose as well. Yet it could not be denied that nightfall always made this place seem a little more distant, and at the same time a bit larger, turning it into a looming presence that made it difficult to think about other things. Sighing, Micail got to his feet and, trying not to think at all, began the long walk back across the plain.

That night, sleep was slow in coming. But in the still hour before the dawn his troubled dreams yielded to a vision of far green hills and a golden pathway whereon he saw Tiriki approaching, robed in blue light.

Spring was always a time of hope in the marshlands, when the earth grew green and the sky clamored with the cries of migrating birds. Whenever the waterfowl settled on the pools, their muted calling turned even more musical, as if the wind gods themselves were singing hymns for the earth. It was a time to gather eggs and tender new leaves, and the increased food supply renewed the confidence and the energy of those who lived around the lake. It was a time of fair weather and improved circumstances, but it was also a time to get back to work on the spiral maze, which after the wedding feast for Kalaran and Selast they had started to cut into the Tor.

Tiriki straightened, digging the knuckles of her left hand into the small of her back to ease its aching, while she rested the antler points that tipped her hoe on the ground. *The priests' caste was never bred for such labor*, she thought ruefully, surveying her segment of the new pathway of the spiral maze that they were making around the hill. The shadow she cast was, she observed, quite slender, and what flesh she had, she knew, was mostly muscle. It occurred to her that she was probably healthier than she had ever been.

The same was true of the rest of them. Ahead and behind her she glimpsed other diggers, bending and rising as their hoes dug into the soft ground. She and Chedan and a few of the others had sung to the earth along the track and loosened it a little, but she doubted that even an experienced stand of singers could have shifted so many particles at once . . . though they certainly could have moved that boulder by the foot of the path much more easily.

Just ahead of her, Domara stabbed her digging stick into the ground and laughed. She had turned five the preceding winter, and a recent growth spurt had stolen away the plump sweetness of babyhood forever. Now Tiriki could glimpse the child she was becoming. Not the woman – thank the gods, that was still far in the future – but the slim, leggy youngster with the mop of red curls. *She is going to be like Micail*, thought Tiriki, *tall and strong*.

The adults might complain about the seemingly unending regimen of strenuous labor, but the children were in their element, happy to dig until they were muddy from head to heels. If only the youngsters could have been depended upon to stick to the work, the elders could have left the job to them, thought Tiriki as the divots flew. But even Domara, who was so insistent on helping in every grownup task that they called her 'little priestess,' could be distracted by a butterfly.

As Tiriki hacked into the earth again she felt something give. The bindings that held the antler tine to the stock were loose again. She sighed. 'Domara, my love, will you take this back down to Heron and ask if he can fix it?'

When the child had started down the hill, Tiriki picked up a bone shoulder-blade and knelt on the path to smooth the earth and shift the displaced dirt to the downhill side. Soon it would be time to stop. She had cleared a full length this morning, and had almost reached the point where Kalaran's section began. Except for Liala and Alyssa, who were sick, and Selast, who was pregnant, everyone in the community was working on the maze, even the Lake folk, although they found this kind of exercise as foreign to their normal lifestyle as did any Atlantean priest or priestess.

Chedan had been forbidden to work. Of course he had protested, saying that inaction would only make him feel worse, but she knew how his bones pained him. He had done his part and more, she had told him, when he had taken the image of the pathway through the hill from Tiriki's memory and translated it into the pattern of an oval maze that wound back and forth along the slopes of the Tor. Starting as if it meant to go straight up the spine of the hill, the way led sunwise around the middle slope and then dipped and turned back. It circled widdershins almost to the beginning before dropping again and skirting the base of the hill, only to turn and start upward again, a little above the initial path. From there it wound back and forth to nearly touch the summit, but instead doubled back in another curve that brought it at last to the stone circle at the crest.

It had taken a year's effort to dig out the full three-foot width of pathway for the initial circuit alone. Now they were working down and around on the first return course. The rest of the way was carefully marked out by sticks thrust into the soil, but already it had been trodden often enough to wear a narrow footpath, scarcely wider than a deer trail, into the ground.

Tiriki swayed with a faint sense of vertigo as she visualized the maze – even Chedan's first sketches had dizzied her, reminding her of a symbol or inscription she was certain she had seen before, though she could not remember where or when. The mage had assured her that its shape was unlike any character or hieroglyph that he was familiar with, and Dannetrasa, who was even more widely read, echoed his conclusion, yet the notion continued to haunt her.

Ancient or new, the pattern worked. She and Chedan had walked it more than once, and each time felt the proximity of another world and touched the inner spirit of the land. This was not the Temple that the prophecies had described, but its power was profound and manifest. When the path was completed, anyone, she was sure, would be able to follow it, and they would find a blessing.

Tiriki scraped the bone blade across the soil again, breathing deeply as the rich scent filled the air. Here, beneath the trees that clothed the base of the Tor, the earth was rich with the humus of many centuries of fallen leaves. The digging would be more difficult on the grassy upper slopes, where the rocky substrate was barely covered with topsoil. She rooted her fingers in the earth and felt its strength flow up into her, as if she were herself part of the complex of life on the Tor, growing from wind and rain, sun and soil—

'*Drink deep . . . reach high . . . we will survive the storm . . .*'

Startled, she lifted her hands and the eerie voice silenced.

Storm? wondered Tiriki, gazing at the cloudless sky. But the old ship gong was ringing to announce the noonday meal, and her belly told her it would be welcome.

Long red rays from the westering sun slanted through the trees above the hedges. To the east, a sliver of moon was rising over the Tor. Damisa stood in the pool of the Red Spring, ladling water with her hands and then letting it pour down over her body. The iron-rich water had passed first through a shallow pool where it absorbed some slight heat from the sun, but its chill still set goosebumps in her flesh.

Taret had taught them to seek the spring, weather permitting, on the day after their monthly courses were done. This, too, was a rite of passage. '*Women are like the moon,*' the wisewoman would say, '*every month we start new.*' Damisa hoped it was true. Sometimes she felt that she would like to start her whole life over. It was all wasted anyway. She had been born into the luxuries of Alkonan nobility and trained to serve the Temple of Light, not to work herself ragged in the gritty world of hoes and cookpots.

For a time, at least, she had found some hope for joy – or at least a little happiness – but that was plainly over now. Not only was Selast lost to her, fixated on her approaching child, but Damisa herself had driven Reidel away. She liked to think that it was honor that kept her from seeking him out again when all she had desired was the comfort of someone's arms. But in all this time, she had found no one else to whom she was willing to turn. She dribbled more water over her head and watched the drops catch like jewels, twinkling red and gold in her long auburn hair.

On impulse, she turned and kissed her hand to the slender rind of pearl that floated in the twilit sky.

> 'New moon, true moon—
> Bring me new luck soon!'

A silly child's rhyme, Damisa thought with a smile, wondering what the moon would have wanted to teach her today.

A sudden burst of wind stirred the treetops and she shivered. As she turned toward the bank where her clothing waited, she remembered that she had promised to bring Alyssa some water from the spring. She stretched to hold a ceramic jug beneath the little waterfall that fed the pool, then climbed out and began to scrub her skin vigorously with a woolen towel.

By the time Damisa reached the hut where the seeress lived, dusk was laying gentle blue veils across the land. She tapped gently on the doorpost, but heard no answer. These days the Grey Adept slept a good deal, but one or another of the saji women who tended her should have been somewhere near. She was tempted to simply leave the jug by the door and go away, but as she bent, she heard an odd sound from within.

Hesitantly she drew aside the hide that curtained the door and saw what she at first took to be a pile of grey cloth heaped beside the hearth. Then she realized that it was shaking and from it came the strange noise. A swift step brought her to Alyssa's side.

'Where are your helpers?' Damisa said, as she carefully plucked the cloth away from the old woman's face and tried to straighten her contorting limbs. It occurred to her that whoever had been here had probably already gone to summon assistance. 'It's all right now – be easy – I'm here,' Damisa said, knowing even as she murmured the words that they were untrue. Alyssa was most definitely *not* all right.

'The circle is unbalanced!' the seeress muttered, 'If they use it they will die . . .'

'What? Who will die?' Damisa asked desperately. 'Tell me!'

'The Falcon of the Sun runs like a serpent in the sky . . .' Alyssa's eyes blinked open, staring wildly. 'The circle is square, but the sun goes round, while the stone unbound grows round with sound . . .'

For a moment then Damisa saw a plain where three vast squared arches stood within a circle of mighty pillars, as if Alyssa had somehow transmitted the image mind to mind. Then the woman's head began to twitch and Damisa had to struggle to keep her from battering it against the hearth-stones.

She heard muffled voices and looked up in relief to see Virja pull back the curtain. Then Chedan came limping in, with Tiriki following.

'She has not wakened?' the mage asked sharply.

'She has *spoken*,' answered Damisa, 'she even made *me* see what she . . . was looking at! But I couldn't understand it.'

The ruddy light cast by the fire on the Grey Adept's face created an illusion of health. But her closed eyes were sunken pools of shadow. She looked like a dead woman already, save that she was breathing . . .

Chedan lowered himself carefully to a stool and, leaning his weight on his carved staff, bent to take Alyssa's waxen hand in his own. 'Alyssa of Caris!' he said sternly. 'Neniath! You hear my voice, you know me. Out of space and time I do summon you, *return!*'

Virja was whispering to Tiriki, 'All day she was sleepy, first I could not get her to eat, and then I could not wake her—'

'I hear you, son of Naduil—' The words were strong and clear, but Alyssa's eyes remained tightly shut.

'Tell me, seeress, what do you see?'

'Joy where there has been sorrow – fear where there should be joy. The one who will open the door is among you, but look beyond him. Little singer—'

They all looked at Tiriki, since that was the meaning of

her name. Quickly she knelt between Chedan and Alyssa.

'I am here, Neniath. What would you say to me?'

'I say beware. Love is your foe – only through loss can that love be fulfilled. You preserved the Stone – but now it becomes the seed of Light. That must be planted deeper still.'

'The Omphalos Stone,' breathed Chedan, as if unaware that he had spoken the words aloud. He had once said he still had nightmares in which he alone had to wrestle it down to the ship . . .

With all else that was lost, thought Damisa, *why could not the Stone too have slipped beneath the sea?*

'You spoke of – a foe – disguised as love?' Tiriki was saying, with confusion. 'I do not understand! What must I *do?*'

'You will know . . .' Alyssa's voice weakened. 'But can you risk all . . . to gain all . . . ?' They listened tensely, but there was only a rasping as the seeress struggled to breathe.

'Alyssa, how do you fare?' Chedan asked, after a little while had passed.

'I am weary – and Ni-Terat awaits. Her dark veils wrap me round. Please – give me leave to go—'

The mage passed his hands above Alyssa's body, but his smile was sad. For a moment dappled light swirled above the body of the seeress, then faded away.

'Stay but a little while, my sister, and we will sing you on your journey,' the mage said gently.

Tiriki touched Damisa's arm. 'Go now and fetch the others—'

As Damisa ducked through the door, she heard Chedan's voice begin the Evening Hymn.

> '*Oh Maker of all things mortal,*
> *We call Thee at Day's ending.*
> *Oh Light beyond all shadows,*
> *This world of Forms transcending . . .*'

For many hours, the priests and priestesses sang in shifts to ease Alyssa's passing, but Chedan and Tiriki stayed with the Grey Adept until the end, hoping for another moment of clarity. Even when they were not seers, the sight of those who stood on the threshold of death often extended far indeed; but when she did speak again, Alyssa seemed to think she was on the isle of Caris where she had been born. It would have been cruelty to call her back again.

They agreed that Alyssa's body would be burned the next night, on top of the Tor. Until then, work on the path had been suspended. Domara was sent off with the village children to gather wildflowers to adorn the bier. It relieved the child from the sorrow of her elders, but Tiriki thought the house seemed very silent without her. With no other duties to keep her occupied, Tiriki decided to join Liala on her afternoon visit to Taret's hut, slowing her swift steps to match the careful progress of the other priestess, who could not get around these days without a walking stick.

'We have suffered other deaths, of course,' said Liala heavily as they made their way along the path, 'but she is the first of *her kind* to go.' Tiriki nodded. She knew what the older woman meant. Even poor sad Malaera had been only a simple priestess, with no special talents or powers. Alyssa was the first seeress to die in the new land. Would her troubled soul find rest or continue to wander, caught between the past and the future?

'It was that last Temple ritual, with the Omphalos Stone.' Without meaning to, Tiriki found herself glancing back toward the hut where that egg of ill-omen now lay. 'Something in her mind broke, even before Ahtarrath did. After that . . . she was never the same again.'

'Caratra rest her!' Liala made the sign of the Goddess on her breast and brow.

'Yes, she walks with the Nurturer now,' said Tiriki, but her thoughts were far away. She had thought to come along to help Liala, but now realized that she very much needed the comfort of Taret's wisdom. The old wisewoman had served the Great Goddess for longer than she could imagine. She would help them to understand.

The door to Taret's house was propped open, and as they approached it, they could hear her saying, in the tongue of the Lake tribe, 'You see, she is here now, just as I told you . . . Come in, my daughters,' Taret added. 'My visitor has a message for you.'

Seated on the far side of the fire was a young woman wearing a short, sleeveless tunic of blue-dyed wool. Slim and supple, her dun-colored hair was caught up in a tail at the back of her head. She had taken off her journey shoes, and her feet were those of a dancer, high-arched and strong.

Seeing the blue tunic, Liala offered the salute of one priestess of Caratra to another – as did Tiriki. The stranger's dark eyes grew wide.

'They both serve the Mother too, yes,' said Taret, her birdlike glance darting between them. 'This is Anet, daughter to Ayo, Sacred Sister for the people of Azan. They send her with news they cannot entrust to other messengers.'

Rising from her bench, Anet bent with liquid grace in the salutation a neophyte makes to a high priestess. Tiriki raised one eyebrow. Did the girl think they would doubt her credentials, or did she have some other reason for wanting to impress them?

'Heralding Stars, child, you need not be so formal!' said Liala with a smile.

'I would not wish to presume,' Anet replied as she settled gracefully into her cross-legged pose once again. Tiriki had a sense that whatever had motivated that salutation, it had not been humility. 'The other Sea People are very ceremonious, especially with us. Very proud.'

Tiriki felt the blood pound suddenly in her ears. 'Sea People? What do you mean—?'

'The strangers,' Anet said simply. 'The priests and priest-esses who came in winged boats from the sea. People of your kind.'

Tiriki barely stopped herself from seizing the girl's arm. 'Who were they? Can you tell us any names?'

'When they first came we thought the old shaman was their leader. The one they call Ar-dral.'

Tiriki gasped. 'Ardral?' she echoed. 'Not Ardral of Atalan! Seventh Guardian of the Temple at Ahtarrath? Ardravanant?'

'I have heard him called that. But we do not see him so much anymore, since their prince—' Anet grimanced. 'Tjalan – with his soldiers, brought the other priests to sing up the stones. But I see now that you two dress much the way some of *their* priestesses do. Maybe you know them too. There is Timul, and Elara—'

'Elara!' It was Liala's turn to be excited, 'Do you mean the acolyte Elara?'

'Yes, that is familiar . . .' Anet nodded slowly, eyes wide.

'And she's a healer? I knew it!' Liala exclaimed with a grin.

'That's—' Tiriki's voice wavered. 'You said there were other priests. *What are their names?*'

'Oh, so many—' The girl paused, blinking prettily. 'There is Haladris, and Ocathrel, and Immamiri – many. I regret I did not get to know all their names, because my father so much wished me to marry their *other* prince to bring his blood into our line.' Anet gave Tiriki a sidelong smile. 'A tall and handsome man with hair like new fire. Lord Micail.'

It was a pity, thought Chedan, that this news should come just now. Poor Alyssa had not even received their full atten-tion at her funeral.

It did not take long to call the community together, nor much longer to hear what the Ai-Zir girl had to say about the Atlanteans and their plans to build a great circle of stones in Azan. Tiriki wanted to set off on the weeklong journey at once, and when they sought to restrain her, she had collapsed. It was ironic, considering how well she had coped with their countless perils, that she should be undone by joy. But it was often so, he remembered, after a long period of mourning.

Once Tiriki had been put to bed, and the guests settled in shelters for the night, Chedan sat for many hours before the council fire. The heavens wheeled above him, revealing both familiar and still unknown stars in the unusually clear night sky. Tiriki had been given herbs to make her sleep, but one by one the others came to join him, minds too awhirl with speculation for speech. By the time the fire had sunk to a smolder of coals and some white curls of smoke, each face could be clearly seen, for it was dawn.

'We must join them,' Rendano was saying, 'and the sooner, the better. These Ai-Zir tribes clearly command more resources than the natives here. We would have some hope of reestablishing our own way of living.' The glance he cast toward the rude structures whose thatched roofs could just be seen through the trees was eloquent of disdain.

'I am not so sure,' Liala put in. 'Before Alyssa died . . . she spoke of danger from circles and stones. Now we learn our compatriots are just on the other side of those hills, building – a circle of stones. Is it not possible that the danger Alyssa warned of will come from *them*?'

'From our own people?' exclaimed Damisa in amazement.

'Not to speak ill of the dead, but we all know Alyssa was crazy,' Reidel echoed her.

At this, Chedan looked up, but he bit back the words. Reidel had made great progress, but he understood nothing about the strange forces a seeress must contend with – no one who had not walked that path could truly understand.

'Since when did *madness* ever prevent one from seeing the truth?' asked little Iriel, who – Chedan suddenly noticed – was not so little any more. In the past six years she had become a woman. At home, he mused, all of the acolytes would have been advanced to full priest or priestess by now.

'Alyssa lived in her own world,' Iriel continued. 'But when we could make sense of her ravings, there was usually some truth in them. So – so I think Liala's right. What if these plains people are forcing our priests to build for them? Taret says they are a powerful tribe.'

'I think that girl did not begin to tell us all she knows,' Forolin put in unexpectedly. 'Her father is the king – if Prince Tjalan has really taken over, how does that sit with the other tribes? If one of them wanted to revolt we would be valuable hostages – something of the sort happened on a trade route I used to travel when younger. I am as eager as anyone here to go somewhere more civilized,' Forolin went on earnestly, 'but we shouldn't rush in. Things are not so bad here.'

'Yes, life is hard, but we are secure.' Selast laid a protective hand over her belly. 'And I can hardly go a-wandering just now.'

Chedan stroked his beard, thoughtful. He was willing enough to let the others speculate on danger from the natives, but Alyssa's words still echoed in his memory. She had not spoken of danger from people, but from the stones themselves.

The others had grown quiet. Looking up, Chedan realized that they had been watching him. He looked from one face to another. 'I sense we may be moving toward some sort of decision,' he observed, 'but if experience has taught me anything, it is that someone always has a last word . . .'

Damisa's frown had been growing. 'Well, no one has asked for *my* opinion!' she said sharply, 'How can we not go? Not only are these our own people, but Micail and a lot of other Guardians are there. Surely whatever they are building is part of the new Temple, just as it says in the prophecy that everybody used to make so much noise about! Do you really believe a lot of savages could control so many adepts and priests – especially if Tjalan is there to guard

302

them? Or is it *Tjalan* you are worrying about? He will protect us too – or don't you trust anybody who isn't from Ahtarrath?'

'No, no, no,' Chedan said soothingly. 'Dear Damisa, where does *this* come from? Selast and Kalaran are hardly Ahtarrans. Indeed I am Alkonan myself, you might recall . . . No, for good or for ill, my friends, we are all Atlanteans together in this new land.'

'It is not Prince Tjalan we doubt,' said Kalaran, 'but the people between us and him.'

Liala nodded. 'Forolin made an important point. If Tjalan has enough men to threaten the tribes, the natives may indeed think of using us as a shield against them. And if Tjalan is not strong enough to deter them – need I say more?

'Why not send a few to make contact?' Liala suggested. 'Some of the younger folk, who can go swiftly. If all is well, the prince can send an escort for the rest of us. After so long a separation, surely we can wait a little longer to rejoin our friends and countrymen.'

'I have been thinking much the same thing,' Dannetrasa nodded.

'So it seems that most of us agree,' observed Chedan. 'Perhaps Damisa should be one of the party, since she is familiar not only with the ways of the local wildlife, but is also Tjalan's cousin. Damisa? What do you say?'

'I will go with some of my men to guard her,' Reidel offered when he saw Damisa's eager nod.

'But should we not send someone – more senior?' asked Rendano.

'I hope you don't mean me.' Chedan shook his head. 'Do *you* wish to go? Besides, Damisa is the eldest of the Chosen Twelve, and thus under law has rank and standing in any Atlantean court or temple.'

'But what about Tiriki?' asked Damisa. 'She'll want to go—'

'But she should not just now, I think. She needs time to

recover,' Chedan responded. Alyssa's words still bothered him, and it would hardly be tactful to point out that the high priestess was not expendable . . . 'But somehow I doubt that she will agree with me. I suggest that you and Reidel gather some men and supplies and leave, soon – as soon as possible,' he added wryly, 'preferably before she awakens. I do not wish to have to tie her up to keep her from following you.'

SEVENTEEN

'Did you hear the news? Anet is back from the Lake lands—'

The voice was that of one of the native slave women the Alkonans had recently bought to help with the work of the new community.

Micail, passing behind the kitchen hut on his way to the gate, could not help hearing them.

'Is she?' another slave said. 'Did she bring her bow and arrows? That's the only way she will capture Fire-hair!'

Micail felt a slow flush burn his cheeks as the women laughed. He had been aware of his nickname, but he had not realized that Anet's interest in him was common knowledge.

The first voice spoke again. 'The news is she travels with strangers. More Sea People – different ones.'

'Where do they come from?' someone asked.

'Somewhere in the marshes. They have been there for years, they say. I hear they don't look much like the new masters; they dress like marsh people. But taller, so maybe.'

'Say, I heard one of them is—'

'Hush,' a new voice interrupted, probably a supervisor, 'anyone could hear you shrieking. We will know all about it soon enough. No doubt the Falcon lords will want to see them.' The scrape, scrape, scrape of the grinding stones never ceased, but otherwise, there was deafening silence from within the kitchen hut.

Presently Micail turned away and began to walk back toward the central court. With a detached curiosity he realized that his heart was still pounding heavily, though he had been standing still. *Perhaps*, he thought, *I had better stop in and see Tjalan . . .*

By the time Anet and her traveling companions arrived, everyone in the community had heard that they were coming. Rumors flew wildly, some less absurd than others. Mahadalku and most of the senior priesthood declined to join the crowd waiting on the commons, but Haladris was there.

A second drop of water struck Elara's head and she frowned up at the sky. More clouds were rushing in to blot out the morning's fragile blue. The natives counted the beginning of summer from a point halfway between equinox and solstice, but one shouldn't try to tell the season by the weather, Elara thought grimly. She pulled her shawl up over her head as the first spatterings turned into a light rain.

Someone at the front was pointing, and Elara realized that she had arrived just in time. A group of people was approaching across the plain. Even at a distance she recognized Anet's dun hair and her easy way of moving, and the two Blue Bull warriors that always escorted her. Behind them she could see a knot of tall, bronze-skinned men in wool and leather, and gleaming from among them, one head of long auburn hair that had never been born to the tribes.

'Who is that?' asked Cleta, stretching on tiptoes beside her and wiping rain out of her eyes, 'Can you see?'

'They are Atlanteans, that's for sure . . . Heart of Manoah! I think it's Damisa!' Elara blinked, trying to reconcile her memories of a gawky adolescent with the young goddess who was striding toward them.

As Anet's group reached the crowd, Micail stepped forward from his place beside Prince Tjalan as if unable to stand still any longer. Some of the stiffness seemed to leave his shoulders, but there was still tension in his stance. Elara

306

felt her heart wrench with pity, then noticed that Anet was watching Micail as well, her expression like that of a fox who eyes a cock pheasant, wondering whether it will be able to fly away. *You still do not see he is not for you,* Elara thought grimly. *Or for me . . .* she reflected ruefully. His rejection of her offer had been polite, but clear. *If Tiriki lives, he will go to her. And if she does not . . . I think he will remain as he is.*

Tjalan, too, stepped forward now, all smiles. Seeing him, Damisa bent in the salutation due a reigning prince, her face radiant. She then performed the proper obeisances to Ardral and to Micail, as lords of the Temple, but her gaze, it seemed, could not quite tear itself away from the Prince of Alkonath.

'Why, it is my little cousin!' exclaimed Tjalan. 'Praise to the God of Roads for your arrival! Now enter in a good hour, and let no fear trouble you while you are in my domain. Welcome! Welcome indeed, cousin. This is joy beyond imagining.'

As Damisa straightened, her blushes barely contained, Elara saw her surreptitiously tug down the skirts of her gown and suppressed a grin. *She has grown taller, too!*

'My prince,' Damisa was saying, 'I am grateful indeed to find you here. I bring greetings from the Summer Country, and from the leaders of our community – the Guardian Chedan Arados and the Guardian Tiri – Eilantha.'

As Damisa spoke her gaze had gone to Micail. *Help him, someone!* thought Elara as she saw the color leave his face entirely. And Ardral stepped forward, his hand gripping Micail's elbow.

'We rejoice to see you, O acolyte. Your message of hope heals our hearts.' Ardral's words flowed smoothly, but was there an unaccustomed roughness in his voice? Eyebrows quirking, his piercing gaze darted to the young man who stood behind Damisa.

She did not wait for him to ask. 'I present to you Reidel,

son of Sarhedran, formerly captain of the *Crimson Serpent*, and consecrated now to the Sixth Order of the Temple of Light—' Under the shocked stares of the clergy, Reidel's weathered face grew even more impassive, but he managed a fairly graceful bow.

Cleta leaned close to Elara, murmuring, 'If they've taken a *commoner* in, their group must be even smaller than ours.'

'Come now,' said Tjalan warmly, reasserting control of the situation with a gesture, 'you shall come in from the rain and claim the rewards of your journey. And when you are refreshed and fortified, perhaps you will tell us something of your adventures in the Lake lands.'

Atlantean tradition required that new arrivals be welcomed with food and drink. Micail was reminded of the feast after Tjalan had brought his ships to Ahtarrath, another occasion on which the superficial courtesies had been like a lid on a cauldron seething with unspoken agendas. Damisa was quick to list those who had found safety at the Tor and to assure Micail that Tiriki was well. But once or twice in her account of how they had discovered the Tor and founded the settlement she showed a certain hesitance or made an overly hasty reply that led Micail to suspect that there might also have been a few things that they had been instructed not to speak of.

Tiriki was alive! Micail's mind seethed with questions he could not ask here. Had Tiriki felt as empty all these years as he had? What pains and sorrow had she suffered when he was not there to comfort her? Damisa said she was in good health – why had she not come with them? It was all he could do not to rush off in search of those Blue Bull warriors and demand that they take him to the Summer Country immediately. But they were with Anet. At the thought of asking her to take him to the woman she must see as a rival, he quailed. Perhaps it would be better to see what Tjalan intended to do.

Tjalan's cheerful summary of events was even less candid. Good manners prevented Micail from interrupting to ask about Tiriki; he waited impatiently for a moment when he could speak with Damisa alone. But before he could do so, the prince effectively ended the session by suggesting that the newcomers might wish to go to the dwellings that had been made ready for them and rest. Reidel seemed unhappy about being separated from Damisa, but once Damisa realized that the facilities included a proper Atlantean bath, she allowed herself to be led away by Tjalan's servants without a backward glance.

Meanwhile, the prince insisted that Ardral and Micail accompany him into the innermost chamber of his fortress, where the other Guardians already sat waiting on benches with richly carven backs ranged around a blazing hearth. Micail had not been in this room before, but he found it entirely unsurprising that even here in savage Azan, where there was a floor of packed dirt under the mats and carpets, Tjalan had somehow managed to surround himself with luxuries. There was even a sort of throne, a good-sized chair, whose posts were carven falcons.

As the servants of the prince bustled about the room, making sure that everyone had a drink or food to eat, Micail allowed Ardral to guide him to a seat closer to Naranshada than to Haladris.

'I am glad we could have this meeting,' Mahadalku was saying, her smile as chilly as the rain that was battering the roofs. 'Chedan Arados is reputed a very strong singer, and I have heard much the same of your princess—' she nodded to Micail. 'They will be most welcome additions, and I do not doubt we will find use for many of the others – although I am not so certain about this . . . sailor . . . Reidel.'

'He seemed a pleasant young man,' offered Stathalkha.

'Yes, he was pleasant enough,' rejoined Mahadalku coldly, 'but he has not been Temple-trained since childhood. How can he hope to channel any real power?'

Naranshada shrugged. 'There are always a few among

the Chosen Twelve who did not have lifelong training, and they have done well enough. This new land is not exactly overpopulated with Atlanteans of any caste. We will face the same problem eventually – even if we find a dozen lost shiploads. And I for one cannot imagine that Master Chedan Arados, of all people, would allow anyone to be initiated who had no potential.'

'I can assure you he would not,' Ardral put in, and there were more than one or two other mutters of assent, for Chedan's fame had been no small thing.

'They have been there all this time,' Micail said suddenly, 'just over the hills. Why didn't you *see* them, Stathalkha? I was assured that your sensitives had searched near and far – why didn't you find them?'

'Perhaps we did.' Stathalkha's faded eyes blinked at him, and she wrenched her withered body around a little so as to confront him more directly. 'We found several points of power in use where the energy felt – familiar. I believe that a hill such as the girl described figured prominently at one of them. But we were looking for a place to build our Sun Wheel. Mahadalku and I felt that if more of our people were here we would locate them in time. And now, you see, we have!' she finished triumphantly.

Micail realized that Ardral was gripping his shoulder, and his fingers slowly unclenched. To strangle the fragile Tarissedan priestess would do no one any good.

'Yes, indeed,' Tjalan murmured thoughtfully, his strong features glowing bronze in the firelight. 'And now that we know where they are, we ought to bring them here.'

'If I might say so,' observed Ardral, 'it is never good to move *too* quickly. There might be some virtue in developing another port on the opposite coast. They are plainly somewhat closer than Belsairath.'

'I doubt it would be suitable,' Haladris countered. 'From everything I have heard, conditions there are – primitive, at best. What use could such a place be?'

Ardral smiled grimly. 'A refuge, if things go wrong here?'

Tjalan frowned. 'What do you mean? It is true that the tribes are restless, but they will not be able to organize any move against us for some time. By then the Sun Wheel will be ready, and we will be able to direct a lethal strike to any point on the plain, and beyond. The Ai-Zir will fall into line fast enough then.'

Micail felt suddenly dizzy. 'What do you mean? The power is to be used to build the Temple.'

'Of course, of course,' said Delengirol gruffly, 'but we can hardly build anything else without an increased labor force.'

Haladris added coolly, 'And the power of the circle may need to be demonstrated . . . in order to suitably impress the tribes.'

'To *impress?*' Micail's skin prickled as if lightning were about to strike from the clouds. Ardral straightened, eyeing him with concern.

Mahadalku nodded vigorously. 'Yes, surely you recognize that we must be able to keep the natives under control. At least, until they have – achieved their potential.' Her practiced grin was heavy with condescension.

Micail fought down rage, his consciousness quivering. Astonished, he recognized the familiar fire – not in all the empty years since he had fled from dying Atlantis had his inherited powers awakened within him – but there was a strange *twist* to everything that was not the same.

How could he touch powers that were his – not as a Guardian of Light but as Prince of Ahtarrath – when the island was gone? As he struggled for control, the tension in the room grew palpable. From outside, the heavens echoed the thunder within and a gust of wind slammed rain against the walls.

Of all those gathered in that room, only Tjalan, unfamiliar with the tradition of Ahtarrath, did not understand the meaning of that distant roll of thunder. In the eyes of

311

the other priests amazement mingled with speculation as they too realized that the powers of Ahtarrath had been restored.

As the Guardians stared at Micail, Tjalan took a sip of wine, and his smile was indulgent. 'I know, I know, it seems so contradictory. In the name of Light, we impose a burden of sweat and suffering. But it is a temporary burden. As they see what we are truly capable of, they will acclaim us. For indeed, how else do you suppose the temples of Atlantis were built, cousin? As you have witnessed, even the greatest mages require the assistance of ordinary men.'

It is Tiriki, Micail thought, scarcely hearing Tjalan. *Simply knowing that she lives makes me a whole man once more. I thought my powers came from my land, yet I have carried them with me. But I will have to be careful.*

Mistaking Micail's silence for assent, Tjalan continued, 'Micail, old friend, after all this time do you not sense the infinite possibilities in this land? With its resources, its population – this place could become greater than all the Sea Kingdoms combined!'

Micail sat motionless, his pulse still racing as he restored control. At the moment, it was not the potential in the land that concerned him, but his own. But perhaps coming here had changed it somehow. His joy chilled.

Tjalan added persuasively, 'All of the temples of Manoah, even the one that you served in Ahtarrath, were modeled after the first Temple in the city of the Circling Serpent in the Ancient Land. You were born there, Micail – surely you remember the marble pillars, the golden stairs? It is your destiny to rebuild that Temple in all its glory. In this place you and I can rekindle all the greatness of the Bright Empire!'

But should we? Micail wondered. His inner turmoil prevented him from answering. Was he questioning Tjalan's motives or his own? Only Naranshada seemed to really share Micail's unease. The faces of Mahadalku and Haladris were composed and serene. When he turned to Ardral, he saw in the senior Guardian's grey eyes a gleam that he could not interpret.

'So long as we do not repeat their mistakes,' Naranshada was muttering. 'There were reasons why the Bright Empire fell . . .'

'*And* the Sea Kingdoms,' Micail muttered, finding his voice at last.

'To be sure,' Tjalan said pleasantly.

'Surely, though, we can agree that we should not make a final decision now,' Ardral temporized. 'Perhaps Tiriki and Chedan are creating something that will contribute to what we hope to achieve. The gods work in mysterious ways.'

'Yes—' Naranshada agreed. 'We are not speaking of a few wayward chelas to be swept back into the fold. Chedan is a mage, and Tiriki, a Guardian. They have ruled their own Temple for five years. We need to hear what they have to say.'

'Which is why they should be here!' exclaimed Tjalan, turning to Micail. 'Gods, man – you are Tiriki's husband! Where else should she be but with you?' The prince shook his head.

'Of course I want to be with her!' Micail snapped. And he did not – could not – doubt that she would want to be with him. But the thought of *ordering* Tiriki to do as he wished appalled him. They had always acknowledged each other as equals.

'Whether or not she wishes to join us, for the good of all, she must be compelled to do so,' said Mahadalku grimly. 'With all due respect, Lord Micail – your wife is not a *senior* Guardian.'

'What do you mean by that?' Micail gritted.

'That it cannot be left solely to her decision,' Haladris answered. 'This very equality of which you speak requires that she must take her proper place in our hierarchy. Only the traditional disciplines can preserve our way of life. Otherwise, our numbers are too few to ensure the survival

313

of our caste. If the great Chedan Arados were *here* instead of there, I do not doubt he would tell you the same thing.'

'Perhaps,' said Ardral soothingly, 'we are anticipating a few troubles more than there are. The community at the Tor may be eager to join us – why upset them with threats and demands? Why not wait until we have had a chance to speak with them? Chedan *is* my nephew, but more than that, I have found him to be a man of no small wisdom. I think we can be sure he will choose a course that will be beneficial to all.'

This time it was Micail's turn to quirk an eyebrow. Ardral's usual response to strife was simply to be elsewhere. But whatever the adept's reasons for repeatedly calming the gathering today, Micail was grateful. In all his dreams, finding Tiriki again had only brought joy, but this discussion had made him very uneasy. With the exception of Tjalan, these people too were all Guardians, dedicated to the same ideals, oathsworn to the same gods as himself. Why then did he find himself feeling as if he were among enemies?

As Ardral began to move toward the door, Micail rose to follow him, but Tjalan took his arm gently.

'I sense that this evening's events have upset you.'

Micail stared at him, not daring to let himself be drawn into further discussion. The surge of power he had experienced earlier had shaken his spirit even as it reinvigorated his body, and he no longer trusted his self-control.

'These people can be difficult – as I know to my own pain,' Tjalan went on. Subjected to the full force of Tjalan's charm, Micail found himself relaxing, just a little. The prince went on earnestly, 'Remember, they are old – would that they had hearts as youthful as yours!' he added warmly to Ardral.

'Haladris and Mahadalku particularly—' The prince smiled and returned his full attention to Micail. 'At home, those two were accustomed to being in charge of their own temples! It does no harm to let them have their say now.

When all of our people are united once more, you are the one who will rule the new Temple. That position was always destined for you.'

But could I bear such a responsibility? wondered Micail, as he and Ardral resolutely left Tjalan alone with his throne, his guards, his dreams of empire at last. *Is this the destiny Rajasta's prophecy predicted for me? It is as if I stand between hungry beasts, trying to choose which one will devour me.*

He made polite noises and permitted Ardral to escort him to the gate, but almost as soon as the senior Guardian had returned into the shadows of Tjalan's fortress, Micail turned around and did the same thing, though by a different route.

After some searching, he found Reidel and one of his men talking in the hall. When he asked what they were doing there, Reidel only pointed through the door, where Damisa sat beside a fire, surrounded by what looked to be most of the acolytes and chelas. For a moment Micail hesitated. They all seemed so young, so vigorous and hopeful. Did he have a right to disturb them with his anxieties? But he had to know.

Their faces turned toward him as he stepped into the light. He saw welcome and speculation, and even an unexpected compassion in Elara's warm eyes – but then she always seemed to know when he was overwrought. Still, it was Damisa who had his attention.

'Will you . . . ?' He cleared his throat. 'Damisa, I do not wish to part you from your friends too quickly, but I would be very grateful if you would walk with me for a little while.'

'Of course—' In a single smooth movement she was on her feet. 'You will want all the news, and I will have plenty of time to talk to these—' she paused, grinning, 'rather less holy servants of Light!'

As they turned to go, he felt again the watchful gaze of the stranger Reidel and almost paused to reassure the former ship's captain that he would return the girl safely. But Reidel was a priest now and outranked even by an acolyte. Surely he had no right to question anything that a Vested Guardian might choose to do.

'That young man,' Micail mused, as he and Damisa walked away, 'Reidel? He seems . . . oddly protective. Does he imagine I might do you harm?'

'Oh, no!' Damisa exclaimed, half-turning to glare behind her. 'I apologize for him, Lord Guardian. He thinks he is in love with me.'

'But you don't return the feeling?' Micail nodded to the guard as they passed through the gate and started along the path toward the river. The rain had stopped, and the sun was setting through bands of cloud that flared like banners of flame above the distant hills. *Tiriki sees that same sunset*, he thought with a surge of emotion.

'To be honest,' Damisa said dully, 'I suppose I gave him some reason to think I might. But it was a mistake. I tried to explain. He doesn't say anything about it anymore, but he . . . looks at me.'

'If he troubles you—' Micail began, but she shook her head.

'No!' She flushed. 'I am sorry. I am so used to the informal life of the Tor and the marshes. I've embarrassed myself in front of Prince Tjalan already. Please, Lord Guardian! Reidel is my problem – my mistake. My responsibility. Please.'

Micail nodded, eyeing her appraisingly. She was certainly not the serious little girl he had met in Ahtarrath, and yet the young woman standing before him still had that precariously balanced intensity. 'You have been well taught, I see,' he said with a smile. 'But you need not call me Lord Guardian. I get enough of that already. Call me Micail. And please tell me about Tiriki,' he added hungrily.

'Of course,' Damisa answered him. 'She's in good health, praise Caratra. It is she who has kept us going these past years – she and Chedan.'

'Then why didn't she come with you?'

'I'm sure she wanted to,' Damisa said quickly. 'But she had already been up all night by Alyssa's deathbed. And to learn you were here – in such a strange way – it was a shock to her. Not that she ever gave up believing she would find you some day, but she had . . . put the hope aside. So Chedan felt it would be better to send someone stronger – more expendable, I guess that means—' she grinned. 'I expect that when she woke up and found we were gone, she was furious at Chedan and let him know it.' Damisa blushed again.

Micail blinked, trying to imagine his gentle Tiriki upbraiding anyone. 'Then it is Chedan who is your first?'

'Not really – oh, in a way, maybe. He always says we're too small a group to need an official leader. In almost every way, really, he and Tiriki share the responsibility.'

As she and I used to do at home. How else does he replace me? thought Micail, with a flicker of envy. But even as the idea burned in him, he knew that he had no right to resent anything his wife might have had to do to survive in an environment that sounded considerably more hostile than Belsairath or even Azan.

A light wind was rustling in the willows, and from somewhere out above the plain came the call of a hunting owl. Oddly, those small sounds only seemed to intensify the quiet. The dark ranks of trees along the river blotted out any actual sight of the plain, but even with his eyes closed he could have pointed toward the henge.

'Chedan might also have felt she ought not to leave the child,' Damisa said into the silence.

Micail's head jerked up, the Sun Wheel forgotten. From his tight throat he squeezed out the words, 'What child?'

'Why hers – yours I mean. I am sure of it now. Domara's hair is exactly like yours! You *really* look like her – I mean she looks—'

'But Tiriki wasn't – she never told me!' He wondered if his pounding heart would burst through his chest.

'She didn't know,' said Damisa, with sudden sympathy.

'On the voyage here she thought she was seasick. She suffered terribly. It was Taret who told her – the wisewoman at the Tor. She has the Sight—'

'A daughter,' Micail whispered.

'Called Domara. I should have mentioned her when I first reported, but we've become so accustomed to having her around, I didn't think— In any case, you must be just as glad not to have had such news in the middle of a meeting! Domara was born at winter solstice, that first year. She turned five this year. A real darling—'

Micail, calculating in his head, scarcely heard. The dates fit, if Tiriki had conceived in those last days before the Sinking. But how – when his seed had never taken root in all their years of peace – how could she have carried a babe to term in the midst of disaster?

Unaware of his turmoil, Damisa continued to talk. 'Selast's child will be born this summer, so you see we have quite a number of children at the Tor. But I suppose there must have been a lot of births among your people too . . .'

'I don't know,' he muttered. To have noticed such things, he suddenly realized, would only have caused him more pain. What he felt now, he was not certain. Pride? Joy? Terror? It did not matter. His heart was singing. *I have a child!*

Obviously, thought Damisa as she sat down in the chair Prince Tjalan offered her, this was her evening for interviews. No sooner had Micail brought her back to the acolytes' quarters than a servant came to summon her to the prince's court, at the center of the compound. Since there was no hill against which the masons might have constructed a more stylish fortress, they had built up the sides with stone and plastered the walls.

She settled onto the cushions, sighing as her body remembered what it felt like to sink into such softness. At the Tor they had a few hammocks, but many more hard stools, and a lot of crude benches made from fitted logs. It had been a long time since she sat in a real chair. Her eyes misted as she recognized the Alkonan patterns of the hangings on the walls.

A silent servant placed an elegant flagon and two fili-greed goblets on a green-and-gold table and withdrew. *I am dreaming!* she thought. *The last five years were an evil dream, and I am awakening safe at home once more* . . . But she could not ignore the bitter lines in Prince Tjalan's face, nor the new silver laced through the black of his hair.

A pale golden liquid gurgled entrancingly from the flagon into the goblets. 'What shall we toast?' said the prince, offering one of them to her. 'The Bright Empire? The Seven Guardians?'

'The hope of the new land?' she answered, a little shyly, raising her cup to meet his.

'Ha! *Yes*,' Tjalan grinned fiercely. 'You are indeed a relative of mine!'

The liqueur was deceptively sweet, but she could feel it burning all the way down.

'It's raf ni'iri,' Tjalan warned her, 'so be careful. I always find it is a little stronger than even I expect.' He eased back in his own chair, cradling the goblet between long fingers to inhale its delicate aroma. But even as he did so, she noticed, he was surveying her with a most ambiguous smile . . . Damisa felt her cheeks grow warm, and could not tell if it resulted from embarrassment or the potency of the drink.

'My dear, you have more than fulfilled your promise,' the prince said at last. 'You have matured from a delicate flower into an enchanting woman. One who knows how to propose a toast, at that!'

She felt her blushes deepen. It was odd that when Reidel said this sort of thing, she believed he meant it. With Tjalan – she shook her head. Of course, he was only being polite. His wife was – had been – a famous beauty, after all.

'You think me a flatterer, eh?' Tjalan chuckled at her discomfiture. 'Well, when I take you to Belsairath, my dear, we shall dress you as befits a princess of the royal house, and then you will see some real flattery!'

But I am a priestess, not a princess . . . She blinked up at him. *He was right; this stuff is very strong.* She held the goblet to her nostrils and pretended to sniff it, as he had done, then set it firmly down on the table.

'When we have rescued the rest of your party from those marshes and finished building the Sun Wheel, we will create a new empire in this land . . .'

Tjalan's eyes brightened as he began to describe the cities he would raise here, the roads and harbors – his words painted a vision of all that they had lost restored, more splendid than before. Part of Damisa's mind was wondering whether this new empire was really possible. From what Micail had said, Tjalan did not have that many priests or soldiers.

Have old Chedan's doubts infected me? she chided herself. *Have I, too, begun to think that what has been lost can never be restored?* She never spoke to anyone, even Selast, about the many nightmares in which she had tried and failed to face the eerie forces that had radiated from the Omphalos Stone. *Chedan said,* she thought muzzily, *I had better not tell anyone that the Stone is at the Tor.*

'And so,' he was saying now, 'when we go to bring them back here, I will rely upon you to help me to explain.'

She roused herself, frowning. 'I'm not sure Tiriki will want to leave. She's put a lot of work into – the place. It would be better for us to simply go back and talk to them – once we can get another guide.'

'You don't know the way?' he said sharply, and a shiver of unease sobered her still more.

'Oh, out of sight of the Tor, one hill still looks like another to me,' she lied cheerfully, 'and I'm sure it's not much different for Reidel. He's always saying it's simpler on the sea.'

Chedan had cautioned her to keep their location vague until she was certain it was safe to reveal it, and she realized that she did not quite trust Tjalan, despite his flattery, or perhaps because of it. *Besides*, she assured herself, *one should not spend all one's resources at once. Information is the only coin I have.*

'That is . . . unfortunate,' said Tjalan. 'Well, you have had an exhausting day. Best you get some rest now. My servant will show you where you are to stay.'

A little surprised by his abruptness, Damisa allowed herself to be led away to a bed that seemed almost too soft. Her limbs had become accustomed to mattresses of deer hide stuffed with straw, and it was hard to get to sleep. She woke long after morning prayers were ended, with a headache that throbbed behind her eyes. By the time she finally did get moving, she found that none of the acolytes seemed to know where Reidel and his three sailors had spent the night.

When she made her way to the gate, thinking that a walk by the river might clear her head, a smiling guard barred her way with his spear. It was then that Damisa realized she was a prisoner.

'Have you seen Damisa this morning?' Lanath took Elara's arm and drew her toward the log benches beneath a trio of chestnut trees where the other acolytes and chelas were waiting. When weather permitted they often gathered there for lessons, but today the senior priesthood were sequestered in its own conclave. Still, Elara suspected that the topic their elders were discussing might be the same as their own.

Since the arrival of Damisa and Reidel, rumors had begun to whisper through the compound like wind in the trees – the tribes were planning an uprising . . . Reidel's sailors were coming to rescue their captain . . . The prince was mounting an expedition to quell a rebellion . . . Lightnings that did not come from the sky had terrified some workers at the henge . . . All that could be said for certain was that Tjalan's soldiers were sharpening their swords and mending their leather armor.

'See her?' Elara echoed as she sat down. 'I *heard* her – cursing out a guard who would not let her through the gate. I met them marching her back to Tjalan's house, and as they passed, she whispered, "Find Reidel!" But I couldn't find him.'

'An acolyte held prisoner?' muttered Galara. 'That has to be wrong.'

'We ought to try to learn where he is,' Elara repeated.

'I don't like it,' muttered Lanath. 'It's like we're going behind our elders' backs.'

Cleta scowled at him, 'Do you think they are going to ask our opinion? What choice do we have?'

'I don't understand why it is such a problem,' put in Vialmar, brushing his coarse black hair out of his eyes. 'Why wouldn't they want to join us? I really want to see Kalaran again, and the others too. Don't they want to see us? I mean, *this* place is bad enough—' He looked across at the palisade as if he thought a horde of maddened Ai-Zir warriors might charge at any moment. 'But from what Damisa said last night, out there they have *nothing*. I should think they would be only too happy to come here.'

'Whatever they do or don't have,' observed Elara, 'they have learned to survive. I don't know how many casks of wine Tjalan and the others brought with them, but when they are emptied, there will be no more. Maybe Chedan and Tiriki are wiser than we, to begin by learning how to live as we shall all have to do one day.'

'Not once the stone circle is finished,' put in Karagon. 'We'll have enough power to deal with anything, then.'

'*Should* it be finished?' asked Lanath. 'There's something about this whole place that gives *me* the shivers.'

'The point is, people should be free to make up their own minds, and locking them up or forcing them to move does not accord with the traditions of the Temple that I learned!' Elara said.

Cleta nodded. 'I agree. In Ahtarrath, Lord Micail was

both prince and archpriest, so there was no conflict – but lately – I don't know. I would feel happier if we knew what has happened to Reidel.'

'He's just some common sailor,' sneered Karagon.

'No, Damisa said he was an initiate,' corrected Li'ija. 'But it doesn't matter. Tjalan should *not* just spirit either of them away.'

Galara sighed. 'All right. What do you suggest we do?'

'I told you I went looking,' Elara said. 'I checked every building. He is not in the compound.'

'Maybe he already ran home,' Karagon offered hopefully.

'Let's not count on it,' Cleta recommended. 'If he is not here, he may be in the village.'

One by one, all the heads turned again toward Elara. She was the one who had developed the most significant ties among the Ai-Zir.

'Very well. I will go.'

She found Queen Khayan-e-Durr at her usual occupation, spinning wool with her women in the warm spring sun. After the customary ceremonious greetings, Elara began to tell her story, but she was not really surprised to find that the queen already knew. The problem, evidently, was how to make her care.

'If Prince Tjalan has his way there will be no chieftainship for your son to inherit. If the prince seeks to corral his own people, do you think he will let yours roam free?' Elara could not tell if she was making any impression. 'Anything that helps those who have different ideas will hobble his power.'

'That's so,' said the queen, 'but many years ago, two of our shamans had a quarrel. By the time it was ended, a plague had struck both tribes. Who will lie dead, I wonder, when your mages are done?'

'Would you rather live safely as slaves?' exclaimed Elara. 'You will have to choose a side!' *When*, she wondered then, *did I choose?*

323

Khayan gave her an odd look. 'So you betray your own people?'

'I don't believe I do,' she answered soberly. 'I think that some of them betray themselves. As for me, I am faithful to my gods.'

The queen sketched the sign of Caratra on her breast. 'This Tiriki, Lord Micail's wife. She is sworn to the Goddess?'

'So I have heard – although she has served the Temple of Light.'

'We will seek to help her,' Khayan smiled. 'But whether the result will be to reunite her with Micail or to estrange them is in the lap of the gods . . . It is not enough to release these prisoners, if that is truly what they are. Soon enough, Tjalan will find someone from the tribes who knows the way to the Lake lands. We do not often go there, but the way is no secret. This Reidel, too, will need a guide, or his enemies will arrive before he does. A guide, and an offer of alliance,' she added thoughtfully, 'else we may all be sucked into a needless war. I will tell this to Tjalan once they are safely gone.'

'Be careful!' exclaimed Elara. 'I would not have his wrath fall upon you!'

'He will be very sorry if it does,' the queen replied. 'Every soul in Azan would rise to avenge any hurt to me! If Tjalan does not understand that, then you and Lady Timul had better tell him.'

As the season turned toward the solstice the weather around the Tor became even more capricious, as if unable to decide between winter and summer. While Tiriki waited for Damisa and Reidel to return, she sought to relieve her frustration by working on the pathway around the Tor.

The day is like my spirit, thought Tiriki, looking from the raw earth of the pathway to the clouds, *perched between*.

To know that Micail lived was ecstasy, but the thought of him with this native priestess was a betrayal worse than

324

loss. Yet at the same time she understood that the duties of a priest or priestess might require a ritual mating to energize the fertility of the land. *I did not do so*, she thought with a rush of passion.

Micail could have slept with this native princess for that reason, she told herself. Anet had not implied that she wanted Micail as a lover, but as a bull brought to the cows – to improve the herd. But what haunted Tiriki's nights was the fact that Anct had not said whether or not Micail had agreed to lie with her . . . and Tiriki had not asked.

And if he took her to bed from simple need can I blame him? she asked herself for the hundredth time. *He thought I was dead. Surely I have often enough wished him alive and able to find comfort – wherever he could. Did I stay faithful from virtue, or because no one presented me with any temptation to stray?* There was no fault in the reasoning, but in her heart of hearts, she could not accept it. If she had been condemned to sleep in an empty bed these five years, Micail should have slept alone as well!

She jammed the antler tool viciously into the soil, as if by removing the dirt she could get rid of her uncertainty. She could not even rail at Chedan for so quickly sending Anet away with Damisa and Reidel while she slept. All spring the mage had been short of breath. He said old age was catching up with him, but she feared it might be something more than a cough that warm weather had not cured.

She looked up as Elis, who had been working on a section of the spiral above hers, gave a shout. 'Someone is coming! He has – black hair. Stars above, it's Reidel!'

'Quiet, all of you!' Chedan's tone, not his volume, cut through the babble of assorted priests and priestesses. 'Obviously all of this is a – surprise. To us all.'

Guided by one of the Ai-Zir hunters, Reidel had cut the journey time by almost a third on his return, but the hollows in his cheeks and the shadows around his eyes came not from fatigue, thought the mage, but from anxiety.

'I could hardly believe the prince would use force to make us join him; he must know how we've dreamed of finding other survivors.' Reidel glanced at Tiriki, whose face, after his first news, had ceased to show any emotion at all. 'But it is hard to misinterpret a guard on one's door! And though Damisa has better quarters than they gave me, she is still a prisoner!'

'What can Prince Tjalan be thinking?' exclaimed Liala. 'He cannot lock up a chosen acolyte of the Temple!'

'An outrage,' Dannetrasa seconded him.

'Yes, yes,' Chedan interrupted. 'But if you will be patient for a little longer, I would like a bit more information from Reidel himself, and for that, it would be helpful if I could hear myself think . . .'

He turned back to the man who stood before him. 'I believe we can be certain that no harm will come to Damisa,' he said soothingly. 'She is Prince Tjalan's cousin. I can assure you, he will keep her in safety.'

'Fear more for the prince,' muttered Iriel. 'Have you *seen* Damisa when she's mad?' A ripple of laughter from around the circle released some of the tension.

'Her anger is what got *me* released,' said Reidel. 'Or at least got Elara to ask the Ai-Zir to help me. I was dumbfounded when the queen herself walked into the house where they were holding me. Tjalan's guards were slumped on the ground outside, sleeping like babies – the queen had slipped a potion into their beer. Tjalan won't suspect her; they knocked out a hole in the wall from inside so it would look as if I escaped that way.'

'I am glad to hear that Elara helped you,' said Chedan. 'Later I will want to hear more from you about the acolytes, but at present it is their elders that concern me. We have made you a priest, Reidel, but you are still our best-qualified military man. In your estimation, what forces, in the physical realm, does Tjalan have?'

326

The young man pulled himself together and began to describe what he had seen. As Chedan had expected, Reidel had made a full assessment of Tjalan's soldiers without even being aware of doing so.

'Over a hundred?' exclaimed Kalaran when Reidel's report was finished. 'Well, we can't defend ourselves by force of arms!'

'By magic, then?' Dannetrasa said dubiously. 'They outnumber us there too. They have *eight* Vested Guardians, you said? And four acolytes – and *other* priests and priestesses?'

'Including Micail . . .' Tiriki spoke without inflection. The unvoiced question hung in all their minds – had Micail been powerless to prevent Damisa's imprisonment, or did he support Prince Tjalan?

Chedan sighed. 'And Ardral. But we have one advantage. All this time we have wondered what use the Omphalos Stone would be in this new land. If they seek to attack us by spiritual means, we can invoke the Stone, and they will do as much harm to themselves as to us. But if it comes to a true magical battle—' He shook his head. 'We will *all* lose. No, we must win them over instead. Somehow—'

'We must meet with them,' Tiriki said, in that unnaturally even tone. 'Or some of them . . . not there, not here, but in a neutral location.' She looked up, her voice breaking at last. 'I will *not* believe Micail could betray me! But I cannot risk the rest of you.'

'We cannot risk *you!*' Liala objected.

'But Chedan could not manage the journey—' Tiriki held up one hand as he began to protest. 'And we must not both go. If Micail's . . . allegiance . . . is in question . . . You must agree he is most likely to listen to me.'

Chedan sighed again. No doubt this was his repayment for having prevented her from going before. He had been right then, and he suspected she knew it, but she most certainly knew that he would not be able to stop her now.

'There are the remains of an old hillfort about halfway

between here and Azan,' said Reidel unexpectedly. 'We camped there on the way. We might arrange to meet them there. I am willing to go back and tell them so.'

You are willing to go back to Damisa, thought Chedan, but he kept silent. Reidel's devotion did him credit, after all.

'Very well. We will take two of your best sailors as escorts, but no more. This is to be a parley, not a fight,' Tiriki reminded him. 'Perhaps Tjalan will come in force while I am gone, so we must keep as many men here as we can. She surveyed the roomful of faces. 'Elis, Rendano, would you be willing to accompany me?'

Chedan did not expect either of them to decline, and they did not, although it would have been hard to say which of them looked more uneasy. Even now, the thought of contesting the will of a famous adept like Ardral would have given him pause . . . Chedan found himself wondering again what position his uncle held in Tjalan's new community. Reidel had only briefly encountered Ardral there, and they had not spoken to one another, but Anet's description of the old adept lingered in Chedan's mind. By now, the canny old man probably knew what was going on better than Tjalan or Micail did . . .

I know all of them so well, the mage thought. *I should be there. But Tiriki is right*, he realized, as a sharp twinge in his knee reminded him of his own fragility. *I really cannot make the journey now.*

'Tiriki,' said Chedan, as they left the meeting hall, 'I hope that it is entirely unnecessary for me to tell you to be careful. But remember – the riddle of fate is that we continually choose our own nemesis. And it is not usually the one we think we are choosing at the time.'

EIGHTEEN

Tiriki was wearing blue.

In the dreams that had haunted his sleep since her messenger arrived, Micail had imagined her wearing, if not the pristine vestments of a Guardian of Light, at least the simple white robes of the Temple. Still, even at a distance, there could be no question that it was her. No one else in these lands had such golden hair.

But she was not alone. Four others advanced up the hill beside her, a balding middle-aged priest in a rather threadbare white robe trimmed with faded red, and two strong commoners in boots and hide tunics, armed with orichalcum-tipped pikes. There was also another woman in blue. *Perhaps Elis?* Micail wondered. *Damisa said Selast was pregnant . . .* He shook his head at the thought of any of them pregnant. He remembered the lost acolytes as mere children, but of course five years would have changed that.

Had Tiriki changed? Had *he?*

Micail's heart pounded in his chest. Were the five figures really alone? From what hidden place in the wilderness of misty hills ahead had they come? A dense grey haze veiled the plains behind him, even this slope where he and Tjalan stood waiting, as if this spot with its enigmatic overgrown earthen walls were no more than a way station in the mists of the Otherworld.

The wind picked up, and suddenly they were close enough

for their faces to be clear. Tiriki looked not so much older as stronger, as if hardship had emphasized the fine bone structure of her face and given tone to her musculature. In fact, she looked, if possible, more like *herself* than ever. Whatever she had been through, it seemed to have done her no harm. She moved with the grace of one at ease in her flesh, and her skin had the healthy glow that comes from being much outdoors.

And now Tiriki was near enough for their eyes to meet – and what he saw in hers made him start to close the remaining few feet between them.

Tjalan laid a hand on his arm. 'Wait! I thought we agreed—'

Micail turned, almost snarling, 'She is my *wife!*'

The prince's bodyguards were just out of earshot, but they tensed and bent closer like falcons catching sight of prey.

'Indeed,' the prince murmured, one hand still lightly gripping Micail's arm. 'But Damisa has had a lot to say about how closely Tiriki has been working with Chedan. He kept her from coming to you before. Would it be so surprising if a woman – left alone – were to transfer her loyalty?'

'Ever since we left Azan you have been pouring this poison into my ears,' Micail growled.

'Just look at her robes,' Tjalan tried again. 'If she has turned away from Manoah, why not from you? I warn you – we should not trust her any more than we do Khayan-e-Durr – or that firebrand Timul!'

'Unless you propose to stop me with that fancy blade on your belt, I am going to talk to her – alone if I may – with you, if I may not!'

Tiriki could not but notice the tension between the two men, the anxious hovering of Tjalan's swordsmen. Micail saw her gaze grow even more expressionless as he frowned.

'My lord Tjalan!' she said, with a formal nod. 'May I present my companions, the acolyte Elis and Rendano, formerly a priest of the Temple on Akil.'

I am not frowning at you, my darling! Micail thought desperately. *What are you feeling? Look at me!* For five years he had lived within an invisible wall. When he learned Tiriki still lived it had begun to crumble. Now he could feel the pressure of his need for her about to burst within him like a rushing flood.

'It is not for me to welcome you to this land, where we are all only travelers . . .' Tiriki went on. 'I perceive that the Great Mother rules here, as at home. Therefore we greet you in Her name – in the name of Caratra, whom we called Ni-Terat in the old land.'

Surely this formality is a defense . . . perhaps I appear equally cold to her, Micail told himself as Tjalan began to reply with something about honor and fortune and meetings. *I dreamed of this day, but there was never any dream like this. How can she be so controlled? She is my beloved! Yet she is like a stranger . . .*

'Tiriki—' It was less a greeting than a groan, but he no longer cared. She looked at him then, and he felt the jolt of contact between them. *It's all right*, he thought in relief. *Words can wait . . . the bond between us is still here!* He stepped forward to take her in his arms, seeking her lips as a man dying of thirst seeks a well.

After an endless moment he realized that Tjalan was speaking once more, and reluctantly he let Tiriki go, though he still kept his arm linked through hers.

'My lady – let me say first that I am very sorry for any misunderstandings that may have clouded what should only be the most joyful of reunions. I am sure that your messenger Reidel was a fine ship's captain, and he is no doubt possessed of other talents as well – but I suspect he may not quite be up to the nuances of communication at the higher levels of society.'

The touch of Tiriki's spirit warmed Micail as if he stood beside a flame, but her expression was contained once more. Tjalan took it as a sign of Tiriki's agreement, and gestured toward the group of folding stools and tables that had been set beneath an awning. On a pole beside it, a circle of falcons fluttered on a banner of Alkonan green.

'Please, let us sit for a while and talk quietly as friends should, for surely that is what we are. We have provided some good local cheese and fine waybreads for your refreshment, along with a bottle of Tarissedan wine.'

'Your hospitality is most welcome, my lord,' said Rendano, and sat down almost eagerly. Elis uneasily took a seat next to him and toyed nervously with the food.

'This is . . . pleasant,' said Tiriki. 'One might almost think oneself on a jaunt to the back country of Ahtarrath. The hills were almost this green in the spring – and as likely to be covered with ruins.'

'Indeed, there are many similarities—' Tjalan began, but her gentle voice overrode him.

'But what will you drink when this wine is gone?' She turned her silver goblet enough that the sunlight touched the ruby liquid within, then set it to her lips and drank it down.

'An interesting point,' said Tjalan. 'It is true that this particular vintage is now hard to come by . . . But we shall have something not too different, once the trade routes have been reestablished. Oh yes, the wingbirds will fly again, my lady! Already we have built three fine new ships, and there are more in the making.'

'You mean to rebuild your principality, then?'

Prince Tjalan smiled. 'A principality? Nay, an empire – brighter than before. The population to support it is here, and thanks to men of wisdom like your husband – the power to rule it.'

Micail suspected that he could not have spoken had he wanted to. Tiriki's fair face – her cool eyes, grey green as the sea – that vision was enough for him, even when her glance turned toward Tjalan.

'It is true,' said Tiriki quietly; 'there is power in this land. And you have been building more than ships, I hear.'

'Yes,' the prince said, and smiled. 'A Sun Circle – a henge. The stones are not yet all sung into place, but when it is finished there will be no end to what we can do. Surely you see, Tiriki, you need not fear to entrust your people to me. We have the resources to house and feed them, and useful work to do.' Tjalan glanced briefly toward Micail as he added, 'This *is* the work of the prophecies, after all – your husband is laying the foundations of the new Temple.'

'Yes! You must come,' exclaimed Micail, taking refuge from his emotion in the superficial talk. 'What I have heard about those marshes has filled me with horror. To imagine you, beloved, scratching for every bite of food – sleeping on straw and skins – eaten alive by insects!' He shook his head.

'Is that what Damisa tells you?'

'She has hardly needed to,' Tjalan laughed. 'It was obvious from her reaction to decent food and lodgings! Yes, though I immodestly say it myself – we have already managed to reproduce most of our old way of life here. Although there will always be room for improvement, I am sure.'

Tiriki smiled politely. 'That is the one thing of which we may be certain, my lord,' she said. She dipped a piece of bread in the dish of olive oil, took a slice of cheese to go with it, and tasted the combination with every evidence of appreciation, although she offered no verbal compliment. Rendano and Elis, however, had by then devoured their own share and were openly eyeing what remained.

'And you—' Tjalan turned to Elis. 'Will you not be happy to join your fellow acolytes? And you, my lord, other priests of your Temple?'

Rendano only smiled politely, but Elis nodded vigorously, saying, 'I would love to see Elara – *and* Cleta! Lanath too. Are they well?'

'Very well,' Tjalan smiled. 'I understand they are making great progress in their – voicing? Is that the term? They have been helping us to raise the stones.'

'It sounds quite exciting,' said Elis, with a sidelong look at Tiriki. 'There is a small ring of stones on—'

'Master Chedan tells me there are standing stones and forgotten monuments all over this countryside,' Tiriki interrupted her, 'but they are all rather small. Nothing sized or shaped like – what has been described.'

'I have always had a passion for colossal stoneworks,' Tjalan admitted, 'but of course the circle is only a part of the complex of buildings we plan. When finished, it will be as large as the greatest temples of the Ancient Land! But soon you shall see it for yourself. I will send men to help you move your belongings, and bearers for any who cannot make the journey otherwise. I am longing to see Chedan again. I have been quite worried about his health.'

'That is kind,' said Tiriki. 'He has indeed been ill. That is why he did not accompany me. In fact . . . I would not like to see him subjected to the rigors of any journey, just now.'

Micail frowned. He knew that look, as if she were staring through you into some great distance. *My darling*, he thought, *what are you trying to hide?*

'Now that we have found each other,' she went on, 'there is no hurry, after all. We have been working with the poor natives of the marshes, and it would be heartless to abandon them.'

'I hardly—' Tjalan's face darkened as he restrained his temper. 'I quite understand,' he muttered. 'You know, you should have met my wife – she was quite sentimental too.' He took a deep breath. 'Micail, I have been thoughtless. You and Tiriki must have so much to say to one another. Why don't you walk together for a little while?' The unspoken words, *and talk some sense into her*, were as clear as a falcon's cry.

Tiriki's hands were warm, just as he remembered, but not so soft, and her fingers were lightly callused. Micail turned them upward in his own, tenderly caressing them, and frowned at each tiny cut and scar and scratch.

'Your poor beautiful hands! What have you been *doing!*'

She smiled a little. 'Building something, just like you. But without as much help.'

He laid one arm about her shoulders, resisting the temptation to draw her even closer. They were well out of earshot of the others, but hardly unseen, and he was uncomfortably aware of being watched by an interested audience. It would not do for a senior priest of the Temple to tumble his wife on the hillside in front of the gods and everyone.

He fought to find words for what he was feeling. How strange that after all this time he should find it so hard.

'I keep thinking I must be dreaming,' he said after a moment. 'It's happened before . . . For most of the journey to Belsairath, and even after, really. You could hardly have called me sane. I don't know how long I haunted the harbor, but I was there day and night, sure that your ship would come in . . . Trying to drive out the vision of the harbor in Ahtarrath where you should have been. But there was nothing! Nothing . . .'

She moved forward a little, and her eyes were as wet as his own as she put both her arms about him and held him close. At last, he began to relax.

'How,' he breathed, 'how in the name of the gods did you survive?'

'By the help of the gods,' she said softly, 'and Chedan. He has been a tower of strength, the architect of so much that we have done. Without his wisdom, I must often have despaired.'

'I am so glad he was with you,' Micail murmured, and he meant it sincerely. *But still*, he thought with a stab of envy, *I should have been the one to guide and protect you.*

'And the people of the marshes showed us how to live in the new land . . . ' she was saying.

'On roots and berries and frogs?' he asked, disdainfully. 'I have heard what the natives eat in the Lakc lands. Even the Ai-Zir consider them savages.'

'Well, they have not been savage to us!' Tiriki said a little tartly. 'Chedan says that culture depends not on one's surroundings, but on one's soul. By that measure, these folk are civilized indeed.'

Chedan says . . . It occurred to Micail that he might come to dislike that phrase quite a lot, quite soon.

'Well,' he said, calmly enough, 'perhaps we can send one or two of our lesser priests to man your marshy retreat – but you and the child must join me in Azan.' Why were they talking about politics when what he wanted was to know more about her and the child in whose existence he found it hard to believe, even now.

'*Must*, Micail?' She gazed up at him soberly. 'That is not a word you ever used to me—'

'We have been so long apart – I have needed you so very much! It is not an order, beloved, it is a cry from the heart.'

'Do you know how many mornings I have awakened with a wet pillow because I had been weeping in my sleep, wanting you?' she replied. 'But before we took our marriage oath, we were sworn to the gods. Chedan says that to break one oath calls all of them into question. At home we worked for the gods together and surely we will do so again. But at present we have other obligations. At least *I* do. The marsh folk have given up their old ways to become part of our community and we cannot simply abandon them. If it is otherwise for you, why not leave Azan and come to live with me?'

About to answer, he realized he did not know what to say. If he told her that it was not the same, that his work with the Sun Wheel was more important, she would be insulted, and rightly so. He could not leave the henge incomplete! And if he told her of the intensity of the power that he had contacted here, would she be afraid?

'You see?' She smiled a little, reading his thought as she used to do. Then her eyes sharpened. 'Or do you have some other reason for wishing to remain? That girl, Anet . . . She seemed quite . . . proprietary, when she spoke of you.'

'There is nothing between me and her but wishful thinking! On her part!' Had he protested too swiftly?

'I could hardly blame you if you had given in. She is quite beautiful and you did not know I was still alive.'

'Well, I certainly might have given in, but I didn't!' he said in a goaded tone. 'But you assume I was unfaithful, don't you? Are you trying to excuse yourself for sleeping with Chedan?'

Tiriki shrugged off his arm and faced him, eyes blazing. 'How dare you?'

He glared at her, taking refuge from his confusion in anger. 'What should I think, when every other sentence praises his name?'

'He is a great mage, a holy man and wise . . .'

'Unlike me?'

'You *were* great and wise in Ahtarrath.' Her eyes were grey and cold as a winter sea. 'I do not know what you are now.'

'Come to Azan and you will find out!' He glared at her.

'It will take some time, then,' she spat back, 'for the more I hear, the less reason I find to leave the Tor!'

'But Tjalan will not allow you to stay there. He – our people *must* be gathered so that our talents can be combined. Even together we are few – and he can protect us!'

'*We* do not need such protection.' Tiriki drew herself up. 'I may wear the blue robe of Caratra, but I am a Vested Guardian of the Temple of Light! Neither you, nor Chedan, nor even Tjalan of Alkonath may give orders to *me!*'

'The temples lie beneath the waves,' he said, suddenly tired. 'Until we build the new one, you and I and all the rest are Guardians of nothing. Help me, Tiriki, to make it a reality once more—'

'Nothing?' she repeated. 'Do you think the gods are powerless without their stone temples, then?'

'No, of course not – but the *prophecies*—'

'There are *many* prophecies!' She waved a hand impatiently and moved another step away. 'It is not important. The cult of Caratra is strong here . . . stronger than it was at home. My mother and your mother made me *Her* priestess long before Rajasta and Reio-ta made me Priestess of Light. I am linked to the Sacred Sisters of this land, and *they* believe that the Tor is where I should be.'

He stared, recognizing suddenly a resemblance between her and Anet, and quelled an odd twinge of unease. The mark of the Goddess? Ni-Terat's temple had been of little importance on Ahtarrath. He had never really had to consider Tiriki's other allegiance before.

'If you would keep hope alive that we may ever be together again,' Tiriki said sternly, 'do not attempt to command me to your side. Join me if you will. If not—'

'I cannot—' Micail broke off. *I do not dare to leave them for fear they will misuse this thing we are building!* At last he understood what he feared, but shame kept him from admitting as much to her. He would make sure the Sun Wheel could not be used to serve Tjalan's fantasies of power and then he could let it go.

'Surely you must have your reasons, Micail.' She seemed to believe in his sincerity, even if she did not understand him. 'I will not question you if you truly believe that you must remain where you are – for now. Our lives are not our own,' she added, and he was relieved to hear some trace of warmth in her words once more. 'You said that to me, long, long ago, and lately I have held it in my heart, for I see that it is true. We must fulfill our destinies . . . together or apart.'

'Only for a little while!' he said desperately. 'I cannot explain just yet—' Micail cast a quick glance up the hill and saw Tjalan watching them. 'Believe in me a little longer, as I believe in you!'

For a long moment she stared into his eyes, then at last she sighed. The prince was coming toward them.

'Tiriki—' he said swiftly, 'do not disagree with me when I tell him that you will be joining us soon.' He waited until he saw the last of her anger leave her eyes. 'Eilantha!' he said then. 'How I love you.'

'Osinarmen, I love *you*.'

In the echoes of their Temple names he heard a vow. For a long moment then they gazed at one another, memorizing every feature, every line and curve, as if they might never meet again. Then she took his arm and together they started back up the hill.

Damisa was sitting beneath the ancient oak tree in the enclosed garden of Tjalan's fortress when two of her guards announced a visitor. She grimaced with annoyance, half inclined to tell them she was not receiving and see if they obeyed her – despite their courtesy, it had become obvious that however protective it might be, she was surely in custody. But Tjalan had ridden off somewhere and she had exhausted the little garden's potential for entertainment. Besides, it might be someone she wouldn't mind seeing.

She half rose, her mouth opening in astonishment, as Reidel was escorted in.

'I . . . didn't expect to see *you* again,' she said as the guard bowed himself backward and closed the gate. She had risked Tjalan's anger to help Reidel. *Staying* saved seemed the least he could have done in gratitude.

'You should have known better.' He seated himself on one of the benches, looking around him with the self-possession that had always characterized him, even on the tossing deck of a ship in the midst of a storm.

'At least you *did* escape – I was half sure they'd just killed you. They showed me the wall you broke down – how did you ever—? Oh, never mind. Why in the name of *all* the stars have you put your head back into the noose?'

'I was sent back with a message. The prince and Micail have gone to meet with Tiriki. On neutral ground,' he added, when she started to protest again.

'Someone else could have carried it,' she muttered.

'Our community is not so large we can count anyone expendable,' he said dryly. 'And I knew the way. Besides – how could you think I would leave you here a prisoner? Although—' His gaze moved from the cushions of the carven chair to the finely-wrought table where a matching flagon and goblet gleamed like orichalcum in the sun, 'they seem to be treating you well!'

'Oh yes, the cage is quite luxurious.' She poured wine into the goblet and held it out to him. As he leaned forward into the sunlight she saw the red mark of someone's fist on his cheekbone.

'Are you ready to leave?' Reidel sipped and set the goblet down.

'Yes,' she said at once, but then turned away, not wanting him to see her blushes. 'No,' she began again, but once more stopped short. 'How can I choose when I see hazards on every road? If only Tjalan would trust me!'

'You *believe* him?' Reidel sprang to his feet, staring down at her.

'He wants to restore the glory of Atlantis. Don't you?'

'Ah. Let me rephrase that . . .' Reidel paced a few steps away and suddenly turned. 'Do you believe *in* him? Do you believe that his vision of the future is what you are meant to promote in this land?'

'I? But—' She found she could not meet his eyes. 'I don't know what you mean.'

Reidel moved closer, replying softly, 'Don't you? Then why didn't you just tell Tjalan how to find the Tor?'

'It is not for me to make decisions for Master Chedan!' Damisa in turn paced away, covering the distance to the wall and back again before she even tried to speak again. 'Or for Tiriki,' she began. 'I mean . . . we all have to choose . . . I don't *know!*'

'Oh, *that's* clear.' Reidel leaned against the oak tree, arms crossed. She was not quite sure, but she thought that the expression on his face was a smile.

What an exasperating man, she thought. Since her cruelty to him after their encounter the year before, he had never again spoken of love to her, and yet today he was no longer radiating that horrid, resentful pain. It was as if, without a word said, they had arrived at a new relationship – or *he* had – and his new certainty made Damisa feel more confused than ever.

'I'll ask *you* a question,' she said. 'You say you came back because of me – if I decide that Tjalan's right, will you support me?'

'You strike shrewdly,' he said, after some moments had passed. 'I'd bet Tjalan has no idea how strong you are, has he? For that matter – do you? I really suspect that if need be, you could climb this tree and get over the garden wall all by yourself. I've *seen* you do things a good bit more difficult!'

Damisa blushed in annoyance as Reidel shook his head and sighed. 'I give you the same answer you gave me – yes and no. What I have seen here convinces me Tjalan is no fit ruler. I do not think I wish to help him. But do not mistake me, Damisa. One way or another, I have had a lot of time to think recently. I realized finally that whether or not you ever care for me, it is my fate to love *you*. And to protect you, I will gladly shed the last drop of my blood.'

'We parted on terms of the highest courtesy,' said Tiriki bitterly, 'but we must prepare to defend ourselves all the same. We have only purchased a little time.' She looked around her at the other members of her community, her *family*, who were sitting on the rough benches around the council fire.

341

It was midafternoon, but she had coaxed a few logs into flame, not for warmth but as a symbolic illumination. In the Temple of Light the altar had borne an eternal flame, fed by some unknown source, burning in a lamp of purest gold. It was a far cry from this simple wood fire among the trees, but the light was the same, a splinter of the sun. *And I am no less a priestess*, she told herself. *That is something I would have expected Micail to understand* . . .

'How?' asked Kalaran. 'You say that Reidel is still – again – their prisoner?'

Elis nodded. 'We have to assume so.'

'You think, then, that Tjalan will find someone to lead his soldiers here – to attack us?' Liala asked, in an unsteady voice.

Tiriki nodded. 'And that is the least of our worries. Micail told me something of what he and the others have spent the last four years building – a structure of stones they call the Sun Wheel. According to Tjalan, it somehow controls sound.'

'Adsar's Eye!' Chedan swore. He looked around at the circle of uncomprehending faces. 'But of course you wouldn't understand. The theory of such devices was always taught only to the highest priesthood. I don't think anyone has actually *built* one for centuries.' He sighed. 'You all know that the vibrations of sound can move matter . . . In a properly designed space the vibrations are amplified. A trained group of singers can focus that vibration into a pulse that will travel quite a long way.'

'To move something?' asked Kalaran.

'To destroy?' whispered Elis, her face growing pale.

'He told me it was meant as a source of power for the new Temple,' Tiriki said quietly. 'But as you know, it can be directed anywhere along the network of energies that already flow through the earth . . . It is not finished. But I believe that enough stones have been placed for it to be used.'

'But they don't know where we are—' exclaimed Selast.

Rendano sighed. 'Not yet. But Prince Tjalan is quite proud of his new kingdom, and while we waited for Tiriki and Micail he boasted a great deal. For one thing, Stathalkha is with them, and she has been training other sensitives. They did a survey of all the power points in this land—'

Elis added, 'Including this one. The prince said . . . they knew we were here months ago. They just didn't think it mattered until now.'

'So you see, they don't have to send soldiers,' Rendano said. 'All they need to do is focus power along the ley line that connects the Sun Wheel to the Tor.'

'Does Prince Tjalan know they can do this?'

Rendano shrugged. 'Not yet, I think. But I suspect he soon will.'

Chedan was shaking his head. 'I do not believe it. I thought Ardral at least would be too wise to allow—'

'He is a great adept,' Rendano interrupted, 'but only one among many: Mahadalku and Haladris *and* Ocathrel of Alkonath – even Valadur the Grey! They are Tjalan's most ardent supporters.'

Chedan's expression grew bleaker with each name, for he knew them all. 'They *support* this madness?' he repeated blankly.

'I too could hardly believe my ears,' Tiriki answered, as she quickly reached to clasp his hands in her own. 'But Micail is not without his supporters. Jiritaren and Naranshada are there, among others, and the acolytes seem to regard him highly. But still, they are effectively out-numbered. And Tjalan somehow dominates them all. But how can any of them truly understand what they are risking! Except for Micail, *they* did not see the face of the power that broke Atlantis—' Tiriki's voice broke. 'They have never seen Dyaus.'

'Hush,' said Chedan. Hauling himself upright, he took his turn in trying to comfort her . . . With a little shock she realized that his beard was now completely white. For a moment Tiriki allowed herself to rest her head against his chest, angered anew as she remembered Micail's jealousy. It was like accusing her of sleeping with her grandfather.

Gently the mage patted her hair. 'Neither Ardral nor Micail will allow them to misuse their powers in such a way.'

'Do you truly think so?' She straightened, wiping her eyes. 'I wish I could be so sure. I thought I knew Micail – but there is something new in him. For four years his whole life has been dedicated to building that ring of stones. I don't know if he *can* abandon it.'

'If they do use it to send power against us – what can *we* do?' Liala asked.

Her voice wavered, and pity wrenched Tiriki's heart. *She is too old to have to face such a trial! And Chedan . . .*

'Alyssa!' Tiriki surprised even herself with the answer. 'She said something in her last ravings – at least I thought she was raving at the time,' said Tiriki slowly. 'She was muttering about a war in heaven and a ring of power, and then she cried out very loudly, "the Seed of Light must be planted in the heart of the hill!"'

There was silence, in which they all stared at Tiriki, plainly waiting for something more explicit.

Tiriki swallowed, and tried, 'I think she meant . . . that we *must* use the Omphalos Stone. You said it yourself, Chedan, before I left.'

'Yes,' said the mage, taken aback, 'but all it can do is balance the energies—'

'No,' Tiriki contradicted, 'forgive me, but no. There *is* more! But how it can be achieved . . . I must rest,' she decided. 'Perhaps when my head stops spinning the answer will come.'

'This is not a map of the physical landscape,' Stathalkha said haughtily, her white-robed arm gesturing at the rainbow-colored parchment scroll that lay spread out upon one of

Prince Tjalan's tables. 'It shows the paths in which energy flows.' With one thin finger she identified the various local points of power. 'You already know of this major flow, passing south to north through both the Sun Wheel and Carn Ava.'

Tjalan nodded eagerly. Micail's expression was more ambivalent. It was always desirable to have accurate knowledge, but the thought of a Guardian using his magical gifts against another Guardian – even for remote viewing – filled him with revulsion. Haladris was powerful, and with the backing of Mahadalku and Ocathrel, there was little he could not do – but Micail had a deeper understanding of the stones.

'Then there is this other very powerful flow—' The old priestess traced another line on her scroll. 'It continues from the southwest, roughly at the tip of Beleri'in, and then runs northeast, all across the island.'

'I still don't quite see how this helps us put pressure on Chedan and Tiriki,' said Tjalan, with remarkable restraint.

Stathalkha tilted her head and stared at the prince, bird-like, then shuffled the pile to produce another parchment upon which a surprisingly detailed map of Azan and the Lake lands had been drawn. 'Our perception puts them – just about here—' She indicated a point on the Beleri'in line.

Tjalan peered at the parchment, then touched two points on the map, asking, 'This is Azan? And this other, the Summer Country?'

Tjalan peered at the map again, angled his head, then examined it more closely. At last he looked up again with a wide smile. 'This' – he held up the map— 'this gives us a significant tactical advantage!' He then turned to Micail and put a hand on his knee, saying earnestly, 'Now I feel *certain* we can conclude this matter without harming anyone.'

Micail bristled, but somehow managed to smile, quelling his anger and disbelief with the thought that if he allowed them to push just a little – enough for Tiriki to comprehend their power – then she would have to admit that maybe Chedan could not protect her better after all.

Chedan's staff slipped on the muddy path and Iriel reached out to steady him. Ahead of them, Kalaran, Cadis, Arcor, and Otter staggered beneath the weight of the cabinet. Battered and scarred by its long voyage from the crypts of Ahtarrath, the wooden chest still contained, if only barely, the Omphalos Stone – although the weight of it seemed constantly to change, as if the box itself resisted their every effort to keep moving it along the path.

'I'm all right,' the mage muttered, 'help the others. Iriel – light their way.'

He was not all right, Tiriki knew, but no human hand could steady his spirit. Just as the Stone, struggling not to be moved, shook and twisted in its cabinet, that same roiling energy shook and seared their souls.

Just ahead of them, the mouth of the cave yawned out of the darkness, its base dimly whitened by the stream that gurgled toward its confluence with the waters of the Red Spring. Tiriki was about to step into the cave, but just there she paused, bending a little to let the light of her torch illuminate the interior. *At least*, she thought grimly, *we do not have to worry about earthquakes bringing* this *hill down around our ears*.

Over the past five years all of them – except, of course, poor Alyssa, whose sensitivities gave her little choice – had tried not to think about the Omphalos Stone.

Chedan had said that much of what they were doing even now had been prophesied, but so long ago that the prophecies had mostly been forgotten. Was everything foreknown and forgotten? Was she only another puppet in a drama, dancing for the pleasure of jaded gods? Surely Rajasta had never predicted that the survivors of Atlantis would war against each other . . . Or had he?

Struck by the sudden return of all her doubts, she turned to look back imploringly at Chedan, but he only shook his head. Closing her eyes, she steadied herself for what was to come. If Micail could not dissuade the other priests from using the Sun Wheel against them, or worse still, if he were persuaded, or deluded, or constrained, to help them, she would find herself pitted against him. As she advanced into the cave, she found herself almost wishing that she, like Alyssa, had died before seeing this day.

As Iriel cautiously followed Tiriki inside with another torch, the mage, summoning an inner reserve of strength, helped to guide the movement of the carriers as they struggled and fought to get the cabinet into the grotto. But Chedan's thoughts were distracted with visions, not of the future, but of the events that had brought him to this dreaded moment. Yet the life that he had lived and the many incarnations in which he had served the gods before that had taught him only too well that death could but delay one's fate, not change it. Putting off destiny only made the next life harder.

But he did wish that he did not always feel so very tired. *It is the Stone*, he reminded himself. *It knows that we mean to use its power, and it* will *have its price . . .*

With heartfelt grunts, the carriers struggled wearily along the passage, following the flickering torches. Often they were not even sure if they were climbing or descending.

The air was cool, at least, but it was dank, and the density of earth and stone above weighed on their spirits. 'We are children of Light, We fear not the Night,' Kalaran began singing, rather grimly, and with relief, the others joined the song—

> *'Let sorrow make a space for joy,*
> *Let grief with jubilance alloy,*
> *Step by step to make our way,*
> *Till Darkness shall unite with Day . . .'*

'Here—' Tiriki's voice echoed back down the tunnel. 'This is the arrow I drew to mark the spot. You see – there is the spiral pattern pecked into the stone. Don't touch it!' she warned as Iriel reached out. 'It has the power to hypnotize us and distract us from our necessary task.'

The footing here was smoother and the bearers could go more quickly – the Stone was becoming less restive too, as if it now understood where it was being taken, and approved. The passage curved around and doubled back upon itself several times, but it did not take long for Chedan to recognize, with a small jolt of satisfaction, that it was in fact the same pattern that they had been carving upon the surface of the Tor.

When walking a maze, the final turnings may draw one inward swiftly. Chedan hurried after the bearers as if caught up in the current of a stream – but this was a current of power, that carried them all into another tufa-crusted chamber, barely big enough for them all.

We have done the right thing to bring the Stone here, Chedan thought as he and Tiriki bent to unfasten the latches. Although the shielding effect of the many feet of earth and stone around it made its energies less disruptive than before, he could feel the power of the Omphalos surging even before the heavy lid began to open.

'Gently, *gently*,' he urged, as Tiriki freed the side panels of the cabinet from the framework and laid them aside. The Stone was already glowing in its silken wrappings like the sun through clouds.

'Truly the gods have guided us,' whispered Tiriki. 'See, there—' she pointed to the center of the chamber. 'A hollow that might have been made to hold the Stone!'

Allowing Kalaran to assist, they dragged the broken cabinet closer, then Chedan set his hands around the swathed, egg-shaped Stone and began to rock it back and forth inside its box. At his touch, its inner fires awakened and the frame cracked in three places, the pieces falling to the ground.

Chedan gasped as a surge of power ran up his arms and hearing him, Iriel dropped her torch and shrieked. Everyone else froze in place.

'Let me help!' Tiriki cried. Her torch too had failed, but the chamber was becoming brighter and the white tufa surfaces glittered.

'No!' he insisted, gesturing to them to stand aside as he ripped away the last of the silken cloths. Alone, he could use the Stone's own power to move it, but it was like trying to hold a burning coal. All at once the Stone's power surged again, teetering dangerously before him for a long moment before it settled onto the waiting hollow. Tiriki caught him as he staggered back, his palms throbbing furiously. He held them up, amazed to see no burns.

'Well then,' he said softly to the Stone, 'well then – have you found a home at last?'

As if in reply, the eerie surface dulled, absorbing its own glow. But then, as if the sun had risen inside it, the chamber filled with white-hot light. They all cried out in wonder.

'*The sacred center is our frame . . .*' Chedan intoned, '*Where all is changing, all the same . . .*'

All together they sang the verses, palms extended toward the Stone, until its overwhelming brilliance muted to something more bearable to mortal eyes. With a long sigh, Chedan groped for the staff he had leaned against the wall.

As the others, too, fell silent, Tiriki laughed a little breathlessly.

'My betrothed died to save this thing,' said Iriel quietly. 'I hope that it will save us now . . .'

'Pray instead that its powers will never be needed!' said Chedan roughly. 'Think only that we have done well to give it a proper setting. Where the Omphalos rests is the navel of the world! Once it lay hidden and unknown in the Ancient Land, until Ardral and Rajasta and I were called to carry it to Ahtarrath. Now it has come to this place. Here let it remain and bring only balance and light unto the world. *May it be so!*'

'So let it be,' the others answered in chorus, voices chastened.

'Now let us go,' the mage said sternly, 'and fervently pray that we need never think of the Stone again!'

But even as he spoke, he knew that they would not be so fortunate.

NINETEEN

After the Omphalos Stone was laid to rest, Tor seemed to glow with rays of light that swirled like red and white dragons twining in a ceaseless dance. Waking, Tiriki could feel them; asleep, they sometimes haunted her dreams. But those dreams were better than the nightmares – the twisted shadowy figures who followed her, only to corner her at last and reveal the leering face of . . . Micail.

After the third night in which such dreams robbed her of rest, she took refuge with Taret. Before Chedan and the others she still thought it best to pretend confidence in Micail's good faith, but keeping her doubts to herself was plainly not helping. Taret was close enough to care about the outcome, but not immediately involved. And the old woman was wise. *Another such night*, she thought grimly, *and I'll be raving like Alyssa – Caratra rest her.*

Leaving Domara in the care of the nursemaids, she started up the path, pausing once to note the condition of her favorite patch of wild garlic, and a little further on, to pluck a spray of wild thyme. She also offered her respects to the old oak tree, thinking even as she did so how surprised Micail would be to know that she could even identify such things. *Here I am like Deoris in her garden*, she thought with a sad smile. *If only we had her here. Destiny be damned! I should have grabbed her and dragged her down to the ships. She could have done so much good . . . And she had so much more experience with Temple politics, and for that matter, in dealing with nobles.*

Prince Tjalan had made it quite plain that his goal was nothing less than continuation of the civilization of Atlantis, and Micail had not seemed to question that. It had not occurred to either man to ask if Tiriki supported that goal. Even two years ago she might have agreed, she thought, as she passed the yew trees that flanked the pathway to the Blood Spring. But from the moment the *Crimson Serpent* had arrived here, the lack of resources had forced them to forsake their old way of life. Only by learning from the marsh folk had they been able to survive.

Was she only making a virtue of necessity? Happy as she was here, she had to admit there was much about the old world that she still missed, and she knew that there were others in the community at the Tor who longed for lost customs far more than she. But Tiriki could not help feeling that those who persisted in clinging to the goals and ambitions of a vanished empire were only wasting their efforts and their resources. Even so, she would not have strenuously objected if any of her followers had chosen to leave the Tor and live as Tjalan thought best. But the prince had not offered them any choice at all.

The thought that this peaceful place might be invaded made her shudder. *That is the* only *argument for giving in to Tjalan's demands. Then at least they would leave the Tor alone . . .* But that, she realized suddenly, was wishful thinking. Whatever the virtues of their intentions, Tjalan's priests were power-hungry, and even without the Omphalos Stone, the Tor had been a place of considerable power. The new currents that writhed about it now would call like twin beacons to Stathalkha's sensitives. If they had ignored it before, they would not do so again. One way or another, there would be a conflict between what *they* wanted, and what she had come to believe she was destined to do here.

But even that certainly brought her little reassurance.

Something Chedan had said the previous night had reminded her that the truest destiny was not a thing to be worked out in a single life, but a greater purpose that arose again and again throughout many lives. What she had begun here was right and necessary, and ultimately its promise would be fulfilled; of that she was no longer in doubt. But that fulfilment might take three days or three thousand years.

She found the wisewoman sitting on a stool before her house, using a flint knife to scrape the outer rind from water lily roots. She turned her head as Tiriki came up the path.

'The blessing of the evening be upon you.'

'The Lady give you rest,' Taret replied, with a slight smile. 'I had thought you were keeping talk-fire with your people.'

'The council fire is lit,' Tiriki said with a sigh, 'but nothing is being said that has not been discussed seven times since breakfast.' She sank down beside Taret and took up another flake of flint. 'So I shall help you pare these roots. My mother used to say there is comfort in such ordinary tasks, an affirmation that life will go on. I did not listen to her then. Perhaps it is not too late.'

'It is never too late,' said Taret gently, 'and I shall be glad of your help.'

After a few moments had passed, and she had cut several roots, she said, 'I suppose that I have really come to apologize,' she admitted, 'for I fear we have brought disaster upon you and your people – and that is poor thanks for all your kindness. I have warned the villagers, but they will not leave. Will you go to them and lead them out of danger?'

'This is the place where the Mother has planted me,' Taret smiled. 'My roots go too deep to pull them up now.'

Tiriki sighed. 'You don't understand! Alyssa's vision led us to move the Stone to the cave within the Tor, but if she saw how it would help us afterward, she did not say, or I did not understand. We cannot all take refuge there – even if our minds could bear to be so near it, there is not room for us all!'

'You look at the Stone. That is good. Now, look at the Tor.' Taret sliced through a root and reached for the next.

Tiriki stared at her in frustration. 'But – how?'

'You can no longer go to one and not be in the wind of the other.'

Tiriki closed her eyes, wondering how her own language could be so hard to interpret.

The old woman did look up, and her eyes sparkled as if she was restraining herself from laughter. 'Sun Girl, Sea Child, you ask too much of an old servant of the sacred waters. But there is one who knows all its secrets. She has blessed you before. Perhaps She will do so again . . . if you ask her nicely.' Taret chuckled. 'Maybe *She* has some house-work for you to do.'

Tiriki sat pensively, remembering. She did indeed have reason to know that the Tor was a place where the many worlds drew very close together.

'Yes,' she whispered, and made the gesture of a chela to an adept in the old woman's direction. 'As always, Taret, you redirect my eyes to the wisdom that lies in plain sight. That was the mistake we Atlanteans made, perhaps – to fix our eyes on the heavens and forget that our feet, like the earth on which we stand, are clay.' She set down the flint and stood up. 'If any come to seek me, tell them I hope to return soon, with better news.'

Once, Tiriki had walked this way by chance, and once, by following the winding ways within the Tor. This time she walked the maze on the surface of the hill with the setting sun behind her, passing between day and night as she sought for the first time by intention, the way between the worlds.

The summit of the Tor wavered and receded as another landscape loomed up around it, blotting out the valley she had come to know so well. Yet she perceived still the cluster of life energies at the foot of the hill, those of the villagers warm and golden, the Atlanteans at once more pale, yet brighter. Her heart seized on the tiny sparkle that was her daughter, then caught at another familiar glow, so incandescent in its purity that at first she did not recognize it as Chedan. Her eyes blurred with a surge of affection for them all.

But this vision showed her nothing she had not already known. She turned impatiently, seeking eastward for the focus of power that was Micail's henge of stones.

Why did I never think to do this before? she wondered then. *I have been so embedded in the daily struggle, I never made time to explore the spiritual landscape here.* She directed her attention eastward.

Most certainly the Sun Wheel was there – a circular pulsing of energy in which the white-hot sparks of the initiates dazzled amid the reddish glows that could only be Tjalan and his men.

As she watched, the ring of light grew brighter, pulsing with a rhythm that even from here she knew was based on song. They were loading the henge with power on which they might draw when the time came. And if she could see them, surely they could sense the Tor. She shivered as the distant beam rippled and quivered like the sun seen from under water.

She had hoped that Tjalan would be content to attack them physically. By the time he had marched his soldiers to the Tor, she might have been able to negotiate some accommodation, either with Micail, or with the tribes of Azan. But the prince had found a new weapon, and her vision suggested that he did not mean to wait until it was finished to try it out.

Disheartened, she sank to her knees.

'Lady of Light, Shining One, in my great need you came to me before, unsummoned. Now I call you, I implore you, hear me. Those who should have been our protectors have become our enemies. I do not know whether they will send the forces of the body or of the spirit first, but I am afraid, for my enemies are very strong. Tell me that we will be safe here, and I will believe you. But if you cannot, then I beg you, show me how I may protect those I love . . .'

The answer came as a gentle teasing. 'Safe! You mortals use language so strangely. You have had bodies before this one and you will have others after. You die, or your enemy dies, but both of you will live again. Why be afraid?'

'Because – we are taught that each life is precious!' Tiriki looked around, hoping to see the one who had spoken, but there was only a shimmering, a fullness in the air. Yet that, too, was an answer. How could she explain her fears to a being whose form was never destroyed, but rather, was constantly transforming, in ways she could not even imagine? 'Surely,' said Tiriki haltingly, 'each life has its own lessons, its own meaning. I would not have this one cut short before I have found out what it has to teach me!'

'That is a good answer.' The voice sounded serious.

'And I do not seek destruction of our enemies, only to keep them from doing us harm,' Tiriki continued. 'Please – *will* you help us?'

As if in answer, the shimmering intensified, seeming to surround her, but the brilliance was fired by a new source, blazing deep within the hill.

'The Omphalos Stone!' she whispered in awe, and saw it pulse in response to her words.

'The Seed of Light,' the voice echoed. 'You have planted it, little singer. Your songs can make it grow.'

'I still say there is no need to do anything just yet,' Micail insisted. 'The Lake people are poor, with no resources to stand against us.' But he knew all too well that he had been saying the same thing ever since they returned from the meeting with Tiriki, and with as little result. And now it was almost too late for talking. With Tjalan's blessing, indeed, with his overt encouragement, Haladris had yet again called the entire priesthood to the henge. They meant to finish the awakening of the stones as quickly as possible.

Within a day or two at the most, Micail knew there would be nothing remaining to prevent the Sun Wheel from being used in whatever way they saw fit.

'What you say would be true if they *were* marsh people,' Mahadalku observed with maddening reasonability, 'but they are in fact priests and Guardians like us. They may have gone native to some degree, but they have got *something more*.' The Tarissedan high priestess clutched her veils tightly against the wind off the plain. 'Stathalkha says that over the previous days the intensity of power at the Tor has tripled. Why should that be happening, unless it is because they now know we are here? Best to deal with them before they strike at us!'

'But the Sun Wheel is not complete,' Micail objected, 'We have not even had time to determine if it will—'

'Unfinished it may be,' Mahadalku interrupted, 'but all preliminary tests show it to be fully capable of containing and projecting the necessary vibrations. Ardravanant and Naranshada have both affirmed this conclusion.' She spoke in a calm flat tone that discouraged objection. With a sinking heart, Micail looked around at the other priests and priestesses who, in return, discreetly avoided his eye.

No doubt Jiritaren would follow him if he walked out now, and Naranshada had expressed more than a few doubts about the wisdom of what they were doing. Bennurajos and Reualen, perhaps . . . if Micail pressed the point. He felt fairly sure that Galara and the acolytes might follow him as well. But was that the best option?

Tjalan would probably place us under house arrest, and use the threat to the other prisoners to ensure I did nothing to affect the outcome . . . But if I stay . . . he sighed. *Then I could end up killing Tiriki myself! And in that case I should cut my own throat and apologize to her in the afterlife . . . and be damned to the prophecies!*

In the days since his meeting with Tiriki, it had often occurred to him that he ought to have gone with her, not meekly returned here. He had told himself that then Tjalan might not have permitted either one of them to leave; he had thought of his duty to the acolytes and the fulfillment of his other vows. Now, though, as he gazed at the sharp silhouettes of the tall stones standing against the blue summer sky, he realized that it was a craftsman's love for his creation that kept him here.

I am like a man whose son falls into evil company. Reason says he must be renounced, but the good father continues to hope that the boy will turn to the right path once more. The henge has such great potential for good . . .

'How does this preserve our traditions?' he tried again. 'Tiriki and Chedan have not been charged as heretics – we have not declared war. It is simply not legitimate for us to act against our fellow priests in this way! And it is wrong at an even deeper level to give over this kind of power to such a prideful purpose.' He gestured at the line of soldiers just outside the ditch and bank that surrounded the circle. It was not clear whether they were there to protect the priests against interference from outside or to keep them in.

'Why should we help Prince Tjalan build his empire?' Micail continued.

'Because that empire will support the new Temple,' Ocathrel answered, and the rest seemed to share his exasperation. It occurred to Micail that perhaps he had better stop talking before they all decided he was not just prone to moral misgivings but actually unreliable – possibly a heretic himself. Then they would take the choice regarding whether he should stay or go out of his hands.

At least Ardral was not present to lend *his* power to this disaster. When the gong had summoned them that morning, the old adept had pleaded wine-sickness and kept to his quarters. But despite the knowing nods of the chelas, Micail knew that Ardral was rarely ill. Was he merely staying away or *going* away?

Wearily turning away from Ocathrel and Haladris and the

rest, Micail sat in the shadow of one of the sarsen uprights, and let his thoughts return to the events of the night before.

He had gone to Ardral's quarters to plead for his support and found him sorting through parchments. Some of them had been burning merrily in a charcoal brazier beneath the smokehole. That sight alone had been enough to strike Micail speechless for several moments – Ardral had been curator of the Temple library at Ahtarrath, after all.

'No, no,' the old Guardian had reassured him, 'I am just clearing out a few odd notes and poems and personal musings. No ancient secrets, or at least none that I feel any obligation to pass on. One might argue that all *my* secrets are ancient! But after a lifetime of study, meditation and practice – all I really know is how little any of us knows.' And he had laughed.

Micail remembered the gleam of firelight on aquiline features as Ardral flipped his faintly silvered hair out of his eyes once more.

'Would you like to join me in the last of the teli'ir?' he'd asked then, as if they had been sitting on a gilded terrace, watching the sun set over Ahtarra's harbor or possibly over Atalan itself. Micail had been too nonplussed to do anything but agree.

It had been a pleasant time. They had spoken of many things, most of them amusing. But by the time Micail managed to bring the conversation around to what troubled him, he'd been seeing both Ardral and the firelit room through a perfumed haze. Yet the adept's diction had remained crisp throughout, even if his meaning was sometimes obscure.

'Do you really think my arguments might move Tjalan when yours have not? I am a fine speaker if I do say so myself, but you are his cousin and, moreover, he considers you a close friend.' Ardral shook his head. 'I admit, I found Princess Chaithala and the children charming, and I enjoyed *their* company immensely, but the Prince of Alkonath and

I have never had much to say to one another beyond the usual pleasantries. And none of them will have much to miss when I am gone.'

'Gone?' Micail had stared, wondering if the rumors of illness could possibly be true. Ardral certainly had not *looked* ill, but then he did not look his age either, and he had been old when Micail's parents were babes in arms. 'You are healthy!' he had exclaimed, not sure whether it was a statement or a prayer. Ardral had quirked one eyebrow and Micail flushed in confusion.

'Of course I am. That is why I must go. Every night, every day, Tjalan, or someone, thinks up another question I don't care to answer. I suspect I have been here too long already . . . and I know too many things that man is no longer *meant* to know.'

Even for Ardral, Micail thought now, that had been cryptic. 'Does that mean you will not join in the Working at the Sun Wheel?' Micail's flogged wits had seemed suddenly sodden, making him wish he had not had that second glass of teli'ir.

'Oh, I will be working.' Ardral's teeth had flashed in a wry smile as he briefly patted Micail's shoulder. 'Do not trouble yourself over me.'

Micail had retained enough wit not to say that it wasn't Ardral he was worrying about, but Tiriki, and perhaps the rest of the world. And then the old adept was ushering him to the door.

'I suspect this will be our farewell, Micail, but who can say what fate intends? Time is a long and twisted trail, my boy, and it has many a side road. Our paths may cross again!'

> *Nar-Inabi in Thy splendor*
> *Against the darkness ever rising,*
> *Grant us tonight a restful slumber*
> *And all Thy – all Thy—*

The first verse of the evening hymn faltered, for night had fallen, fallen finally. Above it, its slayer stood, horned like a bull. Victorious darkness drenched the stars, and all had turned to dim mist and hard stone, grey substances crumbling, adrift . . .

Chedan opened his eyes with a start, surprised to see pale light shafting through the open door of his hut.

'Are you all right?' Kalaran bent over him with a frown.

'I will be,' said the mage. He rubbed his temples, trying to dispel the mists of dream sufficiently to face the day.

Kalaran still looked worried, but he held out the carven staff that had become Chedan's constant companion. As they emerged from his hut he could see that the sky beyond the slope of the Tor was a translucent blue. It was going to be a beautiful day.

'I had a rather odd dream.'

Kalaran looked expectant, and Chedan suppressed a smile. Since he had become so lame, the young people had taken to treating him like some rare treasure that would soon fall apart. It might even be true, he thought then. Besides, talking about one's dreams sometimes brought understanding, and this one could be a warning he should not deny.

'I was back in Ahtarra, visiting my uncle Ardral in his chambers by the library. We were drinking some exotic liqueur from the Ancient Land – that man had the most wonderful cellars, it wrenches the heart to think of those delicate vintages mingling with the salt sea. Anyway, he lifted his glass to me in a toast and said that I must go and he must stay, but that between us we had trained my heir.'

'Your heir,' echoed Kalaran, looking rather alarmed. 'What did he mean?'

'What did Ardral *ever* mean? I would have said it was Micail, but now . . . I do not know.' He shook his head, his heart aching anew at the thought that Micail might have become their enemy. 'In any case, Ardral hardly knew him. At least he didn't then. They may have grown closer.'

'Oh . . . But Master, but when you said "odd" – you laughed. Well almost.'

'Yes I did, because I'd been remembering how Ardral finished his drink and set it down and then – he was sitting cross-legged on a low chair – he simply floated upward and out of the window and away.'

'He *levitated?*' Kalaran's voice squeaked.

'Well – actually I *have* heard rumors that he could. But I suppose it was symbolic, in my dream. Because, you see – though Anet told us he was there, I sent him no message. I could not think what to say. And he sent me no answer. So I suppose we flew away from each other.'

As Kalaran's brows knitted in perplexity, Chedan gave him a fond smile. 'Thank you, my boy. I was afraid I had dreamed something important, and you have helped me to see otherwise. If my dream means anything, it means he has gone away – I thought he might have died, but now I rather doubt that. I think I would know. Still, I have been thinking about him. I suppose I have only made a new song out of words he used to say. When one is dreaming it often happens that way.'

'I have a lot of strange dreams,' said Kalaran, after an awkward moment, 'but everything looks better after a good breakfast!'

'That I will *not* argue with,' said Chedan, and he permitted his acolyte to help him down the hill. As they walked, a thin trail of smoke brought the rich scent of hot meat through the trees. Certainly a good meal would help him get through this dreadful day.

'Have you heard?' Vialmar murmured to Elara. 'Lord Ardral is gone!'

'What do you mean? Prince Tjalan has guards at every gate of the compound to "protect" us. They would not let him simply walk away!'

'That's the best part of it,' said Vialmar, with a grin, 'and I've heard it from several different people now – he just came out of his doorway, floated up off the ground and over the wall – gone! Like that!'

'Does Tjalan know?' came Cleta's awed whisper.

'If he does,' answered Elara, 'he's not letting it interfere with his plans. Look – he's brought Damisa!'

'And Reidel—' added Cleta. 'Does the prince think he can persuade them to join us, or does he simply want to show off our power?' She traded glances with Elara.

How, indeed, have we come to this? Elara wondered. *Surely there are too few of us in this land to be at odds . . .* But so long as her elders were in agreement, her vows required her to obey them.

She had even taken the risk of being late, going out of her way to speak to Khayan-e-Durr, but the Ai-Zir were no match for Atlantean swords or Atlantean magic. She had meant to ask their help and had ended by warning them to stay away. She was not sure, even now, if she had succeeded in convincing the queen of the danger. The shamans might be planning something. She had heard drumming from Droshrad's big roundhouse, but now that she thought about it, that was nothing unusual.

If Tiriki dies because of this – what will Micail do then? Could he live with that? She remembered the raw pain in his face when he returned from that meeting between Tjalan and Tiriki, and knew that he could not bear a more final parting. Her own emotions twisted, and she felt an overwhelming sympathy, mixed with the unbearable thought of a world without Micail in it . . .

There was Micail, she suddenly noticed, sitting by himself against one of the stones. She had not seen that look on his face since they left Belsairath. Why didn't he simply refuse to participate? Denounce them all?

The gleam of sunlight on an orichalcum-edged spear caught her eye. Tjalan had stationed his soldiers at regular intervals just beyond the outer ring of stones . . . *That's one reason, I guess.* Elara blushed again.

Not, she realized glumly, that her Temple vows would have allowed her to hope for Tiriki's death even if she had thought that she had any hope of replacing her in Micail's bed. But how they were to come out of this without serious damage to one side or the other was more than she could imagine.

Cleta tapped her on the shoulder. Haladris was summoning them all to take their places. The ordeal was about to begin.

'I don't understand,' said Damisa. 'What are you planning to do to persuade the people at the Tor to join you? What *can* you do, from here?' Actually, even in her gilded cage, some rumors had reached her. It was just that she found them difficult to believe.

Tjalan turned to her, his eyes gleaming more brightly than the golden dragon bracelets he wore. For a thousand generations those bracelets had been the prerogative of a prince of the royal line.

'Something I would rather not do. But birthing a new empire always requires some initial . . . adjustments,' he said. 'When the Bright Empire gave way to the Sea Kingdoms it was the same. Believe me, my dear, I do regret the necessity for decisive action. But it is clear that Tiriki is going to be stubborn. Better one sharp disciplinary strike than a lingering conflict, don't you agree? Then we can put all our energies into establishing the new order. Come now, you *must* agree, Damisa – for I cannot do all this alone.' His long fingers stroked along her arm. 'Now that I have lost Chaithala, I will need a woman to stand beside me, to bear me sons . . . What use a crown with no heir?'

Damisa's pulse quickened. Was he really suggesting that she might be his . . . empress . . . one day? It made sense – the royal blood of Alkonath ran in her veins too – but after all that had happened, it seemed unreal to be offered what had once been her fantasy. Suddenly she understood why

Tiriki had gone back to the Tor instead of returning here with Micail. *She has become a mover of events, not simply a support to her man*, she thought. *What could I become, on my own?*

But she must not let Prince Tjalan suspect her conflicting emotions. Her glance slid away from his and she saw that soldiers were bringing up Reidel, his wrists still bound. His lip was puffy where someone had hit him – hit him back, she corrected, noting the skinned knuckles on his right hand.

'My prince, you honor me,' she said a little breathlessly. 'But I must not distract you with such considerations now.'

He smiled sardonically, but her answer had clearly satisfied him. His attention was already shifting to Haladris, who had begun to organize the singers within the circle of stones.

Reidel was looking at her, with – anger? appeal? He had no right to either emotion. But even when she turned away, she could still feel his dark gaze.

Tiriki forced herself to look away from the dim haze to the east where she knew Micail and the others were preparing to strike against the Tor, and to look instead into the faces of the men and women who waited atop the Tor to defend it.

She cleared her throat and managed a smile. 'The spirit of this place, the Shining One I call the Queen, has shown me what we are to do—'

'But how do we know if they will act today?' asked Elis.

'Or at all?' muttered someone else.

'I have seen the power building,' answered Tiriki. 'But even if I had not, surely it will do us all no harm to practice our own skills.'

'Ah,' said Iriel archly, 'more *training!*' and the tension eased a little as the other acolytes laughed.

'Yes, if you will,' said Tiriki blandly, and waited for quiet to return. 'We have walked the spiral maze we cut into the hill to get here, and that puts us halfway to the Otherworld already. I would like everyone to sit in a circle and join hands—' Tiriki glanced at Chedan and he nodded.

Despite the exertion of getting up here, Chedan's face was pale. He should have been in bed, she thought then, but they needed him too badly, and in truth, they were all hazarding their lives today. At least Domara was safe with Taret. Whatever happened, she would survive.

Tiriki stood in the center of the circle and lifted her hands to the pure light that streamed down from above. It was the second verse of the Evening Hymn that came to her now—

> '*Oh Holiest and Highest,*
> *Sole wisdom worth the winning,*
> *In Thee, we find our purpose,*
> *Our end and our beginning.*'

She made the sign of blessing on breast and brow, then took her place in the circle across from Chedan.

'Oh great Manoah, King of Gods, and Thou, Most High, who art the power behind all gods, to You we make our prayer—' She added then, 'Not for glory or gain, but for the preservation of life, and of the knowledge You have given us. Protect this holy hill and all who shelter here, and let us bring those who work against us to the path of true wisdom . . .'

Her gaze was drawn eastward once more. What were those opponents – for even now she would not think of them as enemies – doing now?

'We are the inheritors of an ancient tradition,' said Haladris, 'and today we shall demonstrate its strength. Our henge will protect our spirits, and Prince Tjalan's soldiers will guard our bodies. Fear not, therefore, to put forth all of your power. Project a hammer of force from this circle that will strike terror into our foes.'

And what if we succeed? thought Micail grimly. He cast a quick glance at Naranshada and Jiritaren, who stood with him among the tenors near the midpoint of the crescent. Both their faces were lined with strain, their eyes narrowed and haunted by regrets, and in the moment, he knew that their unease was nothing new. *They don't like this either. I should have voiced my protests long ago . . . before things had gone so far . . .* And yet if he had done so Tjalan would have put it beyond his power to act at all, and here, even now, he *might* be able to alter the outcome.

Haladris took his place in the center of the crescent of vested priests and priestesses, their bodies completing the circle outlined by the five trilithons, surrounded by the outer ring. He hummed a series of notes, and section by section, the singers released their tones. One would not have thought that so soft a sound could be powerful, but in a few moments Micail could hear the first response from the stones.

It was only a whisper, like the sound of many other voices chanting somewhere far away, but Micail felt the hairs stand up along his forearms. And then for a moment, pride in his achievement surged above his fear.

When Tiriki clasped hands with Kalaran and Iriel, Chedan felt a tingle of power and knew that the circle of energy had closed. As one, they slowed their breathing, seeking the deeper rhythm of trance. He felt the familiar dip and lurch of shifting consciousness, and he reached out to touch Tiriki's mind. They gathered the attention of the others into a single awareness and opened their lips in a single soft note.

Our task is easier, he thought, trying to steady his nerves as a dozen voices swelled in sound. *Our opponents must shape and guide an unwieldy energy to attack us, but we have only to affirm the power that is already here, at what is now the sacred center.*

The tone grew louder, pulsing as the singers circled their breathing around the sound. Already the pure radiance of the sunlight was altering to the shimmering illumination of the Otherworld. And then, from the depths beneath them, Chedan heard the reverberation as the Omphalos Stone caught and amplified their song. His eyes met Tiriki's then, and for a moment, their wonder balanced their fear.

Elara let her breath out in a pure exhalation of sound, trembling a little as the sopranos' higher note matched it in harmony. Exhilaration tingled through every vein at the energy those vibrations were raising, resounding from the smooth surfaces of the stones. Whatever happened after, Elara thought she would never forget the sheer beauty of this sound.

But even as the thought was completed, she realized that the music was changing. Haladris was conducting the lower ranges into an oddly discordant note that rattled her heart. She heard two or three singers waver, but Mahadalku's glares brought them swiftly back on pitch. She almost *could* see the sound vibrations shifting as they bounced from stone to stone, and spiraled westward toward the Tor.

Tiriki felt the attack as a change in pressure, a tension in the air like an oncoming thunderstorm. She tightened her grip on Selast's hand and felt a ripple of added alertness pass around their circle.

'*Maintain the note,*' came Chedan's mental command. '*Do not be afraid. Remember, all we have to do is hold on . . .*'

As we did when the great wave struck our boat after the Sinking? wondered Tiriki as the first shock buffeted them. Somehow, she forced her focus back to the chambered lattices of stone beneath her and the Seed of Light within them, the twin powers that fountained up from the Red and White Springs in the depths, the vibrant ringing of her soul . . .

The pressure increased, as if, having been rebuffed, Tjalan's priests had turned up the intensity of their own singing. The brilliance flashed and refracted as if she sat in the heart of a crystal, while weird lightnings crackled above the Tor.

She reached deeper, drawing on the power of the Omphalos Stone. She fought to maintain the vision of a bubble, a sphere of protection against which all the waves of power she could feel coming against them would break in vain. She could feel the others setting themselves to resist as well. Handgrips tightened until bones creaked and knuckles whitened, but that was the least of their agony.

For Domara . . . she thought with gritted teeth, *and Selast and her unborn child.*

For Otter . . . came Iriel's plea. *For Forolin and Adeyna and Kestil . . . for Heron and Taret . . .*

For all of those they had learned to love in this land, the litany of names went on, and they *held* on, fiercely enduring in the name of all that they had already lost.

'Damisa, I can't see into the circle!' exclaimed Tjalan. 'Is something wrong?'

Damisa twitched free of his proprietary hand. Already, she had heard what sounded like a distant rumbling from the circle of stones, and realized that the Working had begun. But there was surprisingly little noise. It must be true, then, that the circle of stones captured sound. Now the figures of the people within it appeared to be wavering, as a distant scene might be distorted on a very hot day. But she did not think this country *could* produce the kind of heat needed for that to occur.

'My eyes see no more than yours do—' she muttered. 'It is a byproduct, I think of the vibration. Dust may be rising from the soil, or perhaps the light is simply . . . distorted. You can feel it through the ground.'

At least I can, she thought, though Tjalan's sturdy soldier's sandals might insulate him from the tremor that came through the thin soles of her own sandals, queasily reminiscent of the way the earth of Ahtarrath had trembled before the Sinking. She considered advising him to bend down and put his ear to the ground, but that would probably not have accorded with his dignity. What must it be like to be *inside* the circle, working with all that power? she wondered, repressing a pang of envy.

The stones at Azan were dancing.

Micail blinked, but his vision was not the problem. The ground beneath his feet was shaking, and as Mahadalku guided the singing of the sopranos even higher, the sarsen uprights vibrated in time with the sound. This was not the precise and ordered singing that had raised the stones, but a calculated disharmony that scraped and seared in every nerve and bone.

Micail realized that he was not the only one who had fallen silent, but with three full stands in the choir, there were still enough singers to maintain the vibration. He wondered how anything could stand against this onslaught, but clearly the Tor was doing so. He could feel the distortion as the waves struck something that repelled them and then rolled them back again.

We cannot break through! he exulted. But did Haladris know it? The Alkonan priest was singing even more loudly, warping the harmonies. From the scraped chalk surface within the circle a fine white dust was rising. The priest was pale and perspiring, with the fixed stare of one whose vision is focused within. Micail realized that Haladris could not see what was happening around him. The upright stones had been set deeply and braced in the pits that held them, but they had never been designed to resist such a protracted shaking. Stone groaned and rasped as one of the sarsen pillars in the northernmost trilithon shifted, jiggled, twisted, only kept in place by the knob that linked it to its lintel . . .

Although Micail refused to contribute his full strength to

the Working, even in his detachment he felt the expanding wave that shuddered through the flow of power. He suspected that the resistance from the Tor was about to break. But it would make no difference to the unraveling energies here; in fact without direction those forces would cause far greater havoc, both in the circle and at the Tor, than the simple warning slap that Haladris had intended.

I have to stop this before the whole henge comes down! He reached out to his beloved stones and, suddenly, a voice he knew to be that of his father reverberated in his heart—

'Speak with the powers of the storm and the wind – of sun and rain, water and air, earth and fire!' He realized that this moment was the reason for the reawakening of his inherited powers.

'I am the Heir-to-the-Word-of-Thunder!' Micail cried, 'And I claim this land!'

The line of soldiers staggered, casting frantic glances toward Tjalan, as a tremor ran through the soil outside the henge.

'We're winning!' cried the prince, gripping Damisa's arm. 'No one can stay conscious if that hits them! Do you feel the power?'

'*Never!*' Reidel shouted. 'Not while I live!' As the earth heaved again, he broke from his captors and staggered toward the circle of stones.

'Reidel, no!' cried Damisa. The idiot was going to get himself killed!

'Stop him!' roared Tjalan, but it was all his soldiers could do to stay upright. With a curse he let go of Damisa and lurched after Reidel, drawing his sword.

Damisa was hard on his heels. *Both* of them were idiots. This whole situation was mad. Between fear and fury, her thoughts were scarcely coherent, but with a burst of unexpected energy, she caught up with Tjalan, grabbed his sword arm, and spun him aside. The prince screamed in frustration, but she kept going, and in a moment she had tackled and brought down Reidel. His body was warm and solid, and she held on to him, gasping, as once she had gripped him while they made love.

'You will *live*, damn you!' she whispered as his eyes widened in surprise.

Micail bestrode chaos and wielded thunder. In the Word of his Power he found a new sound to counter the escalating vibrations that threatened to unmake the land. But the energy had to go somewhere. For a hot white instant that seemed an eon, doom hung around him like a frozen explosion. He had time to calculate the forces, note the position of every life-spark and measure the gaps between the stones.

'Get back!' he cried to the others. 'Get clear if you can!' And then he sang out the note that he hoped would angle the energy away from the other singers, holding it with all the strength that was in him as shrilling forces blasted outward through the trilithons.

Chedan felt the ebb of the assault and swayed as if the wind against which he stood had suddenly failed. Only now, when the pressure was gone, did he realize how the effort had drained him. Tiriki, sagging against Kalaran, had gone as white as her linen gown, but she was smiling. In the faces of each of the others he saw the same astonished joy.

We have survived! he thought, feeling his tired heart pound in his breast. And in that moment, the forces that they had thought vanquished came roiling through the relapsing barrier like a stampede of maddened bulls.

Responses honed by a lifetime's disciplined trancework brought Chedan back to his feet with the speed of instinct, his staff swinging outward.

'Begone!' His shout reverberated across the land. In desperation he flung his spirit after it into the windy heavens, driving those terrible energies before him. He never knew when the flesh he had worn slumped to the earth, to move no more.

From the northeast to the southwest sides of the henge the power blasted free, radiating out in a semicircle that toppled the trilithon of the Yellow Bulls in the north, spraying fragments of rock outward to fell the nearest singers. One upright of the great central trilithon of the Red Bull tribe stood firm, but its lintel was flung aside and its partner split into two pieces as it crashed down across the altar stone. From there the burgeoning force rushed outward, toppling most of the uprights on the circle's western side. The soldiers who had not yet fled were pelted by flying stones. A large chunk brought Prince Tjalan down, while shards fell on Damisa, whose body still sheltered that of Reidel.

But at the center of the henge Micail still stood, surrounded by a few cowering figures. Still singing, he stood until the last reverberation faded, and only billowing dust remained to bear witness to the violence that had passed over the plain. Only then did he fall, with the same slow deliberation as the stones.

TWENTY

'The sun is rising, darkness flees,
The flame is rising, the spirit frees.
All hail to the soul ascended,
All mortal ill now mended,
Hail and farewell!'

Smoke swirled westward as if driven toward the shadowed horizon by song as the flames flared beneath the funeral pyre. Everyone who could crowd onto the top of the Tor was present – priests and priestesses of Atlantis mingling with sailors and merchants and the folk of the marshes – united by a common sorrow. Tiriki had seen more splendid funerals on Ahtarrath, but never more heartfelt grief; Chedan Arados had been beloved by all.

It had seemed the most bitter of betrayals to recover from that final attack only to find Chedan's body deserted. Most of them understood what must have happened; they knew that if Chedan had not acted they might all have died. But all their wisdom was little consolation for the loss.

On the *Crimson Serpent*, Tiriki remembered, she and Chedan had been forced to perform an amputation on a sailor whose hand had been crushed by a falling mast. The man had lived, but she remembered how wrenching it had been to see him reach out for something and then realize that his hand was gone. *Now I am as he was*, Tiriki wept, *but you are not here to make me a hook for my missing hand . . . Chedan, Chedan, I wish that I had been crippled in my body rather than being left alone without your wisdom . . . your counsel . . . your patient smile . . .*

'Sun Hawk has left us!' wailed a woman of the marsh folk whose children the mage had saved from the plague. But even as the keening of the mourners faded, Otter pointed upward, and all their tears turned to wonder. A falcon – Tiriki thought it was a merlin – circled above the Tor, hovering high in the pillar of smoke as if Chedan's spirit had taken the form of his namesake for one final farewell. And even as they gazed, the hawk abruptly angled its wings and went spiraling eastward through the brightening air.

'I understand—' whispered Tiriki, bending in salutation as if the mage himself stood again before her. She felt his warmth then, like a palpable thing. Perhaps that was why she found herself thinking about the last evening before the battle, when Chedan had spoken to her – really, had forced her to listen, as he spoke of his continued faith in the prophecy. 'You were not to know, but Micail was elected as my successor,' he had told her, 'and for that reason, despite everything that has happened, I still believe he is destined to establish the new Temple.'

She had not wanted to think about it, but Chedan had persisted, saying, 'Of all the things we mortals are called upon to do, the most difficult is forgiveness; in order to truly do it, you will probably have to behave as if you already have forgiven for quite a while before you have actually done so.'

Even then, when Tiriki dared not think beyond the conflict, Chedan believed that they would survive it, and that when it was over, she would have to go to the land of the Ai-Zir and find Micail.

She managed a smile, and said softly, 'I hear you *now*, old friend. I only hope that this time I understand.'

* * *

By the time the mourners came down the hill, the sun was high. Even Domara's ebullient spirits had been chastened by the pervasive grief, but as they left the ashes of the pyre behind them, the little girl ran ahead, racing the other children down the path.

Only a moment later, it seemed, she was bouncing back again.

'Eggs!' she exclaimed, 'Mama, come see! Big giant magic eggs!'

Tiriki traded an apprehensive glance with Liala and hurried after her. Had the Omphalos Stone somehow burst from its hiding place beneath the hill?

Then she realized that she was seeing whitish stones, lying scattered in the grass that grew along the slopes of the Tor – some almost the size of boulders, others as small as eggs indeed, but all of them rounded and surprisingly smooth.

'Caratra, preserve us!' Liala exclaimed, panting as she reached Tiriki's side. 'The dratted Omphalos has littered! It's clutched! *It's laid eggs!* Don't touch them! The gods *alone* know what they might do.'

Torn between laughter and tears, Tiriki could only agree. The force that blasted from the Omphalos Stone must have somehow produced these replicas. Fortunately, there was no sign that they had inherited their parent's power. *Oh Chedan*, she thought, with another red-faced glance at the sputtering Liala, *is this your last joke on me?*

When Tiriki reached her dwelling she found that the saji woman Metia had prepared food for a journey and repacked Tiriki's satchel. Dannetrasa, now the senior priest, was there as well, offering his well-reasoned protest against her plan, but none of them had authority over a Vested Guardian.

Kalaran all but demanded to accompany her, but with the birth of Selast's child so close at hand, she would not permit them to be separated. The merchant Forolin's offer of help was harder to refuse; all of the sailors wanted to rescue Reidel, so she agreed they could escort her.

In addition to these, she decided, she would take the saji women who had served Alyssa as well. When Forolin protested, she spoke to him as Chedan had once scolded her when she had admitted her own prejudice against them. 'Above all, the sajis are skilled healers,' she finished, fighting back tears at the memory, 'and I fear healers will be needed more than priestesses.'

And though at first blush the idea had seemed presumptuous, she decided to take Chedan's intricately carved staff.

The one thing she did not want was a guide. 'No,' she explained patiently to Rendano, 'I no longer need one. My spirit is connected to Micail's once again. All I have to do is to follow it.' That certainty kept her from despair, more than the knowledge that he was still living; she still was not sure what kind of man Micail had become.

But she had been careful, and wise, for too long. Her people were safe. Whatever had happened to Micail – whatever he had done – she knew that she must seek him now.

Micail struggled unwillingly toward consciousness. Everything hurt, even the softness of the bed on which he lay.

'Is he awake?'

That was Galara's voice. He winced as a cool cloth was laid across his brow, tried to speak but could only groan.

'He walks in a nightmare.' Elara replied. 'I wish Tiriki were here!'

Tiriki? Micail shook his head. He would not be fooled again. Tiriki was dead, drowned with Ahtarrath, her ship crushed by huge stones in the harbor – he could still see them, huge blocks tilting, hurtling through the air. People died where they fell. He had a sudden vivid image of his friend Ansha's blood reddening the white chalk where he had been struck down, and it seemed to him too that he had heard voices raised in an Alkonan chant for the death of a prince. He had only dreamed that they escaped; now the dream was trying to drag him back into its clutches. He would not give in this time. There was no escape. They were all dead – all except him.

I swore I would not survive her death, he told himself sternly. It was time to give up, and let darkness bear him off to the City of Bones.

If only I could escape my dreams . . .

Tiriki remembered the paths they had taken to their meeting with Prince Tjalan. She knew that the plain lay another day's journey to the east, and she had only to keep walking toward the rising sun. By then she could not only feel Micail's wavering life force, but a roil of displaced energies that could only come from the broken ring of stones. Her feet hurt, and a sun that shone with mocking cheerfulness reddened her fair skin, yet she hurried down the last hill unafraid of what waited for her – four warriors with the horns of the Blue Bull tribe tattooed on their brow, and the young woman Anet, who had finally lost her faintly mocking smile.

'Hunters saw you coming,' Anet said, and flinched a little from Tiriki's gaze. 'My men can carry your burdens so we will go faster.'

Tiriki nodded. It was strange, considering how she had feared this girl, even hated her, but she had no emotion to spare for Anet now.

'I know that Micail was not killed,' she said harshly. 'But he is hurt. How badly?'

'He was struck by falling stones. He has some wounds, nothing from which he cannot recover. But he sleeps without waking. He does not *wish* to heal.'

Tiriki could only give a wordless nod. She had been *certain* that Micail was alive – but with every step she had taken toward Azan she had wondered – what if she was wrong?

'Who else was injured?' she asked, as they once more began to walk along the path.

'When the stones – shattered – some flew far,' said Anet,

'others fell nearer. Prince Tjalan is dead, and many of his soldiers too. The ceremonies of his pyre ended only last night. Many of the other priests and priestesses – all are dead, too, or – ran away. If they could.'

As they crossed the plain toward it, the Sun Wheel slowly became large enough to see. Some of the trilithons still stood, proclaiming the skill of those that had raised them; others were tumbled, as if some giant child had tired of his building blocks and left them scattered on the grass.

And there seemed to be a presence there among them, a wiry shadow like a drifting curl of smoke.

I will deal with you later, Tiriki said silently as they passed. Ahead she could see the real smoke rising from the hearth fires of Azan-Ylir, where Micail was waiting.

As they reached the great ditch at the edge of the village, a dark-haired young woman whom Tiriki recognized with difficulty as Elara ran out to meet them.

'Oh my lady—' Elara stumbled as if undecided whether to make a formal Temple obeisance or throw herself at Tiriki's feet. 'How I have prayed the Mother would bring you—'

'And by Her grace, I am here,' Tiriki answered, 'I am glad to see you unhurt.'

'Yes, well, almost,' Elara said distractedly. 'It seems Lord Micail managed to direct the force away from our end of the crescent – only one of the sopranos was killed but Cleta was badly injured.'

In his dream, Micail stood atop the Star Mountain, gazing up at the wicked image of Dyaus.

'By the power of my blood I bind you!' he cried, but the gigantic figure of darkness only laughed.

'I am unbound . . . and I will set the rest free . . .'

Wind and fire whirled around him. Micail cried out as reality dissolved – but he felt a slim arm take hold of him, bracing him against the blast. *Tiriki . . .* He recognized the touch of her spirit, though his eyes were still blinded by chaos. *Have I finally died?* He had hoped for peace in the afterlife – was he condemned to keep fighting the same battles over and over again?

Yet his heart took fire at her strength, and he looked once more for his eternal foe. The tumult around him had eased, but Tiriki was shaking him. Why was she doing that? If he let her recall him to the waking world, she would be gone . . .

'Micail! *Osinarmen!* Wake up! I have walked for three days to get here. The least you can do is open your eyes and welcome me!'

That did not sound like something from a dream!

Micail realized that light was beating against his closed eyelids. He took a deep breath, wincing as his sore ribs complained, but suddenly every sense was clamoring with awareness of Tiriki's presence. Her soft lips brushed his brow and he grabbed her and clung fiercely as her mouth moved to his.

His heart pounded furiously as their kiss burned through his every nerve. In a rush his flesh awakened to the certainty that he was alive, and Tiriki was in his arms!

He opened his eyes.

'That's better.' Tiriki raised her head just enough to let him see her smile.

'You're here!' he whispered. 'Truly here! You won't leave me?'

'I will neither leave you nor let you go,' she answered, sobering. 'We have too much work to do!'

Micail felt his own face change. 'I – am not worthy,' he grated. 'Too many have died because of me.'

'That is right,' she said sharply. 'And all the more reason to live and do what you can to make amends. And the first step toward that is for you to get well!' She sat up and gestured to Elara, who was hovering in the doorway with a wooden bowl in her hands.

'This is stew, and quite good,' said Tiriki. 'I had some earlier. At least in this place there is plenty of food. You are going to eat it – there is nothing wrong with your jaws – and then we will see.'

Wordless, Micail stared at her, but she did not seem to expect a reply. It seemed simpler to allow them to help him to sit upright than to argue. And when he tasted the stew he found that he was hungry.

'Tiriki has changed,' said Galara, handing the basket of freshly chopped willow bark to Elara. 'Not that I ever saw so much of her back at home. She married Micail when I was only a baby. She always seemed to me sort of fragile somehow – you know, soft-voiced and pale.'

'I know what you mean. She has certainly taken charge!' She dipped a wooden spoon into a pot set among the coals, testing the temperature of the water there.

In the week since her arrival, Tiriki had blown through the Atlantean compound like a summer storm, arranging for the dead to be given proper rites and reorganizing the nursing of those who lived. In the practical tasks she assigned, the survivors found a certain relief from their shock and sorrow.

'We are so accustomed to letting men exercise authority,' Elara said, 'but in the Temple of Caratra they teach that the active force is female, and that each god must have his goddess to arouse him to action. Without women, men might never get anything done at all.'

'Well that's certainly true for Micail and Tiriki!' Galara agreed. 'He did things – some of which I wish he hadn't – but without her he was only half there. It's funny. I always thought he was the strong one, but she survived without him better than he did without her! I think maybe Damisa's right, we don't really need men at all.'

'Well don't tell *them!*' Elara laughed. Then she shook her head. 'I, for one, would not like to live without them, though. And I suppose if we did not have them to serve as a warning, we women would go astray just as badly on our own.'

She sobered suddenly, remembering Lanath. He had never regained consciousness after the flying stone had struck him, and she was still not sure how she felt about his loss. She had not loved him, but he had always been *there* . . .

'Will you go with Tiriki to this Tor she's been telling us about?' Galara asked. 'She is still my guardian, and I suppose I will go where she says, but you are of age.'

I do have a choice, Elara realized suddenly. *For the first time since the Temple chose me, I can decide what I want my life to be.* She closed her eyes, and was surprised by a vivid image of the shrine room in Timul's temple. In memory she gazed from one wall to the next, ending at the image of the Goddess with the sword. *How odd*, she thought then. She had always thought she would serve the Lady of Love, but suddenly she could feel the weight of that sword in her own hand.

'I think I will go back to Belsairath with Timul,' she said slowly. 'Lodreimi is getting old, and she will need someone to help her run the Temple there.'

'Perhaps I can visit you,' Galara said wistfully.

'Well, you would be welcome.' Elara spooned up a little tea and grimaced at its bitter flavor, but took the dipper and began to transfer the concoction into the beakers. 'Put a little honey in these,' she advised. 'Cleta and Jiritaren should be ready for another dose of painkiller about now.'

'Do you remember, my love, how you cared for your little feather tree?' Tiriki asked, keeping her voice briskly casual. 'It is still alive – indeed, it is flourishing.'

'In this climate? Impossible!'

'Why would I lie? And after living with it for so many years,' she teased, 'do you think I could mistake it for anything else? When you come to the Tor you will see. I tell you, Elis has a rare gift when it comes to plants.'

She took Micail's arm and drew him closer as they continued along the river path. Tiriki had gotten him out of bed the day after her arrival, and each day made him walk further. This was the first time they had gone outside the compound, though. Imperceptibly he felt himself beginning to relax. His ribs gave a protesting twinge at every movement, but they were only cracked, and would heal.

The greater pain was knowing that people were watching – he could feel their eyes upon him, judging, blaming him for living when so many had died – Stathalkha, Mahadalku, Haladris, Naranshada, even poor Lanath – so many. And there might yet be other victims. Jiritaren, he was told, was not nearly as well as he looked. Micail's guilt was ever more piercing, perhaps, because his own injuries had kept him from sharing the first, anguished mourning with the other survivors. Now, they were trying to get on with their lives, while he was still trying to find a reason for living.

As they neared the river they heard children's voices and found a group of native boys and girls playing in the shallows, their sun-browned skins almost the same shade as their hair.

'Ah, just to see them makes me miss Domara more. When you come to the Tor you will see—' said Tiriki again.

'When I come to the Tor?' he echoed. 'You seem so sure that I should do so. But when I have brought such bad fortune to the people here, perhaps—'

'You *are* coming home with me! I am not going to raise your child alone!' she exclaimed. 'Ever since she learned you were alive Domara has been asking about you. She is only a girl, not a son who could inherit your powers, but—'

His hand shot out to grip her suddenly. 'Don't . . . say . . . that!' he groaned. 'Do you think that magic matters to me?' For a moment the harsh rasp of his breathing was the only sound.

'Everyone assures me that if you had not been able to

wield those powers,' Tiriki said evenly, 'the damage done by the Sun Wheel would have been far more terrible.'

'I thought I had the strength to contain the forces Haladris was using the stones to raise – that is why I let him start,' he whispered. 'This disaster came from my pride no less than Tjalan's. My powers have led *only* to trouble! Because the Black Robes tried to take them, back in the Ancient Land, my father died and Reio-ta was almost destroyed. And I – I all but gave them away! Better they die with me.'

'That is a discussion for another day—' Tiriki smiled. 'You should have seen your daughter, though, standing there with feet planted and her fists on her hips, *insisting* that she should go along and help find her father. Yes, she has inherited more from you than magic. Only you can teach her how to deal with such pride.'

Micail found himself smiling as, for the first time, he thought of his daughter not as a simple abstraction, nor even an inspiration, but as a real person, someone to teach, to learn from . . . to love.

'Your people are healing,' said the Queen of Azan. It was not quite a question. She had invited Tiriki and Micail to take the noon meal with her beneath the oak trees by the village, where a cool breeze off the river balanced the heat of the sun.

Micail nodded. 'Yes, those who will recover have mostly done so.'

Tiriki's gaze sought the new mound that the Ai-Zir had raised over those who had died. She suppressed an impulse to grip Micail's arm and reassure herself again that he was not among them. She had wanted this formal meeting to wait until Micail was stronger, but it was time to begin planning for the future.

'And what will you do now?' Khayan asked, with a sidelong glance at the priestess Ayo that Tiriki could not interpret.

'Our wounded are almost well enough to travel. Many of our people wish to return to Belsairath,' Micail replied. 'Tjalan's second-in-command has taken charge of the surviving soldiers, and he can be trusted, I think, to keep them out of trouble and deal with whatever ships may pass through there. But almost all of the priesthood will travel with us to the Lake lands.'

'There are some,' said the queen, with a swift glance at the shaman Droshrad, who squatted in the shade of one of the trees, 'who have suggested that you should all be slain and allowed to go nowhere. But we have taken your magic weapons, or as many of them as we could find, at least. With them in the hands of *our* warriors, your remaining soldiers are not enough to challenge us.'

That news would have disturbed Tiriki more if she had not known that no matter who possessed them, within a few decades at most, the orichalcum plating on the Atlantean arrows, spears, and swords would begin to decay, and any advantage they might give would be gone. *And also*, she thought with a smile, *we will not need them*. The people at the Tor had another kind of protection.

'Prince Tjalan and some of the others did not understand that we must learn the ways of this new land, not impose our own,' said Tiriki firmly. 'But in the Lake lands, as Anet will tell you, we live in peace with the marsh folk. Indeed, we are becoming one tribe.'

'It is so,' agreed Ayo. 'My sister Taret speaks well of all you have done there.'

Tiriki lifted an eyebrow at this evidence of the link between all the wisewomen of the tribes. In Ayo, as in Taret, she sensed the mark of Caratra. She had no difficulty in accepting the Sacred Sister as a priestess whose status, though different, was equal to her own.

'You promised glory for King Khattar's tribe,' Droshrad growled unexpectedly, 'but you lied. You sought to make us slaves to your power.'

385

'That is true,' Micail sighed, 'but surely we have endured our own punishment. Let the lives we have lost be payment for the harm we have done.'

'Easy words,' the shaman growled, but he subsided at a glance from the queen.

'But why these things were done – that is the thing I do not understand,' Ayo said then. 'Was it conquest only? I do not feel that desire in you.'

'Because it is not there,' Tiriki put in, when it was clear that Micail either could not or would not answer. 'You must understand. From childhood we knew our homeland faced destruction. But there was a prophecy that my husband would found a new Temple in a new land.'

'But I did not understand,' Micail said heavily. 'I thought it must be a great and splendid building such as we had on Ahtarrath and in the Ancient Land. But I was mistaken. I think now that what we are meant to establish is a tradition—'

'A tradition,' said Tiriki, completing his thought, 'in which the wisdom of the Temple of Light – and it is great, though we have given you little reason to think so until now – is joined with the earth power of those who live in this land.'

Ayo sat up straighter, eyeing them intently. 'Does that mean that you will teach us your magic?'

'If that is what you wish, yes. Send us a few of your clever young women and we will train them, if the Sacred Sisters will agree to teach some of our own.'

'And your young men, too,' added Micail, meeting Droshrad's scowl. 'But you will have to send food with them—' He patted Tiriki's shoulder. 'My wife needs your good beef and bread to put some meat on her bones!'

'It is true that our resources are meager . . .' said Tiriki. 'In the vales around the Tor, there is little solid land for farming, and it is a hard trial to be continuously gathering wild food.'

'It is true,' Khayan-e-Durr said, smiling. 'The fields and

pastures of the Ai-Zir are rich. If the Sacred Sisters agree, we will ensure the children we send you do not starve.'

'Young Cleta's leg is still healing,' said Ayo thoughtfully. 'Let her stay with us and send another of your maidens to join her. We will allow some of our young priestesses to join you in return.'

'What about Vialmar?' asked Micail. 'He is Cleta's betrothed, after all.'

'That one!' grunted Droshrad. 'He pisses himself with fear when I look at him . . .'

'If he thinks he is needed to look after Cleta, he will find his courage fast enough,' said Micail.

'Maybe—' The shaman still did not look convinced, but he nodded at last. 'I have a nephew. Maybe you can teach him something. He only makes trouble here! He thinks the sun talks to him.'

The air throbbed as if the plains of Azan had become a vast drumskin, vibrating to the rhythm beat out by the feet of the Ai-Zir. Even the stars seemed to blink in time to the rhythm, their sparkling reflected in the leaping fires below. Damisa had never seen anything like it – certainly not in the modest celebrations that were all that the marsh folk could manage – but it was more than that. There was something here that had not been evident even in the four-day festivals she had known as a child in Alkonath. She fussed with the sling that immobilized her shoulder, trying to make it more comfortable. At least the dizziness that had followed her concussion was mostly gone.

'If it wasn't for us, they wouldn't even know the exact date of the summer solstice,' said Cleta sourly, as they watched the dancers circling the bonfire. Damisa glanced down at the other girl's splinted leg. She supposed it must be hurting again. *Between us*, she thought, *we might just about put together one whole priestess*.

On the far side of the bonfire they had heaped up a low

mound where King Khattar sat in state on a bench covered with the hide of a red bull. Even the firelight could not make him look healthy. Damisa almost sympathized, but she had been assured that in time *her* shoulder would heal. Khattar was still acknowledged as high king, but it was clear that the power was passing to the nephew who sat beside him.

Already Damisa had learned more than she had ever wanted to know about tribal politics, which were beginning to remind her uncomfortably of the palace intrigues she had heard about on Alkonath as a child. It all made clear, she thought, the fact that the differences between the Atlanteans and the Ai-Zir were not so very real.

'Here come our valiant protectors now,' said Cleta, as Vialmar and Reidel threaded their way among the dancers toward them, a strangely painted beaker gripped in each hand.

'Cleta,' said Damisa, with raised eyebrows, 'you are slipping! I do believe that was a joke.' The other girl weakly returned her smile, but said nothing; both of them knew that Vialmar's thigh had been deeply gashed by the first of the flying stone fragments. He walked with a limp even now. And she remembered quite clearly that when the power exploded from the henge it had been *she* who had protected Reidel. As he handed her a beaker she was still wondering what madness had compelled her to do so.

'It's called mead,' said Vialmar with enthusiasm, 'Give it a try – it's pretty good.'

Damisa took a cautious sip. The liquor was sweet and tasted very faintly like teli'ir, but fortunately for her head, did not seem to be nearly so strong. Still it seemed strange to be sitting here drinking when Tjalan and so many others were gone.

They sat talking for a time until Cleta had to admit that her leg was giving her a lot of pain. Vialmar, who was tall enough to do so, simply picked her up in his arms and, limping only a little, slowly carried her back to the compound, leaving Reidel and Damisa alone. Suddenly restless, she stood up.

'This stuff is going to my head. I need to walk a little while.'

'I'll walk with you,' said Reidel, rising in turn.

She flushed, remembering what had happened the last time she accepted his escort from a celebration, but she knew it would not be wise to wander alone in such a crowd. There were not a few among the natives who had no love left for the Atlanteans. Silent, she let him lead her toward the path by the river. His hand was strong and warm, callused from labor, but then her own was not exactly soft and ladylike either.

'I have not thanked you for my life,' he said as the tumult of the festival faded behind them. 'I was mad to think I could have done anything to stop the Working. I never imagined that you—'

'At least you *tried!*' she responded. 'I just stood there watching.'

They walked for a little while in silence, listening to the ripple of the water and the wind in the trees.

'I am sorry for the death of Prince Tjalan,' Reidel said finally. 'I know that you loved him.'

Her good shoulder lifted in a shrug. 'Was it love, or only that he dazzled me?' Even now she felt a tremor at the memory of that lean, broad-shouldered figure and his flashing smile. It had taken her far too long to wonder what lay behind it. 'Even though he was my cousin, in the end, I found I could not trust him.'

She frowned a little, wondering when she had abandoned that dream . . . Her eyes were stinging, and she blinked back tears.

'You're weeping—' said Reidel. 'Forgive me, I should not have said—'

'Be still!' she exclaimed. 'Don't you understand? Until now, I haven't been able to let him go.'

'He was a great man . . .' Reidel said with difficulty. 'And he was royal, and your kin. I wanted you to know . . .' he swallowed, 'to know that I understand now. It was madness for me to think that you and I—' He stopped again as Damisa turned and gripped the front of his tunic.

'There is something I want *you* to know,' she said softly. 'I have had a lot of time to think, lying in that bed while the healers fussed over me. A lot of what happened at the Sun Wheel is blurred in my memory. But one thing I do remember. When the stones started falling, you were the one I felt I had to save. Not Tjalan – you!'

'Yes. You ordered me to live.'

It sounded as if he were smiling. Breath quickening, she dared to look back at him, and very gently, he eased his arms around her. Did she love him? Even now, she did not quite know. But it felt good to stand there in the circle of his arms.

'I will lead you a sad life, Reidel,' she said, in a voice so small she could hardly believe it was her own. 'But I *need* you! I know that now.'

'I'll consider myself lucky to have you under any circumstances.' Now he was the one who sounded breathless. 'I always loved the challenge of sailing into a storm . . .'

In the dark hour that falls just before dawn, Tiriki stood with Micail before the broken ring of stones. Festival fires still glimmered here and there like fallen stars upon the plain. But the heavens were more constant. The moon was hidden, and offered no challenge to the amazing glow of the stars. Chedan could have read their message easily, but she realized that she had absorbed more of his astrological lore than she had thought.

Above, the stars of Purity and Righteousness and Choice glittered in the belt of Manoah – the Hunter of Destiny, as the constellation was named by the people here. A year ago, Chedan had told her that when the star called the Sorcerer and the sun walked in the Sign of the Torch, new light came into the world. But at that time, the Sovereign and the Blood Star had opposed them. Now the Red Star dwelt with the Peacemaker, and Caratra's star had moved to calm the Winged Bull. There was hope in the heavens, but on earth there were conflicts which remained to be resolved.

Her future with Micail was one of them, and that, she supposed, must depend on whether he was able to take up his priesthood once more. During these past weeks she had nursed him, challenged him, loved him – and the love at least would not change. But she was no longer simply his mate and priestess. She had grown, and she did not yet know whether Micail had emerged from his own testing with a strength to balance hers.

Micail had put on the diadem of a First Guardian, but she wore Caratra's blue. Before them, the surviving stones of the great henge bulked blacker than the space between the stars. Only three of the trilithons in the inner horseshoe still stood intact, and there were gaps in the part of the outer circle that had been completed before. Even from here she could feel the power of those stones, confused and angry despite the peaceful night.

Tiriki's left hand was enfolded in Micail's. In the other she carried Chedan's staff, marked with the sigil of a mage. Micail had not asked her about that, and she had not yet decided what to say. In the past week she had gradually drawn him back into the world of the living and watched him gain in strength and sureness with each day. But Chedan had left a powerful legacy unclaimed. Was Micail strong enough to bear it? Was he worthy? In this, she could not afford to be blinded by her love for him.

Why had he brought her, garbed in the regalia of a priestess, to the Sun Circle at this hour? She shivered in the cold wind that blows before dawn. They were to start the journey to the Tor tomorrow. *Perhaps*, she thought, *he has come to say a private farewell. This, after all, was his life and his work for four years – his cruel son, he called it.*

She blinked as a sudden red light glowed on the stones. But they were looking westward – she clutched at Micail, remembering again the lurid glow in the heavens as Ahtarrath had died.

'What is it?' His arm tightened around her.

'The flames! Can't you see them?' Memories overwhelmed her like the wave that had drowned the Sea Kingdoms. 'I can see it all – Ahtarrath is burning – the islands of Ruta and Tarisseda and all Atlantis sinking beneath the waves!' She strove for control.

'No, it is only some guardsman, building up his fire,' Micail said soothingly, but she shook her head.

'That fire will burn for so long as we remember. Why did the gods allow this to happen? Why are we still alive when so many others are gone?'

Micail sighed, but she could feel the arm that held her trembling. 'My beloved, I do not know. Was it a reward to be saved in order that we might fulfill the prophecy, or will we be punished because we carried away the secrets of the Temple – even though we were commanded to do so?'

Yes, he had certainly been doing some thinking. Within her breast Tiriki felt hope. 'Do you think, in lives to come, that we will remember?' she asked then.

'So long as the Wheel carries us from life to life upon this earth, how can we forget? Our mothers' oaths still bind us, is it not so? The manner of our remembering may alter, as new lives bring us new griefs and challenges, but maybe we will dream of this moment. There are some things that will always be the same . . .'

'My love for you, and yours for me?' She turned in his arms and he held her tightly until her shivering began to ease. He kissed her then, and she felt the warmth of life surge through her limbs once more.

'That above all,' he answered, a little breathless as their lips parted. 'Perhaps that is the greatest treasure we brought out of Atlantis, for no matter how we try to preserve the ancient wisdom, it is bound to change in this new land.'

'The secrets will be lost, and the knowledge will fade,' she said somberly. 'Atlantis will become a legend, a fading rumor of glory, and a warning to those who would manipulate powers never meant to be grasped by humankind.'

He turned to look at the henge. The stars were fading as the world turned toward morning. 'I poured all my knowledge into building this – but not my wisdom, for that is not what I was seeking. Only power . . .'

'If you could,' she asked then, 'would you restore the fallen stones, and finish the Sun Wheel as it was designed?'

Micail shook his head. 'The chieftains of the tribes have asked me to do it, but I told them that too many of our adepts died. Let the stones lie. If Droshrad or someone else cares enough to try to restore them through brute manpower alone, so be it. But the tribesmen fear to touch them, and by the time that fear has faded, they will no longer remember what the Sun Wheel was intended to do.'

'They are right to fear,' murmured Tiriki. 'There is still anger in these stones.' She had sensed it in the smoky shadow coiling among them when she had passed on the way to the village. Now her inner senses perceived it as an angry glow.

'Enough of the sarsens remain upright to calculate the movements of the heavens and to mark the crossing of the flow of power. The true Temple is within our hearts. We need raise no edifice of orichalcum and gold.'

'It is not only our love for each other that will bind us,' Tiriki said then, 'but our love for this land. I fought to save the Tor itself as much as I did the people in my care. In future lives, we may fare elsewhere, but I think that these places will always draw us back again.'

'And yet you have changed the Tor by burying the Omphalos there.'

'Do you think I have not had nightmares of what might happen if its power was loosed upon this land? But I had the blessing of the powers that dwell there, and the world is balanced once again.'

'For a time,' Micail said quietly. 'When Dyaus breaks loose, he brings destruction, but also . . . things change. As they must. As they are meant to. We are lord and lady of Ahtarrath no longer. The men of Alkonath who survived have given me the falcon banner – they look to me now to lead them, but the only realm I wish to rule is that of my own soul.'

'That banner is not all you have inherited.' Tiriki suddenly realized that she had made her decision. 'Chedan said you were his heir. This is his staff . . .' She held it out, and after a moment of wonder, he took it in his hand.

'It's curious,' she went on. 'I think I told you the marsh folk call me Morgan, the woman from the sea. But they called Chedan *Sun Hawk*. Or sometimes Merlin. Both are names for the native falcon.'

'I used to dream that Chedan was instructing me,' Micail said in a shaken voice. He turned to look once more at the stones. 'Watch and bear witness, Tiriki! Now I know why I had to come here, and what I must do. When we sang we left a residue of power in the circle. I must sing the stones back to stillness, or there will never be peace in this land.'

She wanted to protest, to haul him away from the angry energies that pulsed through those broken stones. But as a priestess she knew that what he said was true, and as a priest it was his duty to heal where he had harmed. If he could . . .

And so she watched, trembling as he moved past the fallen sarsens and into the circle. With all her senses focused upon it, she could both see and feel the turgid red glimmer that pulsed uneasily from stone to stone. She swayed, wondering how he could bear the red heat, staying upright herself only by grounding into the earth below . . .

Micail's tall shape was a pale blur as the sarsens responded to his presence like coals wakened by the wind. Would he be able to master them? Instinctively Tiriki lifted her arms, drawing up power from the ground she stood on, channeling it toward him through the palms of her hands.

Tiriki could see that he was singing. *Be still!* her heart cried to the stones. *Be at peace! Find balance, and rest . . .*

Micail continued to pace among them, leaning on Chedan's carven staff. But whether because of his song or her prayer, the pulsing glow was – not dimming, but changing – from angry red to sullen gold, which only slowly faded from sight.

By the time he had finished, the sky was growing pale. Tiriki quivered from the cold, but as he walked back toward her, Micail was radiant with the heat of rightly used power.

'It is done,' he said softly, warming her hands between his own. 'Now the ring will anchor the lines of power as it was meant to, and mark the wheel of the seasons. A day will come when people will forget, and this will be no more than a ring of ancient stones. But I will remember what we did here, and I will come back to you, beloved. Through life and beyond life, that I swear.'

'In the name of the Goddess, I swear the same to you.' *For you have returned to me already, my love!* her heart added silently. *Both of us have won our victory!*

'Look—' he said then, pointing across the ring toward the short, southeastern stone.

The plain was dark, the earth still covered by night's veil, but in the eastern sky, the new day was coming, rose-pink shading to a refulgent gold. It was not like fire at all, Tiriki realized, but rather like the blossoming of a flower, whose rosy reflection brought sudden life to the great sarsens.

'Behold, Manoah comes, robed in Light—'

'Ni-Terat is made fertile in His embrace—' Tiriki answered him. The words were ancient, but she had never truly understood their meaning until now.

'Hail Lord of the Day!'

'Hail, Dark Mother!'

A line of brightness flared along the horizon, light washed across the world, and suddenly the dim earth was robed in glowing green.

'Hail Lady of Life—' they cried together as that radiance bloomed, and the Daughter of Ni-Terat and Manoah arose and blessed them with the first sunlight of midsummer day.

AFTERWORD

FROM ATLANTIS TO AVALON

In Marion Zimmer Bradley's *The Mists of Avalon*, Igraine recollects a past life in which she and Uther were a priest and priestess of Atlantis and watched the building of Stonehenge on Salisbury Plain. Such a notion is not, of course, original. English folklore is rife with reference to lost civilizations. They have become the expected explanation for such disputed features of the landscape as the Glastonbury Zodiac, or the more plainly evident spiral path around the Tor. From Atlantis to Camelot, we have been haunted by legends of a golden age, the shining dream of a realm of peace and harmony, of power and splendor, which flourishes for a time, and then tragically falls. In *The Mists of Avalon*, Marion told of the ending of Arthur's kingdom, but long before that book was written, she had addressed the story of a much more ancient realm.

As a rule, Marion was not particularly interested in maintaining consistency among her books. The reference to Atlantis in *The Mists of Avalon* is her recognition of something more personal, a reminder of her first book, a brooding occult romance with the suggestive title *Web of Darkness*. The distinguishing marks of that private Atlantis can be clearly seen in the otherworldly magic of Avalon no less than in the telepathic Darkovans of her numerous science fiction novels, and indeed in almost every other power-plagued individual (and society) of her fiction.

Web of Darkness was originally written in the 1950s. It was a story of occult mysteries, pride and power and redemption, and above all love, set in the temples of the Ancient Land, parent to the Sea Kingdoms of Atlantis. In the 1980s, when the emerging adult fantasy market made publication of such a story possible, Marion was busy with other projects, and asked her son David, who had read the original version as a child, to revise it. It is David's knowledge of this material that has made it possible to write *Ancestors of Avalon*.

In 1983, the year after *The Mists of Avalon* began its ascent to fame, the book, in two trade paperback volumes from Donning Press, *Web of Light* and *Web of Darkness*, at last emerged. A mass-market version was published by Pocket Books the next year. Later it was reissued by Tor in a single volume under the title *The Fall of Atlantis*. The struggles of the characters in that book result in the birth of two children who, according to the prophecies, will survive the cataclysm in which Atlantis is destined to be destroyed.

When I was working with Marion on the revision of *The Forest House*, she told me that she had always felt that two of the main characters, Eilan and Caillean, were reincarnations of the sisters Deoris and Domaris, who in *Web of Darkness* bind themselves and their offspring to each other and to the Goddess for eternity. We concluded that their children, Tiriki and Micail, had reappeared in that book as Sianna and Gawen. After that it was easy to trace the line of reincarnations through *The Mists of Avalon, The Forest House, Lady of Avalon*, and *Priestess of Avalon*.

Clearly there was a connection between Atlantis and Avalon. How, I wondered, did the Sea Kingdoms fall? And how did the survivors of that cataclysm reach the misty islands to the north and find the magical Tor that would one day be known as the isle of Avalon? Clearly another story was waiting to be told.

To interlace legend with archaeology has been a challenge. I am grateful to Viking Books for asking me to tell that story, and to David Bradley for his insight and assistance in developing the setting and characters in a spirit consistent with Marion's original vision. Thanks also to Charline Palmtag for permission to use the solstice hymn in Chapter Nine.

To those who would like to know more about prehistoric Britain, I would recommend *The Age of Stonehenge* by Colin Burgess; *Hengeworld* by Mike Pitts; *Stonehenge* by Leon Stover and Bruce Kraig; and the English Heritage volumes on Bronze Age Britain and Glastonbury. For the Tor, *The Lake Villages of Somerset* by Stephen Minnitt and John Coles; John Michell's *New Light on the Ancient Mystery of Glastonbury*; and the books on Glastonbury by Nicholas Mann are recommended. The article 'Sounds of the Spirit World' by Aaron Watson (*Discovering Archaeology* 2:1, January/February 2000), which I encountered in my doctor's office after I had already decided that the structure of Stonehenge *had* to have had some interesting effects on sound made within the circle, reports on experiments into its acoustic properties.